T, Joy,

Happy
Trip

NECESSARY
EVIL

BOOK YOUR PLACE ON OUR WEBSITE AND MAKE THE READING CONNECTION!

We've created a customized website just for our very special readers, where you can get the inside scoop on everything that's going on with Zebra, Pinnacle and Kensington books.

When you come online, you'll have the exciting opportunity to:

- View covers of upcoming books
- Read sample chapters
- Learn about our future publishing schedule (listed by publication month *and author*)
- Find out when your favorite authors will be visiting a city near you
- Search for and order backlist books from our online catalog
- Check out author bios and background information
- Send e-mail to your favorite authors
- Meet the Kensington staff online
- Join us in weekly chats with authors, readers and other guests
- Get writing guidelines
- AND MUCH MORE!

**Visit our website at
http://www.pinnaclebooks.com**

NECESSARY EVIL

David Dun

PINNACLE BOOKS
KENSINGTON PUBLISHING CORP.

www.pinnaclebooks.com

PINNACLE BOOKS are published by

Kensington Publishing Corp.
850 Third Avenue
New York, NY 10022

All Kensington Titles, Imprints, and Distributed Lines are available at special quantity discounts for bulk purchases for sales promotions, premiums, fund-raising, educational or institutional use. Special book excerpts or customized printings can also be created to fit specific needs. For details, write or phone the office of the Kensington special sales manager: Kensington Publishing Corp., 850 Third Avenue, New York, NY 10022, attn: Special Sales Department, Phone: 1-800-221-2647.

Pinnacle and the P logo Reg. U.S. Pat. & TM Off.

First Printing: April 2001
10 9 8 7 6 5 4 3 2 1

Printed in the United States of America

For Laura

ACKNOWLEDGMENTS

Professional acknowledgments: To Ed Stackler, my friend, editor, and inspiration meister; to Anthony Gardner, my agent, for being a great advocate; to all the creative people at Kensington Books, Laurie Parkin for making it all happen, and Ann LaFarge for her editing and thoughtful editorial assistance throughout the process; to Michaela Hamilton for her creative editorial comments; to Dr. Michael Kinsella, PhD, of the University of Washington in Seattle, for understandable genetics; to Donna Zenor for her thoughtful comments and for slogging through a veritable blizzard of alternative drafts; to Ruth Johnson for her extensive research efforts; to Ed Murphy, Registered Professional Forester, for sharing his wealth of knowledge about forests; and to Eric Wilinski for assisting me with the basics of fiction writing.

Personal acknowledgments: To all of my friends, family and coworkers from whom I have received a large measure of encouragement and inspiration, some who helped with a few words, some who devoted themselves to many hours—even days—of thought and very helpful editorial commentary. I thank you all for your generosity and hard work.

There is some soul of goodness in things evil,
Would men observingly distill it out.
                                    —William Shakespeare
                              Henry V, Act IV, Scene 4

Chapter 1

Calamities, like buzzard birds, arrive in flocks.
—Tilok proverb

Kier Wintripp killed the motor and let the wilderness quiet settle over him. Outside the warmth of the truck, in the gray November dawn, the mountains were dressing themselves for winter, the storm smoothing their wrinkles with the white velvet of snow. Kier knew the mountains well, knew what grew in each microclimate, when it bloomed, what you might eat, and what you would not, the resident birds and migratory visitors, the mammals, the invertebrates, the tracks of all, the habits of each, and their place in the order of things. As winter swept the mountains, sap drew back into the ground, growing things began a silent renewal, and wildlife went from fat to slim in sleep or struggle as the forest awaited the plenty of spring.

The wind-driven snow covered his windshield quickly, obscuring the white stucco medical clinic that might have been snatched from a suburb of San Francisco and set on this low-

lying shoulder of Wintoon Mountain. Behind it, the wildness
of the mountain's rocky pitches and forested slopes contrasted
sharply with the manicured grounds around the building.

Kier was late, and he would have preferred to avoid setting
foot in the Mountain Shadows facility altogether. Although he
supposed it was becoming more commonplace all the time,
surrogate birthing in exchange for a fee bothered him. That
Tilok women were doing it regularly troubled him even more.
Still, he knew his family needed him, so he stepped out of his
pickup and started down the breezeway that led into the sprawling complex where his niece, Winona, was about to give birth.
As Kier understood the arrangement Winona supplied only the
womb.

A gravely injured old rottweiler, hit by a tractor, had made
Kier late. He was able to save the animal, but at some cost to
the quality of its life. Using the latest surgical techniques and
stainless-steel fastenings to hold the bones in place, Kier had
closed the many wounds with more dissolvable sutures than
he cared to count. He had left the grateful owner, given his
hands a quick scrub, and driven to the Mountain Shadows clinic
as fast as conditions permitted.

The clinic was in fact a small hospital, a surgicenter and a
walk-in primary care facility all rolled into one. It was touted
as a charitable effort, serving three Native American tribes and
the nearby community of Johnson City. It was an exceptional
clinic given that there weren't 20,000 people in the whole
county, and Johnson City didn't swell to a population of 3,000
except in the summer.

To either side of the entryway, a trickling stream splashed
over stones meant to look river smoothed. The stone was artificial, the water pumped and chemically sterilized. A large
ceramic bullfrog adorned the edge of a tiny pond. Just through
the main entrance was a spacious lobby with a receptionist's
desk flanked by cubbyhole offices used for filling out forms
and admitting patients.

Kier walked through the lobby with a barely perceptible nod, as if he knew where he was going. Two male physicians in green scrubs turned out of another corridor and walked in front of him for a hundred feet or so. They were apparently arguing over a golf score.

The place had almost no scent, which Kier found disorienting. To the ultrasensitive nose, hospitals usually had the occasional pungent sting of alcohol, the ammoniac aroma of industrial-grade disinfectants, the genuine-article piss smell from all the urine-filled plastic bags, and the lemon-peppermint odors of chemical deodorizers used to mask the first three. Powerful electrical filters, such as those in Mountain Shadows, tended to leave only the faint scent—like that of a hot router in cherry wood. A good whiff of a dirty diaper would have been refreshing to Kier.

Without much effort, he found the maternity nurse's station. Shuffling papers and moving charts, the busy charge nurse barely noticed him at first. She wore a dark green sweater over whites, the various layers of polyester stretched tight across a belly that had seen its own births, and had been hostage to long stints of a sedentary life.

After a moment, she did a quick double take. Kier knew what she saw, and he could read in her face what she thought. With his dark eyes and jet-black hair braided down his back, Kier had the general mien of the Tilok people. The rest of him looked more European, the nose narrower and the face less round. The nurse's glance went to the turquoise stones, silver, and feathers that adorned his braided hair and cowboy hat. Cowboy boots pushed the jeans-clad man to over six feet, four inches.

"Say, you're Kier Wintripp, aren't you? The veterinary doctor?"

He nodded.

"Winona told us to look for you. Room Six down there. She

just got back from recovery. She gave birth by cesarean just over an hour ago.''

"I didn't expect it would be that fast," Kier said.

"The baby was breech and had the umbilicus wrapped around its neck. Couldn't be helped.'' She pointed down the corridor to the right. "They rushed her straight to surgery.''

Kier followed where she had pointed. The floors were gleaming, the walls without a mark and tastefully adorned with watercolor wilderness scenes. In the hallway, Kier passed a defibrillator and brand-new stainless-steel medicine carts.

Before he entered Winona's room, he heard the commotion.

"I want to see the baby just once.'' It was Winona, sounding stressed.

"It's awful, just awful.'' His sister's voice.

As he came through the door, Kier's mother sounded only slightly calmer. "Honey, we've asked them.''

His mother smiled at him, and for just a second, the exhaustion departed her body. She looked back at Winona, whose dark hair hung down around a face taut with anguish.

"What's wrong?'' Kier asked.

"They won't let me even look at the baby. Not even for a second.''

Kier pondered for a moment. "I'll ask them to let you see the baby,'' he said. "But just for a couple of minutes. Then we have to let the baby go. He's not one of us.''

"I want to see him.'' She grasped his hands.

"We'll try,'' he said, seeking to comfort her. "When they bring you this baby I want you to tell yourself something, and I have to hear the words out loud.''

"What?''

"I want you to say: 'He's beautiful, but he belongs to someone else.' ''

"Okay. Okay.''

"I want you to swear I'll hear those words.''

"I said okay. Can you stay with us?"

Kier nodded. "But I have to leave sooner than I'd like. The Donahues have an Arab mare that's due to foal. Jack's out of town, and with Claudie ill, and the storm coming in, she needs me there."

"But you'll get the baby?"

He nodded again.

Kier knew Winona needed closure following this bizarre process. He wasn't sure it would help, but after inducing a young woman to carry a baby for money the clinic could bend a little. Now, with the cesarean, Winona might never have a normal delivery. Anger flared inside him as he approached the nurse's station.

"I am sorry to trouble you. I am here to discuss my niece's request to see the baby for a minute," he said to the charge nurse.

"Your niece didn't say a minute, but the answer's the same. It's against policy." She whispered, "And you don't really want to do this to her."

"It'll only be for a few minutes."

"I'm sorry, I'd really like to help you, but it's against the rules."

"Sometimes it's better to break the rules. This might be one of those occasions."

"I know who you are and how much influence you have with the local community and the Tilok tribe, but we don't break the rules for anyone, Dr. Wintripp."

"I understand. Perhaps I could speak with the person in charge of this hospital?"

"That's the administrator, Mr. Hanson."

"I would like to see him."

"He's with a very important visitor."

"Who is that?"

"The president of the company that owns the clinic. Mr. Tillman."

"I would still like to see him."

"I'll see if the head nurse can make an appointment with the administrator some time this week."

Kier looked in the woman's eyes. "It would be a great kindness if you could tell me how to find him now so that I could work out my niece's problem."

At that moment a nurse with a clipboard hurried toward them from the surgical wing, whispering, "They're coming, they're coming."

Kier looked back at the charge nurse, who glanced nervously to the side, not meeting his gaze. The four staffers around them looked bewildered, as if they were contemplating hiding in the closet.

A small swarm of people and a flashbulb-popping photographer appeared. They surrounded a tall, physically powerful man whose narrow waist and bulky upper body were ill-concealed by his L.L. Bean outdoor wear. Kier assumed this man to be Mr. Tillman. He didn't look the doughboy executive that Kier had imagined. The man's presence, his leathery face, black wavy hair, and hooked nose, the primitive intensity of his gaze, looked anything but soft and corporate.

Kier stepped into the group's path, his sheer size slowing them to a near stop.

"Mr. Hanson?"

A short, balding man with black glasses stepped forward. "I'm Mr. Hanson. The clinic administrator. Can I help you?"

Kier appraised Hanson and the rest of the entourage, noting that Tillman watched him with interest. If Kier had to guess, he would have said that Tillman knew who he was. He addressed Mr. Hanson directly. "I'm Kier Wintripp. My niece is a surrogate mother. She just delivered. We believe it would help her to show her the baby for five minutes, then we'll give the child back."

"We can't let surrogate mothers start telling us how long

they want the baby,'' Hanson said. "It's not their baby. They only carry it.''

"A deviation from that policy might be a good thing in this case. I believe it would help my niece, and it would solve some potential problems for all of us.''

"I'm sorry. We don't deviate,'' Hanson said.

"Excuse me,'' Tillman interrupted, "I'd like to understand what you mean?'' Tillman's voice was deep and smooth.

"I mean following the policy risks disrupting our peace.''

"Maybe you could explain that for me.''

"Well, two thousand Tiloks might take a sudden interest in your clinic, and they might all happen to show up at once, making their arrival look remarkably like a demonstration. Of course, the press from miles around would come. That would generate news articles, I'm sure, about the wisdom of surrogate mothering and things of that nature.''

"What exactly do you want, Mr. Wintripp?''

"Five minutes of the baby's life in the arms of the woman who gave birth to him.''

"We can't give in to this,'' Hanson protested.

Tillman gave him a sharp glance, and he quit talking.

"Five minutes. Then the child goes back to the nursery, and you're out of my hospital.''

"I'm out of your hospital when I'm through visiting my niece.''

Tillman's jaw set hard. Kier could tell he was accustomed to having his way. "We can work something out,'' Tillman said, quickly regaining his composure.

"It's settled then,'' said the charge nurse, appearing relieved. "Come with me, please.''

Kier followed, his body strangely alive with adrenaline. In moments, a woman with a surprised expression had brought the baby into Winona's room. Kier stood to the side, avoiding his mother's gaze. He knew that Winona was about to partake in one of the emptiest moments of her life. Motherhood and the hope of a shared future were supposed to be the reward for the hard work of birth. Greenbacks and five minutes with someone else's child would have to be enough for Winona.

At first, the snow fell lightly. Jessie Mayfield found herself outside a three-chair beauty shop in a town where the men still went to the barber. Visiting Johnson City was a bizarre experience and a greatly needed distraction. Trying not to think about Frank Bilotti seemed to be the antidote of choice until she figured out some way that thinking about him could be constructive.

Claudie had tried to insist that she visit a local hairdresser, but Jessie wasn't in the mood. She had picked up the groceries for Claudie and her kids, all the way down to the Pop Tarts, and had only one stop left. A prescription for Claudie's shingles waited at the pharmacy, where she could also pick up some cold medicine for Claudie's firstborn son, Bren.

The only pharmacy in Johnson City operated out of an old church. The steep-pitched slate roof, steeple, overhanging eaves, and lap siding gave the building a certain character. Something else about it made it poignant, but Jessie couldn't put her finger on it. Entering through the church's original set of double doors, Jessie saw shelves climbing all the walls, even reaching the point where the ceiling rose at an angle to form the steeple. Not short on merchandise, the place was packed with everything from portable toilets to hot water bottles.

"Can I help you?" a beautiful olive-skinned woman said. She looked part Native American, with soft, well-tended hair that dropped over her shoulders.

"Claudie Donahue has a prescription."

"You must be her sister from New York?"

"Word travels that fast?"

"Around here the trees have ears and the rocks talk."

Jessie's face broke a natural smile. It felt odd because her life was distinctly a frown.

In a corner next to the counter, a dark-haired boy was coloring. It required no imagination to suppose that his mother was tending the store. His eyelashes were long and distinctive. Designed for expansion, his blue overalls were rolled nicely at the ankles, his tiny polo shirt bore stripes that handily complemented the denim. Mom worked on this kid.

Jessie wondered at his place in life: Other than waiting for his mother to finish work, which he did rather well, this child's only job was keeping the crayon in the coloring book. He had no conflicts pulling him in opposite directions, no tests looming on his horizon to determine if he would be judged fit or worthwhile. No conscious possibility of flunking life. That would come later. Jessie gave him a smile—her second of the day. She enjoyed the connection as their eyes met, and she silently wished him well.

As Jessie crossed the street to her Volvo, the snow hurled down in blinding torrents. The keys didn't fit in the car door lock at first—probably due to the overanxious shake in her hands—and it took a minute to make them work. She didn't want to drive back over the mountain in this snow, but she had to get back to Claudie. Besides, where else would she stay in this desolate county but at her sister's?

Jessie had never believed that circumstances controlled people unless people allowed them to. She now struggled to maintain that belief. Frank Bilotti would like nothing better than to put her mind in that vise called fear. The hearings at headquarters in Washington would begin quickly if she decided to bring charges. Then, either she would lose her job and be drummed out of the FBI in disgrace. Or, if the truth wriggled free from all the lies, three experienced agents who had served with distinction would lose their shields. In the latter case, more than a few of her colleagues would hate her, although she knew that her friends—and there were plenty of those—would stick by her. There was a third possibility: All four agents—including Jessie—would be fired and forfeit their good names forever.

Frank had been her mentor, her friend, and her colleague. Having mentored many in her own right, she held that relationship sacred, and her trust had been absolute. Frank had breached that trust in the cruelest possible way, and for no purpose other than saving his own professional life. If only it had been just ordinary, gut-wrenching, black-hole-in-your-life adultery, maybe Gail could have survived the traditional humbling. Frank's line might have begun something like: "The wife and I are seeing a counselor." But Jessie's best friend had fallen victim to Frank's demented needs and been publicly vilified.

Jessie's fingers tightened on the steering wheel. She needed to do something with her anger other than drive it down the road. God, if she got stuck while driving over Elk Horn Pass, she could freeze to death. That would be one way to rid her memory of Frank Bilotti. Maybe coming to stay with her sister in the mountains hadn't been a good idea. There was so much silence out here. So many open spaces. You couldn't really hide from your thoughts the way you could at Thanksgiving in New York, knocked around in the crowds like a billiard ball, jostling past the guys with Salvation Army suits on the corner. Instead, she now faced eighteen miles of death-defying driving in blinding snow.

She had no affinity for the mountains, hated bugs, and picnics of every kind, and didn't care for animals large enough that their leavings wouldn't fit in a sandwich bag. So why come to a place you hate? Simple. To help someone you love.

Claudie needed her, and that was a good reason to be here. Jessie hoped that she could deal with her own problems by helping someone else. Grady White, Frank's boss, had told her that it wasn't bad medicine to help others as long as you got around to yourself in the process.

In her own self-analysis, Jessie started out with one major vulnerability: She was frightened to death of failing at anything.

She had spent her early years in upstate New York near the bend in the Willis River. At thirteen, she moved to the Bronx, having personally earned in record time all the merit badges that the Girl Scouts had to offer.

After that it was a different matter: pimples, hormones, periods, boys, parents who didn't understand, downright ignorant brothers, tears, hysteria, clothes that didn't fit, fights about what to wear, and weird cravings for things she couldn't have—a list too long to remember. And the lost-animal home. Even as a child, it was her credo that she had to be tough and perfect. But something inside her was soft. It came out first with the animals. Incredibly determined, she had created a backyard menagerie of those particularly lucky creatures that fell into her hands before they met the ultimate sanction at the city animal shelter. To support her critters, she got a paper route. The animals went at age fifteen. She swore off loving animals as best she could, and at age sixteen, became a somewhat introspective girl who plunged headlong into the world of computers.

It was only with her MBA that she had a sort of social blossoming. Awkward at first, she learned how to reach out to people. Shortly after school, she wed. She thrived at her first job, at Delphi, a high-tech company, where she soon headed the information technology division.

When Gail, her best friend since childhood, suffered an auto accident that broke multiple bones, almost ruined an eye, and generally made her a nervous, quivering person, Jessie gave up the better part of her "free" time to help her old friend. Just about that time, Jessie's husband, Norman, announced their breakup to their respective families.

Gail was the reason Jessie had joined the FBI. Gail had a job in the public relations department for the Bureau in Washington, D.C. Although Jessie was a computer whiz, and she was more or less happily buried in her work, and had lots of friends, she wanted to do something more creative. Gail, for her part, wanted Jessie for a roommate, now that Norman was history, so she convinced her to join the Bureau, effectively arguing that Jessie could specialize in computer crime—no street work—and match wits with the smartest crooks in the business. There was no end to the personal creativity she could bring to the task of hunting down virus disseminators, techno-terrorists, and other computer criminals.

Jessie surprised herself by going for it—the right thing at the right time, she guessed—turning down two promotion offers from Delphi. A lot of things about making the move were painful, including the sizable cut in pay, and the interminable, but ultimately rewarding, training.

She rapidly formed many good relationships, chief among them the one with her boss, Frank Bilotti. She had known him for three years before he did the unthinkable.

Although Gail had been the initial victim, it was Jessie who was the witness on whom the entire case against Frank rested. Without what Jessie saw and heard, there would be no investigation of Frank Bilotti. What Frank did to Jessie was threaten her career, and what she held most dear, her reputation, in order to force her silence. What he really did was break her heart. Then it was a professional war.

Of course, when the Bilotti thing blew up, Gail had pointed out that it was ludicrous for Jessie Mayfield to leave the dung heap of a bureaucratic mess for the dirt roads and insect-ridden, off-the-grid, back-country living of Wintoon County. This was not a Jessie Mayfield kind of place. There were no hot dog stands, Jewish delicatessens, sushi bars, or theater districts—nothing but her sister Claudie.

When Frank found out that Jessie intended to bring him down, Jessie just purchased an airline ticket, found Gail a good shrink and an extra friend, then hugged her good-bye and said she'd be back in a month. Given the nature of the accusations (word of which had immediately filtered up and down the Bureau's ranks), and despite Frank's flat denials, counter-accu-

sations, and old-boy buddies backing him up, the FBI w
have given Jessie a six-month administrative leave of absen
if she'd asked for it. As it was, she was taking a month. Until
then, Frank could sweat.

As Kier wound his way down from Elk Horn Pass, he felt
the four-wheel-drive climb over the billowy drifts and enjoyed
the familiar sounds of his truck's heavy-treaded tires compress-
ing new snow. The mindless driving eased his anger at the hell
Winona had just been through. Kier had noted, but not remarked
upon the infant's dark complexion. It could have been Winona's
natural child, fathered by a fellow Tilok. Tilok parentage
seemed unlikely, though. Few Indians could afford the repro-
ductive technology of this clinic. It wasn't like the measles or
an appendectomy or a normal birth where government dollars
or insurance coverage was available. Could the parents have
been from some other mahogany-skinned race? Kier wondered.
He had been expecting a white child, and this visit had been
an eye-opener in more ways than one.

As the grade lessened and the road met the valley floor, a
thought occurred to him: He wasn't going to get back over Elk
Horn Pass tonight or tomorrow. The snow would be impassable
until the heaviest plows got off other jobs and managed to
break through. This wild valley, being so sparsely populated,
was not a high priority for county snow removal.

Being stuck in Mill Valley would actually come as a welcome
relief—a little time off from his veterinary practice in Johnson
City. He could stay in his cabin and complete the construction
of a bookcase that had been unfinished for months. It all dove-
tailed with his visit to the Donahue ranch. For a mare in foal,
Kier might have sent an assistant into the valley, but the
Donahues were as close to him as family.

The evergreens to either side of the roadway were imposing,
white cones. Interspersed, from ground to sky, the hardwoods

out gnarled winter-darkened branches with iced toppings—
witches' fingers, the Indian kids called them.

Windblown snowflakes choked the air. In the valley, the new
snow would soon melt. But in the high country, winter had
arrived. Nearly vertical, moss-bearded granite faces and green,
conifered slopes rose thousands of feet from the river gorge
that cupped the road on which he drove. According to Tilok
legend, the world began here. A little of the coastal California
mountain range still belonged to the sovereign nations of the
Hoopa, Yurok, and Tilok tribes, but the greater part by far
belonged to the U.S. government.

Rounding the corner at the abandoned Murdock homestead,
Kier looked up the old road past the leafless maples and into
the old orchards that were feasting places for the deer, and
ghost places for men—reminders of a time when small farmers
populated the valley. They lived a simple life, with no radio,
lots of kids, lots of food, hand-me-down clothes, and screen
doors to control the bugs.

Even through the fresh snow at the Murdock turnoff, he
could see the imprints of multiple, deep-treaded tires. His
pickup bounced and fishtailed as it rolled over the big, frozen
ruts. Strange. Few vehicles would be heavy or large enough to
leave such a calling card. Either a loaded dump truck or water
truck had made several trips or, even more unusual, several
heavy vehicles had traveled to the Murdock's in a convoy.

Kier considered turning around and investigating, but the
snow already covered the valley floor, and he needed to check
out the horse. If Claudie was right, the mare would drop her
foal any time now.

Six of the eight miles down from the summit, Kier saw the
tail of a snow-covered, boxy car just ahead of him. It looked
like Claudie Donahue's Volvo, and given the number of cars
in this area, it almost certainly was. Strange that she would be
coming back from town in this weather, especially with the
mare's delicate condition and her own health impaired by a

bout of shingles. Kier thought it odd that Claudie didn't pull over to let him pass, since the truck could break a path through the snow for her sedan.

Now the Volvo slowed even more. The blizzard was whiting out everything so badly that maybe Claudie feared she would miss the turnoff. But that wasn't like her. She knew the road as well as anyone.

Kier flashed his headlights repeatedly, signaling for her to stop, and finally she did. He pulled alongside the car, slid across the seat, and rolled down his window, sticking his face into the wind and snow. Her window lowered, and Kier's mouth fell open. This was not Claudie Donahue.

"What do you want?"

The woman behind the wheel had curious brown eyes like brook-shined stones, wet with intensity. Her brown hair was pulled back sleekly to the top of her head, where it cascaded back down in well-coifed curls. Her dark sweater was embroidered with gold thread, and her lapel sported a gold rose pin. She had the look of the city. Nothing this refined had ever arrived in Mill Valley, much less in a blizzard.

For a moment the words stuck in his throat—not so much because of her appeal as at his shock at encountering this creature that didn't quite fit in this world of dirt, trees, ice-covered mountains, barns, manure, and sawdust.

"You going to the Donahues'?"

"Why do you want to know?"

"Maybe I could help."

"Didn't know I needed any."

"Well, I'm the local vet, and I'm going there now."

"Oh. Hello." Her face softened slightly. "Well, I guess I'll see you there then. I'm visiting my sister to give her a hand until she gets a little better."

He hesitated, wondering if she knew he ought to go first and break trail. Shouting in the storm felt awkward, especially since they hadn't had any introduction.

Her chained tires dug in and she lurched ahead. Perhaps she felt more secure with him trailing along behind.

And then he knew.

He hadn't been thinking. She was Claudie's sister, Jessie. He knew perfectly well from photos that Jessie was brunette and beautiful.

"A woman from New York City, driving in these mountains, in a whiteout," he told himself, shaking his head.

The most he had heard about Jessie at one sitting was a few years back, when Claudie told Kier her kid sister was joining the FBI, her specialty computer crime. Claudie had been so proud. According to Claudie, Jessie was a tough one, the type who kicked guys in the testicles and smiled.

The arctic cold front was doing its deed in earnest. With the truck's wipers losing the fight against the ice, the Volvo quickly disappeared, then abruptly reappeared out of the storm—at a dead crawl. Kier nearly rear-ended her, swerved, and made a split-second decision to go around the car. Now was his chance—he would lead the way.

To his surprise, the Volvo jumped ahead, moving toward the centerline. It was too late to avoid a collison. Grating fenders sent an ugly feeling through his gut. The Volvo's left rear fender crumpled against the oversize tires of the pickup.

Within seconds, Jessie's fist was pounding on the passenger's side window. He opened the door, and she jumped in.

"I have never had an accident." She said it in a deliberate, clipped way. Her cheeks were red, her dark hair flecked with snow. "Now this."

"I'm Kier Wintripp. Like I said, I was just on my way to Claudie's. It's nice to meet you. And I apologize for the fender."

"Jessie Mayfield." She shook his hand in a businesslike manner.

"I can be of more help if I go just ahead of you," Kier

continued. "The truck will pack down the snow, and I know the way."

"I *know* the way." She paused. "Look, you pulled around without any warning," she said more sharply. "I know I sound angry." Another pause.

Kier decided that whatever she was thinking was a welcome distraction from her anger.

"That's probably because I'm pissed," she said, half laughing. He noticed what on a better day would be a terrific smile.

"Don't be. I crashed into your car. You have a right to yell."

"Wait, wait." She shook her head. "I am not yelling."

He knew he should drop it. But he couldn't resist.

"Claudie will understand. Blinding snowstorm. You pulled ahead unexpectedly while I was trying to go around you. To break trail."

"I was trying to get to the middle of this disappearing road, and you neglected to explain that you should go ahead when you stopped me."

"This is no big deal," Kier said. "You're just not used to driving on mountain roads in a snowstorm."

"I'm from New York. It snows every winter."

He stared at her, somewhat amused, somewhat stumped.

She stared back. "My sister calls you the James Herriot of Wintoon County. Says you tame mean dogs just by looking at them. Even tame shrews. So where did that soothing personality go?"

"By *not* looking at them. I just don't challenge dogs."

She opened the door and stepped into the snow.

"Ever try it on people?"

"I treat most anything. If your shrew has a problem, you could call for an appointment."

She shut his door firmly.

* * *

"A cougar attacked Dawn. She's bleeding and won't let anyone near her. She's crazy with fear and dilated like she's going to foal."

Nothing about this day would be easy. At the Donahue ranch, Claudie was waiting for them in front of the house in the full blizzard.

She glanced from Jessie to Kier, seemingly unconcerned about the fender of her Volvo. Even in an emergency, she had those mother's-bliss eyes, now slick with tears.

"Where is she?" Kier asked.

"We put her in the paddock near the woods where she wouldn't be bothered. Ever since that new law where nobody can shoot the cougars, they've come around. But usually they stay away from the big animals." Claudie drew a breath, visibly shaken. "I'll bet she's up the pasture a long ways."

"Just let me get a few things."

Kier pulled a big nylon bag from his truck. In seconds, they were in the old barn, Jessie following. They passed eight stalls that opened onto the paddocks, and walked out into the storm. In the far corner of the paddock, the soil was broken and the electric fence ripped apart.

"Normally, I'd chase her on another horse and rope her, but she's about to foal," Claudie said. "I didn't know what to do."

Kier walked quickly to where the mare had tussled with the cat, trying to read what had happened.

"Swollen and slow," he said. "She looked wounded to the cat . . . easy prey." Kier shook his head. "In her condition, she won't run far. You two can use the truck." He looked at Jessie. "I assume you don't ride horses."

"Just have that look about me, huh?"

It took Kier a few minutes to saddle a horse in the barn. He then took a second horse and clipped a lead rope onto its halter.

"Why are you bringing Shaman too?" Claudie asked, referring to the haltered horse.

"You'll see."

Jessie was both attracted and repelled by this man. In her current frame of mind it was a relief to find anything attractive about any man. Probably the stories she had heard, the healing stuff, influenced her perceptions. He was also handsome and more masculine than a leather tobacco pouch. Now, sitting in his truck she had studied him; the fade of his jeans, and that they were clean; the deep brown of his heavily oiled boots; his leanness—no part of his belly hung over his belt, and his smart-looking khaki shirt.

Now watching him ride in a bulky overcoat, his hat cocked low, leaning into the wind, he looked like a vision from the old West. After a couple of hundred yards, Jessie and Claudie drove up to a barbed-wire fence. They got out and walked to where Kier knelt over tracks in the snow. The flakes were beginning to dance and swirl. Drifts were deepening.

"I doubt she crossed this fence. So she was probably shunted to the far corner," Claudie said.

"Yup." Kier followed the tracks down the fence line. "Damn."

He knelt again at a muddy spot where the snow mixed with soil. There was a cougar track right amongst the mare's hoofprints. A splotch of blood had congealed on the snow.

"He's still after her."

Kier opened a compartment on the truck and removed a large canvas bag, which he handed to Jessie. Grabbing the saddle horn, he vaulted onto the horse and, in one smooth motion, snatched back his medical bag.

"Catch up with me," he said, leaving at a dead run.

Jessie and Claudie didn't have to drive far. Around the next

stand of trees, Jessie saw Kier in the distance, standing next
to his mount, watching the silver-gray mare against the fence.
Coming right to the foot of the mountain, the oak-dotted pasture
made a natural funnel defined by the terrain. The cattle scattered
in response to the activity, then banded together in the far
corner of the pasture, perhaps smelling the blood or the big
cat.

Kier left his medical bag by a lone oak, then swung out of
the saddle and hung from the side of his horse with one foot
in the stirrup, his body facing his mount's rear. From what she
could tell, Kier was approaching the mare while leading the
other horse. The wounded mare tossed her head and began
moving away down the fence.

Kier stopped.

As they neared the scene, Jessie could see the lather and
blood covering the panicked Dawn. Nostrils flaring, the horse
panted wildly, intermittently making a high-pitched, squealing
noise. Jessie could even see the newborn colt beginning to
emerge, a dark spot that appeared to be the colt's forelegs.

Kier waved at Jessie to stop the truck.

Now Jessie saw the blood on the mare's flanks and a horrible
wound on her nose. On her belly a deep, bloody furrow ran
between many smaller gashes. Jessie gasped. What looked like
greenish viscera protruded from the deeper belly wounds. Blood
dripped thickly from more places than she could count.

At the oak tree, the women climbed out of the truck, watching, riveted to the delicate dance before them. Every time Kier's
horse stepped toward the mare, the wounded creature would
begin moving up the fence.

"It looks bad," Jessie said.

"It's worse than that," Claudie said. "From what I can see,
the cat grabbed her nose with his paw, sank his teeth in her
neck, raked her flank. I think she's lost a lot of blood."

Jessie suddenly realized why Kier was hanging off his horse:
By doing so, he remained almost invisible to the wounded

mare. Guiding the two horses to the mare's left side, Kier
stopped them along the fence a good thirty feet from her. He
steadied the two horses, now skittish at the smell of blood, and
kept them tight together.

Still the mare sidestepped away.

Kier moved the two horses again, at least ten feet back,
giving Dawn even more room. The mare still tossed her head,
but this time she took a few nervous steps toward them. Kier
remained stock-still, stuck to the side of his horse. Again the
mare came toward them, then stopped. It seemed she would
come no closer.

Stepping down from his mount, Kier let his horse drift away,
so that he came into full view of the mare. He stood square to
her, focusing all his attention on her now. He raised his arm
and pointed at her and began chanting loudly in Tilok.

The mare pawed and snorted. She backed away at first. But
after a minute, she turned sideways, flicked an ear, then released
a breathy squeal of pain. Another contraction came hard. The
moment the mare flicked the ear down, Kier's chanting grew
softer, and he turned sideways to her as if singing to the horizon—as if he were ignoring her.

As the two horses with Kier calmed down, the mare neighed,
rolled her eyes, and stepped closer. Now, she was perhaps
twenty feet away. Seconds ticked by. Wearily, she pawed the
ground, wobbling as if she might go down. Whinnying sounds
followed breathy squeals in time with her contractions.

Kier's chanting grew louder again, and he once again turned
squarely and pointed at her, fixing his gaze on her. The mare
threw her head and backed up. Still Kier pressed her, even
stepping forward, his arm locked, finger aimed. Again she
moved away, breathing hard, frightened, pitiful. Finally, her
ear cocked and she turned her flank to Kier. He also turned
sideways, crooning softly, seeming once again to ignore her
altogether.

To Jessie it seemed almost as if Kier were in a trance,

unconcerned, unaware of the emergency to his side. Then she noticed his feet; like the minute hand on a clock, they moved in almost undetectable increments. The two horses at his sides just naturally drifted with him. They were almost to the mare when she closed the gap by taking two steps toward them. Kier slipped the lariat off the saddle horn.

"God, this should be on TV," Jessie whispered. "What are the words?"

Claudie shook her head. "Some weird Tilok chant." She shook her head. "As long as it works."

Now Kier moved to the mare, stroking between her eyes. His chant became softer yet as, slowly, he moved to the side of her neck and slipped the lasso over her head. With the rope around her, the mare seemed to calm completely, as if she knew it was futile even to think of running. Gently, Kier tugged her down into the snow so that she lay on her side. In an instant, he was on his knees, stroking her neck and motioning the women forward. Claudie came with the medical bag, while Jessie hung back, knowing instinctively that it would not be good to crowd the injured mare.

With each contraction, Dawn let out an almost human groan. Now a third of the way out of the womb, the glistening wet colt thrashed its forelegs to aid in its own birth. It appeared a spindly, delicate thing as it came through the stretched membranes.

Using large metal hemostats, which looked to Jessie like needle-nose pliers, Kier set about probing the deep ugly wounds on the mare's neck. He pinched off the larger blood vessels, all the while chanting to the horse. Next, he did the same with the fissurelike wound in her belly. Finally, he moved to the colt and helped it slip from the birth canal.

Jessie watched his face while he worked, the calm concentration as his hands constantly moved, touching the mare, stroking her as she released her foal.

At last Kier looked to the women and nodded. Claudie breathed a sigh.

"I need to get back to the kids," she said. Then Jessie felt Claudie's hand on her shoulder.

"You should be more careful about letting that stallion get to the mare in the springtime. This is the wrong season for delivering a foal."

For the trip back to the barn, Kier had the foal on a small pile of straw in the bed of the pickup. The mare, no longer bleeding, would follow her foal at her own pace. The other two horses, now in halters, with their saddles and tack in the truck, would instinctively return to the comfort of their stalls and paddock.

"That stallion's like a lot of men," said Claudie. "Just one thing on his mind."

"I don't know any men like that," Kier said.

He sat next to Jessie, relaxing his legs, aware that her thigh was touching his. He sensed that she was nervous about the contact. Claudie was completely spread out on the passenger side, perhaps oblivious to her sister's situation. Perhaps not. They crossed over Wispit Creek on a small bridge. He took in the pleasant fragrance of Jessie's hair and secretly enjoyed the way she tossed it to keep it out of her eyes. After helping Claudie out of the truck, he offered Jessie a hand.

"You're trying to decide if I'm a human being or a cop?"

"No. I think that's your question."

He walked to the back of the truck to lift out the foal. Its wobbly legs went in every direction as Kier carried him into a hay-covered stall in the barn.

"What did you mean by that?" she said as she followed him to the barn. "Do you have something against federal agents or just women?"

"How long have you been worried about it?"

"I'm not worried about it."

"Am I right that shoving people around, shootouts and the like doesn't detract at all from your personhood?"

She stood openmouthed. "Well, that's hardly—"

"Good, then I guess it's not a problem."

Instinctively he knew that she cared what he thought of her. He hadn't figured out why. Maybe it was the reason he seemed to be talking so much. As the women stood in the doorway, watching the storm, the mare arrived. With the women looking on, and holding lights, he began the tedious job of dressing the wounds.

An hour later, his back hurting, he joined Jessie and Claudie at the barn door. The snow had grown alarmingly deep already.

As he reached for his bag, he looked over his left shoulder and across the barn to a head peering around a pile of five-gallon plastic containers. Kier looked into the dark eyes of Turtleneck, the Donahues' pet llama. As always, Kier silently cussed his failure to save the animal's mother. Tentatively, the young creature walked across the board floor, coming to see Kier.

She was a pleasant diversion from all the troubles of the day. He stripped off his rubber gloves, stroking the rich woolly coat of her back, and in turn she offered her nose and nuzzled his hand. Knowing that she was being weaned from the bottle, Kier hummed a Tilok chant and let her suck on his finger. The furling tongue felt like caterpillars.

Jessie came over. She too began petting the llama. Glancing out of the corner of his eye, Kier noticed a nervous little smile. He would wait for her to speak. Evidently she had the same idea, because the llama was basking in the quiet chant and all the attention.

She cleared her throat. He remained impassive, saying nothing as he rubbed the llama between its eyes.

"I guess maybe we didn't get off on the right foot," she finally said.

"Why is that?"

"Well, the fender. And I guess you don't much care for FBI agents."

"How do you feel about them?" he asked.

"That's like asking how I feel about postmen. Some good, some not so good." She looked at him, apparently expecting some sign of agreement or understanding. He studied the llama's limpid eyes. "Well, for example, how do you feel about Indians?" she asked.

"About like that. Some good, some not so good."

"So do you think maybe we could start again?"

"You gonna be a postman or an Indian this time?"

She breathed as if to speak, then paused, unsure.

He gave her a rare smile. "I'm more or less just kidding you."

"Oh." She looked nonplussed. "Well, it certainly worked."

"Look, I'm pleased to meet you." He extended his hand. "I think women as attractive as you make me nervous. To be honest."

Jessie shook his hand gamely. "Will you be staying for a while? I mean with the blizzard and the pass and everything? Claudie and I would like some company. I'm visiting over Thanksgiving, trying to help Sis with all she's got going. This shingles is a weird disease. Anyway, will you stay?"

"Really, I ah . . . well, I think I better go. I have a cabin, and I have a little building project there." He was amazed and irritated at how nervous he felt. Leaving sounded good and bad all at the same time. "Actually, I've gotta be on my way."

"Okay," was all she said. But it was at that moment that he realized something was wrong. Maybe it was the way Jessie said the word, the shrug of her shoulders, or her tone when she had asked him to stay. Or maybe what was unconscious had just become conscious. He felt as though he had just kicked a helpless creature.

Claudie was coming back through the doorway to check on her horse. Or her sister. Kier wasn't sure which.

"Hi, how you doing?" Jessie said to Claudie, taking her arm. Jessie seemed confident, soothing, and strong. Perhaps he was imagining things. Never in a single day had he had so many catastrophes.

Things would get better, they always did. Perhaps things were actually not so bad. The foal would survive, and the mare would recover. He doubted Winona would be doing any more surrogate mothering. She could work in his vet clinic.

Kier was bidding Jessie and Claudie farewell, still thinking about Jessie, when it happened.

It started as a barely audible roar, but turned into shrieking thunder. The air seemed to compress; even the storm seemed to still. Incredibly bright light flashed overhead, streaming through the falling snow.

Concussive shock waves sent a rolling vibration through the barn, and a series of muffled booms shook the air again. Kier allowed his awareness to expand as his body absorbed the reverberations. He looked everywhere and nowhere, marveling at the intensity of the light. On the wind he smelled kerosene, pungent and foreign.

Then the cold silence of a winter pasture reclaimed the Donahue ranch. Turtleneck had disappeared behind a haystack.

"What in the name of heaven—" Claudie began.

Kier's heart picked a slightly faster rhythm, but his calm remained. Separating things in his mind, like untangling a snarled line, he knew that the explosions, the light, the roar, and the odors had been man-made. No natural phenomenon could account for what he had just experienced.

"That sounded like a jet crashing," said Jessie.

"Like jet engines near full throttle," Kier agreed. "Before the impact."

"Oh my God," Claudie breathed.

Kier squinted into the blizzard, which showed no sign of letting up.

"I'm going," he told them.

"I'm coming too," said Jessie just as quickly.

Kier knew it would only waste time to argue with her.

"Suit yourself," he said and ran into the storm.

Chapter 2

A man who ignores the bear in the night will be
the feast by morning.

—Tilok proverb

Stalking Bear sat on Iron Mountain under the outstretched
branches of a giant Douglas fir. There were two faces to this
tree: the windward (the angrier face) and the lee. On the lee
side, a large boulder created a wall. Between the rock and the
tree, the mountain made a shelter as peaceful as the place for
a babe between its mother's breasts. Despite the storm, the
snow had scarcely dusted the old man's blankets.

A host of men had descended upon Iron Mountain over the
past twenty-four hours. They had guns and walked about with
maps and gadgets, trampling the forest underfoot, and defecat-
ing like sick dogs. They talked on and on, with a separate
complaint for every twig that pressed into their oversized
haunches. Only one among them could listen to the forest, and

this man was driven by something unnatural. The other men seemed no more than careless accidents.

With eyes closed and the blankets over his head, Stalking Bear slept. The pestilence that had drawn so close fanned his dreams into giant flames.

A distant roaring opened his eyes. It grew and tore across the landscape. He heard it making junk of the trees and covered his ears.

It stopped as quickly as it had come.

Stalking Bear rose and stood motionless, watching. He felt the cool in his lungs and the sweat soaking his shirt in the chill of the howling wind. All around, granite cliffs stood in silent witness to this sudden intrusion into the mountain valley.

Above Stalking Bear, kier, the fish hawk, unfurled its wings and slid through the blowing snow to disappear against the evergreens. In the sudden quiet, a slow shiver of anticipation crept up the old man's spine.

In that instant, he knew. He was being called to a danger he did not understand in a place that had been Tilok forever.

Jessie held on to the back of Kier's coat, maintaining actual physical contact and tolerating this lash-up only because it was the simplest way to be sure that they weren't separated. Endless FBI training exercises had taught her to go from an ordinary state to the edge of an adrenaline high in seconds without the mind-spinning disorientation that ordinarily accompanied the shock of extremes. Being in a howling blizzard and looking for God-knew-what qualified as such a situation. She expected to find spilled jet fuel, with maybe more explosions, and probably people at death's door.

This was not the time or place for a triage operation, Jessie realized. Kier's veterinary medicine would do little for people who needed plasma and blood. It would be agonizing for injured survivors. This was also not the time to allow quibbles with this man to prevent their cooperation in a potential disaster.

Only after Kier turned to take her arm did she realize that she must have been dragging. She tried to concentrate on keeping up with him in the snow, an almost impossible task, for Kier Wintripp was superbly fit.

As she put her head down to gut it out, she glimpsed snow-laden branches low to the ground, probably the firs between the field and Elk Horn Mountain road. The whole area around her sister's home was a jumble in her mind. Grudgingly, she credited Kier with an almost inhuman ability to find his way—and to find people, from the stories Claudie told. Jessie assumed he had a perfect map of this mountainous terrain in his head.

More trees—a wall of them, with heavy brush beneath—slowed their progress. They slid through the dense stuff with a slapping of branches and barely audible crashes in the thickening whiteness. Kier paused. Correcting slightly, he headed off at a new angle—away from the road, she was sure. As they topped a steep rise, thigh deep in snowy windfalls, they spied a giant hole through a thicket of evergreens. It had to be the jet's crash path, if indeed it was a jet.

They were trotting instead of running now, Jessie's bursting lungs filling in short gasps. The brush grabbed at her jeans and jacket. Tough, prickly branches raked her legs and shins.

Kier stopped abruptly. "Through the brush," he said, pointing ahead. "It's big, but it's no 747."

She could see the hole through the forest clearly now. Broken trees lay everywhere along the flight path. A small bunch of evergreens—Jessie thought some sort of fir, each tree about a foot in diameter—had been shattered six feet above the ground. Climbing through the downed trees looked impossible, but Kier scrambled over and under, breaking a trail, pulling and lifting her through the hardest spots.

A silver squirrel with obsidian-bead eyes stood on the remaining stump of a sheared-off evergreen. Apparently his tree had snapped right at the roof of his hollow in the trunk, leaving him miserably exposed, shaking and chattering—the squirrel version of "Oh shit."

They came upon more broken trees, oaks still not completely shed of their leaves. Big pieces of sheet aluminum lay about the ground and among the fractured branches. Everything was frosted with snow. She didn't see the jet engine until she had almost run into it, smoking hot and steaming in the cold. Not more than a few feet away a still-smoldering wing looked like the shredded remains of a popped balloon. They followed the trail of mangled foliage until they saw what looked like the main body of the plane. Squinting in the blinding snow, Jessie saw a blurry scene of shadow and white.

The plane had the sleek look of the private jets used by corporate moguls and Hollywood stars. It was the size of a small commuter jet, perhaps a little shorter than a 737. It lay in a tangle of woody debris and earth, the cockpit partially covered with snow on the windward side, a gaping hole near the tail. The fuselage seemed mostly intact.

Jessie stepped over a shoe containing a foot and a shinbone— nothing more. Trying not to slip on the snow-covered rocks and cluttered debris, she muttered thanks to Kier, who briefly steadied her by her arm. As they drew nearer, they found the body that went with the foot spilling out of the wreckage. Caucasian, maybe in his thirties, dead of multiple, massive injuries.

Jessie whisked snow from his face . . . and sucked in a lungful of icy air. There, neat and round as a Concord grape, was a bullet hole in his forehead. Little blood stained the snow. He had been shot in the plane before it crashed.

The man wore an empty shoulder holster, reddish-brown, and twisted bizarrely over his chest. *Think. Draw your gun.* Training took over. Jessie reached under her coat for her 9-mm. semiautomatic, which was housed in its own business- black shoulder holster. Standard issue now was 10-mm., but the recoil was excessive for her light body and she did, after all, spend her time in offices, so carrying a cannon seemed unnecessary. She had never drawn it except to practice.

Breathe deep. Scan. Scan. It was Dunfee shouting in that gravelly, knock-down-a-wall voice she'd never forget. Special Agent Mike Dunfee might as well have been standing behind her. Assuming the stance he'd taught her, adrenaline fluttering her legs and pounding her heart, she pointed her gun directly in front of her and began a 360-degree pivot around Kier. She could see only desolation.

Should she rush into the plane? Better to be careful, she decided as she felt Kier pulling her down into a crouch next to the plane's rear entry. Facing him, she saw calm in his eyes.

"Give me the gun and let me go in there first," he said, nodding at the hulk that had been a jet.

"This is my job."

"Right." He took a deep breath, obviously trying to figure what he should say next.

"Listen. I know you're an FBI agent, but you run computers, don't you?"

"I run computers. You doctor sick animals."

He stared off to the side with his jaw clenched.

"Yeah, well, I hope it doesn't bury you."

"Well, if it does, I died doing my job."

Without saying more, he let his eyes gaze over the landscape, searching, trying, Jessie knew, to devour every inch, to know more than could be known. Kier motioned with his head and they moved just inside the fuselage through the rear hole.

"This is my deal, Kier," she said again, trying to slow him down.

She fought to find the confidence that had gotten her this far in life. She worked with computers because she was good at it, not because she was afraid of the field.

Quickly she surveyed what she could see of the main cabin. In the darkened interior to the left, she could make out a scramble of bodies and debris. Nothing moved. There were papers and blood everywhere. To the right, she found that the tail section contained large plastic pods, most of them broken open and covered with ice. Some were full of documents; others had what looked to be the remains of lab vials. Thousands of small plastic containers were strewn around. Kier was like a shadow standing so close that she could feel his breath as he looked over her shoulder.

"Anybody hear me?" she called.

"Everybody I can see is dead," Kier said.

Quickly she checked the bodies that she could easily reach. Most had visible bullet wounds in addition to crash injuries. All dead.

While Kier began looking through the papers strewn near the jet's rear door, Jessie returned to the corpse outside. Crouching by the body, she wished desperately for plastic gloves. She had studied bullet wounds in pictures, and in bodies at the morgue. This was different. Here there was the nauseating odor of a perforated bowel, the slaughterhouse reek of open entrails. And here she had to hurry. More bodies were inside. Who had done the shooting and why? Had this been a hit man or a bodyguard? Foreign agent? Mafia member?

She searched the body. Blood caked the torn shirt and suit coat—expensive clothing by the looks of it. Under the suit, the chest was spongy, and the steaming innards had popped out through lacerations in the belly—bluish-green, translucent, like twisted sausage.

"This is all lab stuff," Kier called from just inside the plane. He was opening a thick three-ring binder, one of many.

Jessie found nothing in the jacket or pants pockets, not even lint; it was as if the suit had been taken directly off the store rack. No I.D. This man was not law enforcement.

As she moved back to the rear of the fuselage, Kier did not even look up from his reading.

Inside and to the left lay seats for more than twenty people, spaciously arranged. In the gray half-light she counted the bodies, some hanging lifeless in their belts, others squeezed between collapsed seats. Nine. Looking back, she saw Kier still studying the papers.

"We really shouldn't touch things," she said without conviction, knowing the plane could catch fire and burn, leaving nothing but a mystery.

A feeling came over her that she'd forgotten something. She looked back outside the way she had come. There it was. Partially snow-filled footprints circled the jet, ultimately leading off into the brush. She hadn't noticed them before. Someone must have survived, or found the wreck before she and Kier did.

"There are tracks," she called to Kier.

"I saw. They're hard to read." He barely looked up from the black plastic binder.

"What else haven't you told me?"

"I think the person doesn't want to be found." He shrugged. "He's long gone. Probably at the county road."

"I can't believe anybody survived," she said. "What's in the binder?"

"I'm not sure yet."

"You're taking this awfully calmly."

"The bland expression is hereditary."

It struck her as the driest sort of black humor. She watched a moment longer as he pored over the pages.

The smell of jet fuel stung her nostrils. Better hurry. Stepping gun first, she began making her way through the passenger cabin. Teal leather and rose carpets told her the decorator had an eye for the gaudy. Oxygen masks dangled from the ceiling. The fuselage of the jet was crushed in places, but she saw no complete breach, except at the large hole where she now stood, and at the midsection, where a stump had pierced the side of the plane. Exposed wires, like veins on a skinned carcass, ran fore and aft. Blood stained even the ceiling.

The quiet was eerie—pregnant with tension, as if someone was waiting, watching. She took her uneasiness as a warning, and did not struggle with the illogic of it.

Four bodies, facing one another in club seating, sat slightly aft of the midsection. The stretched seat belts were almost ripped from their fittings. Near the first body, Jessie found a gun on the floor. Bullet holes riddled the back of the man's suit.

Struggling through his pockets, vomit tickling the base of her throat, she found no I.D. on this one either. On the other side of the aisle, the next body lay in the seats like a collapsed marionette without the strings. The way the body was compressed between the seats it would take a pathology team to pull it out and determine the cause of death. Only arms in camel-hair sleeves and legs in twill slacks remained visible.

In the next row forward on the left side lay the other two bodies. One had his head back, tongue extended between clenched teeth, and a 10-mm. Glock with a silencer in his hand. She put her nose close and caught the smell of a fired weapon.

Farther forward sat a macabre, five-person huddle—two women and three men who didn't seem to have guns. All of the men had wallets with ordinary-looking I.D., including drivers' licenses. They wore slacks and open shirts. One woman was dressed in a business suit, the other in a pantsuit. All the clothes looked middle-American plain, stuff that could have come from any mass merchandiser—nothing like the slick Italian suit of the gunman.

Kier, now some distance away, still knelt in the tail section with the binders. He showed not the slightest interest in the plane or the bodies.

"Are you finding anything I should know about?" she shouted.

"I'll tell you later."

She made herself continue to the command center of the plane. Beyond a maze of more seats and debris, a partially crushed door had been completely pierced by a heavy object—maybe a person's head. The jagged hole was as big as a basketball. Through that door she would find the flight crew.

She heard a buzzing sound and automatically ducked, squeezing her way between seats and bodies, trying to avoid looking into the sightless eyes of a grotesquely twisted head. Now the buzzing combined with a popping noise. *Of course—electric wires were shorting.* Her gut tightened as her nostrils caught the heavy smell of burned plastic. She saw no visible flame—yet.

"Kier," she yelled. "Kier," she said more loudly. "Get out of here. Take what you can."

She glanced behind her. He was already gone.

Her hands started shaking. An adrenaline intensity overtook her body. There was something . . . a presence. The physical cold mingled with her chilled spirit as the plane made deathly creaks. Outside, the forest was passing into nature's own death: winter.

As Jessie touched the cockpit door, she caught sight of something through the jagged hole: steam—delicate, ghostly puffs of vapor—each wisp so marginally visible she wondered if they really existed.

It was someone's breath condensing.

Chapter 3

Good men kill when the only alternative is more killing.

—Tilok proverb

For a moment he watched Jessie as she knelt over the corpse in the snow outside the fuselage. Then he turned back to the interior of the plane, intensely curious. A feeling crept over Kier unlike any he could recall. It was like being tied to the tracks with train sounds in the midst. There were many large fiberglass pods, tan in color, stored in racks in the aft portion of the cabin. Each pod was about eight feet long, two feet in diameter. Most were broken open, and those that had split had heavy mantles of ice, like refrigerators in need of defrosting. Kier supposed that subzero nitrogen gas or something similar had escaped the pods, leaving behind the icy residue.

Spilling from the broken pods were broken DeWar flasks that looked like metal-clad thermoses. Some had obviously bounced around the cabin and had spilled their contents. Each flask bore an orange-and-black biohazard symbol. Squatting down, he looked inside one of the partially torn open flasks. A vertically suspended carriage with various levels and pie-shaped metal containers hung from the screw-on lid. Inside those metal containers were small, translucent vials, some filled with liquid, some with what looked like a gelatinous material. Each vial was a half inch long and coded with a number and initials. Each had a screw cap, the top with male threads, the vial itself with female threads. Some of the vials were crushed.

"This is all lab stuff," he said half to himself. Jessie, seemingly intent on the body, made no response.

The tiny placards on the scattered vials read variously: AVCD-4, AVCD-4-II, MY-TB, TB-I, TB-2, TB-AV, HP-A, HP-B, HP-C, and a host of other labels. Given the number of pods, if they were all similarly packed, there must have been thousands of vials.

Kier knew that "CD 4" was a name for a protein molecule on the outside of the white blood cells of humans and certain monkeys, but he did not know what "AV" might mean. He knew that "My TB" might stand for mycobacterium tuberculosis. HP-A, HP-B, HP-C were perhaps hepatitis A, B, and C. In fact, it seemed that most of the labels bore initials that were shorthand for an infectious disease. He recognized malaria, typhus, scarlet fever, the bubonic plague, leprosy, and many others. Still more vials, with labels like STAGE 5-MAL MEL, appeared to be shorthand for various kinds of cancer cells. A planeload of human diseases, a veritable Noah's ark of the plagues of mankind.

His scalp prickled. After glancing again at Jessie, who still knelt by the corpse in the snow, he turned his attention to a large black box that lay open. Its contents were five heavy binders. Possibly laboratory documentation.

No ordinary container, this box had a thick layer of rubberized material on the outside. The inside of the box was metal lined and its walls thick. It was undoubtedly fireproof and shock resistant. Beside the box lay two hefty combination locks that obviously had secured the latches before someone opened them.

Carefully he lifted out the binder labeled VOL. 1, opened it, and saw a table of contents for six volumes inserted loosely, as if the set was regularly updated. Looking down at the box again, Kier saw space for a sixth binder of the same dimensions as the first five. If the sixth volume had ever been there, it was now missing.

Jessie edged silently past him, headed toward the bodies in the plane.

After the table of contents came a handwritten page scrawled in blue ink. There was a spidery quality to the writing that was the telltale sign of a fountain pen in a hurried hand.

> *Jack Tillman's going to kill us all, Lord help us. And we have given him the tools. Although I have not yet made him God, I have put him at God's right hand. These volumes must be given to the media and to scientists who can sort out how to responsibly use what we have discovered. If you're reading this (and whether you work for Tillman or not) you must kill him before he kills you.*
>
> *I wanted to help my wife. That's how Tillman talked me into the Wintoon Project with the Tiloks. I never knew that by trying to save her, I would start this nightmare*

The page ended in mid-sentence.

Kier recalled Tillman's arrogant stare. He searched for the remainder of the handwritten diary, flipping quickly through the other volumes, looking for more summary explanations. Nothing.

Jessie, looking at bodies, said something about not touching things. But this was a treasure trove of information and even she didn't sound convinced. Not wanting to start an argument, he said nothing and continued on.

He searched the index for "Wintoon Project," finding only

a reference to Volume Six. But Volume Six was nowhere to be found, unless it was in the forward cabin among the debris.

Kier's eye wandered back to the flasks and vials and then to an index page. In a subheading that read "Adult Cloning Methodologies," he found a cross-reference to "Wintoon Project" at page 67 in the missing Volume Six. In fact, the table of contents showed that the entire last half of Volume Six was devoted to "DNA Reconstruction," "Gene Reassortment," "Gene Expression," and "DNA Chip Methodologies."

Looking up, he saw that Jessie was mostly finished with the bodies, staring back at him, wanting to know what he was finding. Where to begin? "I'll tell you later," was all he said, in deference to the smallness of his real answer as contrasted with the potential magnitude of the discovery.

Urgently, he skimmed the dense material for additional references to Wintoon. He again looked for the missing Volume Six, walking up the aisle partway toward Jessie. Nothing.

He had to get these books out of the plane in case it exploded and burned. Kier carried the binders out into the maelstrom and found the mountain still in the midst of its makeover. Snow blew in swirls—it blew up, it blew down, it covered every offered space.

He let his gaze wander over what he could see of the snow-covered trees and the crumpled jet, using what he observed and felt to focus his thinking. The men in this plane had been experimenting with DNA. They had been engaged in genetic tinkering that somehow involved the Tilok. According to the writer, Jack Tillman was a very dangerous man. He apparently owned the contents of the jet. Was all of this related to the Indian girls and their birth-mother jobs? And the disease agents? How?

As he placed the metal box beneath a fir, Kier felt overcome by a sense of disquiet. He shuddered with anticipation as his mind turned to Jessie. When he had last seen her, she had been walking toward the cockpit. He would check on her from outside the pilot's window.

In a few quick strides, he was at the airplane's front wind-shield, which was badly shattered, but not completely broken through. Even on the lee side of the plane, the same side they had entered at the tail, the snow had drifted halfway to the windows. But it was cottony soft. He sank in to his thighs.

He leaned a large metal bracing structure from the wing against the fuselage and stood on it, still barely able to see inside. It surprised him to find three bodies, one of them facing aft. He pulled himself up another inch. His eyes caught move-ment—the dull glint of metal. The third body was a live man, gun trained on Jessie through the jagged hole in the cockpit door.

Sliding back down the side of the plane, Kier ran, his great steps eating up the distance. As he passed through the rear entry into the cabin, he choked back the scream that threatened to escape his lips. He became a shadow, sliding up the aisle. He could see Jessie now, her hand reaching for the door, the assailant's bloodied face rising.

Jessie saw the ugly circle formed by the barrel of a large-bore handgun pointing through the hole in the cockpit door.

"Oh no," she breathed like a spent balloon.

Just then Kier's huge hand grabbed her thigh, pulling her body to the side of the cabin. A muted pop followed, and she knew that the silenced shot had narrowly missed her.

As she started to retreat, she brought her gun up and pulled the trigger. It felt like slow motion, but the sound of her shots almost ran together, the roar filling the tight space as the gun jumped in her hand. Kier kept pulling her aft. In a panic, they squeezed through the bodies until they both jumped outside.

Once in the snow, she looked at Kier. Both of them were

wet with perspiration despite the cold. "Thanks," she said shakily.

She popped the clip out of her pistol, willing herself to gather her thoughts as Kier peered back into the cabin, no doubt trying to catch a glimpse through the hole that had framed the shooter's face. Thirteen shots. Slowly she slid the clip back in place. *Think. Think. I've got a live shooter in the cockpit. Any more shots, the plane could explode. Talk him out. He's bleeding, it's cold. Time is on my side.*

"This is the FBI," she called into the fuselage.

Nothing. Not a groan, curse, or plea for help.

"Talk to me," she shouted.

Then she had an idea. When she looked at Kier, he was motioning to the front of the plane, mirroring her thoughts. It would be better to check the cockpit from the outside.

At the cockpit, she had him lift her to the windshield's edge. For an instant, she contemplated the feel of his large hands on her, even as the frigid wind iced her wet body.

Swiping the snow from her eyes, she peeked through the side window. Straining, she saw the gunman's torso. The shooter's gun hand jerked into view. She pulled away from the window, and Kier let her drop as the shooter's bullet split the windshield where her face had been.

"This is the FBI. The plane is surrounded," she called out.

"Oh, thank God," a voice called back above the wind. "I thought you were Tillman's guys."

"Let me get on top of the plane and drop in through the broken windshield," Kier told Jessie quietly. "You go inside and cover him."

"You're a civilian," she snapped. "More important, you'll be a wide-open target."

"Have him put his hands through the hole in the cockpit door. Shoot if he moves. I have a better chance than you would."

She knew he was right. Reluctantly, she nodded and moved along the fuselage.

"First throw out your gun," she called from the rear hatch.

"How do I know you're a Fed?"

"Mister, you're gonna bleed to death if we don't hurry, and I'm not crawling up there to do the I.D. bit. Not as long as you have a gun."

"All right. All right." A second later, a pistol, complete with a long, ugly silencer, flew through the hole in the cockpit door and skittered across the cabin floor. Among the five guys in slick Italian suits, Jessie had only found three guns. The man up front might easily have the fifth.

"Now put your face and hands through the hole in the cockpit door where I can see them."

Silence. She sensed Kier behind her; she could feel his body heat. He had followed her. She whispered to him: "You don't dare climb up on top and start smashing the windshield unless his mug is in a spot where I can shoot it off."

Kier nodded. Then something else flew through the hole in the cockpit door. A hand grenade.

"Tillman sent you!" the man screamed.

Kier saw it coming, and he knew the conventional wisdom: If you saw a grenade coming at you, it was probably too late.

Time didn't slow down for Kier. Nothing did. There was no moment of insight or thought; his life didn't flash before his eyes. There was only time for the instinct to survive. And therein lay the telling act, because he grabbed Jessie before he jumped.

Intense heat engulfed them. Pulling her on top of him, he slid down a brushy, snow-covered hillock.

He became vaguely aware that the foliage had quit slapping their bodies. He felt Jessie slide off and watched her sink a hand into the velvety powder, trying to find purchase.

Kier helped her push up.

Half to herself, she asked, "Why'd he do it?"

"Didn't believe you? Knew he'd die anyway? No telling."

"Didn't believe what?"

"Didn't believe you were the FBI. How would the FBI get here this fast? He said 'Tillman.' Tillman's in those papers." He nodded back at the plane.

"What do the papers say?"

"Be right back," he said. Kier climbed to the top of the short rise. Returning in about two minutes, he noticed she looked uneasy. He wondered if she'd ever been alone in the deep forest. Around them the oaks shone stark black against the snow that glazed the upper sides of their gnarled branches, witches' fingers pointing everywhere. Behind them the taller evergreens rose like crystalline spires. For him it was a magnificent place temporarily desecrated by mankind.

"You don't like it here."

"It's a dank forest, in winter. Somebody just tried to kill us."

Kier nodded and decided against explaining his thought. Instead, he showed her the elaborate box that contained the five black binders.

"So people are killing each other over a planeful of lab reports?"

"They're into something they shouldn't be. Genetics and more, and involving my tribe. I think that plane was loaded with every infectious disease known to man. Somebody's got to—"

A mountain of air, followed by a thundering blast, knocked them both on their backs. Debris pelted the trees above them. Without the embankment they might have been killed.

Kier lay stunned, not yet believing what had just happened. Jessie was getting up, but looked woozy.

"You okay?" he asked.

She nodded. "It had to be a bomb. I doubt that fuel could have exploded that violently. We were damned lucky."

They both stood, burning debris on the snow around them, and Kier nodded toward what looked like an impenetrable wall of snow-covered branches. Ducking beneath larger boughs and dislodging a cascade of snow in the process, he knocked smaller dead branches out of the way until he had created a sheltered area just large enough for them to huddle in under the cover of an old evergreen tree. They squatted with their backs to the trunk.

She groaned.

"Sorry I haven't got a chair."

"I'll manage just fine," she said.

He pulled out Volume One and handed her the handwritten page. While she read, he took the volumes out of the heavy box and put them in his pack, abandoning his medical supplies.

"God, what was on that plane?" Jessie had finished reading. "You suppose there's anything left after that explosion?"

"Don't know. Flames everywhere," he said.

"I've got to call for help."

He began crawling out of the brush toward the embankment. "Let's get back to Claudie's and the truck."

Chapter 4

A mighty warrior's thoughts are more deadly than
his arrows.

—Tilok proverb

Out of nowhere a man appeared, initially just a shadow in
the dull light, moving steadily toward the plane. His clothes
were the color of the snow. Jessie and Kier had walked halfway
back from the plane by a circuitous route to avoid the heavy
brush. They had turned down a very wet swale, as evidenced
by the sword fern spread through the oaks. They saw him before
he saw them.

Across his chest the shadow man held an automatic rifle.
The oversize banana clip told Kier it was military, no hunting
rifle. Kier motioned Jessie down behind a big, snow-covered
log. As they dived in the snow, they caught glimpses of two
more men, one to the right, one to the left, both apparently in
a rough line moving through the trees.

The first man would soon cross the pair's original path from the Donahue ranch. Should Kier jump the man bearing down on them and ask questions later? he wondered. The jet had crashed a little more than an hour ago. How did men dressed for combat arrive here this soon? How could anyone know in advance where a plane would crash?

"What the hell?" Jessie whispered.

"I'll be damned," Kier agreed in astonishment.

The first man was still coming directly for them, walking slowly, and looking side to side, now just thirty feet off. They flattened behind the log, burrowing into the snow. Jessie fished out her gun.

"It looks like the army's arrived," she breathed in his ear.

"We'll know soon enough."

But Kier had a sense. When these men moved through the forest, they studied the ground and the landscape, their heads constantly turning. They often stopped to watch. This was no exercise. These weren't just soldiers: they were hunters.

Crunching snow told Kier the man was upon them.

Like a swooping bird, the rifle's barrel came, then passed from view. Kier sucked in his gut until it hurt. He put his finger to his lips and pointed up. The ghost man was standing just above them atop their log. In the dense snowfall and rough ground, the footprints that memorialized their passing were not so easily seen.

In an instant, Kier reached around the log, finding the white boots of the big man, and yanked with tremendous force, sprawling the soldier across the log. Obviously surprised and disoriented, the soldier flailed and started to call out. Kier rose above him, delivering a sharp blow with his right elbow to his solar plexus.

Faster than Kier could comprehend, Jessie thrust her gun in the man's face.

"Shut up," she half whispered.

Together, Kier and Jessie pulled the man into the deep snow behind the log, and under a hemlock with branches low to the ground. Jessie had ahold of the soldier's hair, with her gun still to his head, but he either didn't see it or didn't care. He began to scream.

Kier delivered a moderate two-knuckled karate punch to the man's solar plexus, and the scream turned to a grunt almost as soon as it began. Kier crossed his hands, grabbing the man's jacket on either side of his neck using the long bones of his forearms in a viselike grip, cutting off the blood flow through the carotid arteries. What was left of the groan was choked to a loud whisper. Still the man struggled, kicking out at Jessie. From the corner of his eye, Kier saw a blur, and Jessie's pistol butt cracked the side of the man's jaw. The head lolled for a second.

"Damn it," Kier whispered, "don't do that again." Quickly they peered out from their hiding place under the tree. Apparently the wind and the falling snow had drowned the man's cry. No one seemed to be coming.

The soldier shook, still conscious. Kier moved around his adversary and caught his throat in a lock of his forearm. Legs thrashed for a few seconds until finally the soldier lay still, fighting only to breathe.

Jessie leaned forward, tearing off the man's goggles and pushing back his hood. He was a dull blond with hair the color of soiled straw. His blueberry-blue eyes had a wild look; his cheeks, pockmarked under the stubble, had missed a few shaves. She brought the tip of her gun's snout an inch from their captive's left eye.

"Can you hear me?"

"Yes," he whispered in reply.

His breath smelled like a bad can of tuna.

"I'm Special Agent Jessamyn Mayfield of the FBI. You always have that gap between your lower teeth?"

"Very funny. You broke my jaw."

"Sorry. You got a little excited."

"Who's strangling me? Tonto?" the man said, holding his face, while Kier maintained an armlock on his neck.

"According to your dog tags you're Sergeant Miller of the National Guard."

"You can read."

"Where you from?"

"Omaha, Nebraska. I'm a Sears floor manager."

"Well, then you won't mind if we search you. Just to make sure."

"My commanding officer is Captain Doyle. And I have a job to do."

She hesitated.

"I don't believe him," Kier said. "National Guard wouldn't play around out here. It's wintertime."

He looked to Jessie, who resisted, then relented. "I guess I'll risk an ass-chewing to search him against his will."

Jessie reached under the man's parka and pulled a pistol with a silencer from its holster. Neither of them recognized the make, and it bore no markings. He had three full clips of ammunition velcroed to his holster.

"Well," Jessie said, "this isn't military issue. Shoots .45 slugs, steel tipped to puncture a Kevlar vest. The bullets are called Talons."

"It's mine . . . personal."

"In that case, you're under arrest, because the Talons and the silencer are illegal."

On his belt she found a two-way radio with an exotic-looking digital push-pad. It was turned on and crackling. He also carried a military-issue 9-mm. semiautomatic pistol, ammunition, and a pair of handcuffs.

"These aren't military issue either," she said, nodding at the cuffs. "Where are the keys?"

"Pocket," he replied when Kier compressed his neck.

After they cuffed his hands behind his back, Miller sat and spat out blood, along with a few tooth chips.

In his pack they found a black high-intensity Techna light; Zeiss binoculars; eight more clips of ammo for the M-16; a grenade belt with four hand grenades; high-energy Power Bars; a Sterling compass in expensive-looking brass; a hand-held satellite navigation device; a Bic lighter; a stiletto knife made in Italy; a canteen; a money clip full of hundred dollar bills; an accordionlike stack of plastic sealed cards with hundreds of names and numbers in fine print; and a geodesic contour map, also encased in plastic, complete with elevations. On the map, about three miles north of the Donahues', there was a single red square. The man carried no other I.D. and wore a Kevlar flak jacket with a steel plate across the breast for maximum protection. It, too, bore no indicia of government ownership. They studied the plastic cards, but they were incomprehensible, possibly a code for the radio.

"You have the right to remain silent. . . ." she began in a whisper.

Kier bet she had never spoken the words in an actual arrest situation. He sat stone-faced, impatient, while she gave the required Miranda warning. His eyes never stopped moving as he peered out through the tree branches, looking for more men.

"Did you find the jet?" The man was ignoring Jessie's litany.

"Yes."

Kier shook his head at Jessie, concerned that she not disclose any information.

"What do you know about it?" she asked.

"Did you go inside?" Miller asked, worry plain in his voice.

"Tell me why you care."

"Did you go in the damn jet?"

"Whisper, asshole," Jessie said. "What difference does it make?"

"You did go in the jet. Well, that's just great."

The man lapsed into silence.

It didn't take long to establish that the man was done talking—at least willingly. Kier surmised that he was terrified of his own people. Kier and Jessie exchanged looks, and he knew she understood the ploy. They needed information, and Kier would do anything short of physical torture to get it.

"She's the only FBI. Me, I'm kindred spirit to Goyathlay. You would know him as Geronimo, not Tonto." Kier watched the man through slitted eyes as he spoke. Popping the man's own stiletto, Kier touched the finely honed blade with his index finger. "Uh-oh," he whispered, glancing to the side.

Another gunman had just appeared no more than one hundred feet away. There were going to be lots of men. In seconds, he and Jessie could be trapped.

Their captive's radio crackled. "Every man should be converging on the crash site. Sector seven, northeast corner, seven clicks in, nine clicks down. Stay with procedure. Roll call," the voice said. "Smith."

"Whiskey," somebody answered.

"Jones," the voice called again.

"Scotch," the next man answered.

"Jackson."

"Port."

A name and a password response, Kier figured.

"Jenkins."

"Bourbon."

"Miller."

There was a pause. Their man was Miller. Now they were in trouble.

"Miller, you out there?"

"Unzip his coat," Kier whispered.

He had a plan. Shadow Man Two had turned his back to the wind and was urinating. Good, should keep him occupied.

Jessie raised a brow, and then did as Kier requested.

"Roll over," Kier told the man.

"Has anybody seen Miller?" the voice called over the radio again.

It was the third time. With Miller lying facedown, Kier

removed the cuffs, stripping off the thin, white outer coat. Underneath, the man wore a dark, down-filled arctic body suit, which provided the insulation.

"Now the white pants," Kier said.

"They won't come off over his boots," Jessie said as she began pulling at the laces.

The man in the distance was zipping his pants, then talking on the radio. Holding Miller's radio close to his ear, Kier heard the other man speak.

"Jones, here. Miller was near me. He was to my left. May have gone on ahead."

"They'll shoot if I stand up without my whites," Miller said.

"What are you gonna do?" Jessie put the cuffs back on him with a cold, efficient click.

"Something helpful I hope." Kier was bigger than Miller, but still managed to fit into the suit. He pulled up the hood, put on the goggles, and slid the helmet over the hood just as Miller had done.

"I think we should stay together."

"Can't—they'll find us."

"If you're going to run a distraction of some sort, I need to get these volumes to a safe place."

"Exactly. That's the only evidence there is of whatever is going on here."

"How shall I get out of here. And where will I meet you?"

"I would advise staying right here for ten minutes or until you hear a gunshot, whichever happens first. Best to get out of here when they're distracted. And they'll be distracted."

A dark look crossed her face.

"I'm going to do it without killing anybody," he added, attempting to reassure her. "I need his knife, his radio card, and his watch."

She slapped the items into his hand with a concerned frown.

"Why?"

Kier handed her Miller's silenced pistol after chambering a round. "Safety is off. How about I borrow yours?"

Jessie now pointed both pistols at their prisoner as if she didn't trust just one and told him to roll onto his belly. Then, holstering her own pistol and keeping the silenced weapon, she unlocked the cuffs.

"Lie on your gut with your arms around that tree."

He cursed elaborately as she fastened his wrists on the side of the tree opposite his cheek, which was now pressed against the rough bark.

"I love you too, sweetie," she whispered in his ear.

The other man, the one called Jones, had completely disappeared. Circling around, Kier supposed. Jones would be looking for tracks. Soon he would discover their trail. Their tracks would be visible for a good hour or so before they became misshapen impressions that only a careful eye would detect.

Kier took her aside. "You saw the bio-packs in the tail section. It could be—"

"We might have a disease. Or several diseases. I know, I know."

"If we've been exposed to something dangerous—"

"I won't go near Claudie or the kids."

"Or anyone else."

"I understand contagious."

"We don't have time to go all through this. You've got to keep Miller cuffed and backtrack his trail so you aren't obvious. I'm sure you'll be angling sharply away from Claudie's. Eventually, you should come to the stream. Turn and head down it. Stay in the water and don't leave a single track. You'll come to the bridge at Claudie's driveway and our vehicles. Don't wait for me. Hopefully, all these soldiers will be converging on the plane. Give Claudie and the kids the truck. Take the Volvo and go as far as you can to the north, away from Johnson City. They won't expect that."

"Where are you going?"

"After you—as soon as I can. I'll find something to drive."

Then, carrying the M-16 across his chest just as Miller had done, Kier trotted away with more misgivings than he let show. He was a healer trying to do a warrior's job at a time when he had hoped the world had outgrown warriors.

Chapter 5

To catch a rabbit watch his hole, not his track.
                                        —Tilok proverb

"Stubborn damned Indian."

Jessie watched him run, marveling at the way he let the brush slip past him with long sure strides, even in the snow. Except for the obvious trail in the drifted mounds, he was as elusive as a wild creature in the forest gloom. He disappeared from her sight after running just forty or fifty feet.

She shuddered with cold, then fear. Putting together all that she had heard, and the little that she had seen, the man was the oddest mixture of scientist, mystic, and naturalist that she had ever met. Unfortunate that he lacked so in people skills.

Claudie said that when Kier was young he turned wild for a short time, running with a group of Indian radicals who undertook the survivalist way of life. They were socially aloof, a law unto themselves, fascinated with guns and knives and living off the land. They even plotted to take over the county seat, but it never got that far, despite the fact that Kier and his friends had obtained a frightening array of military hardware. Kier's rebellious phase had something to do with his father's death years earlier, but Claudie never understood the details. Fortunately, before Kier and his band did any irreversible damage, Kier's grandfather convinced him to break away from the group. If Claudie was to be believed, the only vestige of that experience that lasted was Kier's practice of the martial arts.

Beneath the forest canopy it was almost dark, the waning light turning everything a somber gray, which would linger in deathly, freezing, colorless, joyless tones. A purgatory if ever there was one, she thought, until the sun went down and it turned to hell.

Letting memory comfort her, she could almost feel her gray cashmere sweater, see the pearls that lay across it, smell the coffee, feel a yellow pad under her hand, and hear the soft hum of her computer, as soothing as a mother's heartbeat. She lived in seventy degrees, with carpets and Coke machines, bottled water, potpourri air freshener, ionizing filters, the gentle humor of intelligent colleagues, great challenges, but no danger. This freezing forest was not her world.

There were of course things that seemed worse than physical danger. Take Frank, her boss. A man you thought you could respect, a strong guy, a guy who by some miracle seemingly hadn't let the system, or criminals, steal his sensitivity. A man who was clever by anybody's definition, and wise about pain and cynicism and people, beaurcratic or otherwise. Someone you could trust—someone she *had* trusted. Someone so smooth that he could explain how it was that he could have adulterous sex with another Bureau employee and still be the pillar of the office. Someone who could promise Gail marriage with his blue eyes brimming with sincerity—just before leaving on a trip for Hawaii with his wife.

The beauty of this hellish forest was that she didn't need to think about Frank and his threats to end her career—there was enough happening here without digging up that skeleton and worrying it some more. In fact, she'd stay alive longer if she dropped it, before she got to the really horrible part. Before she started in on all the whys. Why did her best friend behave so stupidly? How could Frank be so evil? *Why did I have to discover it?* And she slogged on.

Glancing back at Miller, she wondered what his name really was, where he came from, and what his mother was thinking at this moment. Did he believe he would die? For the second time in her life she thought she might.

One thing she knew for sure. She had to get to a phone and contact law enforcement right away, before anything worse happened to her sister, the boys, or even Kier, a man who might start a small war. In addition, there was the threat of an epidemic of some sort from that disease menagerie in the plane.

Only two hundred feet from where he left Jessie the ground became firmer. Sword fern gave way to bracken fern, like miniature tree stems with fronds atop, growing in every little opening, interrupted by dense clumps of Scotch broom and manzanita. Kier ran in a great arc, staying low, parting foliage by angling himself, letting his shoulders shrug off the clingy tendrils. Ahead a natural opening, dominated by grasses, left a blanket of snow that showed their old tracks like soil on white satin.

Kier knew that he needed to get close—very close—before Jones saw him. With luck, the man would believe he was Miller. Jones stood only a few feet from the tracks left by Kier and Jessie. Running through a last cluster of madrone, Kier kept low, hoping Jones wouldn't look his way. Sixty feet to go. The man seemed occupied with the traces of Kier's earlier passage. He turned as if to follow the imprints in the snow.

Uh-oh. Jones was using his radio again. Already it might be too late.

Kier bounded the last three steps straight at Jones. The man turned, pointing his gun. Kier willed himself to keep the automatic across his chest, his eyes riveted to the black, round bore of Jones's M-16. Jones stared, cocking his head.

He's trying to decide. He's spooked.

Kier swung the butt of his rifle at Jones's jaw. Jones fired. The rifle butt connected with a firm thud as, missing Kier by inches, the shot echoed through the forest, shockingly loud. Kier cringed, knowing the sound would make things infinitely more complicated. Even so, he was sure Jones had not got a good look at his face, obscured as it was by the fur-lined hood under the helmet.

"Jones, say status. Jones, say your status."

The man's radio lay in the snow. Jones had alerted the others, and now Jones wasn't answering.

"Switch Delta, Switch and answer Delta," came the radio command.

They would be scrambling frequencies, Kier knew. And the way it worked, Delta code would not be available on either Jones's or Miller's radio card. Checking Miller's card, Kier saw a series of names down the left side, in alphabetical order. Numbers followed most of the names. Delta was blank. No doubt the printed list was also in electronic form on the phone. Both these radios would now be useless unless they wanted to talk to him.

Kier dropped to the snow, scanning the trees, using Jones's unconscious body as a half-shield. In seconds, another man approached, moving low and fast, obviously casting about for his comrade. Kier slumped forward, lying atop Jones. Like a pointer, this new attacker froze, staring through the snow-laden air. His gun came up. Surely he wouldn't shoot downed men in the snow—especially when they gave every appearance of being his own kind. Kier slipped his hand over the butt of his pistol. From the corner of his eye he watched the man cautiously approach.

"Help, I'm hit," he groaned as the man got very close.

Nudging Kier with his gun barrel, the man bent over, apparently trying to see his face. Kier kept it buried in the other man's parka and moaned. He waited until he felt the man lifting his shoulder. Kier rolled and at the same time delivered a hard kick squarely to the man's chin. He was on his stunned enemy in an instant, choking him to unconsciousness, keeping him silent until his body slumped.

Visibility was improving slightly, but steady polka-dot sheets of frozen moisture still blurred the landscape. Kier did not want to kill. If only these people had not brought their destruction to this place.

Once again his mind went over the facts like a watchmaker sorting the parts of an old-fashioned timepiece. Even if he didn't understand the nature of the power that the scientists had given Tillman or the extent of Tillman's plans, he knew that these men were capable of wanton killing. Common sense told him that escape would require a profound subterfuge. He needed to make them think they had solved the puzzle of their disappearing comrade.

He took Jones's automatic, fished out the rest of his ammo clips, grabbed his radio, his light, and took his money. Then he turned to the second man, leaving his weapons, but taking his money, his knife, his light, more ammunition, and his grenades. Pulling off Miller's field pack, he quickly loaded the booty.

Cringing even as he did it, he turned the second man over onto his belly and aimed the M-16 at the fleshy part of the man's buttock, taking care that the shot missed bone. The single shot blew out a chunk of fatty flesh a little smaller than a walnut. It bled profusely, allowing Kier to smear blood over the back of the man's outer coat. He fired off some more rounds.

"Miller has turned, Miller has turned," Kier said into the radio in the whispered growl of a dying man.

"Code nine, say status, Jenkins. Code nine, say status, Jenkins."

In response Kier fired his automatic and made an ugly gurgling sound into the mouthpiece.

"Code Zulu, switch and answer Zulu."

Again they were scrambling.

He was reaching to pick up Jones's body when a flurry of snow from overburdened branches cascaded to his right, and out from a wall of frosted evergreen boughs stepped another of his tormentors. The man was a good distance away and looking in the wrong direction. Striding directly back up Jenkins's trail for at least twenty paces, Kier heard no shots until he was almost out of sight. He dived for an elderberry thicket, shooting a volley as he flew. Though wild, the bullets made his quarry duck. Kier crawled desperately for cover. Already rounds slammed into the brush around him, missing him by what he knew must be inches. Finding a log, he climbed over it and hunkered down. A tremendous explosion directly behind him numbed his ears and tossed the bushes around him like salad. Somebody was using hand grenades or a mortar. There was no sound but the pounding of his heart; his ragged, too-fast breath came not from fatigue. Panic pooled in him like a reservoir trickling through the cracks of a dam. He needed to calm his mind. Now he would need another unconscious captive to carry out his plan.

"I've got him at sector seven. He's near the northeast corner, south and east of the corner maybe twenty or thirty feet. Repeat. Sector seven. Northeast corner, south and east of the corner approximately twenty to thirty feet."

The man was actually shouting. Kier felt a different kind of chill as he heard the enemy radioing his position. In minutes, there would be armed men everywhere. He dropped and crawled into a dense windfall of criss-crossed fallen trees shot through with Pacific bayberry and overgrown with salal. In this thicket he was all but invisible. But he had not been there ten seconds before he discovered that he shared the spot with one of the enemy.

It was the heavy sound of Kier checking his clip that gave him away. Only a few feet of heavy brush lay between him and the man who now, in panicked tones, reiterated Kier's position. Kier had no illusions. He was in a deadly spot.

Panic in the man's voice meant he was rattled and might do anything, even something that could kill them both, like tossing a grenade in tight.

Lying flat, Kier squirmed forward a foot, sticking his head in the brush, peering through the crystalline corridors formed by snow on branches. Nothing. He couldn't see more than three feet. Again he elbowed forward. An almost imperceptible rabbit trail appeared in front of him. Without thinking, he had been crawling down it. Off to his right the shooter lay waiting. If Kier continued on his current path, he would crawl into the enemy's sights.

He pushed slowly to the right and detected nothing. It was not until the second move that he spied a small patch of white fabric, distinct from the snow because of its flat texture. Squinting, he turned his head right and left, trying to see more, to at least identify the torso.

The man a few feet away would be wearing Kevlar body armor that could easily be pierced by the combat rounds in the M-16. But the silenced pistol he had shagged from Jones would be much quieter. If he could bring himself to shoot this man, he would take a chance on the pistol to gain a soundless assault. Aiming the long, lanky handgun, he rose even higher, carefully discerning the white fabric from fallen snow.

Slowly he moved off his elbows to a crouch. Now he could feel his own fear like a hand on his throat. At any moment he could be seen. His eyes roved. Nothing. With his head buried in the brush, he rose still higher. Oh yes! There was his shooter, just six feet away, his legs under a massive Douglas fir log, his body flat to the ground. Incredibly, the man had removed his helmet, probably to listen. Kier aimed at the man's hooded head.

It was a useless gesture. He would not kill a man who lay unaware and frightened in the bushes. Without another second's hesitation, Kier uncoiled his body from its crouch and dived at the man, aiming the butt of the pistol at the man's temple. If it hadn't been for the tough fibrous vines, the strike might have landed before the man could roll.

As it was, he struck the man's shoulder. Recovering, Kier drove the palm of his left hand into the man's chin, then swung the butt of the pistol into the man's temple with such force he hoped he hadn't killed him. Kier watched the body quiver, waiting for more fight. Then there was no movement. Flopping him onto his back, Kier felt for a pulse and found it. The man was young, maybe early thirties, handsome, with a moon-shaped baby face.

Bullets raked the brush in time with the staccato chug of an M-16. Kier flattened himself.

"Cease fire, goddammit. Crawford, you in there?"

It was quiet. Kier felt blood under his fingers. His eye followed it to the man's chest and a lethal wound. They had hit their own man through an arm hole. At least he had the body he needed, albeit a dead one.

Crawford's radio crackled again. "Crawford, say your status."

He knew what he would do. If it worked, he might live.

He had minutes if he was lucky, but perhaps he had only seconds. They would be coordinating by radio, getting in position for a massive assault. Each one of them knew where he was. Their satellite navigators would lead them straight to his coordinates. There was only one thing they didn't know. They didn't know who he was.

Kier worked quickly, aware that any slip would cost him his life and probably Jessie's. Another Douglas fir log some distance away had the makings of what he would need. It had not been long since the tree had fallen.

Kier put Miller's radio card, stiletto, and money clip in the dead man's coat. Jones's knife and a couple of clips of his ammunition he put in Crawford's pack, along with Jenkins's compass, more ammunition, and money from both Jones and Jenkins. Last he took the index page from Volume One of the lab reports and hurriedly went about untying and retying Crawford's boot so that he could cram the document inside. Every one of these guys seemed to have a black field watch—nothing distinctive there. Even so, he put Miller's watch in a shirt pocket.

Now he would learn whether the fallen Douglas fir had what he needed. Picking up the body, he walked quickly. Between Kier and his goal at the butt end of the tree trunk lay sixty feet of pristine snow. It was completely open for about half the distance. The other thirty feet were heavy brush.

Kier hoisted Crawford onto his back. Leaving a single set of prints, he paused every couple steps to let blood from Crawford's oozing chest drip onto the virgin snow. He dragged one leg as if wounded.

The base of the trunk, which lay in a shallow swale, was propped off the ground by a fibrous wad of roots and earth. The giant root ball had been torn from the ground when the tree toppled in a high wind. As Kier expected, beneath the root mass lay a deep hollow obscured by drifted snow.

After sitting Crawford in the snow, he quickly burrowed into the crater where the roots had grown. If he hunkered down he could get his entire body a foot beneath the level of the ground.

He propped Crawford's body up against a root in front of the hollow and placed his M-16 across his chest. Using Miller's stiletto, he stabbed Crawford's thigh, making an ugly knife wound. Urgently now, he gathered snow and packed a wall between himself and Crawford, verifying that he could seal himself off and retreat under the log. He would not be visible behind Crawford unless somebody dug.

He dug back through his hole, emerging beside Crawford. In order to see the surrounding landscape, he crawled to the lip of the swale. Tense as a hunting cat, he lay on his belly and waited. They would send a team to surround the windfall area, which was maybe two hundred feet across. They would swarm it.

Kier didn't have to wait long. First, he saw a man in front, then one to the right, then one to the left. The three were crawling. He watched, checking the progress of each.

There would be more men on all sides hidden by the brush. His attackers would be confident. They would know that if he was still here, they had him. With any luck, they were certain that they were following a single wounded man and their eyes, as they studied the track, would be clouded to other possibilities. Kier waited until all three of the men in front were visible at once. Pressing his cheek into the hi-tech plastic stock of the rifle, he willed his finger to set off the first round. Controlled, precise shots exploded the tree trunk above the first man's shoulder.

From every side fire poured in, driving him back under the log. Shoving and packing snow madly, he sealed himself off behind Crawford's body. His movements dislodged a powdery dust. Since everything was frozen solid, there was no apparent moisture. Roots hung down around him, and the earth smell was strong. Plugging his ears helped. He could imagine what it must look like. Wood flew as every green thing was chopped to pieces. Grenade bursts that he could feel in his bones—one after another—shook the ground. Four, five, six. His closed eyes began to flash red behind his lids. The log shuddered overhead.

Soon they started with what he supposed was a rocket launcher. Explosions that seemed to bounce the log from the ground compressed the air. The breath of almighty God came roaring through the woods, withering everything in sight. Then, at last, it was quiet. There was no doubt that these men were capable of insane violence. They cared for nothing except to destroy those who opposed them. Quickly, he reinforced the crumbling snow that formed the barrier behind Crawford. A radio crackled when somebody turned the squelch too high, but the tiny speaker was still too far away for Kier to hear the words.

After a time he heard men stomping the brush.

"One body blown to hell. From the dogs, it's Crawford." After a moment came a different voice: "He's got Miller's stiletto and a second radio card. I.D. number twenty-six."

"That's Miller's," the voice came back over the radio.

"He's got an extra watch, and ammo clips."

"You don't suppose . . ." the radio voice began.

"He killed Miller?"

"He's got Jenkins's stuff," the third voice chimed in again.

"And Jones's," a fourth voice called out. "I know this knife belonged to Jones."

"He left a blood trail. Somebody stabbed him in the leg. Maybe Jones. There was only one set of tracks in here. Back there . . . there was a lot, but you can't tell if this son of a bitch was the guy at the plane."

"It's too far for one guy. . . ."

"But we don't know exactly where Miller was, and we don't know if Crawford is in this by himself." There was a long pause.

"He's got a paper in his boot. Some index."

"Read it to me." A much more authoritative voice cut in over the radio. A familiar voice. There was a pause.

" 'Atomic Force Microscopy,' then 'Nucleic Acid Sequencing Strategies,' then a whole bunch of subheadings, then 'Gene Reassortment,' and more subheadings. Then in Volume Two, 'AVCD4 Anti-virus trials,' and after that, in Volume Three . . . 'Cloning—' "

"That's enough," the voice said. "I'm coming out there."

The original voice returned. "If Crawford was the guy at the plane, he just backtracked, is all. . . . He just ran like hell, grabbed what he wanted, and left. The rest of us were walking slow.'' Another long pause. "Hell, there's tracks all through here.''

There was more talk that Kier couldn't quite make out; then somebody raised his voice again.

"You got a better idea? God didn't drop Crawford here. Somebody shot our guys. He's got the paper in his boot proving he stole the stuff. . . . Somebody wounded him and slowed him down. . . . What's more . . .''

"Maybe we've all been shooting at each other. Hell, I don't know.''

Another voice, close in: "If there was anybody else in here, they gotta be dead.''

Still Kier waited. At any moment, his hunters might unplug the hole and see him. Every second hammered in his brain like a sledge on concrete. His nails were buried in the palms of his hands, but he had no sense of his own end until he pulled the pins on the two grenades. He did it with his teeth, but kept the handles depressed. They would all be on their feet, standing around Crawford. Doing what he supposed one should never do, Kier waited with live grenades, ready to throw if they pulled the snow from his hole.

Kier listened for more talk, but heard nothing. Perhaps the men were pulling back. He curled into a tight ball; he hadn't noticed the discomfort of his confinement until now. Water dripped from overhead—the ice melted by his body heat. Inactivity brought on chill. The heavy muscle in his thighs cramped. Tightness of body, the feeling of being closed in, began to occupy a place in his mind. The sense of being caged mixed with his adrenaline to form the beginnings of panic. He knew what to do. His mind went to a different time, to a different place, to the solace of Grandfather's lake. He replaced the pins in the grenades with his teeth and relaxed.

* * *

It is evening. No-see-ums swirl around his head, put off only by Grandfather's liberally applied bay leaf oil on his bare skin. Around the lake stand dense evergreens as old as anyone Grandfather can remember and far older still. They are fir, hemlock, cedar, and pine, forming a velvety fragrant thickness over the earth. Protruding into the water, like creamy brown natural leather, a sand spit simmers in the late-summer sun.

Near the spit there is a small clearing carpeted with spring-fed grasses and edged with the softer verdant hues of huckleberry and myrtle. In the midst of this meadow the cabin enjoys the shade of hand-planted mountain bilberry, the leaves tinged with the first autumn color. There is no breath of wind. The water, soft as satin, glistens under the bursting yellow-reds of sunset.

Grandfather stands beside him and puts a strong hand on his shoulder. Kier wants to understand the power in this touch, a better touch than he has ever felt, a healing salve to his loneliness. His father is dead. For many days there was little feeling. Life on ice. Now a sense of loss has eaten a giant hole out of his middle. All that stands between him and the incomprehensible abyss is Grandfather's hand.

A fish hawk rises on the wind. Kier watches his namesake, and something about the bird stirs him. There isn't a way to say what he is experiencing except that it is a longing. So he lets the sense of this go through him without trying to understand it. There is a gentle squeeze on his shoulder and once again he is aware of the hand. It is as if it is guiding him to the bird.

"A man might know the currents on which he glides and then he would be free," Grandfather says.

As Kier waits and remembers, he wonders about the currents. In his mind is a puzzle, the pieces of which are strewn about—very few of them put together. There is his mother and her iron will. That is part of the puzzle. His dead father. That is a bigger piece.

Immediately after his father's funeral, his mother had moved them another ten miles from the Tilok reservation. Before this precipitous relocation, they had been a good two miles outside the reservation and on the outskirts of Johnson City. Their new house was in the forest to the far side of town and surrounded by white people. His mother said only that the world was mostly white and not red and that he better "get used to it." She worked for a local groceryman and was said to be very good at keeping his books.

Kier went to a public school and worked by the lamplight every night under his mother's tutelage. Grandfather moved off the reservation in order to be with them, and with him, Kier escaped to the forest to learn Indian ways. Tracking became a passion. His mother tolerated that part of his life, maybe even in her own way encouraged it, but it was always subserviant to his studies, always trivialized.

Nathaniel Wintripp, Kier's father, was a half-blooded Tilok Indian whose own father had been of Spanish descent. By trade Nate was a stonemason. He had been the most prolific and artistic craftsman in the rural areas nearest mountainous Wintoon County. But Nate Wintripp had a certain reserved aloofness about him. He'd grown up with his grandparents and struck out to live on his own at age seventeen. Although he ably supported himself through two years of Chico State University, he quit after the second year to work full-time in his growing business.

Kier had struggled to know his father. He wanted to get beyond the pats on the head to something undefinable, to something he didn't understand. On October 12, 1969, his father flew into a rage, banged Kier's wrists on a washbasin, stalked out the door, and never came back. A month later, Nate Wintripp was dead, never having let his son, Kier, find the bond that he so fervently pursued.

After his father walked out, a quiet desperation seemed to grip Kier's mother. It ran so deep that for years he couldn't bear the thought of stepping from the groove that she was charting for him. Although she was pure Tilok, he could not determine what she wanted to be—except for one incontrovertible opinion that she held with utter conviction. Even though he must be a success in the white man's world, even though he must have the best university education, even though he must bear no trace of his lineage in his speech, he would marry an Indian woman or certain calamity would befall him. After all, Nate, her own husband, being half white, could never really accept an Indian. How would a white woman ever accept Kier?

In the secret places of his soul, Kier wondered if his father could ever have accepted him. Or if his father accepted no one. Or if Kier wanted something from his father that was not to be found on this earth. It seemed to Kier that just before his father's death, they had been somehow reaching for each other. There was, he had imagined, a peaceful joy that lay just beyond his reaching fingers, that was forever snatched away at the very moment of his most profound awareness. He could not reconcile the shame he felt when he thought of his father.

He did not try to create this missing bond of communion with his mother. Theirs was a union fashioned from the mutuality of their struggle to survive on little income in a mountain town and from their shared tragedy.

Kier did not sort out the cauldron of emotions that he buried in a place in his mind and covered over with layers of keen intellectual musings. When he met his first wife—a white woman—the uneasy feeling was passed off by the simple observation that he had never made a genuine friend nor found a genuine love. He knew only male comrades in adventure and female partners in sex. This he supposed was a good and sufficient reason for the temporary loss in equilibrium. When he reached to grasp and share his new bride's love, he floundered as if drowning, with no concept at all of swimming. It frightened him.

Now he relived the feeling. His breaths grew deeper and there was tightness inside him. He felt the shame. His mother's raw determination still felt like a dead weight crushing his soul. This stew of old emotions had brought him to a place where he could not taste certain of life's flavors. He could not, it seemed, taste the flavor of love or savor it with another.

What he didn't know was why.

Jessie had heard nothing during the several minutes since Kier had left. Then she heard a single shot.

As Kier had suggested, she put Miller in the lead, with his hands cuffed behind, and backtracked on Miller's trail.

Shortly they heard more shooting.

"Tonto's a bullet-ridden carcass," Miller said.

"Shut up," she said, wondering if he was right and feeling a lot more than she expected. They traveled easterly, then angled to the north, heading away from Claudie's and the Volvo, until they came to the creek. Finally, leaving Miller's track, they turned south down the creek. Jessie understood Kier's logic. New tracks that took a different direction heading off toward the Donahues' would need explaining.

Walking in the water, she discovered a torture more exquisite than any she had known—save one. The pain was bluer than the dead blue of a particular glacial lake that would forever stand in her memory. The sensation spreading in her feet was like the lifeless cold of that pristine water: A horrible, bone-deep ache that would, she knew, eventually cut her feet from her body. She had thought they would simply go numb; well, they did, but only after pain like a twisted gut. Kier's strategies and this wilderness seemed to demand suffering.

At first, as she and Miller walked, Jessie thought of survival, of spotting the next paramilitary trooper before he spotted her.

After a time, though, as the sounds of the battle receded and the frothy air and dense forest closed in around them, her mind departed the macabre of Wintoon Mountain for the ordinary macabre of her office, of her nightmare with Frank. Tears came to her eyes and she cursed herself. How, when she was barely alive, when she had come here to this godforsaken brush patch at the other end of the United States to escape—with this place turning into a war zone, people maybe dying—could she think about Frank and his sick friends?

She wasn't going to do it. The one thing that had to remain hers was her mind.

As she began to wonder whether Kier were dead or alive, something crashed in the distance, the woods resounding with numerous explosions and the staccato of automatic weapons. More firepower than she would have thought possible was unleashed in the next minute. She felt unusually alone.

Using a small stick between fingers that still clenched a grenade, Kier cleared a hole at the far edge of the log. It seemed from the conversation that at least two men had remained with Crawford. They had walked a little way up the hill now, by the sound of their receding voices. Kier listened as best he could. After a time, he heard nothing. Still, they could be watching. It would be more dangerous to come out slowly.

With a quick thrust of his elbows, Kier cleared away the snow, rising in silence, and bursting from the hollow. *Go ahead, think about the guys who just tried to kill you.* His mind prepared itself for slaughter. Hands ready to rise from his sides, biceps straining, and pectorals tight with anticipation, his breath rushing from his throat—at the last instant he held the grenade handles tight. He didn't throw. There was no one within sight, though Kier could now hear someone talking nearby.

They had taken the bait. The leader hadn't arrived. The men were assuming Crawford was a safely dead enemy and Miller was one of his victims.

Kier slithered away on his belly.

Chapter 6

The fire that succors a family will burn the enemy.
                                                    —Tilok proverb

Jack Horatio Tillman walked to the crashed jet with long, unflagging strides. He planned to work his way methodically along the track until arriving at the thicket where the men had found Crawford. They had come up with a neat little theory that had Crawford as a turncoat who stole the journals.

After arriving at the two unconscious soldiers, it took Tillman only a minute or two to determine that his men had not carefully read the signs. He managed to slap Jones awake; Jenkins was still out cold. His men had run past with barely a sideward glance, more interested in catching the attacker and obtaining the possible reward. Whoever took out Jones and Jenkins had a weak stomach. They had gone to great pains not to kill. It wouldn't be Crawford.

Tillman himself hunted big game when not occupied by the running of his pharmaceutical and medical research businesses.

If it was feasible, he would gladly run his empire from a canvas tent in the bush.

Tillman's father had inherited money. Not so much that he couldn't spend it all, or drink it all, but enough that it enabled him to hunt most of his life. For as far back as Jack Tillman could remember, when his father wasn't drinking, he was hunting. He had endured his father's drunken beatings and reveled in his hunting expeditions. The only thing they had done well together was track and kill for sport.

The track in front of him now—this so-called Crawford's track—was made by an athletic male much stronger in the legs than Crawford. Whoever it was had backtracked so perfectly, so rapidly, that his high-step rivaled that of a Tennessee Walking horse. Crawford could not have maintained this gait for a dozen paces without kicking snow.

The mystery man had kicked no snow. To lay this track was close to impossible. Carefully, Tillman pulled the loose snow out of a footprint until he reached the packed ice crystals beneath. The foot had been held much straighter than that of a duck-walking soldier. Crawford couldn't have left an imprint like this one. As the foot had landed, it hit the ball as much as the heel. Only a stalker moved this way naturally. The man who left this track, even while fleeing, was trying hard to confuse his men.

The runner was large and long legged, his pace steady and purposeful, not panicked. Each stride was approximately the same length. There was little deviation in the direction of travel. The person knew this terrain. Most obvious of all, the foot was much too large to be Crawford's. It was barely possible that it was Miller's. But if it were Miller, Tillman knew he had vastly underrated him.

A chill unrelated to the cold passed through Tillman. Not fear, he thought, but acute anticipation. His face burned with anger at the stupidity of his men. Doyle was out here, which frustrated him more. Of all his men, Tillman had begun to suspect that the new man, Doyle, was the kind he could count on. But during all the radio talk, Doyle had been strangely silent.

Things were going badly, badly enough that Jack Tillman could be prosecuted for serious crimes. But he didn't intend to be a candidate for capital punishment.

In his forty-eight years nothing had ever threatened Jack Tillman quite like this. The likelihood that the jet would crash at the drop site was infinitesimal, and yet it had happened. No doubt his men seriously underestimated Marty Rawlins and his four cronies. Most likely a fight had erupted when the scientists were told about the drop.

But even with that bit of bad luck, what were the odds that one of his own men turned or, even more unlikely, that combat-ready strangers had meddled with the crash site? Tillman had obtained background on all the residents near the drop site. Meticulous people had done the research. Tillman knew about the Tilok vet, Kier Wintripp, an outdoorsman who had been written up in magazines.

His home was in Johnson City and his summer cabin was up the valley from the Donahues' ranch. He had led a manhunt for five militia-types that had raped and killed two Indian girls. The vet had tracked ahead of the sheriff's group. According to the story, he had told the authorities the wanted men had ambushed him. There was a firefight. The vet carried a lever action 30/30 while the men he hunted had submachine guns and other military hardware. All five of the men were dead by the time the sheriff arrived. The Indian didn't have a scratch. As a combat-hardened survivalist, this man would have the ability to kill, even if he lacked the stomach for it.

Tillman already knew a great deal about Kier Wintripp. And he had more information available—much, much more. He knew the very stuff of which the man was made and considered

him the only immediate resident who was potentially dangerous. On the reservation, twenty miles distant, other Tiloks might
pose a threat, but fortunately, several mountain ridges divided
the Donahue ranch from the Tilok tribal lands.

Until now people and circumstances had always behaved
more predictably than the wild animals Tillman hunted. His
pharmaceutical firms succeeded because he understood ordinary people's fear of disease as well as the scientists who
sought to conquer this fear through the power of healing.

Tillman had become an industry giant almost overnight
because he also knew how to turn other people's failures to
his advantage. His first venture was a dying company that had
bet all its stockholders' money on a drug that failed its first
major double-blind study. It was supposed to perform near
miracles on the healing of wounds. In fact it only made the
wounds less painful, which, when discovered, caused the stock
to plummet.

Tillman talked his way into the company and was elected
president mainly because he was the only interested and
remotely qualified candidate. But he knew that the drug's anal-
gesic properties could be enhanced to make surgical wounds
less painful. By adding other compounds to the cream, company
scientists made a new topical pain killer used on everything
from wounds to babies' gums. Spectacular sales enabled Tillman to parlay profits from the pain remedy into a sophisticated
laboratory with scientists he could use for more substantial
projects. Research, Tillman knew, was made ridiculously slow
by absurd rules and artificial constraints. Tillman undertook to
solve the problems with the bureaucracy and succeeded again.

With the money came time to think, to devote himself to
issues of global importance. Disease, it seemed to Tillman, was
often associated with dysfunctional lifestyles. Poverty and the
idle hand from which it stemmed created a host of maladies.
Gluttony was tributary to a different set of diseases. Careless
sexual habits spawned numerous others. It seemed that the

flaws of mankind nurtured disease. The scourge of disease was nature's discipline.

Society needed a more advanced approach to disease than merely curing it, for to cure all disease was to take away nature's ability to chastise, which in turn slowed the process of evolution by promoting the dysfunctional. Disease was a thing to be used. Mankind could advance only by curing selected people and certain plagues.

Controlling disease, then, was essential to enhancing its function. The ability to cure was just a single component in such control (and not unhappily, a source of great wealth). The creation of convenient disease and its selective use, the natural corollary to cure, while profitable, would be appreciated only by a much more advanced culture.

Tillman saw himself as a man ahead of his time. His theories could not be broadly disseminated in his lifetime, for he would always be mortal, unable to escape the bonds of aging. No cure for aging was close enough to save him. He could only prolong his life. The ticking clock required that he conduct progressive research, the key to which had always been keeping each chief scientist at the various Tillman laboratories isolated from the work of the others. It was usually desirable to convince each team leader that he was the only one bending the rules, the only one in on the real secret, and the only one sharing in the big money. Only two pseudo-scientists on the business side knew nearly everything. These men Tillman trusted implicitly.

Then came Marty Rawlins—a genius whose abilities crossed many disciplines and who made brilliant technical decisions in every research program that he touched. A man like Marty could do far more if he knew the whole, and so the seduction of progress had led Tillman to deviate from his usual operating plan.

Ultimately, he let Marty and his team synthesize and direct DNA research on a wide-ranging basis, coordinating the work of three separate laboratories and many subgroups within those laboratories. By the time Tillman realized how much Marty had figured out and how pettily squeamish he was, it was too late.

Viewed in isolation from the circumstances, Marty Rawlins's death shamed Tillman, and Tillman regretted it deeply. He took no joy in killing good men, but this was discipline and necessity. This was order. And, in a sad way, progress.

Tillman took his own introspection as clear evidence that he was not a sociopath. Rather, he had an uncommonly large vision and a sense of the future that other men lacked. He was becoming something unique and possessed a grand tool for the good of mankind. He knew he was not perfect and that some of his decisions might ultimately be found wanting by wiser men who would come after him. But these men would realize that cutting through modern man's emotional prejudices could only be accomplished by violating sensibilities pinnacled on society's metaphysical vanities—those spiritual grand illusions that impeded advancement.

At the giant log, Tillman asked to see the document taken from Crawford's boot. Doyle handed it to him. It was as he feared. Rawlins had made mention of a Volume Six, titled "Adult Cloning, Gene Mobilization and DNA Chips," with various damning subheadings that included "DNA Chip Gene Expression by Disease Category." Worse, the section subheadings bore the designation: "Adult DNA Cloning," and under that were I.D. numbers. Rawlins had gone insane.

"Look on the other side of the log, gentlemen," Tillman said to Diggs and Doyle.

Diggs, a small wiry man with chin whiskers, swallowed audibly. "I swear those tracks weren't there before."

"I just got here a couple minutes ago." Doyle pointed into the woods. "I was up that way, trying to sort things out."

As Tillman pondered the wisdom of shooting both men in

the head, he studied the neat red sideburns that Doyle kept perfectly shaped. He felt the butt of his revolver, even as he realized that he was telegraphing his thoughts. The quiet concern in Doyle's eyes confirmed it. He dropped his hand from the pistol.

"He tricked you." Tillman spoke in deadly, quiet tones. "He waited until you relaxed before he came out. He carried Crawford's body, knowing that you would focus your small minds on the fact that there was only one set of tracks."

Rage came to Tillman as naturally as tides to the sea. Now these men knew something of the cloning and DNA work. And that something was too much.

"I recall reading of an Indian tracker with a summer home in this valley. It was in the materials we were given to review. Whoever we're chasing didn't want to kill," Doyle said.

Tillman could not help but be impressed, but he said nothing. He needed to create the hard edge of hatred in his troops. He needed to define the enemy. Talking wouldn't do it. Old tracks in the snow wouldn't do it. What he was thinking would be a hard thing, but it was rational.

"Gentlemen," he told Diggs and Doyle, "I want to show you something. I need you to put these on."

As nonchalantly as a drunk fondles a whiskey glass, he tossed them each a pair of handcuffs. He studied Doyle's clean-shaven face. There was professionalism even in the way he stood.

"Just on the right wrist please."

Diggs looked at Doyle nervously. Doyle betrayed no emotion. Neither moved, each holding his silver-gray manacle like spoiled food.

"Gentlemen?"

Diggs shuffled his feet, casting his eyes downward. Neither man dropped his M-16. Tillman hated what he was about to do with Doyle.

"Indulge me, gentlemen." Tillman spoke in good-natured tones, but with condescension, as if to schoolchildren.

Diggs put on his cuff.

"Now we're going to test your athletic prowess," Tillman said, nodding to Diggs. "I guess Captain Doyle no longer works in our little army."

"Wait a minute," Doyle said, moving to snap on his handcuff. The loyalty caused Tillman a stab of pain.

"Step over here."

Doyle did as he was told and placed his back against a fir maybe eight inches in diameter. Tillman cuffed his hands over his head so that they were locked behind the tree.

"Well, do you want your job, or not?" Tillman said to Diggs, who, pursuant to Tillman's nod, stood against the same tree with his back to Doyle. Both were soon secured, with their guns on the ground and their hands over their heads.

Tillman popped open a stiletto with a slender blade.

Doyle cocked his head, eying the knife, but said nothing.

"We did the best we could." Diggs looked as though he might cry. "Please don't."

Doyle remained silent.

"Don't what?" Tillman asked. "Don't what?"

"Don't hurt me." Diggs struggled against the cuffs.

"Oh, this won't hurt." Tillman allowed the contempt he felt for Diggs to rise inside him like a screaming demon.

"Open your mouth. I want to see your tonsils."

"What?"

"Just do it."

Like a careful dentist Tillman positioned Diggs's open mouth, then took the knife from behind his back and, quick as a mantis tongue, punctured the side of the man's throat. Blood welled up in the mouth. He had hit the carotid artery. Tillman pushed up on the chin firmly with his left hand while Diggs choked on his own blood.

"It's a fast way to die," he said to no one in particular.

Grabbing Diggs by the forelock, Tillman let the stilletto's tip cut to the skull and describe a rough circle around the top of the head. He knew that, once started, the human scalp peels like an orange. Using his thumb and forefinger, he separated scalp from skull and held up his gory trophy.

Doyle looked sideways to see what was happening with Diggs. Tillman walked slowly around the tree and dropped the scalp at the feet of Doyle, who didn't move a muscle.

"I understand what you're doing," Doyle said. "You think it's the Indian, Kier, and you want to bloody well make the point to the men. You could never trust Diggs with what he read in that paper. Two birds, one stone. But I think you sense that you can trust me."

"I'm impressed."

"I'm the man to help you catch the Indian."

Tillman removed the cuff from Doyle's wrist.

They hiked back to the burned-out jet, where Tillman let Doyle explain this latest atrocity to the shocked troops.

"A dangerous and cunning Indian has scalped Diggs. He's made fools of every man out here today," Doyle concluded.

Now the hunt would begin in earnest.

Chapter 7

Men will kick an apology ahead of them like a
stone, thereby ensuring that they never quite catch
up to it.

—Tilok proverb

"Miller, or whoever you are, if you're out there, give me a
jingle."

It was the voice Kier had heard before—calm, authoritative—coming over the operative channel on Miller's radio. He
assumed it was Tillman. Kier heard the rage only at the edge
of his tone. He knew that to talk—even to talk as he ran—
would be a death sentence. First, it would totally eliminate their
confusion as to whether Miller was indeed whom they were
looking for. More important, they could triangulate his position.
Over time, they might even determine his direction of travel.
They probably had the best equipment available.

"Listen," the voice said. "We can make peace. You'll never
get out of these woods alive unless we make a deal. Even if

you do, you'll be a hunted man forever. You've got the journals, haven't you? We've figured it out. Okay. We're pissed, but you've got something we need, so let's deal."

Kier believed that they had figured out nothing except that some guy in a white camouflage outfit was killing and maiming their people. Tillman had perhaps twenty men, probably ex-soldiers. Maybe Special Forces men who couldn't find anything else to do in life—hired mercenaries, pumped up with some concocted story about how they were doing the world a favor. Or maybe such people didn't care for abstractions.

At a flat-out run, Kier took the trail directly to the Donahues'. Even if Jessie had traveled at a much slower pace and had covered more than twice as much ground, she should have long since arrived and departed. But he had to make sure.

From the densest thicket, as the last light faded, Stalking Bear scrutinized every detail. He placed the object that would be the salvation of his people in a safe place—a place where, if need be, one other would find it. With it, he left a written note.

Now Stalking Bear was pulled in two directions.

A pregnant Claudie and her two little boys, Bren and Micah, climbed into Kier's truck. Theirs was the immediate peril. Tomorrow would always lie with the children. Even if the Donahue boys were not Tilok, they were friends to the Tilok. And Stalking Bear's grandson had no greater friends than Jack and Claudie Donahue.

Moving like a shadow with easy strides, Stalking Bear vaulted into the bed of the pickup truck as it passed. He folded himself into one of several storage compartments barely large enough for him, making himself very small, and slowed his breath, his heartbeat. He became the sleeping bear. The tension flowed out of his body, and he listened, dreamed.

* * *

"Sorry I startled you."

Kier piled into the driver's seat of the Volvo as Jessie slipped over the center console.

"What the hell happened?" she asked.

In the backseat, Miller groaned.

"I didn't kill anybody, but Miller's friends killed one of their own." Kier glanced at his watch. "You were supposed to be gone two minutes after you got here."

"So I'm a slow walker. Only one dead?" she asked, her voice sharper now.

"I think so."

"It sounded like a war. I'm sure you saved our lives."

"See how long that lasts," Miller said.

"Miller here is getting quite a reputation," Kier said.

"You mother—"

"We better get you out of here fast." Kier stepped out of the car and opened the back door. "These guys want to carve you up." As Kier dragged Miller back to the car trunk and locked him inside, he watched the treeline in the last of the gray light.

"We need to hide for a while. We have to figure out what the journals mean," Kier began, back in the car. He turned the car left, toward Johnson City, driving as fast as he dared, forcing the Volvo over the drifts and the chained tires into the roadway.

"We've got to head for civilization," she said, her fist gently tapping the side window. "Why can't we just try for Johnson City like Claudie?"

He didn't answer. Instead, he looked for a turnaround. They came to a drive marked MOLLANDER. It was the only nearby dwelling—a summer cabin about a half mile from Claudie's, usually unoccupied this time of year.

"You're not talking."

"I'm thinking."

When he reached the end of the narrow roadway to the cabin, he turned the Volvo around and got out.

"Now what are you doing?"

"I'm still thinking."

"You're lying in the snow."

"I'm removing the chains."

"What if I want the chains to go to Johnson City?"

"They'll have men at the pass. They'll kill you. If you try to walk around them, you'll die in the snow."

He removed the tire chains quickly and dumped them on the floor in back.

"That's my choice," she said.

"Uh-huh," he said. He would hog-tie her if he had to, but he certainly wasn't going to say so.

" 'Uh-huh.' What's that mean?"

"It means I'm listening."

"You're driving back toward my sister's and away from Johnson City."

"If we go back without the chains, it'll throw them off, at least temporarily."

"We need to get to a town, to telephones. I've got to insist."

"This side of Elk Horn Pass you're off the grid. No power except home generators and no phone but cellular. With luck, they're confused. They'll suppose that people fleeing would more likely head toward Johnson City than away from it. Our only choice is to lose them in the wilderness and come out in our own time and our own way."

"What about the cell phones?"

"There's one in my truck. Claudie's got one. We don't have either of them, and they won't work unless you're higher on the mountain. We can't drive that high in this snow, even if we had one, which we don't."

"Listen, that plane was full of some medical research, including every disease in the *Merck Manual.* They could be experimenting on those Tilok girls, for God's sake. We've got to tell the world—''

"You can't tell anyone anything if you're dead. They might let Claudie past, but they're never gonna let us through. And this car won't make it over the pass anyway. No chance."

"So we should run off into the mountains in a blizzard, maybe with some deadly disease? These people could be back out on the county road by now just waiting for us around the next bend. I say we make a plan that moves us toward town, even if we walk."

"That's what they expect. They'll likely have snowmobiles. It won't work."

"Why?"

"Resources. I saw their truck tracks. They weren't driving around with empty trucks. Either they have a lot of men, or men and snowmobiles. Whatever they have will be directed at Elk Horn Pass if they lose our tracks."

"If we aren't going to make definite progress toward a phone, maybe I should go by myself."

Kier slowed down and looked at her.

"You do that and the odds are very high that you will die. Be patient. I will get you to civilization. I promise."

Her jaw hardened, and he knew she was trying to control her anger.

"So I've got to live with you because I can't live without you. That's what you're saying. So what are the odds of an epidemic of some sort?"

"I have no idea." He paused. "Those guys were killing each other before the jet crashed, right?"

She nodded.

"There was a firefight in that plane."

"Okay," she said with a reluctant tone. "And you're going to say the grenade guy feared Tillman enough to die killing us—or just to keep a secret, or for some other damn reason. So we ought to be a lot more afraid of those guys who'll kill us instantly than a disease that will take time, and that we may not even have. That's your point?''

''Something like that.''

For a time Jessie didn't say anything more. Finally, ''What makes no sense is the private army. How did they know this jet would crash in these mountains?''

Kier shrugged.

''I think this decision making needs to follow democratic principles.''

''I think that before I let you kill yourself we're going to have a serious fight.''

''I've got a gun.''

''That's my point. To win you'd have to use it.''

He watched her bite her lower lip.

The square-hewn beams of Douglas fir that ran from the eaves to the ridgepole at the peak of Kier's cabin shone golden in the soft light of the propane lanterns. Simplicity gave the place an elegant look. A large oval carpet adorned the board floor. In the center of the carpet stood a black oak dining table that gleamed with innumerable coats of varnish. Six cane chairs surrounded the table. On the walls pine bookcases held an assortment of fiction, from Hemingway to modern thrillers, as well as books on all manner of biological subjects, a stack of *Scientific American* magazines, and a collection of *National Geographic*.

An old rocker was centrally located beside an irregularly shaped coffee table crafted from a redwood burl; a long-stemmed carved pipe with a pouch of tobacco lay on it beside a picture of a smiling brunette. On one wall next to the bookcases hung perhaps a hundred pictures of Indian kids, all in the mountains, all in camping settings. On another stretch of wall pencil sketches of native villages and landscapes were on display.

Jessie began pacing the moment they stepped in. "How long do we dare stay here?"

"Right here? Only a few minutes. Underneath us is a cellar of sorts. We can stay there for an hour or two, then we gotta go. We can't risk them finding us."

"It's got to take them a while. The way we sneaked here, hiding the car, walking a half mile, and crawling through the damned brush—"

"Don't forget in a raging, deadly blizzard," he said with a sly smile—the first she had seen since the barn.

"How could I?" She and Kier had beaten a trail through the snow to the creek in back. Next, they had set about leaving tracks haphazardly behind the place. "I've frozen my ass off in it three times now."

While Jessie read over his shoulder Kier flipped through the laboratory binders, skimming only certain small sections of the voluminous work. Occasionally, he glanced at his watch, concerned about their pursuers.

"Waited as long as we dare," he said, finally rising to fill a pack with food.

Jessie continued flipping through the binders. "What do these small print tables in Volume One mean? Row after row of As, Cs, Ts, and Gs?"

"You're probably reading a decoded gene or segments of it." He finished in the kitchen and leaned the pack against the wall. "'A' stands for adenine, 'T' for thymine, 'G' for guanine, and 'C' for cytosine. Those four molecules, the nucleic acids, go together in pairs to make a DNA strand."

"Do all vets know this stuff?"

"Certainly the ones who keep up a little on their biology do."

Kier knew the basics cold. A gene was a unit of DNA. Each gene specified the sequence of amino acids that defined a specified protein. Each gene was therefore responsible for the production of a unique protein, proteins being the building blocks of the body.

DNA was structured like a ladder twisted in a corkscrew shape. Each rung on the ladder was a nucleotide base pair. A nucleotide base pair can be adenine/thymine or cytosine/guanine.

"Everything genetic is determined by the order of those four paired nucleic acids. You could safely say that the order and placement of the nucleic acids in your genes account for your good looks."

"I think we can dispense with the compliments."

Kier did his best to give her a look of mystified innocence.

"Look, I don't mean to be rude, but—"

"You're still pissed about the telephone."

"I'm pissed because I don't think you take me seriously. There is this definite undercurrent that you're the damned chief and I'm the Indian."

"I'm not going to let you kill yourself, taking off into a blizzard trying to find a phone booth."

"So either I've got to do what you want or shoot you. I know. Let's get back to genetics."

"Okay. Now, the DNA of a virus has, say, tens of thousands of base pairs. A bacteria like tuberculosis probably has one or two million. The plans to the whole of every creature down to even bacteria and the lowly virus are in the form of these nucleic acid pairs. These guys found a new way to read those blueprints. On a human they have to read three billion nucleic acid base pairs to fully map all forty-six chromosomes. The government's Human Genome Project is mapping our DNA, but Tillman's group did that years ago. Some other private groups have rough maps. But Tillman's done a lot more than that."

"How did you get all that out of the fine print?"

Kier came over and put his finger in the text to a spot he

had marked by dog-earing the page. "You see this paragraph where they're talking about deciphering genetic code—

" 'The scanning, tunneling, atomic force microscopy working in combination with the Cray Sequencing Program produces outstanding results, accurately sequencing one hundred million base pairs per hour. Our early autosequencing technology sequenced only 100,000 base pairs per day. Methodologies available to the government still produce only about 100,000 base pairs per year for each electrophoretic processor.' "

"What's that mean?"

"They're talking, I think, about how fast they can read a strand of DNA using new electron microscope technology, combined with some processing technology they developed. This is phenomenally fast if it's what I think it is. Imagine a horse and buggy and the space shuttle. That's about the difference between what these guys say they have and what the rest of the world has."

"But what does it do for them?"

"If they can map a human's chromosomes down to each of three billion nucleotide pairs in thirty hours . . . If they knew which genes did what . . . But whether they would know that, I don't know. . . ." He trailed off.

"They're doing the same thing as the Human Genome Project. Right?"

"It begins with that. But it will take everybody else years to do a crude job on one hypothetical human. Tillman can do an individual human, distinguishing him from all other humans, in about thirty hours. That's phenomenal."

"So they're figuring out what makes each human unique," she said. "So why are people killing each other over this?"

"You want a wild guess? All right. But remember we're speculating here."

"Yeah. Yeah."

"The whole idea behind this research is to figure out the function of each human gene. Knowing the genome map is only the first, tiny step. To really know enough to alter a person's genetic makeup intelligently you've got to understand the function of each gene and how they interrelate.''

"I've read *Time* magazine too. If I knew how to alter genes I could, let's see, grow human organs, cure cancer, make designer babies, fix birth defects. I guess if I really had that ability I'd about own the world, and that's maybe what the guy with the diary meant, when he said he hadn't made Tillman God, but he had put him at God's right hand. But that's a lot of ifs.''

"Well, the table of contents does make it sound like they're able to alter genes. That's why we've got to read these volumes, and figure what they were actually doing.''

"But where is the evil in all this?''

"I'm not sure, except it's clear they were engineering viruses for various purposes. Maybe they were developing viruses to deliver altered genes to mutated cells as a form of gene therapy. Maybe that got dangerous. Somehow it led to something they call the Wintoon Project, as in Wintoon County. Here.'' He pointed at the floor. "Unfortunately this Wintoon thing is covered in Volume Six, and that's missing. But somehow it involves my tribe.''

"I wonder if it's like germ warfare.''

"I can't see how a bunch of girls being surrogate mothers would relate to germ warfare. And you wouldn't possess every disease in the book if you were experimenting with germ warfare. You might start with something like ebola or anthrax, but you wouldn't have the Noah's Ark of man's infirmities.''

"God, do you think they're cloning people?''

"Monkeys. At least the reference was to macaque monkeys. But of course, that could have been for starters. They're primates and closely related to man. Give me time. Reading the journals is slow going. They're summarizing years of work.''

"Well, I guess we'd better check on Miller before he freezes to death.'' Jessie closed one of the black volumes and tossed it aside.

"I haven't changed my mind," he said. "We're going to the cellar to study these." He held up one of the black volumes. "Then, unless I discover something new in here, we're going into the mountains. And for your information, it's now thirty-six miles to Johnson City on the road."

"For God's sake, these people have to be stopped! If we can't go to Johnson City, isn't there some other place?"

"I'll get our friend from the porch. Then we'll go to the cellar, where it's safer—"

"A town with a phone wouldn't be safer?" she cut in.

Kier walked over to her until his chest was six inches from her nose. Looking down into her eyes he sighed his frustration, then said in a very soft voice: "Are you ready to use the gun?" There was such intensity in her silence that for a second he wondered if she was thinking about it. "Then I'll get him." He walked out the back door.

Chapter 8

A mother's cleverness for her children is double
that for herself. Her ferocity is tenfold.

—Tilok proverb

Jack Tillman regarded the old man and his wife silently.
CAROTHERS read the little sign by the driveway. There was
shiftiness to their eyes that Tillman couldn't trust. Tire tracks
led into the forest, past the Carothers' snug little tin-roofed
cabin. Tillman was almost certain that these tracks matched
those that had come from the Donahue farm. Nobody was going
to make it over the Elkhorn Pass now. At any moment Tillman
half expected his men to tell him they had found the vehicle
in the woods out back.

"Doc came by earlier," Mr. Carothers was saying when
Doyle joined them.

When Doyle had come to Tillman from England, Tillman
had made him second in command of the field people. More
and more, though, Tillman felt tempted to promote him over

Brennan. This red-haired Englishman embodied the no-holds-barred, kick-ass attitude that Tillman liked.

Like Tillman, Doyle was a big man. Together they towered over their reluctant hosts. With the addition of three of Tillman's other men, the two-room cabin was almost filled to capacity. Everybody stood away from the door, near the stove that dominated one wall.

Carothers apparently noticed Tillman's naturally dark complexion and asked if he was part Indian. Tillman took it as a compliment, feeling as he did that he was in touch with his primal self and therefore much fitter than many of his softer counterparts.

"Well, the National Guard is here on government business." Tillman eyed the frail man as an owl might study a mouse. "And we can't do our job unless we know the whereabouts of everybody in the valley. As I said, we found the Donahue place empty, but freshly so, like they'd left in a hurry. Two vehicles went in this direction, but only the truck, which was first to leave, kept going. The car may have turned around. I don't know for sure." He paused. "Coincidentally, there are tire tracks coming right into your place here—"

The door opened and Brennan stomped in. "We got 'em," Brennan said. "Just up the road, in the woods."

"Thank you for your cooperation," Tillman said on his way out the door to the old man.

The Donahue woman had driven the truck up an old logging skid trail well into the woods and had been working in the dark to obliterate her tire tracks when his men found her. She had a long way to go if she had intended to complete the job all the way back to the county road. Now Doyle had her in the cab with the kids.

Claudie Donahue struck Tillman as a handsome woman, even though ripely pregnant in a heavy overcoat and peering out from under her dowdy stocking cap. He spoke through the open driver's side window. At first he proceeded slowly, showing his fake I.D. and explaining his military status. He was careful to let her study his driver's license, and even showed her his dog tags. Oddly enough, he joked, he was General Grant of the National Guard, no relation to the Civil War hero. That her expression remained too impassive to read irritated him. Her cool skepticism cut him like a knife.

"Take the kids," he told Doyle finally. "I'll ride with Mrs. Donahue." He opened the door of the king cab truck.

"The kids stay with me." She said it calmly, but forcefully. "And where are we going?"

Tillman held up his hand, signaling Doyle to wait.

"Back to your house, ma'am. It's necessary."

"The kids can ride in back," she said.

"We need to talk, ma'am. Things that aren't for kids."

She hesitated, studying him. He supposed she was trying to decide whether he was really a general of the National Guard.

"I can get you out of here on a snowmobile if you cooperate."

Hope flickered in her eye. "Can we talk here?"

"Fine. Take the kids to the house," he told Doyle.

"Let's go, chaps," Doyle said with a big, friendly smile.

Getting in the cab beside her, Tillman spoke in conspiratorial tones. "We're searching for a downed plane, and we thought maybe you could help."

"Don't know anything about it." Her response was too careful.

"You heard nothing this afternoon?"

She hesitated.

"Of course, you did. Why are you afraid to talk?"

"I don't know what I heard. A boom. Later, I heard what sounded like guns, more explosions."

"Two vehicles left your driveway. You were driving one. Who was driving the other?"

"Frankly, I don't know."

"Who was staying with you? Come on, ma'am, we need your cooperation. We've got an emergency here."

"Why are you here?"

"That's classified, ma'am, for your own protection. Now, I'm the one asking the questions, and I need your help."

"My sister was staying with me."

"Who else?"

"No one else. But our friend, Dr. Kier Wintripp, was visiting."

"How do you know him?"

"He's been a friend of ours for years."

"This is an important government operation, ma'am; we know a lot. We just need you to confirm it. Tell me about your sister. Where's she from?"

"Back East."

"What's she do for a living?"

Again Claudie hesitated.

"Mrs. Donahue, I really need your help here. I don't have a file on your sister because she doesn't have a place near Mill Valley. Now, she could be in real danger ... so please help me."

"She's with the FBI."

"A special agent with the FBI?"

"Yes." The woman sighed.

"Was she there when you heard these noises?"

"No. Later."

"Did she go investigate?"

"I don't know. She suggested I go to town before the snow got deeper."

"This is the vet's rig."

"We thought I could make it easier in the truck."

"Why didn't your sister come too?"

"She was going to stay and watch the place."

"Ma'am, forgive me, but I don't think you're being candid here, and I need your full cooperation."

"I've told you everything I know."

He was certain she was lying. An FBI agent would have gone to investigate. That would account for the second set of footprints. That left the third set of tracks at the wreckage. Any of the three could have the lab summaries.

"Ma'am, I'm going to insist that you be candid and tell me what you know. Right now! People's lives could be at stake."

She looked at him squarely, without fear. "I've said everything I have to say for the time being, and I want my kids back."

Glancing around to be sure everyone was still inside, he reached under the woman's cap and grabbed her long brown hair, yanking back her head. With his right hand, he clamped down on her neck. The instant after he did it, he knew that, right or wrong, he was committed to a course of action that must end in her death. Her hands went to his, trying to break the chokehold. She was strong, but not strong enough.

"Stop fighting me," he hissed, increasing the pressure.

He had to get his wits about him. From under his coat he pulled a black-handled knife and popped the blade. He put it to her neck.

"I'm not going to waste any more time on you. And before I start cutting you up, I'm going to kill the kids."

He heard himself speaking, but it was as if he were listening to a stranger.

She groaned an animal groan: "No."

"If you don't talk . . ."

"Noooo."

". . . and talk fast, I'm going for the oldest. I'll bring him out here and slice his throat while you watch."

"What do you want?" came her hoarse whisper.

"I want to know exactly what happened, and if I think you're lying, I kill the kid."

"Kier went looking for Jessie in the storm. While they were gone there was an explosion. It was at one-thirty or so, maybe a little earlier. They didn't come back. There was another large explosion, then shooting, then more explosions. Far away. Finally she came back. She was frightened. She told me to leave. She wouldn't explain or come near, insisting that she remain outside. Just an epidemic or a disease or something she said Kier had found. She begged me, so I went. She said to head for Johnson City and avoid strangers. That's all.''

Tillman could feel her submission. It felt good—like victory. He realized that he was breathing hard. The colors in the cab had become more vivid. Confidence filled him. He put a hand on her belly. She stiffened.

''If you don't cause me any trouble you may yet have another child.''

He felt an unaccustomed urge to continue touching her body. The new clarity of thought that now possessed him enabled him to see that his power over her was for the good of the whole project. His hand moved to her breast, and he studied her face as he felt it. It was not the hefty breast that impressed him, but his power to incite her loathing.

''I will take you to Johnson City. If you tell a soul of our little talk, I will kill you.''

Watching her face, he knew this woman was too strong to believe that he might let her live. She would not anesthetize herself with false hope, like some. He could have saved his breath.

He radioed Brennan. For what he was about to do, Brennan was the right man.

''Get the snowmobile and follow me.''

Tillman laid the back of his hand against her cheek, experimenting. It satisfied him that she did not pull away, even though he knew her body shook with the desire to escape. Her fear mingled with hate was a form of respect that he had come to cherish.

When Brennan's snowmobile pulled behind him and the kids were in the small jump seats in the back of the oversize cab, he told Doyle to take the other men and go on ahead to the Donahue ranch.

Other than the occasional quiver of her lip, Claudie looked almost normal as she drove. Mothers always tried to keep up appearances for the kids. It was a shame these boys weren't younger. If he could have saved them without them having any troublesome memories, he would. He didn't kill kids when it wasn't necessary.

"Mom, Bren keeps poking me and won't quit," Micah said from the back.

"You boys hush."

He could tell by the way her eyes darted that she was thinking. A strong woman like this would be grasping at any straw.

"Stop the truck."

An uneasy silence fell all around. Reaching under his coat, Tillman pulled out a grenade, holding it low so the boys wouldn't see it. "You know what this is?"

She looked down at his hand and nodded. He pulled the pin and held it on the seat.

"If I let go of this lever, you know what happens?" Again she nodded, saying nothing.

"Don't even think about driving off the road. If I relax my hand, this cab becomes an inferno."

She nodded again.

The boys were quiet now. Tillman figured that like all mammals they were alert to the presence of danger, even if they didn't understand it. Idly, he wondered at all the things he could make their mother do. Her arms seemed locked in place, her hands frozen to the wheel. He studied the way she bit her lip. He was winning. He could smell the kill. Oddly, he found himself wishing he had time for sex. He shook it off.

"Please let them go. They won't understand . . ." It was starting, he knew. "They won't remember, they don't understand any of this."

"We're letting you all go. You have nothing to worry about."

Her mouth quivered and she began to sob.

"Please, please," she whispered, "not the boys . . . they're just little boys."

"Mommy, Mommy."

Just around the next bend, Tillman recalled that a sheer drop of over five hundred feet plunged to the river. Nothing could survive that spill. Taking his radio, he spoke to Brennan and told him to hold back. The lights from the snowmobile disappeared behind them in response.

They came to the bend.

"Stop," he said.

In her eyes he could see the knowledge of her own death and the terror at her children's. But shockingly she didn't stop. In an instant, he knew her thought. She wasn't going to let him win. He would die with them.

"Bastard," Claudie said as she drove for the edge.

Holding the grenade tight, Tillman opened the passenger door and pushed with everything he had. As the front wheels slipped over the edge, he reached for the ground, aware of the abyss ahead. His fingers, clawlike, grabbed a large rock at the drop off. He watched as the truck teetered. Then the engine roared. It was in reverse, and the rear tires were biting through the snow to the rocks. Far below the grenade exploded. A horror filled him as he realized she might drive away.

Tillman clambered to his feet, drawing his pistol even while considering whether to use another grenade. He had never searched the truck cab for guns. He had been stupid—careless. Aiming at the cab, ready to fire if the truck were freed, he waited. He began walking in a wide arc toward the driver's side. As he moved, the outline of the truck was almost lost in the snow and darkness.

* * *

Tillman remembered nothing until Brennan bent over him.

"Where's the woman?" he said. Pain shot through his head. He felt his own hair matted with blood.

"I don't know. You've only been out for a few minutes, but I just got here. I haven't been to the truck."

With his head pulsing, Tillman rolled and looked toward the motionless vehicle. He could see nothing but the glow of the taillights. He struggled up, determination overcoming his pain, dizziness, and caution.

"Let's go." Then he paused. He had killed clever men and cunning animals. It was a mistake to let his anger drive him.

"You circle that way," he told Brennan.

"Why not just turn on the M-16s and be done with it?" Brennan asked.

"How do I explain a bullet-ridden vet's truck at the bottom of the canyon? If I'd wanted that, I'd have stuffed a grenade in the cab." He asked, "Did you hear the grenade explode down over the cliff?"

"Yeah, seven or eight minutes ago. I hung back like you said."

Tillman shook his head, trying to remember.

"There's no cover to approach the damn thing," Brennan said, nodding at the truck. "I say we just unload an M-16 and be done with it."

"Nobody asked you."

In a matter of two minutes, Tillman had circled around and begun his approach. He went slowly, completely in control. As he got closer, he expected a trap.

But they found the truck abandoned, its doors left ajar, and the snow gliding inside. All the footprints led to the cliff. Tillman followed the trail along the cliff until it abruptly ended. His captives and their rescuer had climbed over the edge to escape. In the beam of Brennan's flashlight, he looked for individual tracks, but the trail from the truck along the cliff was stirred up as if they had gone back and forth. To sort it out and count prints would take time he didn't have. He looked down the face of the cliff, but could see no more than twenty or thirty feet in the dark. At the edge of the abyss where the tracks ended, he found no sign of a rope. Casting about, he found a heavy branch with a barely discernible rope burn. They had used a line and somehow pulled it down after themselves.

"It would take serious climbing gear to get down that cliff," Brennan said.

"Maybe somebody left pitons in that wall."

"I doubt it. And without gear it wouldn't be that easy to use them."

Obviously the truck's vet cabinets had made a hiding place. The person who hid in the compartments had circled behind Tillman, clubbed him, and led the family over the cliff.

Perhaps it had been the veterinarian. But then who had been in the other vehicle? He had no time to go down the cliff after them, and without equipment in a snowstorm, it would be extremely dangerous—probably impossible. Kier and the FBI woman were far more important to find. What were the odds that a woman and two kids could survive in this weather anyhow, much less on a cliff?

"They're dead or on their way to being dead," he said. "We'll send men back to make sure."

Returning to the truck, he yanked open the storage compartment doors and examined every space. Most of the storage areas were chockful of medical supplies and equipment. He found only one cavity possibly large enough for a man to hide in, but far too small for Kier Wintripp.

At the tailgate, Tillman shouted, "Push." He threw his chest against the truck. Brennan heaved as well, but the truck didn't budge. They began rocking it on the edge, until they felt it slip just an inch, then again. At last it groaned, slid forward, then plunged down over the cliff. The crashing sounds it made on the way down were smothered in the pillows of snow.

Normally a comfortable ally, the darkness now thwarted Tillman. He could not penetrate its murky depths, and the mysteries it enfolded were likely to multiply. He needed to improve his odds. At Elk Horn Pass on the road to Johnson City a cellular phone would enable a man to call anywhere in the world. He would dispatch someone on a snowmobile immediately. If only the weather cleared, even slightly, an infrared-equipped attack helicopter would perform wonders. With the thought of that power unleashed against one Indian and an FBI woman, Tillman's mental edge returned. With it came the realization that until now he had never met a hunter that was truly his equal. Even lacking the technology, given enough time, he would hunt and kill Kier Wintripp.

Stalking Bear stood on a ledge under a rock overhang that created a shallow cave. Claudie's two boys sat huddled beside him next to a coil of rope. From above came the sound of the truck grating on the edge of the rock. After a moment the scraping of metal ceased, and for a couple of seconds there was silence. Then a crashing noise ended in a muffled thud far below.

He listened for Claudie's screams, but heard none. He had gambled her life on the assumption that the men would be in a hurry and would be distracted. They would be searching the ground for tracks and staring over the edge of the cliff.

Using a rope he had pulled her up the tree next to the truck to the first branches. From there she could climb to over forty feet above the ground, hidden in the pitch black of the heavy boughs. By laying a clear path that dead-ended along the abyss, Stalking Bear hoped to distract the men from Claudie's hiding place. To lower themselves they had passed a rope around a tree leaving two strands dangling. Once safely on the ledge, they had pulled in one end, snaking the rope back around the tree and down over the cliff.

Even if the men didn't find Claudie, he questioned whether she could climb out of the tree. He waited perhaps an hour before he began searching the face of the rock with his hands. Climbing the cliff unassisted would be difficult, but not impossible. The two boys huddled together and he suspected they were cold. He considered how he might ascend, then felt one last time and discovered what he was looking for—there was a line dangling from above.

Two tugs on the line were answered by two tugs from atop the cliff. Claudie had made her way out of the tree and was signaling her success by dropping the rope to him. Fastening his rope to the one hanging above, he and the boys continued down the cliff to a treacherous but passable trail. Claudie traveled by a different route to a cave near the bottom of the canyon far below them where they were all reunited.

Knowing their pursuers would send more men, Stalking Bear led them to a cave three miles distant and there built them a camp.

Chapter 9

A wise man treats every new cave as if it had a
bear.

—Tilok proverb

Kier suspected that, for Jessie Mayfield, a root cellar had
the ambience of a snake pit. The heated rear porch had large
windows and a spacious workbench against the outside wall.
Under the workbench Kier kept his chainsaws, hoses, and gardening paraphernalia, although he did no gardening in the conventional sense. Against the wall nearest the house stood some
shelving put together in a manner similar to a series of bookcases. One six-foot segment of shelving on the end could be
swung away from the wall to reveal a trapdoor. The construction
was elaborate, but it all worked to effectively hide the opening
to the cellar.

"Actually, it's not that bad," Kier said, sensing her hesitation
at the black hole before them.

Tentatively, she placed her foot on the first rung, testing it with her weight. When she seemed satisfied, she climbed down the ladder with deliberate, careful, steps, reaching the earthen floor without difficulty. At the bottom, Kier snapped on a single naked light bulb hanging from a wire. The place was walled in with two-by-six boards—moldy and probably rotten. He began sliding the tongue-and-groove boards on one wall, lifting them out of slotted uprights until he exposed a heavy metal door set in a concrete wall.

"The wine cellar is through here," Kier said pointing into the concrete vault.

"Every time you want a bottle of wine you go through this ritual?" she asked, sounding incredulous.

"When I'm here I leave the boards out."

"Unbelievable."

They walked into the climate-controlled cellar. It was about eight feet by fourteen, board lined on the walls, ceiling, and floor. Wooden bottle racks on all four walls surrounded a small table in the middle.

"Don't tell me you sit here and drink wine."

"Only when I'm tasting."

"I've got to tell you, this is like finding a cathedral in a whorehouse. Nobody, but nobody, would ever guess this was here. Or that you're a wine guy."

"I was more or less counting on that." He paused and allowed himself a half-smile.

"Are you laughing at me?"

"I'm just enjoying your amazement. Surely you'll grant me that. We should move our stuff out back in the woods. We can bring the binders down here."

"We'll be trapped if they catch us in this cellar."

"We've got to be out of here before they come." He put the bag with the food in the corner before they ascended.

Back in the cabin, Kier picked up one of the five journals on the table. He wanted to devour them.

"There's almost nothing in plain English except this diary

fragment,'' Jessie said, leaning over his shoulder. Together they studied it again.

"This guy is certain that Tillman, the architect of whatever is going on, is a monster,'' Kier said. "I told you about our little meeting at the clinic.''

He turned to Volume One. "In the applied lab they were looking at disease processes and the interaction with genetic variability. It looks like they were doing some work on a virus. They call it AV-TR4 and I can't figure what it is. But it's not unusual to be working on viruses. Man-made or otherwise.

"Then they've got a ton of research on some sort of immunity issue. They keep referring to 121258-533561289. Which they abbreviate to 1212.

" 'Whether 1212 is typical of the Tilok race or an anomaly is not yet evident,' it says. Apparently they were studying the Tiloks from a genetic standpoint.''

"What do you suppose 1212 refers to?''

"Maybe a gene nucleotide sequence. I don't know. These tables here reference 1212 and contain the nucleotide sequences for part of a gene. I'm sure of it. Maybe they think Tiloks have some important genetic immunity.''

"Could a particular group of Native Americans have an immunity not common to the rest of us?''

"Sure. Cherokees don't get Alzheimer's disease at near the rate of other races.''

"Do you think they were reproducing Tilok genes in animals to study some genetic trait of the Tiloks?''

"We're getting far out now.''

"Why all the diseases in the plane then? Could they be correlating disease processes with genetic profiles?''

Kier shrugged. "Maybe the government knows why all that disease was in that plane.''

"The government wouldn't condone experimenting on Tiloks or hauling around a freakshow of deadly organisms.''

"Who says these people would be truthful with the government? We can't assume anything until we know exactly who and what we're dealing with.''

He was about to continue reading when a muffled scream came from the back porch. Miller's voice, calling through the gag, sounded his desperation. They went through the back door.

"What do you want?" Jessie asked, loosening the gag.

"I have my rights."

"Okay," Kier said. "We'll untie you and you can sit in the living room."

"If we sit around we're dead, man. If they have the slightest inkling you were near that plane, we are in the ground six feet down. You get me?"

"I was figuring on leaving you here to explain things," Kier said.

"You can't do that. If you leave me, it's murder."

"Why are you so afraid of your own people? The National Guard, they protect our country." Kier gilded his words with sarcasm.

Miller said nothing.

"Well, we're packing to leave. If you're right about them coming, they should have you untied in three or four hours."

"You mother f—"

"What are you afraid of?"

"They'll kill me and you know it. They'll shoot the cabin to pieces and burn the place to the ground. Then they'll ask questions."

"Now tell me, how do you know they'll burn the place to the ground?"

Miller glanced around, starting to look as though he might talk. "Will you take me with you?"

"If we believe what you say."

"There's a chemical—steno for short. A few molecules will slowly kill you. If you got in the plane, you could have it on you and in you. They'll be scared to get near you, so they'll burn the place, because fire neutralizes the chemical. But they may send somebody in. They'll want the black books you took. Damn. It hurts to talk." He touched his broken jaw. "They told us if we went twenty feet from the plane, we'd be quarantined. If we went in the plane—we were dead."

"What kind of sickness?"

"I don't know. . . . It's a chemical. Top secret." He seemed to be loosening up now. "It's probably just a line. Nobody knows for sure. Maybe there was radioactive stuff. I don't know."

"Why are these black books so important?" Kier asked.

"I don't know."

"So why does the sickness spread if it's a chemical?"

"I told you it only takes a few molecules of the stuff to kill you. It can spread just by touch, like poison ivy. But they said it spreads easier than that. It can atomize in the air."

"Who's the leader? Who hired you?"

Miller knotted his fists and looked from side to side, straining at the rope across his chest.

"How do you know about the books?" Kier asked.

"If we found any books, they told us we'd get $100,000 extra. If more than one of us found them, we'd split the money. Of course, they were supposed to be in the plane, so we figured unless it busted open and the books fell out, we'd never see the money."

Kier leaned close to the man. "And how did you know to be there when the plane crashed?"

Wham! Something slammed against the front door. Suddenly, bullets were flying through the sides of the cabin, chewing wood, and sending splinters like darts through the air. In an instant, Kier grabbed Jessie, literally sliding her into the hole, motioning her to drop. As she stumbled down the ladder, Miller's head exploded in a red fog, splashing blood everywhere. Kier tossed the volume through the trapdoor, then jumped for the hole, catching the third or fourth rung down. By pushing a button near the top of the ladder, he was able to cover the trapdoor with the cabinet. In a minute, the gunfire ceased. Then there was silence. Something slammed against the front door. Then came the sounds of one man walking, and something—maybe the bed—being thrown against the wall.

"One light is on, but nobody's here except a dead-ass Miller."

The voice came from directly above them.

"They knew we were coming." Then a pause, and more walking. "Well, looky here, four black books."

"Door out the back's open." A radio crackled. "You guys see anything?"

Kier couldn't make out the muffled reply.

"They must've had ten seconds, plenty of time to run out the back."

"This place is surrounded. We'd have seen them."

"In this damn snow?"

"There's tracks all over back here. Burn it and let's see what comes out."

"They'll find us," Jessie whispered. "Only a matter of time. How did they get here so fast?"

"Snowmobiles, probably," Kier replied. "It's been an hour and fifteen minutes since we left Claudie's. But it's incredible they worked this fast." He paused a moment. Then he stood. "You can hide here."

"I'm the FBI," she snapped. "Remember?"

"Forget the FBI stuff. This is in my backyard."

Kier could discern her determination even in the semidarkness of the small flashlight. Her hand gripped his wrist. They heard the rushing sound of fire. "Listen to me. I can help you."

"Jessie. In the dark, alone, around my place, I can do something. You'd be a handicap. This isn't a computer thing."

"Well, it's not a house call for a sick dog either."

There was very little time before the fire would be too hot to allow their escape. He could hear the crackling flames overhead, and knew he had to come up while the structure was still standing.

"I can cover you," she argued, still gripping his wrist, pulling on him.

"Okay. But wait sixty seconds at least before you come." He reached down and grabbed the book.

Kier stepped to the ladder. At the top he gave her a quick salute. He pressed a button that activated the hydraulic arm moving the shelving away from the wall. Sliding through the trapdoor, he closed it quickly, squatted on it, then flipped down the metal tongue that fitted over a recessed steel loop. Instead of a lock, he placed a piece of wood through the latch, jamming it so the trapdoor wouldn't open.

"Jessie," he called out, his face to the crack. "I've changed my mind. Wait there until I call you. Get in the wine cellar and put the boards in place. If I'm not back in forty-five minutes, get out the best you can. There's a crowbar—"

"Kier, don't be an asshole."

"Please, Jessie."

"I'll kill you for this."

Then he swung the shelving back over the door.

Overhead, flames boiled under the roof. The heat was intense but bearable. A good portion of the rear wall was on fire; he had only seconds. Crawling to the still-open rear door, he saw one man nearby, mesmerized by the burning cabin, his M-16 at the ready. The hunter toyed with a grenade in his left hand.

Kier had to knock out the double-pane side window on his left, then dive through without being seen. Spying a chainsaw gas tank, he considered how he might use it for a diversion. The heat now felt ferocious on his back. He had to move or die.

He opened the cap and hurled the tank at the window to his far right. As he huddled behind the woodpile, the explosion blew past him. With the acrid stink of his own singed hair filling his nostrils, he threw an axe into the closer window, on the left, then got on his knees and used a maul to clear out the rest of the glass. The fire, gobbling oxygen, left nothing but smoke for his lungs. He had to get out. Launching himself through the window, he cleared the windowsill in a flat dive.

Work with what you have, Jessie told herself, standing on the ladder. Forcing herself to be calm, she considered that fighting the trapdoor would only distract Kier and perhaps draw the attention of their attackers. She retreated to the wine cellar, boarding up the interior wall so that she would be invisible to anyone who came to investigate. After the boards were in place, she closed the metal door, turned on the light, and caught a whiff of fresh air from a vent. She scarcely glanced at the wine bottles on their neat wooden racks or noticed the thermometer, which indicated fifty-seven degrees.

She had marked the time and would wait the forty-five minutes. Then, she would go up and give the world a piece of her mind.

Chapter 10

A man falling from a great cliff needs neither courage nor fear. But those who remain need both.
                                        —Tilok proverb

When Kier hit the ground, he started crawling like a mouse under a rug. He had been visible for a split second against the light of the flames, but since there had been no bullets, he assumed he hadn't been seen. A small pump house stood forty feet from the blaze; he stopped there and hid the fifth volume.

He examined the tree line, looking for the safety men— those who would stay well back to assist the hunters nearest the cabin. He would disable the reinforcements first.

The snow still fell in great sheets, blown sideways by a piercing wind, the cold soothing his burns that, despite the pain, were minor. His primary concern now would be frostbite. Kier was immediately conscious of the bone-aching pain of bare hands on snow. Soon they would feel like dead flesh. Wearing only his long underwear, pants, a shirt, and a sweater, he could not stay out for long without more insulation. He lay on his belly, sinking down into a couple of feet of fluffy snow.

Slowly crawling past one tree trunk at a time, he scrutinized every outline in the night. Sometimes he tested with his rapidly freezing fingertips, feeling for leather or fabric. A cacophony of wind noises, the creak of the trees, the howl of the air around every edge, the rustle of every leaf, the swish of every branch, the crackling roar of the nearby fire: all made sound an untrustworthy ally.

After many minutes, he didn't know how many, he reached for yet another outline in the night. The touch was almost casual, as he expected another tree. He felt the roughness of bark. But right next to it, planted at the sapling's base, lay something smooth—too smooth. It was a boot. Kier's weary body came alive. He had found a soldier's foot. Moving again, he put the boot between himself and the fire. Yes—there was a silhouetted leg against the light from the burning cabin.

By the position of the heel, he verified that the man faced away from him. Kier rose slowly, absolute stealth imperative. He could not risk a miss or a struggle.

He waited, letting his breath run over his hands, warming them from the horrible, tingling pain. After many seconds, he heard a raspy breath like a quiet sigh. Slowly he put his hand out into the night wind—listening, feeling, waiting. Then he cupped his hand back toward himself. In an instant he felt a snow-capped dome—a helmet—icy-smooth plastic on the leeward side. It was the lip at the back of the man's neck. Fast as a cat's paw, Kier's hand drove under the man's helmet, chopping the bony knot at the base of his skull. At the same time, he grabbed the man's chin, yanking it upward.

In one motion, he applied a chokehold. The man's arms windmilled as he struggled vainly against the silencing of his mind. Finally, he sagged. A small body for a professional thug, Kier thought.

He expected to find a duplicate of Miller's equipment, and

he was not disappointed. First he put on the man's down-filled mitts. Only the trigger finger had an independent sleeve, and they were very warm. In seconds he had the all-important pair of handcuffs. Although there was no stiletto, a sharpened knife hung on the man's belt. Trying not to think of what he was about to do, he pulled off the mitts just long enough to untie the heavy laces of the man's right boot. With some difficulty, he removed the boot, along with two pairs of socks. Holding the man's heel with his left hand, he took the large combat knife and held it against his Achilles tendon.

How deep should he go? Certainly he needn't go all the way to prevent the man from following and make him worthless as a soldier. He couldn't see; fishing through the man's pockets, he found his flashlight. It would be suicide to turn it on in the open, so he hunkered down. In the instant he could see, he sliced into the flesh, cutting well into the tendon, but not completely through. With utter disgust, he crammed the man's foot back into the boot, not bothering with the socks. If he didn't die of the cold, it would be weeks or months before the man walked unassisted.

Now Kier had a two-way radio, a penlight, an automatic weapon, four grenades, a 10-mm. pistol with a silencer, and several ammo clips. He stripped off the man's thin overcoat, which would provide Kier some slight additional protection. There was no time to remove the insulated body suit, and he didn't want the man to die.

The odds were starting to change. Running his mitted fingers over the automatic rifle, he knew it was not an M-16. These guys were not even pretending to be National Guard. Pulling back the bolt, he quietly ejected a shell, the sound a slight *click,* lost in the wind. Feeling the round, he knew immediately that they had the latest in technology. He couldn't remember what it was called, but this gun left no empty casings. Hundreds of shots could be fired without a trace. The powder was solid and affixed to the bullet. Next he found the bolt release and the safety. Without a sound, he continued his crawl along the tree line.

"Bulldog—silver. Boxer—gold." The unconscious man's radio crackled. "Pit bull—iron. Poodle—quartz. Shepherd—copper. Basset—" Silence. "Basset—" Kier said nothing. "Basset, say the code."

The burning roof now created a brighter light, and the snow did not fall as thickly. Kier moved into the forest, continuing in a circle around the cabin, which was rapidly becoming a pile of his smoldering treasures.

In case Jessie tried to emerge as the fire began dying, Kier had to get these men away from the cabin or disable them all quickly. Knowing every square inch of the terrain was about the only thing in his favor. It wasn't enough. The others would be much more cautious now, nervous that he was hunting them. They would not stand in the open, nor would they hide in obvious spots like the tree line. He needed a radically different strategy.

He had an idea.

"I want to live my last few days in peace," Kier spoke into the radio. "Since the 'chemical,' as you call it, will kill me anyway, why worry about it?"

He began to run even as he spoke, hoping they couldn't immediately locate him from the transmission. It was a risk.

"Stay here and you'll die one by one. Unlike you, I have nothing to lose. I'm dead any way you slice it. I know the ground. You don't."

"You'll be a sorry son of a bitch if you don't give up. You'll die slow," an angry voice replied.

"Stay with procedure." It was Tillman's calm, authoritative voice.

"Some of your men aren't taking to these mountains." Kier ran through the trees toward the cabin's front. "Tillman, can you hear it in his voice? Your man's moving off-center. Maybe we should all start lobbing grenades around in the dark.'' Kier chuckled into the radio.

"Whatever you might have we can fix.'' Tillman again. "If we agree to pull back, we want your promise that you'll stay and negotiate.''

"I'm a doctor. I'm not going to leave and risk spreading something around.''

"Make sure you don't then. We're withdrawing. We'll hold our fire. After we pull out, I'll call you. We'll meet.''

It was what Kier had hoped for—a misguided attempt to trap him on his own turf. If he were lucky, at least some would make a show of leaving. Nearing the road, where he expected to find the snowmobiles, he moved slowly in a crouch, alert to every shadow, every vertical line or hump that might be a man. Then he stopped.

There would be someone with the snowmobiles, at least one guard. He crawled in a serpentine pattern, first approaching the driveway, then moving away. Time and cold were working against him, but he knew his edge lay in patience. Animals stayed hidden because they spent minutes and hours without moving, oblivious to the disquiet that the passage of time created in humans. Pausing frequently to put his head above the snow, squinting against the tiny wind-driven flakes, Kier found no one. Surprised, almost bewildered, he drew to within fifty feet of the road. Still he remained alone.

Something—he didn't know what—told him to backtrack. It made sense since he was leaving prints in the snow, but mentally, turning around was tough. After only a few feet, he saw two shadows and a small light. They were following his trail. He vigorously shook a tree, and night tracers lit the air over his head, the bullets chopping the tree in half. Some truce. In a blink, he touched off a dozen rounds of his own. The two men disappeared like chaff in the wind. He had aimed high, over their heads, but it would keep them down for the seconds he needed.

Now the race was on in earnest. Most of the men would be nearby, coming down the driveway to the waiting snowmobiles. They would be right where he wanted them. Turning, he ran carelessly, knowing there was no way to make it safe. His legs churned through the snow, and in seconds he could feel the stress. His muscles burned, and the air frosted his throat.

He made an angle for the road. By coming back from the north instead of east from the cabin, he hoped to have a split-second edge on the guard. The man would be watching in the direction of the cabin.

Kier hit the public road at a dead run. He didn't see the parked two-man vehicles until he was almost on them, didn't see the guard until the man turned to fire. Kier dived, bullets tearing past him. The muzzle blast flashing in the night made an easy target. Kier rolled and killed him.

He went to the first snowmobile, his fingers searching wildly. There was no key. And he knew without looking that the rest would be the same. Only seconds stood between him and several men with automatic weapons. No time to search the body. His last chance to carry out his plan would use up the precious remaining seconds. He would do with his feet what he had intended to do on a machine, and it would be the most important footrace of his life.

He fired a wide volley toward the cabin, hoping to slow his pursuers, and ran. Not with measured strides or with an eye toward pacing himself, but full out.

"Catch me if you can, assholes," he shouted into the radio.

It was some six hundred yards to where he was going— about three-eighths of a mile—but it was in deep snow and far enough that his pursuers could easily reach sixty miles per hour by snowmobile.

Staying to the edge of the road, sometimes to a trail just off it, made him a harder target. Still, why would a man run down a road? Hopefully, they wouldn't think about it much. He didn't. Instead he focused upon the pain dancing in his mind; fire, burning up and down his legs; lungs that were melting butterfly wings; and a body that couldn't get enough oxygen. He wanted air. He wanted away from the pain. But he could only run.

He had gone almost a quarter mile—he recognized a tall pine—when he saw the first lights behind him. For a moment, he almost slowed at the hopelessness of what he intended. They would catch him in one hundred yards unless he stopped to fight or slunk into the woods.

There were six lights, a pack. It was all or most of them, and they hung relatively close together.

He jumped off the road just before the first bullet came. When he fired back, one man went down. The lights scattered and the firefight began. Events were developing all wrong. And it would have stayed that way except for their one miscalculation.

The enemy was also patrolling the road. Around the corner, from the opposite direction, a snowmobile roared into Kier's sights. The gunrack across the front told him enough. He crouched. At the lights from the pursuing vehicles, the new man slowed, presenting an easy shot. Kier fired right into the man's steel breastplate, literally blowing him off the seat, and ran for the careening machine. He was on it before his startled pursuers fully grasped what had happened. Kier turned off the lights and exulted in the power of the machine. He revved the engine in neutral from behind a tree, sending an unmistakable message.

"Catch me if you can," he shouted again into the radio before taking off.

He sped away from them at forty miles an hour in low gear, wanting it to sound like sixty. Two bends and he saw the small side road that was critical to his plan. He went straight ahead instead of rounding the third bend, down into an old creek bed and skid trail used to slide logs to the river in the early 1900s.

At night, up was not so easily discerned from down as one might think. At night in a snowstorm, up from down was even harder to perceive. On a steep grade it was even more difficult to determine. Kier knew the chute grew steeper as it went. And it only went down.

He lay flat on the machine, barely able to glimpse the occasional light in the rearview mirror. He dodged and weaved around the curves, jinking up and down the banks of the gully like a luge in a track. He could barely hold his speed to forty in a dead coast. Now he was dropping like a plummeting bird. Wind whipped in his face. He clutched the snowmobile between his legs as if it were part of him. They were gaining on him. He screamed his mirth into the radio.

At the last possible second he rose on his machine, jumping clear to the side and up the bank. He felt like a pebble falling down the mountain. He tried to slide, but bounced terribly. The earth, his mountain, pummeled him. Snow-covered brush whipped him. Frantically, he grabbed and dug in, first with his feet, then with his hands and elbows. He cartwheeled in the blackness, slapped and thrown like a child in the clutches of a monster.

But it slowed him. He stopped on the lip of the chute, out of the slick, as the first machine passed by with its engine dead and the driver screaming at the horror of the abyss. A second man shot by with only the sounds of shifting gears. Kier lost count of the machines that reached the end of the chute and flew the fifty to one hundred feet to the river's bottom. There was a big, deep stretch at the head of a rapids into which the unsuspecting would fall. They might survive, but it would be a struggle to make it through the rapids, and it would be hours before any survivor could make it out of the canyon a couple of miles or more downstream.

Walking back to the cabin driveway was an ordeal. Frozen to the skin, numb from cold, his muscles no longer did his bidding, his fingers worked only minimally, and a shrapnel burn irritated his leg. He needed rest.

Fear formed in his gut. When Jessie freed the trapdoor, she'd be dead if any of the remaining killers saw her. That spurred him on. When he reached the driveway to his cabin, he pulled out the radio.

"This is your new leader. Wanna talk?"

Nothing. He could not believe that every last man had followed him. Slowly he advanced along the tree line, looking for any shadow in the falling snow. The cabin still burned.

He moved back into the trees, keeping the cabin barely in sight until he was behind it, near the now-burned back porch. As he emerged from the trees, Kier saw a form backlit by the firelight next to the pump house. He moved forward, stealthily at first, then stood, relieved. He knew it was Jessie from her size and form. Silently, she raised her pistol, pointing it at him. He stared intently and raised a hand to waive. *Pfffft.* The silenced shot missed his head by mere inches and made a hollow *thunk* behind him. Kier whirled to see a man fallen in the snow. Jessie had shot him in the face.

She came forward with her pistol still leveled in his direction. Her demeanor telegraphed her anger. As she closed the gap between them, she finally began lowering the pistol. He found himself sighing in relief.

Tillman sat quietly in the Donahue kitchen, his large hand wrapped around a sizable mug. He squeezed the ceramic vessel rhythmically as if his hand were a beating heart. His men were spread around the house, leaving him alone except for Doyle, who sat nearby, seemingly engrossed in an old magazine.

Tillman had twenty men left, a formidable group with him in the lead. What stopped him from undertaking a manhunt around the burned cabin was the fact that he didn't want to underestimate the Indian's resources again. Eight men were now dead or incapacitated. Sheer numbers would accomplish nothing for Tillman unless he could outthink Kier Wintripp. He now expected the Indian to flee to the mountains he knew so well. It was what Tillman would have done. Troops could block roads and search cabins easily. It was tougher to find a trained survivalist in the wilderness.

From his reading, Tillman knew that the Tilok was histori- cally a highland, not coastal, tribe. Before Europeans arrived, they had been hunter-gatherers, living in the mountains and migrating to the high country in summer. Kier's ancestors were people hardened by migration and living off the land. Any man could learn what Kier knew, but if heredity counted, Kier had a better beginning than most.

Tillman had to remind himself that he had bigger responsibili- ties than killing this Indian for his own satisfaction. Admiration for the man's skill was all well and good. A sporting sense and its attendant need for victory were as normal as *Monday Night Football*. But this hunt was about none of those things. The Indian and the woman had to be neutralized.

Lesser men allowed petty concerns to overcome common sense or anger to compromise their morality. It would not be so with Jack Tillman. A living, breathing Doyle was proof of that. He glanced at Doyle, who still held his eyes on the magazine.

"Order the men on the road to move to the area around the Indian's cabin. They should be there in five minutes. Tell them I'd prefer the Indian and the woman alive, but I'd rather have them dead than escape. Leave the men around the plane in place. Leave two here. I'm taking five men with me to the cabin. You and Brennan follow me in ten minutes with the rest. Radio to Crebbs at Elk Horn to hurry up and get me the helicopter. I want to know the minute they have one lined up."

Doyle had that puzzled look.

"The weather won't stay like this forever," Tillman said. "The minute it changes, we can use the chopper. This Indian is going to be more difficult than you might imagine. I can feel it.''

Doyle nodded as if the mystery had been solved. "I wonder how long he can survive," he said.

"You mean you wonder if he's a match for me."

"I wouldn't underestimate Brennan either," Doyle said.

"Of course, you wouldn't. He's your superior officer."

Tillman was amused at the subtle maneuvering. He knew he had thrown Doyle a bone by telling him the plan first and letting him tell Brennan. Soon he would do the reverse for Brennan. Competition was good. It kept men from becoming complacent.

"We're going to need some food. Tell the men to butcher that damn llama. And tell the men who stay here to search through those family albums over there. Have them figure out which one is Jessie. There must be pictures. I want to see what she looks like."

"I've already done that." Doyle walked to the counter and returned with a picture.

Tillman turned the photo in his fingers. She was a brunette. Proud and confident, she showed a slight cockiness in her understated smile. This was a woman who might stir him.

For as long as he could remember he had been attracted to such women. They were the opposite of his mother—a short, bespectacled, obsequious person who always acted afraid. She had been a shadow over his life. He hated her and frankly admitted it to himself. Early in life Tillman had understood that identifying such unconscious hostilities was an important part of growing up.

Probably his most vivid recollection of his mother was of her cowering in a corner as his father ranted and raved in a drunken fit. He was nine at the time. Shortly thereafter he'd been sent to a boarding school. He never saw his mother again. She disappeared one night and his father never mentioned her name or acknowledged her existence. After age eleven, Tillman missed a lot of school in favor of hunting trips. He spent a cumulative total of three years in Africa before his eighteenth birthday.

From the beginning Tillman had known he must be his own parent. At eighteen, he joined the military; at twenty, officer's candidate school, followed by army intelligence training and secret ops in Cambodia after Vietnam.

As comfortable as he had felt at war, army life did not ultimately suit Tillman. Its structure became for him a mental straitjacket. Business and science, he decided, were his calling, and he used the GI Bill to earn an MBA and a degree in pharmacology. Still, his military training and hunting experience proved useful more than once in his business life. Now it would help him catch the Indian.

And with luck, the woman.

Chapter 11

When people of the plains come to the mountains,
the mountains get no flatter.

—Tilok proverb

Kier probably could have stopped Jessie's stinging slap, but
he didn't try.

"You son of a bitch. You ever lock me up again and I'll
have you prosecuted for interfering with a federal officer."

"I thought you had decided to become a postman."

"It's no joke."

Kier looked into those eyes, thinking if it were another life,
he'd kiss her. He gave her a little smile, waiting to see if she
would smile back. She didn't.

Overcome with fatigue, he bent and put his hands on his
knees. "My cabin's burned. Let's get some supplies before
they send in the next wave."

She turned without another word and led him toward the

burning cabin. He stopped briefly at the pump house to recover the remaining volume.

His body, covered in sweat and snow, was out of adrenaline, out of energy, and numbing quickly. Even with the heavy wool shirt, sweater, and the thin white topcoat, he would weaken and eventually suffer the effects of exposure unless he got more insulation or warmed himself. They went to the heat of the burning cabin. They would need to pull supplies from the root cellar as soon as the fire cooled enough. While they waited, they could strip some of the clothing from the bodies of the men who had come to kill them. Quickly his mind began cataloguing what they would need.

Then, like one more symptom of a deadly illness, he heard the sound of snowmobiles.

"Let's go."

"We can't. We've got no supplies, no clothing. Nothing."

"We have all we need," he replied and grabbed her arm, pulling her into the forest.

A second wind is a strange thing. Athletes near the goal line, soldiers in the heat of battle, mountain climbers struggling against the elements, all accomplish far more than even they— the champions of the flesh—imagine might be possible. And they do this after their bodies tell them that exhaustion is complete.

Despite their fatigue, Jessie and Kier went at a bounding lope up the mountain through a tunnellike opening in the trees that marked the trail. They used only the small light that Kier had taken from the fallen mercenary. He slowed to a brisk trot a few hundred yards later to lead her along a rock face that had shed boulders now slick with snow. Crouching to scramble over chunks of granite, scraping her shins and banging her knees—it reminded Jessie of screaming FBI drill instructors, of competition, of gutting it out on pure desire.

Moving with an ease and grace that she could not duplicate, and that utterly astounded her, Kier occasionally slowed and turned, as if to measure her endurance and progress. At other times, he wordlessly reached back to pull her up a particularly troublesome spot, seeming to anticipate her difficulty.

After myriad tiptoed and hopping steps, they cleared the boulder field and began winding up the mountainside through heavy tree cover. Flickering off the boughs on either side of the trail, their dim, hand-held light gave only sufficient illumination for the next footfall.

An hour and a thousand vertical feet later, Kier stopped. He shone the light on a house-sized boulder projecting from the cliff. Its overhang sheltered them from the weather.

"Dig," he said, throwing snow away from the cliff's base to expose what looked like a small cavern beneath.

When Jessie began knocking the drift out of the way, she discovered dead leaves on the floor of a little cavern. Farther back, wind-driven whiteness gave way to a cave floor spongy with moss.

As they climbed under the overhanging rock and out of the wind, Kier removed his heavy sweater and cut the sleeves off his shirt. Stuffing the shirt sleeves full of moss and leaves, he made what looked like a sausage and tied it over her ears, then did the same over her nose and mouth. After putting his sweater back on, he began taking huge handfuls of the green moss and stuffing them between his sweater and his long johns, even down his arms.

He nodded at Jessie. "You do the same."

Then, over the moss, he packed in leaves until he looked like a scarecrow in a white camouflage windbreaker. They finished packing Jessie's coat and stuffed their pants before tying off the trouser cuffs with ribbons of cloth cut from Kier's sleeves.

"Now if we keep moving we might live and avoid frostbite until we get to shelter."

"Can we build a fire?" Outside the little hollow she saw nothing but icy blackness. She hated the hint of weakness in her voice. "I suppose they might find us more easily if we did that," she added, trying to redeem herself.

"Sometime I'll tell you what frightens me and you'll laugh."

"Who said anything about being frightened?" Her voice came to life.

"No offense intended. I know the mountains aren't your favorite place."

"Yeah, well, you put up with things in this world. We don't always get what we want." But her mind leaped ahead to her one phobia. "Are there any really steep drops where we're going?"

"In the mountains we call them cliffs."

Hanging her head and gripping Kier's belt, Jessie once again struggled to keep up in the thigh-deep snow. Labored breathing, screaming muscles, icy air like razor blades down the throat— all commanded her mind.

After climbing across the mountain's face for more than an hour, they came to the knife-edged spine of a ridge. When she saw the ground fall away sharply, she stopped and tugged on his coat.

"This is steep," she said.

"Not very," he replied, turning to continue on.

She forced herself ahead, most of the time unable to see the drop she knew must be there. At the crests where it became the sheerest, the snow tended to scatter on the dull gray rock, keeping it shallow. No matter, she would have rather walked through the snow.

The icy wind punished her—aching the bones, freezing the flesh, pounding the inner ear with dull, thick pain. Thinking ahead was debilitating, grist for despondency. Misery was better contemplated one moment at a time, she thought to herself, remembering grueling hikes through bug-infested swamps at Quantico.

Other people's troubles had kept her going then. Her mother's waitressing work, followed by a quick marriage and grandkids. Dad's tunnel vision of Jessie as the supplicant daughter, obedient, grateful, bound to marry a good boy with a not-too-threatening job. When she announced she wanted to go to college, and had a partial scholarship, and a research assistant's position at the university, her parents had been dumbfounded.

They were good people, lovable in their way, and even adaptable to change. Once she graduated from college, her younger brother followed, and then her older brother began night school. Claudie never went. What really blew the Mayfields away was Mom's decision to go to college. After all, she said, the kids were grown, and it was the way of the world. That had been a blockbuster. Jessie smiled, remembering how close she had finally felt to her mother when she enrolled in junior college.

Such thoughts helped keep her mind from the bleak present, where each step was labored, where she sometimes foundered on rubberized muscle. Then she began wondering if the next step would come. But it always did, and they kept climbing for what seemed several hours. In the dark her watch was useless.

Abruptly, she noticed that they were out of the snow. Only rock and leaves lay underfoot. Kier stopped.

"We're here," he said. "It's called Bear's Cave."

As Kier shone the light around, she was able to make out rock walls and ceiling. There was a fire pit, dry wood, a brown backpack hanging from a pole spanning the cavern, along with three pairs of snowshoes.

"Was there ever a bear?"

"None that ate people."

She thought he was smiling.

"I wasn't sure the bag would be here," he said. "Inside that pack there are blankets, twine, a hatchet, things that aren't necessary but very nice. We don't let the boys get in it. They make do with what the mountain provides, and so do we. We bring the young boys here in the summer. The older ones come in winter.''

Kier quickly climbed the almost vertical face of the cave, which had only the most meager handholds; then, twenty feet off the cave floor, he went hand over hand along the pole, which bowed under his weight. Loosening the leather thong that held the pack to the pole, he dropped it at Jessie's feet. Then he dropped two pairs of the semi-oval snowshoes.

For a moment, Jessie's weary frustration gave way to exhilaration. She marveled that she could have such feelings over a few blankets. Pulling open the pack, she took out two, wrapped them around her shoulders, and promptly began shaking.

"We can have a fire, but only in the night, or during the day in very heavy snow. Otherwise they will see the smoke." Kier had climbed down and joined her. "Even without the smoke they'll find this place quickly."

Once the fire was burning, Kier went out into the darkness without a word.

"What are you doing now?" she muttered out loud, and was not surprised when he didn't answer.

Kier returned to Bear's Cave, dragging long pine bows. He stripped the smaller branches off. Then he went out to retrieve two more twelve-foot branches, each roughly three inches in diameter. By cutting one into three equal pieces, he created a four-foot-tall tripod, binding the three poles together at the top with a short piece of line. Next, resting one end of the last branch on top of the short tripod and letting the other lie on the ground, he had fashioned the sloping ridgepole of a tent or lean-to.

"But why in a cave?" Jessie asked.

"There will be no fire tomorrow. We will want to be warm enough that we can sleep by day."

"How can I help with whatever it is we're doing?" She rose with a groan.

"Lean the shorter sticks against the low end of the log," he said, even as he began placing the longer branches at the high end of the ridgepole near the tripod.

Each leaning piece of wood lay close to the next, just inches apart. Kier corrected Jessie a couple of times, then nodded his approval, and disappeared—only to return a few minutes later, dragging two small trees. Once again stripping the trunks, he cut them into short segments and lashed them and each of the smaller vertical pieces to the ridgepole. They had what looked like the upside-down keel and ribs of a crude boat. Kier finally wove some sticks horizontally through the vertical ribs.

When at last the skeleton seemed sturdy and complete, a giant pile of needled boughs remained. From this Kier made two beds, side by side. He put one blanket on each.

"Try it out," he said.

She did, and he followed. Rolling toward her on his elbow, he studied her face in the firelight. He found himself thinking about one large bed. Without a doubt she wanted to tell him all over again how dumb it was to run into the wilderness, but instead she just shook her head.

"We might as well get used to each other." He broke the silence. "Say what's on your mind."

"I think it's this overwhelming sense I get that you don't respect me."

He allowed himself a puzzled frown, as his way of asking for more information.

"Well," she began, as if he had actually spoken, "there's the 'one man against the evil empire' mind-set that seems to be operating here. You know what I mean?"

"You want to go to the city, the government."

"I want to work with people who can do something—people whose job it is to do something."

Kier remained impassive.

"So what's wrong with that? If my horse were sick, I'd call you. If someone were breaking the law, I'd call the police."

"This is different. First, we can't get to the city any time soon. Second, this is no normal crime. This is huge. You know that."

"All the more reason—"

"The government could be involved," he interrupted.

"Just what is it with you and the government?"

Kier rubbed his jaw and decided to tell her.

Chapter 12

The shadow that stalks you grew old when you were little.

—Tilok proverb

"It helps a man to know himself," Grandfather had explained as he removed things from his pack in the narrow beam of an old flashlight. He lit two torches, one at either end of the pool, then sat cross-legged on the flat stone next to the water's edge. In the dancing light of the torches, the place took on an eerie, magical quality.

At first Kier expected a story, but Grandfather simply asked him to look in the pool. The most respected leader of the Tiloks sat straight as an iron pipe, seemingly lost in thought. Kier studied the lines that already had begun to wishbone around his grandfather's mouth. From his face he could discern nothing of what was to come.

Kier could not see the bottom of the oval pool; shadows

blackened its surface, hid its rocky bottom from sight. The darkened water's seamless mirror reflected the torches.

"Get closer," Grandfather said, moving nearer the pool.

Kier did the same. At the edge, he found a perfect reflection.

"What do you see?"

"I see me."

"Is yours a good face?"

Kier studied himself, realizing that he hadn't thought about it. A broad, squared-off chin gave him a look of strength, even at age thirteen. He supposed he liked his face. Perhaps his eyelids drooped slightly because he had secrets. He did things that were forbidden. Although his mother did not know, he slipped out even on school nights to go into the forest. He wondered if Grandfather suspected. Kier looked away from the pond, nervous. Perhaps such things couldn't be hidden from his grandfather. Everybody said he knew everything—never missed a thing in the woods. It was said that even crickets were safe when Grandfather walked by, so sure was he of every step he took.

"What do you see in your eyes?"

Kier fidgeted. Now he knew Grandfather could read his face as plainly as if he'd admitted to sneaking out at night. What they said was true. Grandfather was a Spirit Walker. Kier still said nothing, his heart starting to hammer in his chest. Words wouldn't come.

Grandfather waited. Kier's eyes returned to the pool. He tried not to think of the secrets. His body felt smaller. With hunched shoulders, he looked again at Grandfather, who appeared to have hardened to stone. Silence stretched before him like a desert road shimmering to the horizon.

He's thinking about me. He knows about the secrets and he's just waiting.

Could Grandfather know about the trips to Lotta's? She lived a little way into the forest in a cabin. Kier sometimes went there at night. Kier's face got hot. Usually he went exploring, looking for tracks. Occasionally though, he went to the cabin and watched Lotta's shadow against the shade as she brushed her hair.

When finally he looked up again, Grandfather's form seemed to reach the top of the cave. Something needed to be said, but he didn't know what to say. Tears wanted to spring from his eyes. With all his energy, he froze his countenance. To cry would be unthinkable.

"What is your fear?" No longer did his grandfather's expression seem hard.

"I don't know . . . what makes me feel unhappy sometimes."

After a moment, Grandfather spoke. "So, tell me, if you could change one thing about your life, what would you change?"

That was easy. "Father."

"Tell me."

"He left us and got killed."

"And do you wonder why he left?"

"I don't know if I think about it."

"Why do you think your father left?" Grandfather persisted.

Kier felt his shoulders fall, a sort of shrug in response to the question. His mind wandered. He felt tired all of a sudden, as though he wanted to sleep.

"Do you think about why your father left?"

Kier let his mind drift. He just wanted to go home.

"Your father did not accidentally shoot himself, nor was he shot by the man who struggled with him. A government man killed him thinking he was someone else. Your father never really left you."

Kier could not believe his ears. He knew his stinging eyes betrayed him.

"Your father was visiting friends in Arizona. When he walked out of your house, he intended to come back. He was just going away for a time, to think. The FBI was looking for an Indian man who looked something like your father. The man they were hunting had been in the house your father was visiting. When your father showed up, well . . . they had the wrong man.''

Kier felt sick. ''Why didn't someone tell me? How do you know he was coming back?''

''I talked to him after he left—''

''But Mother said . . . She said he might not ever have come back.''

''It's probably what your mother believes. She warned him not to go. There was bitterness in her when he was killed. A bitterness that he didn't listen to her. You remember the day your father left, don't you?''

''Yeah.''

''You thought he was angry with you.''

''He yelled. He pounded my wrists on the sink.''

''So you thought maybe you were part of the reason he went away.''

''I don't know.'' So much had changed in just a few seconds. ''Why didn't someone tell me?''

''You were young. Your mother didn't want you bitter with hate.''

''But my mother said he left.''

''Your mother is a good woman, but stubborn, hotheaded. Your father would have come back. They would have talked. Everything would have been fine. He went away once before in the spring of the year. Sometimes you know how your mother gets.''

''Yes. But I asked her—''

''And she told you all the time that he went off mad and got himself killed.''

''But I didn't know . . . I mean . . . I thought . . .''

''You thought you were the reason he left, that maybe you had done something. And he was never coming back. I promise you that your father loved you and never would have left you.''

Kier thought about what Grandfather said. The kids at school, always wanting to know why he didn't have a dad, said things. This was all such a relief. Or at least it seemed so at the moment. If only someone would have told him sooner.

"What happened?"

"FBI man got anxious. He thought your father was someone else. Two Indian men started fighting, and the FBI man shot in the night. He killed your father, who was trying to stop the fighting, trying to calm the situation."

"What happened to this FBI man?"

"Nothing. And nothing will ever be done. They claimed that one of the Indians your father was trying to stop had a gun. There was an investigation . . . testimony . . . but in the end they said the bullet was lost before it could be tested. The government people swore no one from their group fired a shot."

Kier sat and stared at the pool, at his own eyes, promising himself that he would never make his father's mistake. He would never trust the white man's police.

As the years passed, Grandfather's explanation seemed to raise more questions than it answered. And the words never answered the need of his psyche to know *why*. Not why his father had died, nor why the FBI man was never punished, but why he could never touch his father's heart.

Chapter 13

When young lovers make their lodge together, they must build fires in the rain.

—Tilok proverb

"You can see why I might have a problem with the FBI." Kier poked the fire and tossed on another log. "It's why when I turned eighteen I became a gun-toting, paramilitary radical."

"But you became a vet, an educated man. How . . . ?"

"Let's not argue. You asked me. I told you."

"True enough. We'll come back to it later." She would bide her time.

After they were warmed by the fire and rested, Kier rose. "Now for the hard part. Getting our little house together. Pick up the small end and help me carry this thing down the canyon. We'll leave the supporting tripod here for another trip. It'll be heavy even without that."

Jessie let her amazement show as Kier began to separate the tripod from the rest of the structure.

"You're going to leave this fire?"

"A lot of people know about this cave. Tillman's guys may trick somebody with some story or other, and ask where I might go. They probably won't come tomorrow or the next day even, but I still want a margin of safety when we sleep."

She stared incredulously out into the night.

Around the face of the bluff and about one hundred yards down the hill, there was a dense stand of young fir. They walked in the beam of a flashlight. Kier had tramped a clear trail in the snow past the stand, but instead of staying on the trail, he lifted the skeleton of their shelter into the trees and directed Jessie to jump off the trail to the base of a young fir. She did as directed, landing in a large hollow in the snow created by the sapling's overhanging branches. After Kier had also jumped, they pushed their way into a thicket of intertwining limbs, then proceeded, with great effort, to carry the skeleton down through the trees two hundred yards to another overhanging rock face, where the forest looked more open. They proceeded down the rock face for a half mile. There, Kier uncovered a small cave largely concealed by snow. Clearing out the drifts, they placed the makeshift tent under the rock and out of the weather.

After returning with the tripod and backpack, they repaired the structure from damage suffered during the move. Then they cut boughs from nearby trees, lashing them onto the structure until a foot-thick green coat covered the outer framework and the inside floor. Digging down in other spots, Kier began scraping up fir and pine needles, leaves, sticks, and vines. Soon he began piling the fluffy mixture over the exterior boughs. Jessie, her fingers freezing even in her mitts, tried to emulate Kier, who worked like a man possessed. Losing all track of time, she only stopped flinging debris when she felt Kier's hand on her back.

"Now I understand your strategy. We work our asses off to keep from freezing to death," she said.

"We need more sticks and boughs and any heavy chunks

we can find. Let's look for a windfall," Kier said, guiding her back into the forest.

"Quantico was like Disneyland compared to this," she muttered.

She studied the terrain in the faint beam of the small flashlight. The snow was still falling but, thankfully, the wind had died. Weird shapes appeared like surreal sculptures, the snow molded over the skeletal remains of downed trees, plants, and boulders.

Suddenly, she realized she was totally disoriented. Barely able to stand, she looked for Kier's light, saw it disappearing over her left shoulder. She felt a stab of panic shoot through her belly. Struggling to move through a tangle of trees, brush, and vines, she cursed herself for being weak. Knocked loose like some ghostly dust in a horror film, snow showered from the trees around her. Surely, if she was calm, she could find her way back without Kier. But even as she thought it, she continued chasing the receding light. Unconsciously, she began running.

By the time she forced herself to walk, the light was coming back toward her. Kier had turned around. In seconds, he had seemingly floated over the forest floor in a few large bounds. Then his face was near hers. His hand on her moss-padded shoulder felt good.

"We're almost done," he said with a rare smile. "I'm sorry I got so far away from you."

"Oh, no big deal. You actually like this place . . . this . . . ?" She waved her arms.

"More than a few people have the same attitude toward New York."

She said nothing more.

Kier led the way back to a big blowdown—a tangle of old branches and wood hunks where two large trees had fallen in the forest. Several backbreaking trips, dragging large branches and bark chips, were required before they had the materials to armor their hut. When they were finished, three to four feet of fluffy debris were sandwiched between two layers of boughs, all covered over with heavy branches and sheets of bark.

"Only one thing remains." He took her by the arm and led her back up the mountain.

"Yeah. You gotta bury me."

After they had returned a couple of hundred yards toward the cave, they headed off at an angle down the mountainside, following rock formations familiar to Kier and to generations of Tilok before him. Occasionally he would stop and shine the light on the rocks, verify his location, observe Jessie, and then continue on. Now she was shaking from the cold, and he was starting to worry about her getting so chilled that he would never get her warm. Ever since his childhood, he had enjoyed a great tolerance for the elements, but she had spent almost her entire life indoors. Eventually, after what seemed at least fifteen minutes, they came to the base of some trees with ruffled, reddish, paper-thin bark.

"Madrone," Kier said, casting about until he found some car-sized granite formations. Once they'd scooped the snow from the rock ledges, they could see crevices, and in those crevices, leaves. These they gathered onto two of the blankets. In two trips, they were able to build a large leaf pile at the hut's entrance. After packing in one third of the leaves, Kier tapped Jessie on the shoulder.

"Crawl in and roll around," he said.

Shining the light at his face, Jessie didn't move and said nothing. Finally he reached out and turned the light so that it shone partially on her face, revealing a frozen mask of discontent.

"It will break down the insulation, make it effective," he

said. "More importantly, it will keep you warm and start to unthaw you."

Groaning, she got down on her knees. "Is this a squaw thing to do?" Then she began rolling.

"Not that kind of unthaw," he said. "Are things starting to tingle?"

"I can feel needlelike hot points in my feet and legs."

After a few minutes, Kier crammed in more leaves. "Roll again. We've got to hurry this up."

"If I were a male FBI agent, would it work this way?" Once more she shined her light on him, only this time from inside the hut. "Well, would it?"

"We're thawing you out so we don't have to cut things off you, like toes and fingers. All right?"

"Thank you. I appreciate the sentiment," she said. "See— we're a team." She gave him a mocking smile in the dim light. "We share. After thoughtful discussion and explanation, we work together."

Kier began fashioning a plug for the entrance using unidentifiable debris.

"Sometimes when people are dying there's no time for discussion," he said.

"But there's plenty of time to pound little pieces of wood in the trapdoor so your partner will be stuck in a hole."

Kier said nothing while she matted the leaves and he greatly narrowed the entrance so the plug would be effective.

"Now we're ready for the blankets," he finally said. "For this, you need to get your wet clothes off."

He knew that by now the warmth of the hut would have made her clothing sodden. Removing her clothes and eliminating the moisture was the only way to get her really warm. Kier dropped to his knees and helped her out of her coat.

"I'll do the rest," she said sharply.

"As long as you don't fall asleep during the Tilok sex ritual."

* * *

After Kier disappeared, to give her privacy she supposed, Jessie took off her boots and pants, wishing that her panties were more like military briefs, cursing that they were damp. It was a struggle that took far longer than normal, manipulating the soggy material in the cramped front portion of the hut. "It's still freezing in here," she said aloud, wondering if he had returned. It was silent. Now the cold was piercing. Rubbing her arms helped almost not at all.

"I'm freezing," she called again.

"That'll change."

She wondered about her shirt, realizing that it, too, was damp, then decided to ignore it. "Bring in the blankets," she said through chattering teeth.

When Kier reappeared, he was completely naked—astonishingly so. He fingered the fabric of her shirt. "You can take that off later."

She gave him an unappreciative look in the dull light.

"If you don't, you'll feel a chill. Unfortunately it's not wool or one of the new moisture-wicking synthetics."

"I took survival," was all she said, trying not to look at his contoured body. *He's beautiful,* she thought.

They proceeded to line the leaves with the first layer of blankets.

By now their shelter looked like a tiny hole in a mound of debris stuck in the face of the rock. After shuffling leaves to get a thick layer above the blankets as well as below, the hut was ready for the final touch.

"Now I'll wait outside while you get out of the rest of your wet clothes."

"Why?" She sighed. "It's freezing out there. Just turn out the flashlight." When it was dark, she removed her shirt. The bra and panties would stay, damp or no damp, she decided.

As if reading her mind, he said, "Please, no wet clothes,

You can wrap yourself in a blanket, so our skin definitely won't touch.''

"Damn straight it won't."

"I didn't plan the crash so we could be naked together."

"So why don't you find some way to holster your pistol before we go night-night."

"Are you afraid it'll grow on you?"

"Don't flatter yourself."

"Take this blanket," he said.

She saw nothing, but felt it against her shoulder. When, after some struggle, she had wrapped it high on her nude body, under her arms, she felt better.

"We'll be very warm," Kier said, snapping on the light.

The roof of the hut had over three feet of insulation, not counting a foot of woody boughs. Inside, there would be a foot or more of leaves covering the double blankets over them, and at least that much under them.

Working quickly on his belly, his head under the blankets, Kier pushed through the leaves at the foot of the hut, then proceeded to put one more blanket down. Watching the ripple of his muscles as he worked, the taut skin on his ribs, she marveled at his lanky frame.

After smoothing the blankets on his side, they switched places. In an awkward moment, she slipped over the top of him.

He was circumcised and large, she observed, with a shudder of disdain for her curiosity. She didn't equate penis size or shape with anything of significance, but she wondered if other men would envy this one. Men were that way. She imagined describing it to her friend Gail and smiled involuntarily. Her eyes went to Kier's, hoping he hadn't caught her staring.

"Don't mind me," she said. "I'm just hysterical. I was daydreaming about a cup of hot chocolate and drifting off to sleep."

"Does hot chocolate interest you that much?" He asked it

so smoothly, with just enough—she didn't know what, maybe with knowing amusement, something under the surface—to let her know he had noticed her looking.

The bastard was thinking she was attracted. How male.

She yawned hugely to underscore her lack of interest. "This hut is so small. Well, you know, in emergencies you think about things in certain ways . . . get cravings, like for chocolate. You're not normal . . . like being pregnant. . . ." *Oh God, why did I say pregnant? What's that got to do with hot chocolate?* "I'm just tired, and I'm rattling on."

She closed her eyes to make sure she didn't stare again.

"I'll be back," she thought she heard him say. A moment later she was sure she felt his hand smoothing her hair. Then again maybe it was only a dream.

Chapter 14

No bobcat ever did so well with a mouse as a woman with a man.

—Tilok proverb

Back at the Bear's Cave, Kier added a log to the low blaze and opened the last two blankets on the tree boughs, creating the impression that two had slept by the fire. For a moment, he imagined her lying there, her ears still covered by the makeshift headcover, wispy tendrils hanging over her forehead, her pensive smile. Then he remembered her as he had first seen her. So confident with her beautifully coifed hair and glossy lips. Tonight he had noticed her lean body, her breasts firm even under a wrapped blanket. Now she was in bed, in their hut, curled among the leaves. But it wouldn't do him any good.

He pulled a hatchet and a large knife from the pack, testing each with his finger—both were satisfyingly sharp. Setting them aside, he removed a large black cook pot and packed it full of snow before setting it in the fire. Last, he took out a stiff wire with a large sliding loop at one end. With the hatchet and his light he hiked sidehill to a tall, young sugar pine. He chopped it down, limbed the top ten feet, then dragged it back to the big cave. Propping up the thicker end, he used the knife to peel the outer bark from the trunk. Next he removed long, thin sheets of the inner bark layer—a softer, white material—which he cut into ten-inch strips. After packing the pot with the pine strips, he left it to boil.

With the wire loop in hand, he snowshoed down the trail toward the hut, but continued on past the turnoff, tromping hard, making the trail as well worn as he could. This time he went a good four hundred yards before he slowed. Casting about with his light, he verified his location by a clump of pine and the edge of an old forest fire that had crested the hill years before. At the margin of the burn, the trees were smaller and younger; there were older, now completely rotten logs, which appeared as gentle hillocks under the deep snow. He moved slowly, listening within himself. Trying not to think about rabbit trails or rabbit tracks, he let his mind drift while his gaze wandered over the terrain illuminated by the small light.

After he had traveled through the trees some distance, perhaps fifty yards, he located an old trapper's cabin completely fallen in. Each time he saw the cabin, he witnessed the progression of its melding into the earth. Anything that could disappear so thoroughly, reverting to its origins, was a marvel. He went to the back of the ruin, close to the place he would set his trap.

He smiled, and thought of the old ways, of Grandfather . . . of a day when he was young, and very hungry. At twelve, going two days without a significant meal had been excruciating. On one winter camp trip, Grandfather sat by the fire and waited for Kier and his two friends to find food. Enthusiastic hunters, they had set off to shoot rabbits or squirrels or maybe a porcupine. But it was the dead of winter, and the animals seemed to have disappeared.

Using everything they knew, they searched. They stayed out

of the deep forest, looking for openings, or creeks, burned areas, logged patches, areas of transition from one forest area to another—all places they would expect to find rabbits and squirrels. But they were overeager, and the one time they did see a rabbit that might be susceptible to their razor-sharp arrows, they missed.

As their hunger increased, their abilities waned. Sheepish, they returned to camp, announcing imminent starvation. Slowly Grandfather rose and led them into the woods. His blanket almost touched the ground as he moved easily in his snowshoes.

"Stop thinking about food," he said. "Relax your mind, let your eyes take in everything—not just a few things. Let your gaze remain unfocused. Open your senses. When your mind is used up with failures, listen to your instincts."

Grandfather went slowly for a time, about one hundred feet from camp, as far as he had gone the entire trip. "Now tell me where you feel like going," he had said.

"Well, there are no rabbit tracks around here," young Kier said.

"Where?" Grandfather asked softly as if he hadn't heard. Kier gave him a confused look. His two friends appeared even more perplexed. "How do I know where to go, if I don't think about it?"

Then Grandfather walked on and began telling them a Tilok story about the beginning of the world, talking as if nothing but his story mattered. The boys trudged along behind, utterly demoralized, until Grandfather stopped.

"This is where I feel like going," Grandfather announced.

Ahead was a large blowdown that the boys had passed many times before. Here the hillside broke straight away from the ridge top on which they walked, and the wind often roared up to the forest's edge. Half a dozen trees had been knocked down from the winds several years ago. They were still only a few minutes from the camp.

"Now where do you feel like going?" Grandfather asked.

Without reply, Kier crept into the giant tangle of old fallen trees and new madrone, black oak, and tan oak that had grown up among them. After he'd walked maybe twenty feet, a rabbit jumped out, bounding away. Then another flitted past—before he could shoot. When the third rabbit stopped to look, Kier pierced it cleanly with an arrow.

He said the hunter's prayer his grandfather had taught him: "My brother, I take your life so that I may survive. I thank you for it."

Tonight he turned, following his instincts again, and walked four paces. He found a fresh rabbit track in the small, round beam of light. Was it luck? He shook his head, amused at the way his so-called formal education had caused him to doubt himself.

Having set his rabbit snare, Kier moved quickly to create his alarms. He wanted to know if anyone came up the mountain. Removing some fishing line from the canvas bag, he went back down the trail that led toward the valley below. It was a short way to an area where the walkway passed between two mammoth rocks. Here the trail was no more than four feet wide and bounded by thick huckleberry, so that the visual corridor was barely a foot wide. Carefully stretching the leader, he hid it in the snow. For a few moments, he considered how he should lay the grenade. If he placed it under a lip of the rock face, the explosion would alert him to an intruder, but probably injure no one.

He put a heavy, forked stick in a tiny pocket of rock that would shield the blast. With a secure bowline knot, he affixed the trip wire to the pin on the grenade, which he placed on the far side of the fork. If someone caught the line, it would yank the pin.

It took thirty minutes to do the same thing on the less-traveled alternate route because of the difficulty in finding a spot where those on the trail would be largely shielded from the blast.

Finally he set another grenade just outside the cave under a wheelbarrow-sized boulder.

Whether he wanted to or not, in his mind he would be waiting.

Jessie was half asleep, letting her mind wander, too tired to rein it in. The wooden steps grew green with fungus in the damp shade under the bushes. Fourteen steps led to the side door of Frank's summer home in upstate New York. She knew, because she had helped repair them. She was to meet Frank and the others on Saturday, but she had come early Friday afternoon without telling him. She knew Frank wouldn't care. He was a hang-loose kind of guy.

It was a happy moment when she found Frank's car and Mitch's in the driveway, along with a third she assumed to be Fred's. She thought it would be fun to surprise them, so she sort of sneaked up the fourteen steps, past the patio furniture, past the huge, now-empty garden planter, up to the window.

Then, in an instant, Jessie was back on a bitterly cold mountain in a tiny hut, barely surviving, maybe about to die. Tears, remnants of the memory were clouding her eyes. Why did she keep doing this, reliving the moment in her head as if maybe history would change itself?

The truth was, it was better here on this damned mountain than on that patio.

Someone was moving outside the hut.

"It's me."

Relief flooded her; she even felt something akin to good will. But no sooner had she relaxed, than the feeling of foreboding returned. But this was a different foreboding. Fear of possible disease, of the unknown, gripped her. She wondered if she felt ill.

Feeling herself descend into obsessive worry, she checked her pulse, then tried a hard swallow to test her throat. She probed the glands in her neck for swelling. Her skin felt clammy.

Was that a symptom of something? Poking her stomach, she thought maybe it felt tender.

Stop! she told herself. There was nothing to be done.

Kier had now removed the door plug. When he pushed his clothes through the opening, she turned out the light, knowing he would be naked. Outside, she could tell, it was dawn. His wide shoulders were silhouetted when he came through.

"I could use a little light," he said.

Okay, so he didn't care about being naked. She turned it on. He came through the opening inches from her nose. There was a bronze smoothness to his skin that made him seem earthy.

Kier replaced the plug, sealing them in. He spread his clothes next to hers at the head of the hut, then slipped in beside her. She doused the light. Still wrapped in her blanket, she lay spoonlike, six inches from his back. Falling to about the level of her calves, her impromptu wrap left her well covered. Only her feet and shoulders were actually exposed to their mutual bed.

The chill from Kier's entry still hung in the air; no longer was she completely warm. Of course, the solution was obvious. But she couldn't imagine herself just cuddling up to his body as if they were lovers. She would give no false messages about wanting him.

"I could hug your back and you would be much warmer," he said out of the darkness.

"Uhm." She cleared her throat. "I think maybe that would be uncomfortable." She felt him roll over and face her. In the black, she tried to see his eyes, but couldn't.

"Relax. You don't have to like me to keep warm."

"I never said I didn't like you."

"You're chilly and mad. I propose to solve only the first problem."

"Cute." There was silence. "It's not as if I don't have a good reason."

His hands went to her shoulders. "Turn over," he said. She

rolled, disquieted, but saying nothing. She felt his large body behind her, enfolding her, and it was blessedly warm.

"What do you use for lust suppression?" she asked, trying to determine if she was going to allow this.

"Your tender disposition should do fine."

She let her body move a little closer. Waiting, she felt no pressure from his thighs. After a few moments, she let her body mold itself to his shape, luxuriating in the warmth of it. She was careful not to sigh.

"This togetherness-for-warmth business changes absolutely nothing."

"I believed you would die if you came out of that trapdoor right after I did."

"I could have died staying down below. Why does your risk assessment apply when it's my life we're talking about?"

"When it's someone you care about and you're in a hurry, you just do it. You don't convene a debate."

"Someone you care about. Me?"

"Bizarre, isn't it."

There was a long silence that let the need for a conclusion hang between them.

"So you're saying you think in some sense you care about me?"

"You're sister to my best friends."

"And that's the way you care about me. As a relative of your friends."

"Well, at least that. I suppose I'm feeling some chemistry that is obviously one-sided."

"Obviously," she said. "What do you mean you 'suppose'?"

"You don't know the meaning of 'suppose'?"

"So you're really mystified about what you feel?"

"Let's get some sleep."

"Chicken."

"Uh-huh."

* * *

Tillman leaned back in the chair and took a sip of black coffee. This time he sat alone at the table.

The Indian had finally done as expected and taken off for the high wilderness. Climbing rocky ridges where the snow played a constant game of musical chairs, tracks wouldn't last long. Tillman probably could have followed if he had done so immediately, but most of his men would have been incapable. And Tillman was not yet ready to commit to the chase. Kier had the woman with him and therefore could not travel at his full potential. He would walk most of the night, then rest. Probably he would go to either a natural or a man-made shelter. In the morning it would be smart to press him with the troops and wear him down a little.

After visiting the charred cabin and watching his men chase about like angry beagles, Tillman had left in disgust and returned to the Donahues'. He and Doyle had spent only about twenty minutes to sort out the real trail. He wondered whether the all-night march and the chase would wreak havoc on the woman's nerves. Maybe she was really tough. Tillman could almost hear them bicker under the stress.

As he savored the acid taste of the black coffee, he decided exactly what he would do.

"Doyle, Brennan," he barked.

He took another sip while he listened to their heavy-booted footfalls come from the family room.

"I want you"—a nod at Brennan—"to take snowmobiles and go to the Tilok reservation tonight. Just start knocking on doors. Tell them that a plane crashed and Kier went into the mountains looking for survivors. Tell them we need to know the shelters up on Iron Mountain where he might stay. Offer them money if you think it'll help. Get them to show you on a map. If you think it's absolutely necessary, offer to pay one of them as a guide, but only take one Indian and no more.

Keep in mind that whoever you take will have to have a serious accident.''

"What if they come up here on their own looking for their buddy?''

"Tell them that Kier doesn't want people walking around because it will interfere with tracking survivors. Tell them we need to find him only because we've lost radio contact and need to get him another radio. Explain that the government is using armed soldiers to keep everybody out of this area to allow Kier to do his job unhindered. Then, if you have to, that's when you offer to take one as a guide and representative.

"Doyle, you'll stay here. Brennan, you will then lead one of three groups up the mountain. He'll go the route we consider most likely after interviewing the Tiloks. We'll put two other groups up on different ridges in the next most-likely areas. Everybody will look for tracks. In some of those snowfields any idiot can see tracks.

"I'm going to head out by myself on the heels of Brennan's group. No one is to know this. Absolutely no one. Tell the men I've returned to Johnson City. Brennan and I will talk on a scrambled channel. Doyle will stay here at the command post with the other men.''

"You're going to hunt Kier while Kier hunts Brennan's group," Doyle said.

"Precisely. You'll have a chance to test your defensive skills against one of the best," Tillman told Brennan.

"How many men will I have?'' Brennan asked.

"Ten starting from the cabin," Tillman said. "You may have to split up, because there is more than one ridge. But when you find him, if you find him, we'll bring them all together and bring in the other two groups.''

"If the men don't know you're out there, they may confuse you with him.''

"I'll worry about that. You and I will talk. I'll know where the men are at all times. If we have to tell the men someone else is out there, we'll just tell them it's a hired tracker, working alone.''

Kier approached the hut, proud of the food he had managed to gather in such a short time. She had slept through the early morning and into the afternoon. He had taken fairly lengthy naps, and as soon as they ate he intended to sleep several more hours.

Concerned that he would startle her from a deep sleep by slipping into the hut, he pulled the plug and whispered: ''It's okay.''

''You found a phone booth?''

''You have a cozy house with food. Technology is over-rated.''

''Did you say food?''

''Turn over on your belly and sniff straight ahead.''

''Gosh, I didn't know starvation could do that to your nose.''

''Up here you don't take the simple things of life for granted.''

''What kind of food?'' He heard the eagerness in her voice.

Kier crawled under the covers, settling in beside her. ''Today the mountain offers up rabbit and bread.'' He reached back to the entrance to retrieve some tinfoil packages.

''I'm hungry,'' she said, once again breathing in the smell of the freshly cooked food. ''Unbelievable that a scent can be so glorious.''

''Breakfast in bed.''

He pulled in the plug and turned the interior dark until he snapped on a light.

''Where did you get bread?''

''Reach out your hand.''

Her fingers touched something that felt like a cake of oatmeal.

''What? Do I just . . . hhmmm . . . Well, it's not terrible.'' She chewed the cake.

To Kier it tasted slightly bitter, bland, with maybe just a hint of sweet. The subsequent bites he knew would be a little better as their appetites grew.

"You've got to tell me how you did this."

"In the night, I boiled the inner bark of a sugar pine. I got up a couple hours ago, pounded the boiled strips into a mash, and then pressed them into cakes before putting them in the fire. Using tinfoil from the canvas bag was cheating, but faster than trying to bake in hollowed-out stones. Here, now try this."

The rabbit was juicy, warm, and tender from slow cooking.

"God, food never tasted this good." She took a second mouthful, this time a huge hunk. "I see where you got your reputation. We've been here a night and most of a day, and you have created a house with dinner. Really, your prowess at survival is remarkable. If only you were a little more . . . maybe conventional is the word I'm looking for."

"You wish I thought like a white man from New York."

"I wish you were at my mercy instead of me at yours."

"Would you be nice?"

"I'd be horrible." She gave him a wicked smile. "And I'd wish for a phone, a bathtub, central heating, and paintings on the wall. But one of us decided to run around the mountains and the other of us had little choice but to follow. Still, I would like to thank you for the food. That and this book are the only things I can think of to be thankful for at the moment."

"Because of that book we know a lot more than he wants us to."

"We know the guy who wrote the diary figured Tillman was out to kill them and we know they're all pretty damn dead. From what you've been saying it sounds like he's got some incredible technology."

"I think he can predict the effect of genetic mutations. And I think he can create them."

"What are you talking about?"

"They have a giant computer program they call the God

Model. Tillman can plan a specific change to your DNA and predict its effect. Like his scientists could maybe grow you a new scalp and turn you into a redhead.''

"My hairdresser can do that.''

"Or more to the point they could use a computer to randomly generate potential mutations in a gene related to your pancreas, predict the effects of all the various mutations, and then choose one whose effect would be positive for adult onset diabetes.''

"I'm beginning to get the picture. But why haven't we heard about this 'God Model'?''

"There's a reason. We just have to discover it.''

"If he's manipulating Tilok genes, they might hang him for that.''

"Not if they never find out," he said.

"Yeah. The troubling part is that the proof may be incinerated. He's got everything except us and Volume Five. And he doesn't have Volume Six. Have you come up with any ideas about who left those tracks by the plane?'' She hunkered down under the covers and got a little closer to him for warmth.

"It appeared to be a lost man unaccustomed to the forest. But I'm not completely sure.''

"What do you mean?''

"He moved away from the plane up a small rise before going downhill again. Most lost and confused people just go downhill right away. They take the path of least resistance without thinking. So it doesn't quite fit. If I'd had time to follow, maybe I could have figured it out. Tracks talk even when their makers don't want them to.''

"Doesn't seem like anybody would have walked away from that crash.''

"Doesn't seem like a lost city type would be hanging around in a blizzard." Kier reached under the clothes pile, and pulled out the heavy binder. "For the moment we better read what we've got.''

As Kier read, he tried to organize in his mind the big picture concerning the research of Tillman's laboratories. He understood that the government's genome project would only map DNA structure. The real trick was understanding how slight changes in the order of the nucleic acids of the DNA would ultimately affect the proteins formed by the body.

He could see that what they dubbed the God Model was a very sophisticated computer program that was able to anticipate how a change in DNA would affect the amino acids that were expressed in a cell and then create impressive three-D projections of the protein molecules that would unfold in the body. Kier was also intrigued by Tillman's extensive work with viruses. For years scientists had attempted, sometimes successfully, usually not, to use viruses to transport altered genes into an organism. This could serve either the purpose of repairing a damaged gene or replacing a gene defective since birth. Viruses were simply little strands of DNA wrapped in a coating that allowed them to enter cells easily. Once inside the cell, the injected DNA could become inserted into the cell's host DNA, carrying along any nucleic acid chains that had been added to the virus.

One of the many difficulties with this approach was the problem of deactivating the carrier virus, known as a retroviral vector, in such a way that potentially infectious viruses could not be reformed in the body.

He stopped reading when Jessie stirred.

"So what have you figured out?" she asked.

He saw that her blanket had loosened, partially exposing her breasts in the soft light. In response to his gaze, she pulled the blanket tight around her.

Then she said, "My theory is that they wanted to discover the gene for stubbornness and came to the Tilok. The logic is inescapable. Either that, or they wanted great hunters with large dicks."

He thought she wanted to smile, but it never came. "Tell me what *you've* figured out," she said.

Kier began by going over all the basics of human genetics, then plunged into the more exotic work of Tillman's labs.

"It's not surprising that if you can crack DNA sequences and manipulate their structures, you have a massive shortcut to disease control. All the labs ended up with a major emphasis on genetic research. They built viruses to deliver repaired genes to treat humans. Scientists often use viruses as biological delivery wagons, but neutralize them so they are supposedly harmless. I'm reading here about how they used an altered African virus that way. It was some kind of a rare virus that they liked because it could invade so many cells and was harmless."

"Okay. I got that. You might take such a virus—"

"They call it 'RA-4T'."

"Okay, RA-4T or whatever, change the sequence of its nucleic acids—that's the same as its DNA, right?"

"Yup," he said. "You'd do that to make sure it didn't replicate. Usually they take out so much genetic material from the original virus that the chances of it activating into a serious and complex virus is miniscule. Only I think there might have been a hitch in this case. They call the vector RA-4TV, and apparently they purposely removed some DNA from it to deactivate it. There is a lot of technical material in here about that."

"For all your whole-earth philosophy, Kier the doctor is steeped in science. You know this is telling me a lot more about you than it is about viruses. I can picture you in a college lab explaining things. There's another side to you, Kier."

"Never mind about me. The fact is, I think they cloned people."

"I knew it! Carbon copies of grown people, right?"

"Yes. Listen to this."

" 'We introduced a diploid nucleus from a cell of HO 121249533561289 into a fertilized egg from which the nucleus had been removed and introduced it into the uterus on the first day of what we had determined to be a very regular twenty-eight-day menstrual cycle.'

"Supposedly these are monkeys. But they have a thirty-seven-day menstrual cycle. At least chimps do. Humans have a twenty-eight-day cycle. When they identified the monkeys by I.D. number, they would begin with 'MA' for macaque. I think 'HO' is Homo sapien. I think it was a revealing slip of the pen. They're so into their research they occasionally drop the fig leaf."

"Why are they cloning people?"

"Believe me, I'm trying to figure it out. But you can't speed-read this stuff.

"There's another reason I think they're cloning people. In another section is a summary of the experimental vaccine and the AVCD-4 antivirus for another viral disease. I'm not sure what it was. But I'm suspicious that it was RA-4TVM, which I believe is a mutation of the vector virus. Which is a puzzle because it was supposed to be a harmless vector for delivering genes and there would be no reason to develop a vaccine and antivirus to attack it. It says here:

" 'HO 1212 and HO 0814 infants who did not receive the vaccine had a spike in plasma antigenemia two weeks after injection with RA-4TVM. After four weeks, high levels of the virus were present in T-4 cells, with only 1,000 to 10,000 PBMCs needed to recover culture. The nonvaccinated infants then received the vaccine and antivirus, with the result that after sixty days we could not recover any of the challenge virus from ten to the sixth PBMC's, in HO 1212 clones. To achieve the same result in HO 0814 clones took 150 days.' "

"Just tell me what it means," she said.

"Well, I think it means that they took cloned humans and used them to test a remedy for this RA-4TVM. Anyway, it worked. When they injected these infants with RA-4TVM, they were all cured by the combination of the vaccine and the antivirus. But one set of clones had much better genetic immunity and was cured much more quickly. Another reason I think it was humans is because when they are experimenting on monkeys they use SRA-4TV, or SRA-4TVM, which, I think, is a version of RA-4TV that infects primates. Here the reference is to RA-4TVM.''

"I'll take your word for it.'' Even though they had talked about it, seeing it in print obviously shocked her. "God. That seems really far-fetched. You're telling me they cloned babies and then gave them some disease and then cured them?''

"I'm just suggesting. I didn't say it happened.''

"If they cloned babies and thereafter infected them with a disease, that would explain why they so desperately want these volumes back.''

"Right.''

"But what is this disease? Is it like a common virus?''

"I doubt it. The notes indicate it was an African virus that started out harmless. Then they made a vector and it looks like from the research that it became a problem.''

Before he could continue, she cut him off. "Look, I've got the gist and I'm never going to master the details. It's a given that if you can fix genes, you can cure most disease, right?''

"Yeah. Most pharmaceutical companies study genetics so they can develop drugs to interact with the proteins to affect disease processes that actually get their start in defective genes.''

"Genes can be defective at birth or they can get defective because some kid swallows lead paint or the like. Right?'' she asked.

"Right.''

"You can be born with genetic weaknesses or something in the environment can cause a mutation. It's why people buy organically grown vegetables.''

"Right again.''

"You're telling me that Tillman's guys are trying to work at the beginning of the chain reaction instead of the end. Instead of trying to fix the screwed-up proteins or the run-amok cells, they're trying to fix the DNA that started it all. To fix DNA they make harmless viral vectors out of disease viruses to be used as carriers for the repair genes.''

"That's it."

"See, I've been listening."

"So with all their great ability—the computer and the God Model—what would possess them to begin experimenting on people?"

"You've got to have empirical proof. It would have a lot of advantages for everybody except the poor clones that served as guinea pigs. Getting human genes into mice and then experimenting on the mice is really tough and slow. Many so-called cures work on mice but not on people. When your data comes directly from people you don't have those problems. That's kind of an obvious answer. But there may be a much subtler answer. It may be that cloning people and deliberately changing just a few genes in the process enabled them to *create* these computer models. Ultimately, you'd forget the human experimentation and just use the computer, once your model was good enough."

"So when you were far enough along, you'd tell the world that the whole thing was just a computer exercise," she said.

"Yeah and show them a bunch of empirical work with mice and monkeys."

"The link to the Tilok surrogate mothers is obvious, isn't it? If someone were cloning people, they would need human mothers, wouldn't they?"

"That would be far easier than trying to grow an embryo in a lab tank."

"So if someone worked at it, they could take an adult person and make an exact copy. Like they've done with animals."

He shrugged. "It would be spooky if they did."

"This all still doesn't quite explain why they had a planeload of diseases."

"True. Let me keep reading."

She lay next to him, her head on a pile of clothing, soaking up the warmth of his huge frame. He tried to push from his mind the feelings generated by this closeness. He could not recall ever wanting a woman this badly. Ignoring it would require some effort.

After she had dozed for what seemed like minutes, she propped herself on her elbow. He gave a furtive sideward glance and smiled. She was reading the text. This section of the volume was describing a means of analyzing gene function using DNA chips. When he next glanced over, he saw that she had fallen fast asleep again. The image of her face took hold of him, bringing about a peculiar concentration. It was as if he were trying to discover her essence in the pleasing lines of her face. Maybe it was infatuation. Feeling strangely reenergized, he went back to his study.

Day faded into night. They alternately ate, slept, talked, and argued. Kier read. Finally, he crawled out of the hut, dressing in the falling snow, exhilarated by the frosty air.

Taking a pinch of snow, he crawled partway into the hut and sprinkled it on her forehead. She twitched her nose. Watching her, he broke into a large grin. It felt as if his cheeks would crack. He sprinkled some more, this time across her partially exposed breasts.

"Kier, what are you doing?" She awakened, pulling her blanket around. Then she smiled. "Gentleman don't peep."

"Who was peeping?"

"You do have a certain boyish charm, even when you're lying."

She shoved him out of the hut and began dressing. As he looked around at the beauty of the winter mountain he realized that, aside from all the violence and the chase, he was happy in this place, even in the dead of winter. Snow covered the good and the bad, until the thaw when it would all come out. New life. Decaying remains. Everything. Jessie needed a spring.

Something was hidden, something was troubling her. With the decay might come something new and good. He wondered if he would be around to see it. At first glance, she seemed a difficult person. Hostile, cynical, irritable. Some vestige of a sense of humor remained.

But this was not the essence of Jessie. It was what he sensed but couldn't completely define that attracted him the most, her passions and her willingness to throw herself headlong into life. For him it was like looking at someone through bottle glass. Very little was plain, but one could see shadows, glimpses of what might be.

Crawling out of the tiny cave after a twenty-minute struggle with her clothes, and then having to stuff them with leaves, didn't improve Jessie's mood. Kier nodded his greeting.

"We will gather more food, eat, and sleep tonight. Then try to make it to a very wild place by tomorrow evening."

She groaned. "We will have to build a new hut?"

"There is already a better hut. You'll see."

"Man, it's cold."

Kier looked her over. "If you're cold, then your clothes need more leaves."

"I can barely move as it is." She demonstrated her stiff-legged walk to his stony stare and concealed amusement. "So what did you learn with all the homework?"

At that moment an explosion shattered the mountain's solitude. Echoes reverberated. Kier reached in the hut for the four blankets, stuffing them in the bag. He plucked up two of the automatic weapons, handing one to Jessie. She felt her pockets for the ammo, checked her pistol, then took two of the remaining four grenades.

Moving almost parallel to the false trail that Kier had laid from the main cave, then angling in toward it, they slipped through the trees, their automatics ready to fire. He turned and stopped.

''They tripped a trap grenade I set. I need for you to go way down the trail,'' he said. ''If anybody gets to you, kill them.''

''What trail? There is no trail except in your brain. It's been snowing all morning.''

''There'll be an indentation in the snow where I tromped it down last night. I went a few hundred yards past where we turned off to go to the hut. You'll see it, near the granite cliffs, up near the ridgetop. If you don't find it, I'll find you. If I don't come, follow water downhill.''

Chapter 15

There is no good way to deal with a skunk.
                                   —Tilok proverb

Kier had to know how they had found him so quickly. Whatever they had done might work again.

He sprinted to within fifty yards of the turnoff to the hut, then jumped into the trees, waiting. Seconds after he stopped, another explosion reverberated in the still mountain air. A familiar voice shrieked his name.

"Kier!"

Now he understood. The impulse to run up the trail was overwhelming, but he did not. Instead he held his fist against his head and waited for the boy's screaming to stop. But it didn't. The voice was that of James Cole, a Tilok teen as tough as they came.

Then it struck him. If James was in trouble, he would never shout in an out-of-control voice. This caricature of hysteria was meant to tip Kier off. James had far more discipline.

Kier tried to imagine the scene up on the hill. As they approached the cave, the lead man would have hit the first grenade. They would have been approaching in a loose, spread-out pattern with the second man at least fifty feet behind the first. After the initial grenade blast, they would be more careful. But they would have seen the cave, the dying fire, and the two empty beds. Finding no more grenades on the trail, they'd enter, believing they were on the heels of their quarry. They would suppose that the beds were still warm from the occupants. Nobody sets a grenade in the middle of his camp.

And that was why the first man in the camp, a little overeager to rekindle the almost dead fire, had tripped it.

Sneaking quietly through the forest, Kier approached the bend where he and Jessie had jumped off the trail to go to the hut. Twenty feet from the little tree with the hollow base, he waited and listened. He heard the choked whispers of excited men. Putting his radio to his ear, he clicked through all six channels. He heard nothing. Either they weren't speaking, or they had changed the code. Just in case they had something to say to him, he turned back to the channel last used at the cabin.

Then he heard a footfall, the faint whoosh of a boot in deep snow. A silent pause distilled his tension. He was waiting between steps. After several seconds, the sound of branches on fabric came from over his left shoulder.

The stalker was very close, just on the uphill side of the trail, apparently moving back toward the cave. James was calling only occasionally now, but when he did, it was the same anguished cry. Kier turned his head toward the nearby sounds, but could see nothing through the tangle of branches. Then came the noise of two quick steps, and Kier's ears filled with his own heartbeat. Taking a deep breath, he reached to his belt, pulling out the silenced .45. By now the movement was just ahead of him. Several steps brought the man even closer. Maybe he was trying to come back to the path. Standing on the downhill edge of the tunnellike passage, Kier moved his head just enough to get a clear view of the trail in front of him.

The camouflaged barrel of an automatic rifle was the first thing Kier saw. In a moment, the man stepped out of the brush. Not more than five feet from Kier, he stared down at the ground, obviously worried about another booby trap. The hood of his parka hung on his back, so he could listen. Salt-and-pepper hair at the fringe of his helmet indicated the man had a little age.

"Don't move," Kier said in a loud whisper. "Drop the gun."

After a moment, the man loosed the automatic rifle and it fell to the snow.

"We've got your friend the boy back at the cave. We'll make a deal."

"No deal. What was on that plane?"

"Just a bunch of research that you stole."

"Tell me what you know if you don't want to die."

Just then, the third grenade went off, not more than one hundred feet away on the little trail to the hut. Kier flinched. So did the man. That one would have killed somebody, Kier knew.

"You're gonna die," the man said. "You're pissin' us off."

"How many on this ridge?"

The man wouldn't speak again.

"Put your hands behind your head," Kier ordered. He frisked the man, removing all his weapons. There was a silenced .45, four grenades, his automatic, a field knife, and a smaller pistol on the man's calf. "Facedown in the snow," Kier said, proceeding to pull off the man's coat. "Take off the shirt and the arctic underwear. Drop your pants to your ankles."

"I'll freeze to death."

"Not if you talk to me."

Kier placed the silenced pistol to the back of the man's head. The man removed his clothes.

"I want to know how many of you there are." Kier shoved

him down and kicked snow over the man's bare back, thighs, and buttocks. "If I don't like the answer, I'm just going to invite you to lie there in the snow."

The man said nothing, but began shaking.

"Suit yourself. I guess you won't be needing these." Kier picked up the man's clothing and set them in a pile. "Make a nice fire." Then Kier knelt down and began untying the man's boots. "Toes get frostbite really fast. Bad circulation down there at the feet." Kier yanked off the first boot. "They turn blue and rot. It's not a pretty sight."

He pulled off the second boot, then the thick wool socks, thrusting the man's feet into the snow.

"I'm freezing," the man said through gritted teeth.

"Not yet, but soon." Kier kicked more snow over the man. "You ever see a man who's lost half his foot to frostbite? Hobbles around—can't keep his balance. One guy I heard of actually lost both feet. And your nose and fingers will probably go in the next thirty minutes. Notice how they're going numb now? Already feels like dead flesh, doesn't it?"

"If I talk, can I get up and put on my clothes?"

"Tell me how to fix this radio and I'll think about it."

"They'll kill me if I do that."

"The nose. The fingers. The toes. And guess what else goes? You're lying on your belly, you know."

The man cursed in long, elaborate phrases that seemed to have no end. Kier had never heard anything quite like it. "All right, all right. Press star, then punch the year 1776 into the key pad, then the date 07-04-76, then star again."

Kier did as instructed.

"I don't hear anything."

"It's because nobody's talking. Now can I get up?"

Suddenly, the Indian boy's screams took on a calmer, but more robust tone. James Cole was in real pain now. The boy's agony carried in his cries.

"What are they doing to the boy?"

"Probably ripping off his nails with a set of pliers."

"Call and make them stop or you're dead."

"Won't do any good."

"Do it." Kier held the radio to the man's lips and gritted his teeth through the boy's next scream.

"Base, this is Oregon."

"Go ahead, Oregon."

"Stop with the boy or I'm dead."

There was a pause.

"Say again, Oregon."

"Stop with the boy or I'm dead!"

"Sorry—" Something cut the man's voice off. There were muffled choking sounds over the radio, then quiet.

Kier grabbed the radio and listened, but heard nothing except static.

James Cole let out a war whoop that rang through the forest. Then there was only the silence of the falling snow.

"Guess we can go back to the number of men on this mountain," Kier said, mystified as to how the boy might have gotten free. It was unthinkable that James could have overcome a trained soldier, especially since they would have had him in cuffs.

"Ten went up this ridge of the mountain, but only six went up this fork of Hobbs Ridge with the Indian boy. Brennan thought you probably wouldn't go someplace a lot of people know about. They called Brennan and the other four on the radio when the grenade went. They're split in pairs. One pair is at least four hours away. The other is more. Now let me up."

Because of his shaking, the man's words were almost unintelligible.

"You said this ridge of the mountain. What about the other ridge to the northwest and the ridge to the southeast?"

"At least three on each, nobody on the back side of the mountain yet. Of course, that doesn't count the law. Soon you're gonna be a fugitive, you know. The story is you're a thief trying to get rich off other people's research."

"Who do you work for?"

"Oh, come on. They're gonna tell a grunt like me? I'm a mercenary on contract. I work for the colonel back down the mountain. Who he works for, I don't know and I don't care."

"What's the colonel's name?"

"Goes by Brennan, but nobody uses a real name."

"Who does he report to?"

"I don't know. Guy doesn't come around much. Think he goes by Grant."

Kier sensed that the man wasn't giving him everything. Saying nothing, he began pushing even more snow on his captive.

"No," the man said, sounding panicked.

Kier withdrew his knife and held it to the man's Achilles tendon.

"Please, don't cripple me here on the mountain."

Pressing, Kier drew blood.

"All right!" the man said. "Brennan and Doyle report to a guy who goes by the code name Grant, General Grant. Brennan called him 'Mr. T' once, then shut up real fast. That's all I know."

"So where is Mr. T?"

"Johnson City. I don't know."

Kier kicked more snow, then stepped on the man's feet, driving them deeper.

The man half screamed. "Last night they found a lady named Donahue. Let her go, I guess. Command station's at Donahues'. General Grant's in Johnson City. Or maybe at that clinic of theirs. That's all I know."

"Tell me everything you know about the general—Mr. T."

"He's rich. Got a company of some kind, and he's a big hunter they say. He was out looking at the tracks you left. He's got the clinic over by the reservation. I don't know any more than that. He talks to Brennan and Doyle, not me. I lied about the law. They're scared of the law until we find those volumes. I swear that's all I know.''

''Tell me about the clinic.''

''I've only been there one time. I don't know.''

''What did you do there?''

''Nothing just . . . moved stuff around.''

''Tell me exactly.''

''Took papers from the wreckage there by snowmobile. Most of it was all burned, but what was half burned or still readable, we put in boxes and took there.''

''Where exactly did you put these boxes?''

''I don't know. I'm telling you I was blindfolded to get down there. It seemed like a basement—it was all concrete. Now let me up or I'm gonna die.''

''Did they tell you about a virus or bacteria—danger of infection from the plane?''

''Huh?''

''Yeah, *huh*. They had an infectious-disease freak show on that plane, with viruses and bacteria and a few special things developed by the geniuses who hired you. I could have been exposed to something.''

''You're bluffing.''

''Why do you suppose Mr. T's ass is so far away? Have you seen him get near the plane? Why would I make this stuff up?''

''That would explain the suits. We didn't go near the pieces of the plane. Some other guys with special suits did. You . . . you touched my clothes.''

''If I was you, I wouldn't take them back. Or I'd make sure I got medical treatment. Maybe you'd like to take the clothes from the guy just down the hill here. He hasn't been near me.''

''You bastard. I can't even wear my boots.''

''Quite right. With any luck the dead guy didn't get his feet blown off. Then again, maybe he did.''

''Look, I'm freezing. I got to get up.''

"Talk to me."

"Listen, you gotta let me up. I can't feel things anymore." The man's voice had risen to a shriller pitch.

"How did you guys get to the crash site so fast?"

"Damn it, I don't know this stuff."

"Your balls are gonna look like purple plums unless I get some answers."

"Savage. Bastard." Kier waited while the man swore epithets more vociferously than before. "Have you no human bone in your body?" the soldier said through gritted teeth, his whole body convulsing as he tried lifting his middle out of the snow. Kier put his foot on the man's buttocks, holding him down.

"We were waiting for the plane to drop something. It was to drop a . . . a . . . bunch of pods. It wasn't supposed to crash. We don't know why that happened."

"What was the plane supposed to drop?"

"Something for a damn experiment. And a bunch of papers, that's all I know. They don't tell us."

"You must have surmised."

"Look, I don't know."

"You guessed. You speculated."

"I'm gonna die, mister," the man cried, obviously starting to break.

"What did you imagine?"

"We thought maybe . . . it was some military experiment. Something to sell to the military . . . worked out by the government. And then there was . . . something to do with the Indian reservation."

"Why did you think that?"

"Because they seem to know a lot about the Indians, that's why."

Kier's blood ran cold. Every Tilok on the reservation was a potential guinea pig—including his own mother.

"Be more specific. What do they know about the Indians?"

"Well, they had us go to a mink farm and take some minks. In the middle of the night."

"What did you do with the minks?"

"Brought them to the lab."

"How many of you were involved in this?"

"Just me and another guy. They said they thought the natives might have gotten something from the minks. We just went and got about five. It was for some kind of test."

"What kind of a test?"

"One of the science types whispered about a test. 'When the test was done,' he said. And we had supplies for a few days. I swear to you, I don't know—they told us nothing except what I already told you." The man shook so badly he seemed to be convulsing. "Then more men came. We were supposed to get stuff dropped from the plane. I swear to God that's everything I know."

"There was a fancy black box on that plane. It had lab summaries. Why do they want it so bad?"

"There were s- s- six volumes. Number five and six are still missing. They're going nuts over Volume Six especially. I don't know why! Le- le- let me up. Please!"

"Tell me Mr. T's name. You must have heard something."

"Tillman, I think. Tillman, damn it."

Fortunately, the dead man lived up to his name—"Texas." He was big, with boots that would suit Kier's purposes. Apparently Texas had tripped the wire, then looked in horror to see what he had done. Since it had taken a moment for the grenade to blow, it had caught him in the face, with the result that there wasn't much of the head left. Blood was everywhere, and the clothes riddled with shrapnel.

"I have some disappointing news for you."

"What?" the man said, standing on the dead body to try to keep his feet out of the snow.

"You're going to wear his boots, and my shirt."

The man just stared vacantly.

"Don't take it so hard. If I've got a virus or bacterial infection, it's inside me. It's my breathing on you or touching your skin after I've blown my nose or wiped my ass that could kill you."

Kier gave the man the boots with no socks. Then the man put on Kier's shirt. Kier took his captive's outer clothes, which were tight but wearable.

"I don't have time for the truth-or-consequences test. So we'll cut straight to the good stuff. You are going to get on this radio and say exactly what I tell you. If you say anything else, I will shoot you instantly. If you do it right, I'm going to let you run straight down this mountain in those oversized boots. You say exactly the following:

"The Indian stripped Texas. He's headed down the mountain. I'm circling."

After the man uttered the words, Kier took back the radio.

"Run. And if I were you, I wouldn't come back here. Your friends are jumpy. They'll shoot an ordinary shirt in a second."

At that the man fled at a gallop.

Chapter 16

The cries of bad men carry on the same breeze as
those of the good.

—Tilok proverb

Jessie could find no more leaf piles to further insulate her
clothing, so she was limited to rearranging what she had—and
exercise—to keep warm. She longed for the comfort of the
hut. Maybe there would be clothes from the bodies of the
enemy, she told herself.

She walked in a large circle, satisfied that she had managed
to find her beginning point after she had broken down the trail
and stepped off it in a way that would disguise her exit. Having
watched Kier, she made several false leads and hid near one
of them at a spot where she could observe both the main trail
and the false lead.

Now inactivity made the cold a bigger menace. She had
heard of jumping in a snowbank for warmth. At the moment,
it was a frightening thought. The logic behind hiding in snow—

the elimination of wind chill and the insulating qualities of the fluffy white stuff—paled before the mental image of freezing to death in a smothering white prison.

So she remained in her hiding place, rubbing her arms through the leafy insulation, occasionally jumping up and down. But that used energy. Shivering used energy. Thinking used energy. Being ready to kill used energy. There was no more food, and she had little body fat. She imagined her body devouring its own muscles and organs to stay alive.

Looking around, she saw that the trees in this area were young. Kier had explained that forest fires killed the old trees and allowed the forest to regenerate. The young red fir trees had interlocking branches that created a wall of delicate green boughs.

In places where these evergreens weren't as thick, there were leafless hardwoods and underbrush that tore at her legs, dislodging the insulation in her clothes and rustling when she moved. It was hard to see much beyond fifty or sixty feet, even in the openings. In the thickets there was no visibility.

She decided that she needed to emulate Kier: to be a ghost in the woods, moving much more slowly, placing one foot directly ahead of the other, as he did.

Suddenly, she heard a crunch, then a branch swish. Was it Kier? If so, he was making noise on purpose, and that was unlikely. Could those men have killed him with a silenced shot and gotten past him? A hollow feeling entered her chest—a foreshadowing of panic—and she felt so alone. These mountains were so vast, so foreign. While she listened, she made herself take deep slow breaths and consciously relaxed her muscles.

By the direction of the sounds, she could tell there were two of them. So it wasn't Kier. They were on either side of the main trail that she had broken down. They were on her circle, or, perhaps just off it, trying to avoid booby traps. Lifting the silenced pistol, she readied herself. Then they stopped. Why?

For what seemed like minutes, there were no more sounds. Then she heard a snap. Dear God, they were on top of her. She noticed the fog from her own breath. Crazily, she wondered if it would give her away, like a chimney. Now her heart thundered. She aimed straight at the sound, her finger wanting to pull the trigger. But she dared not. Why didn't he move again? A muscle in her shoulder tensed, pulling. Her arms started to ache from bracing in the firing position. *Relaxed control. Relaxed control. Breathe, breathe.*

Another swish. And there was white against the green. Kier was wearing white. She saw an arm through the trees, then above the arm a shoulder. Was it Kier? She had to be sure.

She aimed just below the shoulder. All she had to do now was squeeze. Got to do it. Just a face—something—there! It was a wisp of brown hair. *Pop!* Down he went. She had been dead on, she was sure.

Her breaths were sharp and jerky, her hands shaking. God, I'm a mess. *Think. Think.* Where's the other one? Then she was at Quantico in a shoot-out. Look behind you. Always behind you, Dunfee intoned. And she whirled, like at Quantico.

Bullets compress air, and when they come very close, you can feel their passing. The instant her head turned, the bullet sliced the air where her jaw had been. She heard the little puff of the silenced muzzle.

Without a thought she dropped and rolled into the snow, ready to shoot on her way up. But she had no target. Then all hell broke loose—the thumping of an automatic rifle tore up the woods. She crawled madly on her belly back toward a log she had stepped over. Wood and ice flew everywhere. She held her automatic as she crawled.

Then it was dead still again. Nothing remained of the tumult except the chattering of an angry squirrel. She was behind the log. *Never shoot what you can't see.* Dunfee again. Out here it didn't matter. There were no bystanders. Maybe she should pepper the bushes herself. No—it would only give away her location as it had his.

Breathing heavily, she aimed at the spot that had spewed out the hell. She was shaking. Could she survive this? Then it occurred to her that she had a grenade. But was he still there? And why hadn't he used one? Obviously because he was too close. The trees were maybe a foot through and weren't a sure cover for shrapnel. But she was behind a big log. As if it were happening in slow motion, she watched her finger pull the pin. She stretched back her arm, then swung it forward in an arc, releasing the grenade. She waited for what seemed enough time for a slow yawn. Then, *wham!* The ground shook with the explosion. Damn, the ringing in her ears. Next time she'd cover them better.

Now the silence was overwhelming. Even the squirrel had shut up. Slowly, she stuck her head up. Concentrating again, she listened and looked, with the automatic ready. There was no point in being quiet now. The secret was out.

Then she heard something faint, like whispering. Of course, he would be using the radio. He had the luxury of staying put and waiting for reinforcements.

"Help." The voice was no more than a hoarse whisper. "Help."

She was stunned. It sounded genuine, like a person badly hurt. Dying. *Of course it sounds genuine, you lunatic,* she told herself. If she were going to fake it, she would make it sound real.

"Help," the voice came again.

It was unnerving. All her life she had thought of herself as someone who would help. Without thinking further, driven by something she couldn't explain, she began to crawl in a circle. Crawling straight away would be much safer—make him come to her. But she ignored her own safety in favor of the more powerful seduction.

After several minutes of crawling, she stopped. He hadn't

moved, and was still calling out to her. Now she was opposite the log behind which she had hidden, on the far side of the shooter. By continually calling out, he was giving away his location. She could throw another grenade and wipe him out, unless he was behind something solid.

"What the hell are you doing?" she shouted in frustration.

"I'm dying," the faint voice said. "I don't want to die alone. They're . . . leaving me . . . leaving me for dead."

"And I'm supposed to worry about this?" There was silence. "You tried to kill me!"

"You want me to apologize?" The voice laughed a feeble laugh. "You're gonna forgive me if I say—" She heard an ugly cough. "If I say, 'I'm sorry'?"

"How do I know you won't blow us both up with a grenade if I come in?"

"I'll throw 'em out."

"How do I know how many you have?"

"You've killed enough of us. Four per man."

She wasn't sure from the sound of him how much longer he could talk.

"Okay, you throw them off to my right and blow 'em." She lay in a swale behind a natural earthen berm covered with snow. Then she heard a thud in the trees, and nothing more.

After a time he called out. "Okay," he gasped.

"They were supposed to explode."

"Too weak. I'd blow my ass off."

"Well, I only heard one—and I have no way of knowing it was a grenade."

"I'm not strong. I threw three . . . they're close by."

"Crawl toward me."

"I can't."

"Then you're just going to have to die."

"Please." He was choking again.

"I'll think about it."

She crawled toward the spot where she had heard the grenade

fall. But after she'd crawled twenty feet, she realized how stupid it was to look for a hole in the snow. Still she kept on.

"More to the right."

Damn. He could hear her. Feeling crazy, she crawled straight toward him until she found a log. Thank God. She couldn't see him, but she was sure he was less than thirty feet away.

Wedging herself way under the large log, she called out. "All right. Tell me who you are, and how many of you there are." It smelled musty under the log, even in the snow.

"Please."

"Listen, you bastard. How do I know you won't cut loose a grenade and blow us both up?"

"I'm dying. Please." The man's breathing sounded as if he had been in a footrace. "I'm no hero."

"Why would blowing me up make you a hero?"

"You stole top-secret—" He gasped for air.

"So what do they think we have?"

"They won't tell us."

"Who won't tell you?"

"Tillman. Not supposed to know his name."

"What's he scared of?"

"Don't know." There was more coughing. "Illegal stuff, probably."

"What do you mean?"

"Buddy of mine took two eggheads to the reservation. He heard . . . about some mink farm . . . something with the mink. Now, help me." He sounded like he was fading fast.

"Tell me about the mink first."

"I will. Come." She hesitated. "Please," he said with a certain haunting resignation in his voice.

Something inside tugged at her. He sounded alone and pathetic. Coming to an adversary on his terms was contrary to the rules of engagement she'd learned at Quantico. Dunfee would be appalled. Setting aside the warnings in her mind and ignoring her profound sense of foreboding, she started crawling.

She approached with her gun drawn. But even under the trees, the snow was deep, causing her to stop regularly to push her head above the drifts. Finally she spotted a bloody leg. Low-hanging branches kept her from seeing his torso, his hands. Still hiding behind the tree trunk no bigger than a man's thigh, she looked for a safe vantage point. There was none.

The man stirred. ''Where are you?''

She said nothing. Another tree about six feet away would provide minimal cover and maybe a better view. Very slowly, inches at a time, without looking up, she crawled toward it, conscious of every sound. Raising her head, she found him through a break in the foliage. Her breath caught in her throat. Each of his hands clenched a grenade. How could she be so stupid? If he let go, they would both die. She began crawling away. In a minute, she lay back behind the berm, shaking.

''I saw the hand grenades, asshole,'' she shouted.

A second later the forest rocked with the explosion.

Chapter 17

The hairs on a Tilok neck are better than a friend's warning.

—Tilok proverb

"It wasn't confirmed," the authoritative voice said.

Kier listened to Tillman tell his men about the way Oregon had phrased his last radio call. And of course, Oregon wasn't answering any longer.

"Target One wants us to think he's headed down the mountain without the Fed. Oregon's either dead or useless. He's probably dead. Do we have one man with the boy?"

"Negative that. Somebody came and got the boy; left California unconscious."

"Say again!"

Kier could hear the shock in Tillman's normally smooth voice.

"California is unconscious, the boy is gone. Only one set

of tracks came into camp. We can't figure out how they jumped him. Whoever it was just walked right up to California.''

"You are saying some unknown person walked into camp and left with this boy?''

"That's affirmative, sir.''

"Tell California to stay at the cave. They may come back,'' Tillman said quietly. He had obviously reacquired his grip.

"This is California,'' a voice cut in. "I can't walk. They cut me.''

"All the more reason to stay put,'' Tillman replied.

"Nevada and Arizona are on a track. By the look of it, it's Missy the Fed,'' another voice cut in.

Kier's jaw clenched and his fingers went tight around the automatic.

"Switch and answer after colors. Switch and answer after colors.''

Colors? Kier shook his head. Another radio scrambling code.

"Red. Magenta. Green. Yellow.''

There was a pause. "Black. Red. Blue. Orange.''

No more talking. They had changed frequencies and he couldn't follow. Switching quickly back to the channel on which he had last spoken to Tillman, he waited to see if he might try to contact him. In seconds, he did.

"Medicine man, are you there?''

He debated answering, but reminded himself again that the signal could be triangulated, and that any broadcast would enable them to locate his whereabouts.

"You should be sensible and talk to us. You were exposed to almost every deadly virus and bacteria known to man. I know you must have figured that out. You and the woman need treatment.'' It puzzled Kier that Tillman admitted to having the disease organisms. But then Tillman's men were logged onto a different frequency. Perhaps he was trying to get Kier's trust by appearing candid.

Kier had moved away from the stripped body of Texas to listen to the radio and wait for the mercenaries that he knew would arrive. Crouching now in a dense grove of young red fir fifty feet from their grenade-riddled comrade, Kier could hear men coming.

Above him was a tan oak that was outgrowing the fir. Eventually, Kier knew, that in the fight for sunlight the fir would overwhelm the broadleaf. But able to survive in shade, the tan oak would still stand after it lost the race. Kier hoped for a fate at least as good as that of the tan oak.

Near the tan oak, a wild onion had found a little bare soil, and there was just enough of a root to make a walnut-sized tuber. The first bite took half. It had the crunch of a fresh apple but no sweetness and the dry, stinging tang of the most potent domestic varieties.

Then he heard the *bang, bang, bang*—like a fast vibration—of automatic-weapons' fire from farther down the ridge. They had found Jessie. Forcing himself to wait, he knew the soul-wrenching pain of being helpless.

As luck would have it, the two men were beyond the trail on the side opposite the grove where Kier hid, making it impossible for him to see them. All he could do was follow and wait for his chance. It was getting late. More than two hours had passed since he left Jessie. He would need to find her soon.

Moving quietly through the trees was almost impossible, even for Kier. Branches heavy with snow dumped their loads when he brushed by, making sound. Worse yet, he was leaving a trail that a half-blind man could follow. He had to stay away from them, and behind them, so they wouldn't accidentally cross his track. It was spooky, and very dangerous. If one of them got behind him, it would be a simple matter for them to follow, guess at his direction of travel, and use radios to trap him. If they got him before he got them, Jessie would be next.

* * *

The man code-named California sat with his head hanging almost to his chest. A sizable gash gaped open across the back of his scalp. His brown hair was matted with blood, and his hands shook as they continually touched the wound as if exploring the damage would make it better. Blood oozing from a severed Achilles tendon spread in a huge crimson stain through the fabric of his camouflage suit. Tillman strode back and forth in the snow, filled with rage at the neutered soldier in front of him.

"You gotta get me back down the hill," California said.

"You're a damn coward. What happened?"

"I never saw him. I'm telling you he came out of nowhere. I was doin' the kid like Brennan told me, but I was bein' careful and lookin' around. Then Oregon called. He sounded scared. Said I had to stop or he was gonna die, then *wham!*—something hit me. Then he cut me. I can't walk. I'm gonna die up here."

The soldier's voice was cracking. No dignity remained in the man. The intensity of Tillman's feeling stemmed as much from this man's cowardice as the collective failure to capture Kier. He continued pacing, conjuring his next move. Occasionally, he directed an icy gaze at the man in front of him.

"I was looking around. I swear."

Tillman cursed himself for getting so far from the cave. He had been making a circle, figuring he would cross Kier's track as Kier came to save the boy. Then Oregon had called on the radio, panicked. Within seconds, California's attacker had come like a quiet breeze in the night. From the mark in the snow it was obvious that only one man had crawled here on his belly after dropping from the rocks above. If it was Kier who had held Oregon hostage, then he could not have gotten the boy. And if Kier rescued the boy, he couldn't have captured Oregon. The FBI bitch was way down the ridge dispatching two of his other men, so she couldn't have done it.

Someone besides the Indian and the woman was out playing in the snow. And that someone was intimately familiar with the wilderness.

"Please, you gotta get me off this mountain," California said. Tillman noticed the man had unconsciously moved to his knees. Then he was literally clinging to Tillman's boots.

Revulsion filled Tillman. Ridding himself of this soldier would be like weeding a garden. Like General Patton, he had no appetite for coddling cowards. The Romans killed them outright. Alexander the Great made men brave or made them dead. He reached down and took the man by the hair. A calm came over him as he reminded himself that this man was the only one who could place him on this mountain. The others believed he was in Johnson City speaking through a relay transmitter at Elkhorn Pass.

There was no equivocation on Tillman's part as he sank his knife an inch into the man's neck, making sure to take out the vocal cords.

Kier and the woman were near, and he would hunt them down.

A battleship-gray rock scarp the size of several high rises protruded from the mountain at the place Kier thought to undertake his ambush. Where the granite was vertical and smooth, little grew except lichen. Here and there, where the stony surface was flat enough to hold a sprinkling of soil, there were dabs of deer fern, five-finger fern, bleeding hearts, and huckleberry. Now the plants were mere lumps in the snow. The top of this massive rock formation was overgrown with evergreens.

Kier positioned himself on a high ledge under a dwarfed wind-sculpted pine. From his vantage point, he looked out across a shallow canyon with steep sides going to ridges five hundred feet above him on the opposite side. Most of the canyon was covered in forest. Fifty feet below him, there was the shadow of the trail on which the men would come. They would move slowly and watchfully. They would be spooked by the booby traps and fearful of ambush. Down the trail a short way was the small cave in which he and Jessie had taken their shelter.

The two men who now approached would be easy to hunt. They were both of average build, less than 190 pounds, and not accustomed to the wild. They missed obvious detours around thickets, tending to go straight down, their eyes mostly focusing forward. They easily became boxed in by terrain and windfalls that forced them to backtrack. Leaving a wide trail, they made a lot of noise and had a poor sense of balance. If they stood still, it would never be in mid-stride, but always with both feet planted firmly on the ground—putting them at a considerable disadvantage.

When at last they appeared, he realized he could kill them several times over. They walked single file, with at least twenty feet between them. After every step or two, they would look, but they saw little. When he was about to shoot the trailing man in the leg, something told him to wait. Perhaps it was because of the way they moved, or maybe the lengthy unexplained delay in their arrival, or just a hunch that it was too easy. The man who directed these men understood how to hunt an enemy. Why were these two neophytes sent by themselves to follow a trail, even to walk into an ambush? Why weren't they circling away and coming back?

The man nearest drew closer. After a few minutes of this stop-and-go travel, he would pass beneath Kier and out of sight. The hair stood on Kier's neck. He kept the open sights of the M-16 near his target, but lifted his cheek from the stock of the gun and watched. On they came. There appeared to be no one else.

Kier's eyes roved the hillsides and the canyon, famished for a clue. After a time, he turned his head to look above and behind him. Nothing. There was only the inner voice, the sense that not all was as it should be.

Where do you want to look?

Grandfather's voice came to his mind just as it had that day in the dead frozen winter when hunger was overtaking him. He opened his eyes, looking again to the opposite hillside four hundred yards distant. A movement, then nothing. Waiting, he watched, uncertain as to where exactly he had detected the motion. The first man walked below him, then the second. Almost ten minutes had passed since he first saw them. Any minute now, they would be gone from his sight.

There was another glint of something on the hillside and his eye found what it sought—a white-suited man moving against the snow. This man was very good, doing exactly what Kier would have done. By stalking his own comrades, he would find the other stalker. This one moved with his head up, stopping irregularly, always looking.

Kier aimed for the torso, waiting for one more movement to define his adversary against the far slope. But it never came. The man must have dropped to his belly. Why? Kier slipped back a foot, lying flat on the rock in a depression that hid him from view.

Grasping a branch that hooked over the lip of the snow-covered granite, he moved it slightly. *Smack! Smack! Smack!* Three bullets spattered against the stone, followed by loud, echoing reports. The man across the canyon had found him, perhaps using field glasses. Obviously the man was in a hurry and unwilling to take his time shooting. That was good. That told Kier that Jessie had killed somebody. Perhaps they believed they were running out of men, out of time. Darkness would soon come and there could be few, if any, new recruits.

Kier sidled back to a cleft in the rock completely hidden from view, then looked slowly around the canyon. Across the white silence, he found no movement; on the far hillside, there was no sign of anyone's passing. In the spot where the man had been, he could see nothing. Undoubtedly the shooter would have moved on his belly out of sight. Again the snow was starting.

A deep, tunnellike groove in the cliff enabled Kier to descend to the canyon floor without exposing himself. By the time he reached the trail to the hut, snow was falling in sheets and the far canyon wall became just a memory. Using his radio, the shooter would have alerted everyone on the mountain to the white-clad figure that was Kier—including the two men ahead of him. They would be halfway to the hut, wondering about the trail left by Oregon that headed mysteriously down the mountain.

Kier crept quickly through the forest parallel to the trail, staying in the young stand of mixed conifers, hunting the same two men. On his flank, he knew, would be the other stalker, a man who knew the woods and how to conceal himself. But it would take that man time to arrive—and during those minutes, Kier intended to disable the bait.

Chapter 18

A strong spirit is the best medicine for a sick body.
                                        —Tilok Proverb

Once Jessie had composed herself, she left the shrapnel-shredded soldier to locate the body of the man she had shot. He had fallen just off the path, with his head buried in snow-covered brush. Pulling the head from the snow, she studied the man she had killed. His blue-gray eyes were open and looked large and dull, like those of cod on ice.

Clean-shaven, he appeared relatively fresh for a guy who had obviously been living in the bush. There was a single gold earring in his right earlobe bearing a cross emblazoned on a small round button. Oddly, he reminded her a little of her younger brother—about the same age and build. No identification except dog tags. He carried no wallet, but had a money clip just like Miller's.

Forty-five-caliber slugs were big and the bullets traveled slowly, working well with silencers. When the hefty slug had finally arrived at its target, it had done serious damage, hitting with fiercely destructive power. In this case, the talon bullet had missed the steel breastplate and struck the edge of the Kevlar at the arm hole. At least portions of the specially made slug had entered the body. The result sickened her. While not piercing the Kevlar, the other portion of the bullet had cratered the vest, pushing the material through the man's ribs and into his body. Undoubtedly the energy transferred to the chest cavity, stopping the heartbeat.

The bleeding had been heavy, but most was under the flak jacket beneath the down-filled arctic suit.

By the time she had donned the man's coat and body garment, most of the blood had coagulated and frozen. Since the clothes were much too large anyway, she pulled them on over her own coat and clothing, substantially increasing the amount of her insulation. Her revulsion at his bloody coat felt trivial compared to her relief from the encroaching cold.

In his pack she found power bars and hungrily she opened one. As she bit into the bar, she noticed a small piece of translucent tape running along the edge of the wrapper. Instantly she realized the possibilities. Her jaws froze in horror. If only she hadn't taken a bite before she noticed the tampering. Immediately she spat it all out, then rinsed her mouth with handfuls of powdery snow. She had swallowed nothing, she was sure. If there had been more time, these men probably would have used some method for invading the wrapper that was completely undetectable, like a fine needle or a syringe.

In training they had taught her about poisoned food, and she now realized it had been incredibly stupid to eat what was in the man's pack. Obviously they would have anticipated that food would be taken from corpses or the wounded.

Thinking calmly, she decided that some of the power bars must be free of poison. Three had tape on them; twelve others did not. Further, the three with tape had been stored within easy reach, in a pocket on the outside of the pack. That was about as far as she got with the logic before the first cramp hit. The convulsion in her gut made her throw up. What was left in her stomach came up. She felt clammy; her heart pounded, and her head throbbed. Her insides churning, she vomited again. Instinctively, she curled into a ball, wondering how quickly she would die.

Maybe it's a virus, she thought, as she began to fade.

Probably the fittest seventy-two-year-old in California, maybe in the country, Stalking Bear hiked at a pace that was an honor even to the young man who followed him down the mountain. The men in the white suits had seen Jessie's track. Stalking Bear knew his grandson, Kier, was fighting. They were perhaps a quarter mile from the Bear's Cave trail in the thickest brush to be found. He made a great circle around Jessie's old trail. He studied her steps, read in the ground the story of her ruse.

He sensed where she'd be. A feeling came over him. Something was wrong.

After passing through an oak thicket and a stand of tall fir, he found the small cave.

"I must sleep," he told James Cole. "You go ahead down the mountain. Go to the reservation. I will come after."

James hesitated.

"You can help them best by continuing on," he reassured the young man.

James thought a moment longer, then turned and trotted down the mountain. Unrolling his bedroll, Grandfather sat straight-backed, closing his eyes.

In his dream, Grandfather walks on. After heading across the mountain, through the windfalls, past the cabin, and into the red fir, he sees her track again. It is just where he expects. He follows for many paces. She

*circles and comes back. Tirelessly, he follows. When the
time is right, he looks down into the dying face of Jessie
Mayfield. Urgently, he bends over her. She must drink.
Nearby is a rivulet. Using all his energy, he watches her
drag her body. He waits until she drinks deeply.*

   *Grandfather gently touches her face. As his flesh
presses hers, his spirit leaps within him.*

He wondered at it as he awoke in his cave. He rose and
followed the boy. He knew that he must return and try to save
the Tilok people.

After swinging wide into the canyon to get below the men,
Kier drew close to the rock wall, still moving downhill through
the brush while working toward the hut. He expected that the
men would be cautiously approaching his previous hiding spot
on the ledge. By now the shooter on the far hillside would have
alerted them. It wouldn't take long for them to find his trail in
the snow.

   Near the hut a large crease ran vertically across the rock
wall. Kier pressed into it. Then, peering around the sharp edge
in the granite face, he saw the shelter he and Jessie had built.
It looked like a giant ice cream cone stashed in the rock, the
door plug a small lump of white next to it. He saw no fresh
tracks anywhere.

   The men had obviously turned around before getting this
far, no doubt to search the ledge where he was last seen. Kier
laid a track to the mouth of the hut, dusted the snow off the
plug, inserted it, then very carefully walked backward in his
own footsteps until he reached the smooth, gray granite of the
cliff. An experienced tracker would be able to detect what he
had done, but a novice would not.

   Quickly, he found a sheltered area under a tree with a reason-
able view of the hut. And then, down a slight incline from his

hiding spot, two men appeared, just barely visible. They had come much faster than he had expected, but these were the novices, not the stalker from the hillside. They looked to be thirty or forty feet from the hut entry, one of them talking on the radio. Where was the man who knew how to hunt? What was he thinking at this moment?

As if to egg Kier on, one of the men fired a long burst with his M-16 into the hut. Kier's trigger finger tightened, the shooter in his sights. But he didn't want to kill if it could be avoided.

"Drop your guns," he shouted at the men, who looked up, bewildered. A four-shot burst by Kier brought the men to their knees, guns thrown down.

He left them naked, huddled under the leaves in the hut, and burned their boots and clothes before their eyes. Next he destroyed their radios and rendered the rest of their equipment useless. It was better than a prison. Kier doubted the stalker would even bother to look for them, and if he did, they would do him no good without shoes and clothes.

Angling carefully up the side slope of the canyon away from the men, Kier found something that stopped him cold. Grandfather's track, headed down the mountain. So that was how James Cole got away.

Kier crossed their tracks and continued on. He picked up Jessie's trail about a mile farther along the ridge from Bear's Cave, and he began following it, relieved that the stalker had not yet arrived. Jessie had made a giant circle. He smiled. With a glance, he saw her first false side trail, but knew it was a dead end by the way she had backed out. It would fool the inexperienced. He found a more recent side trail that could be easily missed. She had jumped from the main trail to the base of a tree as he taught her. A cursory glance would reveal only the dislodged snow that had fallen from its branches.

Seconds later, Kier found a track through the trees. After twenty feet, she had stood still. A shell's dull brass finish caught his eye. She had fired the gun.

Tracing the general direction of her shot by the angle of her toe, he studied the terrain. She had run to a fallen tree. He could see where she had crawled.

Looking up, he saw that bullets had ripped through the woods. His heart pounded. A grenade or mortar had exploded. She had hid behind the log, then crawled again . . . his eye followed. Quickly, he moved down the track.

A great sigh of relief escaped his lips when he came upon a man who had apparently been blown to pieces by a grenade. She got him. But where'd she go? He found the berm, then followed her track to the first shooting spot, then into the woods.

Oh, God, there was another body—a man, sprawled, partially stripped. Kier's eyes took in the food wrapper, the vomit, the partially eaten bar, and the spot where she had spat in the snow. Drag marks. She had crawled.

He found Jessie lying in a fetal position with her face next to a barely flowing stream. Her tousled hair fanned from under the helmet. When Kier saw the blood over her stolen white coat, his soul seemed to shrink. A moan escaped his lips. He rolled her into his arms and cradled her head. He pressed her neck.

A pulse. Her chest rose in shallow breaths. Frantically, he tore at her clothes, exposing her body. The delicate white skin bore no marks that he could see.

She was still alive because she had ingested only a minute quantity of the poison. Judging from her distended belly, she had thought enough to drink lots of water. He redid her clothes to keep her warm.

Certain he had too little time, he cast about for a more secluded spot, placed Jessie over his shoulder, and crashed into the brush, making no effort to be quiet. Scrambling over two large logs, he forced his way through a thicket of branches, crushed them to the ground, and cleared a small area surrounded by windfallen trees and brush. Returning to the dead man, he obliterated the evidence of the poison, then moved the man's body a hundred yards down the trail. The man who hunted him would easily find them, but the heavy brush would make it difficult to approach in complete silence, and the soldier's body would provide a momentary distraction.

When Kier returned, she was leaning against the log where he had left her.

"Bathroom." She tried to rise.

"Okay."

Kier moved her through the heavy brush to a spot twenty feet away. He found a foot-high log to sit her on with a smaller six-inch log suspended in the brush pile over which he could drape her elbows. It was what nature had to offer in the way of a convalescent toilet. Using mittened hands, he cleaned the snow off both logs.

She groaned. He lifted her eyelids. She looked barely conscious. Gently, he shook her. Nothing. He shook her again—vigorously this time. With a flutter she half opened her eyes, seemingly more aware of her surroundings. Putting his ear to her belly, he heard bowel sounds and knew that what was coming would not be pleasant.

"Bathroom," she muttered again, made more alert by her discomfort. "Get out of here."

Her fingers began struggling with her coat. Without saying anything, Kier unzipped it. He took the large overcoat off long enough to strip down the arctic overalls underneath, then put the coat back on her for warmth. When he began to unbutton her jeans, her hand grabbed his.

"Get out of here," she said again, her voice hard.

Kier stepped back. "You can do this?" he asked even as her body seemed to wobble on the log.

"Get out of here," she repeated evenly. "I'll do this myself, or die trying."

Then, as if the effort of asserting herself was too much, she began to slump forward. Kier jumped and grabbed her. Maneuvering behind her, he reached around and stripped down her pants. When she tried again to grab for his hands, he put them back on the small log.

"I don't like this any better than you do. Stop struggling and let's do the best we can," Kier said, hot with embarrassment. "Just go." His large hands supported her thighs with her knees draped over the log. "Come on, come on, push, push, push. It's poison. Let's get it out."

Somehow, he thought, if he made it seem like some kind of weird athletic event it might be less horrible for her. Her humiliation made a lump in his throat.

"I'm going to hate you forever for this," she said through clenched teeth.

Then she evacuated her bowels and peed for more than a minute.

"I thought I had already earned that distinction," Kier replied, grabbing toilet tissue from the dead man's pack.

"If you wipe my ass, I'll kill you."

Chapter 19

When the Great Spirit sent down woman, he required that she obey man just as Coyote listens to Rabbit.

—Tilok proverb

"I need you to stand on the log," he said after he had packed things and was ready to move.

"What for?"

She appeared miserably weak. Her belly was still cramping after two more incidents. "I can't go standing up, if you'll recall."

"I am happy to see that your sense of humor is returning. I am going to carry you piggyback–style."

"No way. You can't carry me down this mountain with a full pack."

"Just until you're feeling a little better."

When Kier had first arrived, she could barely speak. Able to walk a little now, he knew she hoped she could go on her own. Undoubtedly, she was struggling for every shred of independence she could find. It was important to this woman to be dependant on no man. But her dependence was a fact, and he hadn't a clue as to how he could change it. She said nothing when Kier hoisted her up. Putting her arms around Kier's neck and her legs around his waist, he felt her leaning into his back, supported by his heavy forearms under her thighs. He was able to hold her securely despite the field pack and two M-16s between her and him.

At 115 pounds, her weight alone would not slow him down much. But he had another 40 or 50 pounds of equipment hanging off him, making the long hike a real challenge. Last time he had checked, he was a lean 230 pounds—most of it solid muscle.

Before starting out, Kier threw a line around her back, tying it across his chest. It gave her something to lean against. Once on the trail, he began a smooth jog, which with snowshoes was really more of a fast shuffle.

"This Tillman man is a dangerous hunter," he said. "It will take him no more than another fifteen minutes to find the spot we just left—assuming he went back to Bear's Cave."

After a time, Kier stopped. His labored breathing seemed to fill the quiet. They were in a grove of large pine.

"It's like a park, as though someone cleared all the underbrush," Jessie said.

"People have camped here and burned everything near the ground." Kier kicked off the snowshoes. "Also, the treetops keep out the sun, so only plants that like shade will grow, mostly broadleafs or hemlock."

"Are we going to stop here for the night?"

"We can't." Kier paused. "We've got to keep going."

"Where?" she said.

"A cabin. You'll like it."

"I wanted to tell you, that the guy who I got with a grenade talked before he died. He said his group was doing something with a Tilok mink farm.''

"Yeah. I had a captive briefly who told me the same thing. They took five mink to the clinic.''

"Why, I wonder?''

"I haven't a clue. They were waiting for that plane to drop the pods and that's why they were here.''

"Instant army.''

"The crash according to this guy was unexpected.''

"Undoubtedly, they were shooting holes in the plane while they were shooting at each other.''

"I did some more reading while you were asleep in the hut. I'll tell you about it when we get to the cabin.''

Kier led her through the woods beside the open trail.

"Give me just the good stuff of what you read,'' she said as they walked.

"I want to show you some more passages.''

"Fine, fine, but tell me the guts of it now.''

"I want to show you why I think they felt the need to clone people. I've got to explain the research. At the cabin. I'll show you.''

After backtracking one hundred feet, they stood five feet off the tunnellike passage through the forest that was the pathway.

"Move your feet just slightly, like you would if you were waiting impatiently.''

"When he sees this, he will think we are trying to ambush him?'' She was catching on.

"He will wonder, and the wondering is enough. It will make him cautious . . . slow him down.''

"Why am I moving and you're not?''

"Because he knows I wouldn't move.''

"What? So I'm supposed to be stupid?''

"You'll learn, and then he'll read your knowledge in your track. But if I had said nothing and we had been here for twenty minutes, wouldn't your feet have moved just a tiny bit? If there was no movement, he would think we had only waited for a short time." Kier pointed behind her. "Take one step back." She did as he suggested. Squatting down, Kier flicked on a small light. "Now look at the size of your track. See how large it is and how the borders are blurred? Now look at mine." Kier stepped backward. "If he looks at this, he will wonder if we waited twenty minutes trying to catch him unawares.

"He'll know from my prior track up the trail that I was carrying you, that you were sick or wounded. Then he'll see that here you walked along after me. See the angle of your feet, compared to mine? And the way you stood next to me? He'll think you were waiting for me while I was looking up the trail, probably with my gun at the ready. When you step, you don't raise your feet high. You walk tired."

Kier touched her shoulder. "Let's go. I think he'll get our message. The illusion is at least confusing."

When they returned to the pack, Kier pointed to a log.

"I can walk now," she said, obviously anticipating him.

"I want to jog," Kier said.

"Are you always so . . . dismissive?"

Kier turned to her, stepping so close that she looked up at him. Reaching out, he touched her face. He let his eyes say the words that he felt.

"Oh, God," she said, meeting his gaze. He thought he saw confusion and uncertainty in her face. Seconds passed before she lowered her eyes.

Kier dropped his hand and turned to pick up his pack. "I'll carry you. It will be faster that way. When you are stronger, you can go on your own."

"Come over here next to the log and I'll climb on."

Chapter 20

Stars are the spirits of our forefathers. On cloudless
nights we are overcome by their smile.

—Tilok proverb

Once again, Kier gave her a line to pass behind her shoulders
to provide support for her back. Since she held on without
much conscious effort, she soon fell into a stupor. After an
indeterminate period of jostling, she prodded herself conscious
and saw no snow falling. A hole in the clouds revealed more
stars than she had ever seen and a bright moon against the
black-velvet sky shone so clearly she could make out its surface
texture. In its light, their shadows danced behind them on the
satin shoulders of the mountain. Kier walked now at an ordinary
pace.

"So tell me again that we're going to sleep in a cabin with
a fire."

"In a cabin, by a fire. But it will be tomorrow."

"So I wasn't imagining things," she said with some hope that it was really true.

"The only other guy who knows about the cabin is in Montana. But it's up to us to get there."

"What do you mean?"

"I would like you to consider just trusting me and not having me explain it. How do you feel about that?"

"Why don't you wish to discuss it?"

"It's one of the reasons I am carrying you."

Confused, Jessie looked around. To her left stood a sheer granite wall. Instantly, she looked down to her right and sucked in a breath. It was a straight drop. In fact, she couldn't see what Kier was walking on.

"Is this a trail?"

"Of sorts," he said cryptically. "I need to concentrate on keeping my balance. Try not to move."

She noticed now that he was carrying his snowshoes.

Her gaze wandered over the outline of the tiny ledge that they traversed. For the first time she observed the long stick in his right hand that he held in front of them, feeling along the rock ledge. As she considered the danger of such tenuous and blind footing, she could feel her heart beginning to pound. Her cotton mouth made swallowing difficult. For a moment, she shut her eyes tightly, telling herself to relax. A few slow, regular breaths helped.

Again she looked. They were moving across a cliff on a narrow ledge. Below there was an almost vertical decline. Directly overhead occasional rock overhangs blocked out the clear night sky.

After a time, the rock wall to the left disappeared, and there was nothing but snow to both sides and below them. Ahead was another mountain, rising gently from the end of their ledge. Far below she could see where the landscape turned dark in the moon's glow—a forest. Kier snapped on a light. He was knee deep in snow on a razorback ridge. Now, on both sides, an abyss invited her mind to take leave of thought and embrace panic.

"Oh my God." She meant it as a prayer.

"I would like for you to carefully consider something."

"What?" She could barely speak.

"Loosen your grip around my neck just slightly, so as not to choke me."

"Oh. Sorry." She realized that she had pulled her wrists into his Adam's apple. "I don't mind telling you I'm frightened."

"I know what I'm doing."

She forced herself into a sort of calm. "I'm better now," she said after a time. "Can I help?"

"In a few minutes, I'm going to need to let you down."

Each of his deliberate steps followed much poking with the staff. The flat mountain surface ahead lay less than a stone's throw away. She longed to lie on it, touch it, kiss it. It was so massive, not nearly so steep as the ridge on which Kier now balanced. And it had trees, blessed trees. In front of them, she could just make out a tree near a large, dark area, like a cave. Actually, it appeared that the mountainside had an overhang. It was as if she were looking down the tube of a giant, curling wave. Ice and snow in the moonlight were the foam atop the breaker.

"There," he said, running his staff into a spot in the snow that seemed to have no bottom. "How would you feel about my loosening the rope and your getting down?"

"Not good. But I'll do it."

Slowly she slid from his back, letting her feet sink into the snow until she found a foothold on the rocky surface. Removing the pack, Kier pushed it down into the snow like a candle in a cake. He motioned for her to sit on it.

"Have you ever seen that?"

She knew exactly what he meant. On the horizon a planet shone jewellike. She threw her head back, staring. Bright stars and lesser stars occupied every tiny patch of black, and the

Milky Way was a shimmering cloud of light. Her cold fear mixed with awe. She looked into eternity. And it was so quiet. There was not a sound.

"It sounds really corny, but I feel like I'm part of God," she said. "How could I ever describe this?"

"What are you feeling?"

"Peace, I guess. This is all so crazy. We're dead meat. There's no peace for us. I wonder if the men who hunt us could ever feel this. God, when I look at this . . . all this . . . I have never seen a sight to match it. . . . But it is not just in the seeing . . . it's . . ." She didn't know what to say.

Kier tried. "It's the experience of a spirit—a very thirsty, parched spirit—that wants to touch another. Grandfather says that by knowing your own smallness you can find a way to the whole. Under these stars you are finding your smallness. You touch the whole."

They both fell silent. She let her gaze trail along the length of the Milky Way and pick among the stars.

"Grandfather brought me to this place."

"I must meet your grandfather."

"He was on the mountain today. Not half a mile from you."

"An old man, with a bag around his neck. A leather bag and a heavy green coat."

"That's him. Where did you see him?"

"I didn't, I dreamed him. When I was sick and passed out. I dreamed he came. He told me to crawl. Begged me, really. So I crawled to a stream and drank and drank and drank." Kier didn't stop her. "It was a dream, wasn't it?"

"There were no tracks near you. It was a dream. On my wall at the cabin I had a picture of him in that green coat. You would have seen it."

"And the bag?"

"No. It wasn't in the picture. A great-grandchild was holding the bag."

"I saw him with the bag."

"Your mind supplied the bag. It's something that used to be common for Indians."

"Do you realize you always have an explanation for everything? It sounds like you believe in nothing but molecules."

"I don't know what I believe. I just keep going."

"Since you went off to college, right? You always quote your grandfather. You don't state your own convictions."

"You felt what you felt. That's real." Kier pulled out two coiled lines, one of which he cut to make a third.

"I need to show you a knot."

"Why?"

"We're going to do some mountain climbing and you're going to need it."

She studied while he wrapped one line around the other. All the while her sense of foreboding grew. When she could do it, he nodded. Getting down on his hands and knees, with the guns still on his back, he felt around in the snow. After a while, he grunted what sounded like approval.

"Did you find something?"

"Oh, yes," he said, sounding relieved. "A piton."

She knew what that was. It wasn't good. It was a device used by people who climbed cliffs. It would be anchored to the rock and mountaineers would dangle from it.

"Do we need a piton?"

"Maybe I could offer a suggestion."

"A suggestion? Here we are in the middle of the night on a freezing precipice with one lousy piton? I just met God, and I'm still scared, and you think with a few words, you can just . . ." She hesitated. What was she trying to say? "Just get on with it. I'll be fine. Just fine."

It was night. Dangling at night was almost unthinkable. It seemed to Jessie that where they stood the ridge's top wasn't more than a couple feet wide. Covered with snow, it created the illusion of a knife's edge. To the left, the down slope appeared walkable, if dangerous, but to the right it fell away almost vertically for several stories. Kier reached down with the line and pulled it as if he were running it through the piton. Just next to him was a sheer drop created by a massive split in the granite right where the ridge joined the shoulder of the mountain in front of them. It was as if a giant had pulled lengthwise along the ridge neatly severing it from the mountain and leaving a straight-walled, U-shaped, vertical fracture.

"Perhaps you could go first, and I could help lower you down. What do you think?"

She was determined to show him no more of her fear, although she hadn't a clue as to how she would do what he asked. Kier wrapped the line around her thighs and waist, then passed it between her legs.

"Have you ever rappelled?"

"At the academy we did it a couple of times. But that was in broad daylight on an artificial rock wall. We had equipment. I had eaten. I hadn't been deathly sick. I had strength. I'll manage."

"Okay. Well, this will be very similar, only I will lower you. But if I slip or let go, this safety line, which you will pay out, will also be through the piton to stop your fall. You must hold the safety line and not let it slide through your fingers, except when you want to go down. Now lean back and I'll hold your weight."

She stood with her back to the sheer drop. Kier held the main line a foot from her chest. It went around his shoulder, across his back, down to the piton, then to her waistline.

"Go ahead and squat down."

Warily, she lowered on her haunches.

"Now lean back and let the rope take your weight."

She froze.

"Go ahead, just lean back."

God, dear God, she prayed. Her heart pounded and her hands shook. She felt humiliated. She was not a weak person and what was being asked of her was not extremely difficult.

She continued trembling. It was getting worse. By now a minute had passed. Kier squatted down close to her. His light illuminated their faces.

"Let's rest a minute. Just sit." He pulled her back from the cliff to sit on the pack. "I remember when I was a kid, I saw this movie on TV about Cheyenne Bodine, a man who was sent to a forest to hunt a creature that was killing people in the night. These guys would sit around the campfire and something—before it attacked—would throw dirt out of the bushes. It scared me bad . . . had me shaking under the covers. Turned out it was a bear."

"I'm trying—" she said.

"There's time," he continued firmly. "I'd lie in my bed, scared out of my mind. Now, I know what you're thinking. It's in your head that I was just a kid, that you're an FBI agent, and this story is demeaning because—"

"The story is about normal childhood fears," she interjected sharply. "This is about two adults on a mountain. If you'll shut up, somehow I'm gonna do this."

Gritting her teeth, she stood, went to the ledge, and held the rope in her left hand.

"Well, pull on the rope, give me some resistance."

He pulled firmly. She clamped her jaw, willing herself to lean back, trusting him to hold her. She took one baby step down the rock face. He played out a few inches of line, and she took another. The first few feet were not as frightening as she had expected. She was near him, and she could see. As she descended, though, the shadows deepened, and Kier became a monolith in the soft glow of the penlight that he held in his mouth. It was like descending into a well. By thinking about the smooth rock and occasional bush she passed, she did not dwell upon what might be coming.

After she'd taken perhaps fifteen downward steps, Kier stopped, and she felt the pain of the line cutting into her thighs.

"What's going on?"

His light shone over the edge.

"Look behind you." A few feet away on the other side of the chasm a snow-covered tree—some kind of needled evergreen—grew from the opposite wall. It looked gnarly, old, stunted, the base emerging from a crack in the vertical rock wall. The thick trunk made an L so that the top grew straight up, parallel to the cliff. Behind the top of the tree Kier's light shone upon the lower lip of a cave mouth in the cliff face.

"You'll need to throw your end of this line around the tree; then I'll show you how to use it to swing across."

Her heart sank as Kier dropped another line. Throwing the lariat to catch the treetop would be tough. The notion of somehow swinging her body through space, across the chasm, was terrifying. She couldn't even imagine climbing from the tree into the cave.

"I've got the end of the line. You need to get that loop at your end of the line around the top of the tree. From up here I'll work it down past one or two of the larger branches."

"Why did you get me down here and *then* tell me this?" Kier was silent. "Never mind, I know."

Only a vigorous throw would catch the broken top of the main trunk in the loop of the lariat. Turning sideways, she studied the tree. Maybe twelve feet away horizontally, the stubby treetop waited to be noosed some two feet above her height. From the top of the tree to its gnarled base was about twenty-five feet. The floor of the cave stood at eye level.

Jessie's first toss hit the tree's broken top. But when she tried to pull it tight, it slipped off. Three more throws were equally useless.

"I can't," she called.

"When you throw again, think only of the tree."

As he said it, she realized that she had been thinking of the rope, not the tree. With nothing to lose and a sense of wild abandon she threw the loop as hard as she could. To her amazement, it fell neatly over the treetop.

"Very impressive," Kier said. "In a minute we'll have a bridge line."

She felt a surge of satisfaction.

From his higher angle, Kier shimmied and shook the line down past the first stubby branch and pulled it tight, catching the main trunk.

"Grab this," Kier said as he dangled another length of line until she had it firmly in her grasp. "This is the swing line. Pull the bridge line taut and tie this swing line to it the way I showed you. Tie it as close to the tree as you can."

She tried it three times before convincing herself that she was doing it right. Then Kier took the belly out of the bridge line, pulling it taut to the piton, forming a single line bridge across the chasm on a steep angle from the cliff top down to the treetop.

The swing line was attached to the bridge line at about the middle of the chasm and was now well above Jessie's head. She would have to push off the rock wall and, in a pendulumlike motion, reach the tree.

"Okay. There should be a ledge there. Stand on it."

She did as he said, clinging to the rock wall.

"I'm going to loosen the line that holds you so I can let it out as you swing yourself across. If you don't make it, you've got to turn feet first to this side so you can push off again."

There was silence. If the tree on the opposite side gave way when Jessie swung, she would slam back against the rock face, dangling from her safety rope.

Taking a deep breath, she grabbed the swing line.

"Ready?"

She hesitated. Could she make herself do it one more time? The black of the abyss below engulfed her.

"Look at the stars."

She did and drank them in. Something in that vast beyond made the chasm less important, her own mortality more acceptable. She pushed off into the jaws of her terror, leaving her spirit in the arms of the universe.

Swinging easily she covered the eight feet to a branch.

"Pull yourself in."

She grabbed the branch like a cat over water, hauling herself to the tree. For a moment, she laid her cheek against the trunk of the pine, concentrating on the rough texture of the reddish brown bark, its sharp scent.

Her eyes cast about for a way to get to the cave. Using her light, she could see that the rock surface was indented with small but numerous hand- and footholds. A large branch just above her looked to be the best bet. Then she saw another branch, less stout but closer, that would take her nearer to firm footing. She tested it and it seemed to hold her weight. With one step on the branch and a hop she could make it to a man-size, two-foot-deep pockmark in the rock wall, then climb to the cave. Feeling confined in the rope harness, she decided to remove it. After a brief struggle she was free of the lines.

She placed her foot on the branch and reached for the rock. The snap was so abrupt she had no time to react. She dropped as if through a trapdoor. Her gloved hand caught a branch as she went. The spindly wood slowed her, then strained downward. As it broke, she got an arm over the bend in the tree where the trunk made its L-turn at the cleft in the rock. Twisting wildly, she eventually wrapped both arms around the base of the trunk and hung there.

She heard the sounds of a child crying, then realized it was she who was crying in ragged breaths. Air sucked into her lungs in great gulps. Her head spun. Something was terribly wrong.

"Don't breathe so hard!"

Kier was shouting at the top of his lungs. *Why was he doing that?* She took a deep, slow breath.

"Get your feet on the rock."

She felt with her left toes and found a small ledge. It seemed too narrow to support her weight.

The tree is solid, the trunk thick and strong, she told herself. She could count on it. It was her muscles and mind that were jelly. She would use her legs, the strongest part of her. She searched around with her right foot. In seconds, she found a secure shelf. After her right toe was well placed, she lifted her body with both arms and the strength of her right leg.

Gripping branches in her hands like the rungs of a ladder, she worked her way above the base of the trunk and climbed up the tree, regaining the dozen or so feet that she had fallen.

The cave beckoned, only a couple body lengths higher than her head. "Have you no suggestions?" she called out.

"Love the mountain. Remember the stars and the feeling you had."

Was he out of his mind? She would never love this cold son-of-a-bitch rock.

"This mountain is killing us. It's freezing. It has cliffs. It hates all civilized people." She risked letting go with one hand to lift her middle finger and aim it at Kier. "I suppose I could be more one with the sucker if I let go and went splat."

She hung her head, too tired to shout anymore, and regarded the dim outline of the rock. Okay, you solid son of a bitch. She crouched down on a stout branch. Crawling forward, she reached out a hand and touched the rock. She concentrated on the granite, putting her other hand out.

Now her knees were on the branch and her hands firmly clinging to the mountain. She would need to drop a foot and find a ledge on which to park her toe. As she reached out, she glanced down. Cold blackness greeted her. To put a foot down into the unknown, to teeter on that branch, seemed a thing too hard to do. Yet if she could do this one last thing, she could rest. In a cave. On a flat spot.

"I love you, you solid son of a bitch," she whispered.

Her boot shot down in a smooth motion and found a foothold. In less than two minutes, she clambered up into the cave, where she knelt and kissed the rock. Grateful.

Chapter 21

Coyote howls to awaken your fears.
— Tilok Proverb

Until she looked at her watch, Jessie had no idea that dawn was still two hours behind the mountains. The solid flat ground on which she lay was a balm to her frazzled nerves. Kier still had not come in.

"There may be a roar," he called.

"Okay," she muttered to herself. What now?

She didn't move as it started, first with some solid knocks of rock on rock, then a clattering, followed almost immediately by a rumble that sent vibrations through the stone under her fingertips. Thunder filled the cave. After a minute of what sounded like the mountain ripping open, the sound stopped.

"Throw down the rope," she heard Kier call out.

She wanted to sleep, not move. She felt as if she had been drugged. Forcing her eyes open, she crawled the few feet back to the cave entrance and the tree.

"The rope?" he called out again. He was at the bottom of the chasm, she realized.

"Just a minute," she said. The rope was hanging from the tree. "Kier."

"Yes."

"The rope's in the tree and I'm in the cave. It'll take me a minute." She knew how weary her voice sounded.

The next thing she knew, his hand was gently shaking her shoulder.

"What time is it?" she asked. "Did you get your rope?"

The roar had been an avalanche. It would look as though they had been sucked away in the flow of rock and ice, he explained as she stretched herself awake. He had lain beside her and let her sleep for sixty minutes or so, but now they needed to move deep inside the innumerable passageways of the cavern where it would be impossible to track them.

Near the opening a wide fire pit had been used many times by the youth groups that he took on wilderness excursions. In the circle of his light beam it appeared full with fine gray ash and the remnants of blackened wood chunks. Beside it was a small pile of rough-barked logs, neatly stacked and split and ready to burn. He could tell that no one had used the place since his last visit.

Jessie reached in the pocket of her coat, withdrawing a light that she used to explore the nearby walls and ceiling. They could barely make out a trail of soot above them, the remnants of a river of hot air that had picked its way over the rock, always rising, sucked by the draft until it found the mouth of the cave.

"Who comes here?"

"We bring the boys when they turn fourteen."

He told her to take off her snowsuit just as he was removing his. "We need to cover ourselves with charcoal," he told her.

"When they figure out the avalanche trick, and they can't follow us over the granite, they're gonna think about dogs—tracking dogs. Fire smell is common in the wild and will mask our scent, make our trail old fast and confuse a hound's nose. But we don't want to turn the snowsuits black."

With that he knelt and grabbed a sooty stick.

She snickered. "Oh, great. I'm already filthy."

Kier gave a concerned glance in response.

"I'm sorry. I've got an attitude. For a moment there I was really happy to have made it here."

"Your cynicism will weaken you."

"It's already kicked the stuffing out of me."

Kier examined her arm. A deep groan escaped her lips when he moved it.

"If we're lucky, all you did was bruise things."

As he helped her out of the snowsuit, he was sure that she was at ease with his touch. He had sensed it previously when she was sick and when she lay against his back, but he suspected that she could never acknowledge it. Discussing it seemed pointless, so he applied the ash in silence while enjoying the closeness.

Since he was a boy, Kier had been in these caverns many times. The first time he came with Grandfather they had used a little-known entry called *witsu ka*, or Worm's Way, a tiny hole with just enough room for a man to crawl in on his belly. It was much more difficult to undertake the long crawl through Worm's Way than to climb to the cave they had just entered—aptly named Tree Cave. When they brought the boys in summer, they would climb the mountain to the bottom of the chasm. One man would reach the cave using climbing gear. Once at the cave, he would drop a rope ladder.

Another entrance by way of a different cave opened onto a treacherous but passable rock ledge in the middle of a thousand-foot cliff. For as long as anyone could remember, this opening had been called Man Jumps, although there was no evidence that anyone had done so. Another cavern passageway led to a surface cave that was the fourth entrance, but a portion of this route was almost vertical, useless without climbing gear.

Two white men lost in the cavern for days had located a fifth tunnel into the caverns. For them it was an escape exit. Some months after their safe return, they had attempted to show the Tiloks the tiny hole in the rocks from which they had emerged, but were unable to retrace their route. Grandfather had found it, but Kier had never taken the time to learn it.

Because the cavern was sacred to the Tilok and on reservation land, no maps of its sprawling labyrinth existed. The only maps were in the men's heads. The Tilok had learned to traverse the interconnecting caverns from Tree Cave to Man Jumps. A few men, including Kier, could make passage from Tree Cave to Worm's Way, but those who made errors in navigation could pay a dear price. The caverns were fraught with drop-offs and confusing turns. Two Tilok men attempting to map the routes had disappeared when they either got permanently lost or, more likely, fell into a chasm. Some of the vertical shafts, which seemingly fell hundreds of feet, had never been explored.

Using the charred piece of wood he had picked from the fire pit, Kier began at Jessie's boots. He smeared charcoal and ash over her liberally. She seemed so exhausted, it did not even occur to him to let her do it herself. Trying to ignore the way he felt when he was near her, the desire he felt when steadying her, touching her, he sought to adopt a clinical air—to move with the precision of a good physician rather than the exquisite sensitivity of a lover. He dipped the blackened stick over and over in the pit so that when he was finished, her clothes would be impregnated with the fine powder. As he worked his way up to her thighs, she put her hand over his.

"I've got the idea," she said, taking the stick and beginning to apply the ash herself.

Embarrassed, he wondered whether his desire was too strong to remain undetected. Always things with women got this way—everything a nuance, every gesture a speech. He hated thinking about it, but he was drawn to her despite his vow never to be with another white woman.

Jessie seemed to be fighting her own feelings. He could feel it as surely as the spirit of the Tiloks in the mountains. But whatever monster gnawed at her, he knew that his was possessed of many more heads, and breathed a far hotter fire. There was a head for every member of his family—his mother, his sisters, his myriad cousins, the whole tribe. All were expecting him, the darling of the white community, to marry an Indian. To marry Willow.

Within minutes, they were covered with ash and soot. Next, to be even safer, they rubbed themselves with needles from the pine at the entrance, which took only a few minutes more. Then it was time to leave. Turning his light on Jessie, he used his free hand to hoist the pack and gave her a questioning look.

"Are you strong enough to hike?"

"I'd like to try."

"Stay directly behind me. Keep your light pointed at the ground."

"Do we have steep places in here too?"

"Stay close."

He put a hand gently on her shoulder, and was sure her head moved almost imperceptibly toward his fingers, as if she wanted to touch them with her cheek.

"I'll tell you when there's a bad edge. It'll be fine."

He squeezed her shoulder in reassurance, and surprisingly she covered his hand with hers.

The crackling of the radio made them both start. The garbled transmission continued as Kier swung his light to the source and retrieved Miller's unit. Jessie stood close while he fiddled with the squelch.

"Click twice if you hear me, Kier. The best triangulation equipment around won't locate you on a couple of clicks."

Tillman.

"Is it true?" she asked.

"Don't know. But two clicks would tell them we're alive. Right now that's a lot of information."

"Cat got your clicker, huh? Well, never mind." Tillman chuckled. "That was a gutsy bit of ridge-walking you did tonight. Especially lugging the lady around."

Kier's insides shrank.

"If you hadn't moved on that ledge when you did, I'd have shot you."

Kier's fist tightened involuntarily. The implications flooded him. So Tillman was the stalker, or at least he wanted Kier to think so. Knowing it as opposed to suspecting this finalized Kier's assessment of their predicament. Tillman, who had experimented on his tribe, the man who directed the search, could hunt and track like a Tilok.

There was no more chatter for a few moments. Then: "I'll be right behind you."

Tillman would likely be unaware of the caverns. He didn't know if his prey were dead or alive. The fact of their survival in the avalanche could only be gleaned on hands and knees, by studying every shred of evidence. Kier shut the radio off and put it away. Deeper in the caverns, it wouldn't work anyway.

Kier focused on the route to Man Jumps, the seldom-used exit that would eventually bring them to the cabin. It was a snarl of passageways until you came to a fork where the stone in the middle was covered with ancient pictographs. Kier supposed that his ancestors used the caves often on their migratory passages through the high country. They would have stayed in these caves during the summer months, when game and berries were plentiful, before the salmon runs and acorn crop.

Near the Tree Cave entrance, years of moccasined feet had rounded and worn smooth stone edges on the floor of the cavern. Missing, however, were the deep gullies in the rock, exactly the width of a human foot, which Kier had seen in places occupied steadily for hundreds of years. As they moved into a train-tunnel-size passageway that would lead them to the next chamber, fingerlike formations of dripping limestone appeared.

"I tell the kids it feels like a ghost convention in here," he said.

"You take them in here?"

"There's more than just me taking them, but yes."

"So I'm not sure why that makes me feel so humbled."

"We don't come here in November. And never in a blizzard, I promise you that. So don't bother feeling humbled. And for the walk through the caverns, Grandfather comes to show the way. He knows them better than anyone."

"I keep saying it, but I must meet your grandfather."

They should only use one light where possible, Kier explained, and then they would be assured of batteries for a couple more nights. She desperately hoped they wouldn't be necessary once they were out of the cave. Hunger gnawed at them, making them more susceptible to the dank cold. Even the insulated snow clothes they had taken off the men required a certain amount of body heat to be effective.

After a time, Kier stopped.

"How do you feel?" he said putting his hand to her forehead.

"I'm dizzy and I've never been so hungry."

"Your hunger will get less with time. It's when it comes again that you really have to eat. You can go days without food. Fortunately you won't have to."

"Let's hold that thought."

At first the drop in elevation was slight; then the path steepened to a downhill hike. Sounds of water dripping came and went. As the passageway became more nearly vertical, it also became more twisted, so that in places it felt like a spiral staircase. In his knees he felt the pounding of the long footfalls and realized how easily she could injure herself. He wondered how long she could walk.

The narrow margins of his light probably made it hard for her to place her next step without stumbling, so he suggested that she use the second light despite his desire to save the batteries.

After walking what seemed a mile or more down into the mountain, the passage leveled out, and they came to a maze of tunnels. Kier paused at each turn, constantly scanning. By developing a habit of always looking, always being conscious of where he was going, he had an extraordinary memory for even the most subtle landmarks. In addition, Grandfather had left piles of pebbles on the main route that could be found about twenty feet before every right turn and at the junction of every left turn. Of course when there were several passages off a large cavern, that method didn't work. In that situation there was either no marker, in which case memory was imperative, or there was a small pile of pebbles at the beginning of the correct passageway.

The primary drawback to this method of navigation was its ambiguity. There were several routes and they crossed one another.

"How do you know where we are going?" she finally asked.

He explained the rules.

"It was better not knowing," she said.

At last, they reached another flat where the walking was easier. After two sharp bends and a hundred yards on the level, they came to a rock wall that separated two passages. On the wall was a thirty-foot-long ancient pictograph. Kier shone a light onto the scene that was painted onto the smooth limestone. She stood close to him, in awe of what she was seeing. Multicolored figures, in earth-red, turquoise, and yellow, depicted people or spirit beings. The arms and legs of the figures were represented by three lines, and torsos by four lines.

"They are the sky people or spirit people who affect things here on earth." Kier pointed at certain of the figures that appeared to hover over the landscape.

Below the sky people were the hunters—tiny red men holding spears and rocks, chasing deer or elk. Between the hunters and the sky people was the sun and, to the right, a smaller sphere—the moon. They hunted in the twilight.

"This fellow here, near the hunters, has the ceremonial headdress—that is good medicine." Kier outlined the barely discernible hat. Two imposing figures stood side by side with a radiant halo depicted over their heads. Between the haloed pair stood a smaller figure. "Maybe the small fellow is on a vision quest, and these two spirit figures are standing over him."

"Or maybe they are man and woman. The halo is their love, and the smaller person their child."

"We always thought it was about sacred dreams. Maybe love is your dream."

"I know part of it is about love," she said.

She took two shaky steps to the wall and plunked down in the dirt. Kier took off his pack and set his light on a ledge, directing its rays at the painting. Then he sat close beside her. When he touched her shoulder, guiding her back to recline against him, she did not resist. He knew his large body was much more inviting than the rock. After a moment, his arm went around her, allowing her head to rest against his chest.

"What does it make you think about?" she asked.

"You first."

"My mind feels like it's floating with fatigue, a little like being drunk."

"Where is your mind wandering?"

"You think I'm imagining things when I say those two people with haloes are about love. You think it's because I'm hung up on the subject."

"I never said that. I'm just listening."

She nodded. "I guess I'm just hoping I'm not one dimensional. When I was young I seemed to have so many sides. You know? I felt more than just desire, anger, and satisfaction.

There were really good people back then. Why don't I know any great people anymore? Did they change, or did I?

"You were like a fairy tale come true if my sister was to be believed. Grounded. Got a whole philosophy about life and nature. According to Claudie, you were gentle with everything. She said you had no guile, Kier. I thought maybe all that bigness I knew as a kid could come back when I watched you with the mare. Then you ignored my wishes, dragged me away from civilization, and tricked me, locking me in a wine cellar against my will. So much for the resurrection of my youthful idealism."

Kier stayed quiet for a while, wanting to deal squarely with his need to reconcile things with her.

"Let's cut through the baloney," he said finally. "The wine cellar isn't the issue. What we're really talking about is this rock-hard inner self of mine that—yes, is stubborn—but more than that, can't consider a white woman as a mate. And we're talking about one more thing. A bigger thing I think."

"What's that?"

"Whatever happened to you, that has you so angry."

"You dragged me around in a blizzard instead of driving to a phone booth."

"But that's not it," he said.

"Are you a mind reader?"

"Is it the divorce?"

"No."

"So what is it?"

"You first. Why do you think I care what you think of white women? You're going to say that I'm somehow attracted to you and that this is some kind of issue with me."

"You're trying to say you're not?"

"Kier, all the problems in life don't revolve around you, for God's sake."

"My unwillingness to be with another white woman, in your mind, is just a rejection of the white man's civilization and ultimately of you. Same with the government. But the reason it bugs you so much—"

"Kier, please spare me. Why are you talking about my feelings? Talk about your feelings. Don't tell me about mine. That's my job."

Kier's anger exploded inside him. He quit talking and sat staring at the dreamers on the wall.

"Okay. Okay. I'll just listen. You talk," she said. "Let's not degenerate. You just talk."

"You're sure?"

"Definitely sure."

"Now I don't know what to talk about," he said.

"Stop stalling before I scream."

"It started with my mother. All my life I have felt my mother's love. Always I have wanted to please her. But more than that, bigger than that, I wanted to be like my grandfather and never betray my heritage. Indian people are being swallowed up. We haven't preserved what is Indian. Often we're not good at what is white. I have gotten along pretty well in both cultures. That's what I was raised to do. But I can't let myself disappear into the white man's world, get fat off peddling Indian mysticism. I almost did that once."

"So you're going to marry an expectation instead of loving a person. It makes poor Willow sound like a political statement. God. I thought I was cynical."

"Ah. So you know all about Willow."

"Well, Claudie told me. I'm a snoop at heart. That's why I'm a cop."

"So now you've decided I'm not in love with her when you don't know either of us."

"We got naked in the same hut. I know you."

"Well, let me explain my side of this."

"Go ahead."

"I guess," he said, sighing, "I don't quite look at my relationship with Willow the way you and Claudie do."

"Let's leave Claudie out of this."

"Okay, the way *you* do. You know the saying about 'stir-the-oatmeal kind of love'? It's not Hollywood, but it's caring." He watched her with eyes that pleaded for her understanding, even as he supposed it was something that she did not intend to give.

"You see there, you've just admitted it. This is some dog-eared old affection that's like friendship. It's not really love."

"It's what I want. I'm not looking for anything else. Anything glamorous."

He heard her take in a deep, ragged breath. "So that's it. Okay. I can respect that. I suppose there're a lot of happy families out there stirring the oatmeal. Personally, I'd rather be passionately in love, howling at the moon, screwing my brains out till we knock the bed over."

Kier thought about that and realized that nothing good could come from continuing the debate.

"I judge from the long, Indian–like silence that we've exhausted that topic. Let's try another unfinished topic."

She leaned closer against him, placing her hand on his chest. He surmised that the rummy, frivolous feeling that accompanied exhaustion was relaxing her. He took hold of her shoulder and pulled her tight. She let her body meld to his.

"Back there on the cliff you were starting to tell me about your boyhood fears of the TV bear. I interrupted you."

"Well, it wasn't just the TV bear. To this day when bears come to a camp in the night and they wake me, my heart races for a few seconds. Like when I was a child."

"Kier afraid of a bear?"

"No. I'm afraid of things that I can't control. It just happened that the TV bear captured my imagination when I was young."

"How about love? You can't control that. Or the pain of it."

"Never thought of it that way."

"Maybe it's time you did. I still remember certain very

powerful emotions from my growing up. When I was a little girl, I always wanted my daddy's attention.''

"Every little girl wants that.''

"Yeah, but this was a big deal in my life. Really big. He wasn't the cuddling type. Never touched me. I'd sit for hours and daydream that I'd found a way to impress him. I have these memories of getting all excited about something, trying to tell him, and him not even looking up from the paper.''

Kier held her close, but said nothing. She put her head on his chest.

"Is it something to do with your dad, that you're upset about?''

"No, it's not.''

"Let me ask a question?''

"Okay.''

"Why were you visiting your sister?''

"I'm not up to this yet.''

"Can't talk about it?''

"Not now. Tell me about Willow.''

"What's there to say? In a couple months we'll get engaged, get married, the whole thing.''

"Did you ever tell Willow all this . . . this stir-the-oatmeal and native-loyalty stuff?''

He made no immediate reply. As he thought about her question, he was not searching for an answer, but searching for a reason. He could not think of one, except the anxiety that accompanied the thought.

"No.''

"Well, I pray for the poor woman's sake that you do before you propose.''

Chapter 22

There is no single day when green fruit turns to
summer sweetness.

—Tilok proverb

"The view definitely takes your breath away."

They looked out over several hundred thousand acres of
snow-covered rock and timber. Rock under snow and ice made
blue-white mountains stretching to the horizon.

"It looks as good as a Bierstadt," she said.

"You can't feel the solitude in a painting."

"You don't freeze your ass off or die from exposure in a
museum," she said. He caught himself frowning. "Oh, all
right. But it would be a hell of a lot easier to appreciate it over
a hot cup of coffee."

Man Jumps cave emerged far enough down the mountain to
be below the sub-alpine forest and in the true fir belt. By the
look of the trees, they stood at 5,500 feet, maybe slightly lower.

Below them grew the mixed conifer forest with its Douglas fir, white fir, ponderosa pine, sugar pine, and incense cedar.

"We're up in the true fir, aren't we?" Jessie said. Obviously she was beginning to discern the different species, which served as a primitive altimeter.

To reach the forest from the mouth of Man Jumps cave they had to go laterally along a narrow rock-strewn ledge that followed the face of the cliffs for about a thousand feet.

Kier knew she was trying to look unafraid, even calm, but her head nodded an involuntary "yes" when he asked if she'd like to ride on his back.

"I should walk on my own," she said.

"You don't look like you believe it."

"I'll walk."

"And *I'm* stubborn?"

A foot or two wide most of the way, the ledge was just sufficient for walking, but narrow enough to be painfully tenuous, bordered as it was by a breathtaking vertical drop. Fractured rock and a dusting of snow along the ledge added to its already treacherous texture.

They moved single file, roped together so that if Jessie fell, she would get a second chance, provided Kier was surefooted enough to hold her. If he fell, they were both dead. Brooding dark clouds hung in the mountains, their tentacles reaching into the valley, portending more bad weather to come. As they walked, he tried to keep her talking in order to keep her mind from the fear. To a degree it seemed to work. Either that or she was becoming more accustomed to heights.

"The cabin is close, just under some Douglas fir down on that ridge. The way the air is warming, I'd expect these next clouds to drop buckets of rain in the valley. Melt the snow. Make it impossible for them to follow us down the mountain."

"I'm growing to hate this business of leaving footprints everywhere we go. I'd just love for the snow to melt. And food. I have this wishful vision of the cabin with plates full of spaghetti and meatballs. Does this cabin have a table and chairs? Can we get something to eat?''

"Table and chairs, it does have. Food, we will get any way we can."

"Why don't you people leave food?"

He found himself smiling. "If we left food, you might be sharing your bed with a bear. Besides, we like to keep it fresh and kicking."

"What is it that'll be kicking?" She set her foot beyond a large loose rock and reached to the wall for support.

"Beaver. Beaver tail is excellent, although I hate to kill them."

"Tail. Oh God."

"Well, there's also cattails. Use the rhizomes on the cattail for flour, young ones for something like asparagus, and the heart, which is hard to describe, maybe like a rich potato. And bulrushes. They're sweeter than the cattails. There's arrowhead there too. Like yam, sort of. Those are all things we can get quick. From the sound of it you'd like an early lunch."

"Well, at least it's food."

"The water there is the key. The creek is dammed up by the beaver, and the pond makes a lot of food for everything."

The ledge came to an end in a rushing stream that plummeted thirty feet down a chute seemingly too treacherous to walk. At the base of the near-vertical drop the stream hit a gentler slope that by the look of it could be traversed.

"I know you won't walk in the snow, so I won't remind you."

"Yes, that way we can pretend you don't think I'm an idiot."

Kier took a line, tied it around himself, then braced against a boulder. With considerable effort, she was able to keep her feet against the rock as she walked backward, going hand over hand down the rope.

Kier, in a hurry and having no good place to tie the line, opted for sliding down the rock variously on his feet and butt.

"You could have broken your leg," she said when he rose stiffly.

He shrugged and started down the watercourse. Still flowing in the middle of its bed, the water cleared the snow and made it possible to walk and leave no track. By following the stream, they could travel downhill to the cabin without leaving any sign. Their hunters might circle the entire mountain and never discover their path.

Tillman squatted alone in the gray light of early morning, studying Kier's footprints. The track led across the bottom of the chasm and disappeared into the head of the avalanche.

Having spotted the prints from the knife-edged ridge above, his men had concluded that they ought to bring in hounds to search the three-quarter-mile-long path of mountain rubble and snow in an attempt to find the bodies.

But before his men arrived, the mountain had told Tillman something was amiss. Scrutinizing the far wall of the chasm, he saw, in the blotchy pattern of white on greenish-gray rock, tiny points and ledges, some no wider than a postage stamp, that lacked the expected dusting of snow.

If Kier climbed the wall, what did he do with the woman? It was a certainty in Tillman's mind that Jessie Mayfield had not scaled the wall either before or after Kier. Not enough snow had been disturbed, even if he assumed that Kier climbed to the top and hoisted her up on a rope. Then he focused on the pine in front of the cave perhaps eighty feet over his head. It would be gutsy, but maybe Kier had strung a line and pulled her across. And if he did, they both went in the cave. Limestone mountains were notorious for caverns and the rock formation he now contemplated was geologically suitable. His research had indicated a network of caverns in this area.

If the cave above were an entrance to those caverns, the tracking would be greatly slowed. Tillman ground his teeth.

Putting men inside the cavern would only give Kier an incredible advantage. Tracking on the stone passageways would be useless. Kier probably had a map of sorts in his head, whereas neither Tillman nor his men would have a clue as to their whereabouts. The Indian would slaughter them.

Iron Mountain was a long ridge with a high spot rising as a summit. Other ridges intersected. Finding where Kier and Jessie might emerge would be time consuming. He would break the men into pairs and have them move fast, looking for any track. If Tillman were Kier, he would emerge from the caverns near a stream that could be followed downhill to avoid leaving sign in the snow. He would instruct his men accordingly.

He considered bringing Doyle up from the Donahue house, but he needed Doyle to lead the next group in. He would summon Doyle when he was closer to trapping Kier. Without further deliberation, Tillman knew to follow his instincts and halt any search of the avalanche. He radioed an alert to watch for tracks on the slopes of Iron Mountain. And he assigned no fewer than two men to search each creek.

Jessie celebrated seeing the cabin with her first smile in hours. They approached the place tentatively, as if it were too good to be true. It was small, she supposed twelve feet wide and perhaps twenty feet long. The peeled logs of its walls were caulked with a black substance in neat horizontal lines that emphasized the uniformity of the cabin's construction. The roof consisted of wooden shingles that still had the color of new straw. Through the roof at one end protruded a rock chimney shaped in a perfect rectangle.

Nestled as it was under the trees and close to a sheer drop, the cabin remained invisible from any direction unless one were within a hundred feet—except perhaps to someone with powerful binoculars on a faraway mountain. Directly in front of the cabin's covered porch, within a stone's throw, a waterfall cascaded into a small pool. Down fifty paces, the stream disappeared over another bluff. The setting was idyllic, and on a sunny, clear day, the view from the front porch would be inspiring to the point of rapture.

Suddenly it struck her that this was not an Indian design. There was nothing Indian about it.

"It's beautiful, but isn't this a white man's design?"

Kier's look told her that he was pleased with the observation. "Yes, that's right. But it's built only of natural materials found on this mountain. Except the windows . . . they were a real compromise. We do use other people's ideas."

Kier did not even try to open the door. Instead, he crawled under the cabin, which sat on a stone foundation. After he disappeared for a moment, she heard a clunking sound, as if he were pounding with a rock on wood. Shortly there was a clattering, as if something had been knocked loose.

"Door is fastened at the bottom, so it can't be opened unless you first release a catch."

The door was made of several layers of criss-crossed, rough-hewn boards and once released, it would not open without a hefty push. In lieu of hinges, the door was fastened to the wall by leather, which she took to be rawhide of some sort.

"My friend's bride is half Cherokee, but grew up in suburbia," he said as he walked in. "She wanted a miniature English cottage. This was a toughly negotiated compromise. My friend and I wanted a miniature Chumash longhouse. But she's an architect, and she designed the cabin."

Something about this revelation made Jessie smile broadly. Kier suddenly seemed more accommodating, a man among men, not an Indian among white people. And for some reason, at this particular moment, he looked unusually desirable. It hit her hard, like a wave that gathers force as it breaks on a steep beach. Overcome with her sudden attraction to him, she consciously stifled the feeling.

"So they're going to live here for the summer?"

"Well, a month, anyway. Then they're flying to Hawaii for a couple of weeks."

Sitting on the wooden bed platform, Jessie began to muse. She didn't know why, exactly, but after a moment she laughed. When she glanced at Kier, he seemed utterly puzzled.

"It's just so . . . so very American. I mean, two weeks in Hawaii, an architect, a cute little dollhouse, a cabin that you two slaved to build. It's so . . . sweet."

She then realized he was studying her. "Well?" She wondered what was going on behind those dark eyes.

"You seem to like the idea," he replied.

To give herself time to think, she turned around and studied the room. Nearest her was a built-in double bed without a mattress, and next to it a simple table with two chairs that reminded her of Amish tastes and methods. Some containers for water that looked to be made of skins hung from the overhead beams. A lovely, rustic-looking cabinet stood against the wall. Its open face had been made from a slice off a log, complete with the bark. A couple of lanterns hung from the rafters, and two fat, wax-bearded yellow candles sat in the middle of the table. A small chest of drawers had been hauled in, and various pegs protruded from the wall for hanging clothes.

When the reality of their situation came rushing back, she felt foolish for allowing herself to be occupied with such trivial distractions. "I can't believe we're discussing this when we could easily be dead in thirty minutes. Where's the food?"

"Just a short way down the creek is the beaver pond."

"Let's go get it."

"Would you like to stay here?"

"No," she shot back, determined to do her share.

"You can help carry the food back."

"Whatever you do, I do." She said it before she could ponder what she was getting herself into.

On his way out, Kier snatched some leather squares from a

peg. There was something vaguely familiar about them, but she couldn't place it.

The short walk turned out to be a brisk, fifteen-minute hike down a steep path made slick by the misty rain. The clouds had come down all around them cloaking the land, making a hazy gray of every vista. Kier announced that when they returned, they would be able to build a fire because the smoke would be invisible. For that she was grateful. If not for the gut-wrenching hunger, she would have chosen fire and sleep immediately.

At the beaver pond, Kier moved to a tree and, to her surprise, began stripping off his clothes. From his large pack she saw him pull the leather squares she had seen earlier. It was a loincloth. He hadn't worn one before and she didn't know why he would bother now. At a distance of twenty feet, she watched unabashedly while he prepared himself. She loved the hard, lean contours of his body, and she hadn't grown weary of observing him.

When he was finished, he walked toward her in nothing but the leather piece fastened with rawhide about his waist. He carried a wire snare and a pistol.

"Here." He held out the other loincloth and waited. She blinked her eyes, but otherwise stood unmoving. "After a half hour or so I'll get cold. If you're going to help, I suggest you get going."

"In that?"

Leaving it draped over her shoulder, Kier walked on. "You can help carry the food back if you have a thing about your breasts."

"I have no thing about my breasts. They're just private, that's all. Unlike some people I don't go around with my genitals hanging out." She caught herself doing it again. "Not that there's anything wrong with them."

"You seem to have a fascination."

"That's not true. That is so silly and so male."

She watched him wade through the rushes without reply and swim toward a teepee-shaped mound of mud and sticks that she knew to be a beaver lodge. *He's got to be crazy to swim in that freezing water,* she thought. But to show him she could do it, she wanted to go after him. If she was going to be his equal, she had better find a way to go. Almost running, she went to a tree, where she struggled out of her clothes while watching Kier out of the corner of her eye. He disappeared under the water twice, then climbed out on top of the beaver house.

She heard silenced pistol shots in rapid succession, and the heavy thunk of .45 slugs plowing into the mud and wood. In moments, he was pulling on something, a wire snare she assumed, to haul in a large, flopping brown mass. Two more shots and the animal stopped struggling.

Clad in her bra and loincloth, she deposited her clothes in the backpack, then went to the water's edge and stepped in, grateful that there was no ice crust. She considered that her bra, if wet, would only make her cold after she emerged. She pulled it off and tossed it on the snow. The cold water hit her ankles, then her legs, aching all the way to the bone. She gasped, but forced herself into the water, wondering all the while if the cold might do her in.

She could feel Kier's gaze even though he pretended to be busy with the beaver. As she walked briskly forward, the pond bottom felt like mush under her feet. An icy burn moved up her legs to her thighs, then to her belly. When the water was a little over waist deep, she began to swim. In less than a minute she swam the forty feet to Kier, who hauled her out atop the beaver lodge. The air actually felt warm. She crossed her arms across her chest.

He seemed to send his eyes everywhere but to her body. "Pull this to shore. Get dressed and wait for me. I'll be right behind," he said. He handed her the stick, which was still attached to the wire snare. She managed to take it in hand without moving her arms. Obviously, Kier had snared the beaver by driving the animal from its stick house. The noose was still tight around the beaver's neck.

"Okay," she said, jumping back in without further comment. "Oh God, oh God," she muttered through gritted teeth as she swam back.

The cold held her like a monster in its jaws, gripping and crushing all the way to her innards. It felt as though the chilly water were sucking the life from her, constricting her lungs, narrowing her vision. It frightened her. From her survival training she knew this kind of cold could incapacitate a person in minutes.

Towing the dead animal, she swam in a sidestroke, pulling with her left hand, while grasping the stick in her right. The beaver was heavy and made the going much slower, but she had only gone a few feet before she discovered that she could touch bottom. Getting a purchase with her toes, she pushed ahead quickly. At waist deep, she tried to run, pulling with all her strength. Stepping out onto the land gave Jessie one of the most triumphant feelings she could ever recall. The pleasure of it overcame the pain of the cold—something she would not have thought possible.

She pulled the dead creature to the water's edge and, still exhilarated by her success, watched Kier, who stood waist deep among leafy plants that looked a little like ivy atop the pond. Making herself ignore the cold, she reentered the water to join him. In a few seconds, she was at his side.

"What can I do?"

"Run your toe down the plant stock to the bottom. Dig in the mud with your toe and then follow a big root out 'til you come to a ball. Break it off with your . . ." He grimaced in concentration as he spoke, and a white ball floated to the surface. "As I was saying . . . with your toe and you'll get one of these."

Doing as he said, she sent her foot down the stock and tried to find the lateral root. But by now everything ached; her teeth chattered and she felt faint. Still she wanted to do it.

Squirreling her foot around in the mud, she tried to find a root. But it eluded her, while Kier popped up another, then another.

"Are you all right?" he asked.

She watched his lips move in seeming slow motion. Her world was swimming in glue. If only she could just get one of those damn tubers.

Abandoning the use of her foot, she ran her hand down the stem, determined to grab one. She went under. On the bottom her hand found a root ball, then a large strand. She yanked. Up she shot. There it was . . . a white tuber.

"Yes!"

"Come on."

Kier was walking toward the shore with his hands full. Pushing herself, she struggled to follow him, clambering with numb feet up onto the bank. She watched while he deposited the edible portion of the arrowhead plant in the snow. Before returning to the water, he glanced in her eyes, perhaps to determine how she was managing in the cold. Methodically, he bent over and began pulling bulrushes. She could feel him discreetly studying her and wondered if he was admiring her or merely concerned for her survival.

"Grab like this." He showed her to hold fast to the base of the young plants to get the root ball. They pulled up ten or so and moved to the cattails. Kier showed her some smaller plants, no more than a foot high.

"Like this," he said, grasping the cattail inside the two outer leaves and pulling. Then they worked in calf-deep water, side by side, harvesting cattails in earnest. Occasionally, she glanced his way, and when she did, she had a feeling that, even as he worked, he was totally aware of her. After they had half a dozen of the smaller plants, Kier began on the larger ones. But when she tried to stand next to him she discovered that her legs felt like flimsy stilts under a drunken clown.

"You can help most by getting dressed so we can break the plants into the parts we need," he said.

Gratefully, she struggled onto the shore, her feet like dead flesh, and made her way to the backpack. Fumbling through Kier's clothing, rope, ammunition, and hand grenades, she found her clothes. As she pulled out her things and set them on the pack, she looked for something to dry herself.

"Use my shirt," Kier called out.

Turning away from him, standing as near the tree as possible, she shucked the loincloth and toweled herself vigorously.

On the way back to the cabin, hauling the food, Jessie began to feel a chink in her armor. Although she couldn't put her finger on what had changed, there was something about the shared adventure in the pond, the toughness of it, maybe the acceptance of his challenge, that bound them. Whatever—she was developing hope. It was a startling admission, but Jessie had grown weary of denying it. And this hope was a damnably dangerous thing.

Chapter 23

A man with a handsome face is good for a summer,
a man with a sharp eye and strong bow is good for
many winters.

—Tilok proverb

Stretching in the heat of the wood stove, Jessie decided that
nothing had ever felt so good. Both candles on the table were
burning. One lantern glowed and a little natural light shone
through the windows. The sounds of the boiling water and
crackling fire, the smells of cooking meat—these things
charmed the senses. Cattail sprouts and two kinds of tubers
steamed over a saucepan while the beaver meat sizzled in its
own fat. At one end of the cabin all of their clothing but what
they wore hung from a line strung wall to wall. Kier, shirtless
and wearing almost-dry jockey shorts, tended the food as Jessie,
clad tentlike in his T-shirt and her panties, stood close by.

She could have sat or leaned against the wall. It wasn't
necessary for her to be near him. Of course, she was also close

to the food. The newest shoots from the cattails, now six months old, could still be eaten raw, and she had already eaten quite a few.

Sweat glistened in the hollow at the base of Kier's throat. She noticed it, and the bulk of his arms. Although his arms were long and a little bit lanky, they were the size of a thin man's thighs. Veins in his flesh stood out just like those on hefty athletes. His chest was massive and hairless, smooth.

She could feel the heat of him. When his eyes caught hers, she had a great urge to smile, as if they were sharing some secret joke. Whenever she looked up, his gaze was there, waiting in ambush. The eyes were deep brown, smiling. Aside from mirth, they looked full of desire. Maybe love. Again she looked away. She hated to think she was embarrassed.

"Prolonged eye contact is a form of boundary testing," she said in as detached a tone as she could muster.

When next she looked, he was concentrating on the food, no longer staring. As he pressed the meat with a fork, she studied his face, looking to see if there was any hint of his emotions. She could read nothing until he glanced her way with a little smile.

"What?" she asked.

"Are my eyes such a force?"

For a moment, her gaze followed her hand as it reached for a cattail sprig, then returned to his.

"It's your desire."

Kier turned from the frying pan, inches from her, looking down into her face. The warmth of him washed over her as she tried to decide ... what? She reached out with her hand, even as things tumbled in her mind. Her hand hovered over his chest, waiting. It was a perfect parody of her indecision.

"You're right. I'm sorry. I was flirting," he said, breaking the spell. "It's an unnatural situation. We're both tired."

He was right. People in harrowing circumstances felt compelled toward one another for strange reasons. She and Kier would never work. Looking at him now, he seemed relaxed. The tension had departed, leaving only the cooking smells and the comfort of the fire. Yet something inside her wouldn't let her leave it alone.

"Do you think that some hurts are so big we never really get over them?"

"I don't know. A lot of times I think that sort of thinking is just an excuse."

"Did you ever think about the downside of love?"

"What's that? Loss of freedom?"

"No. The fact that it ends. Either in life or in death." He looked perplexed. "You don't have the faintest idea what I'm getting at, do you?"

"Afraid I don't."

"Do you think you ever just decided to go it alone because the risk of it all ending was too great? I mean when you were a little kid. When your dad died. When your first wife left you. Did you ever say to yourself: 'Kier will take care of himself. Kier doesn't need anybody else'?"

"Everybody needs to take care of himself. But I think I understand what you mean."

"Your first wife left you."

"Well, it was complicated."

"Don't complicate it, Kier. You taught at the university together, Claudie told me."

"Yes."

"You wanted to come to the mountains so you both moved here."

"Yes."

"She left."

"Okay. She left."

"So this stir-the-oatmeal kind of love that you're longing for—how risky is that?"

"I've heard the old saw about afraid to fall in love. I don't think that's me."

"God no. Kier couldn't be afraid of anything. So let's not talk about fear. I want to know what you did with all the pain."

Kier shook his head with a half-smile.

"I felt the pain," he said, looking irritated.

"Which caused you more pain, your father's dying or your mother's need to prove that her son could be somebody even without a father?"

"Where do you get all this?"

"You forget. You've spilled your guts to my brother-in-law, and we both know that Claudie owns him. I put it all together."

"So you're a shrink as well as a cop?"

"I'm a disillusioned woman, Kier. Maybe numb from the pain myself."

He put his hand to her face for just a moment, then shook his head. "I guess I don't like depending on other people."

"What if we changed the word to 'trust'? What if we said you don't like the feeling of needing to trust someone?

"When you were at that university, with your wife, where she was the hotshot, where she knew everybody, came from a prominent family, knew her way around, how did that feel? Did you maybe worry just a little bit about what if she cut you loose?"

"I think I was confident of her loyalty."

"So when you moved back to your turf, where you knew everybody, where you were the hotshot, where you were in control, did that feel different? Did you really need to trust her back here?"

"Any of us feels insecure if we're out of our element."

"That's not what I'm talking about. I'm talking about you not being able to love somebody when it takes a lot of trust. Actually, I think I'm talking about you not being able to love somebody."

"I can love Willow. Are you questioning that?"

"Love can never be built on a lie. Until you tell her what

you have in mind for love—this passionless caring sort of thing that you call 'stir the oatmeal'—then you can't love her."

"Well, no one can fault you for not speaking your mind." He gave her a little smile.

"No, I speak my mind well. Go ahead and change the subject. I know you're dying to."

"Remember I was going to tell you what I read, something I figured out."

"Yes," she said.

"It's something that I only barely understand. I think I have an idea of how, at least in the early stages of their research, they created the God Model that enabled them to figure out gene function. They call it DNA chip technology."

"I remember reading something totally unintelligible about that."

"I think I understand the basics of how it works," he said. "Are you ready for more biology?"

"As long as there's no lab."

"Just the theory."

Kier began putting the food on the table as he talked.

"In each cell is a little factory that produces one or more types of protein. Instructions to the factory regarding what kind of protein come from the messenger molecule RNA."

She dished up the beaver tail, trying to cut a sizable hunk for herself. But her mind was mostly occupied with Kier's explanation and didn't focus on the fact that she was using an ordinary butter knife.

"Wait, wait. Let me make sure I've got this. When a cell wants to send a message to make some particular protein, it sends out RNA."

"Right. Let's use this," he said, pulling out a sharper knife.

"This RNA is unique to that particular gene."

"That's right. The RNA is just a mirror image of the DNA that makes up the gene."

"Beavers are tough guys," she said.

"They are." They both took a few bites, saying nothing. Then Kier began again with his mouth full, obviously intent on his thought.

"So at a given moment in time if you collect the RNA that a cell is giving off, then you will have a fingerprint of both the involved DNA and, if you know enough about the process, the protein that is being created. Another way of saying it is that you will know which gene is activated."

They both ate ravenously. Kier stopped talking to take a few more bites.

"The quantity and type of RNA that is given off by various cells may change as circumstances change. Such changes could include stress, disease, hormonal surge, tough beaver tail, passionate sex. . . . The patterns of the proteins made by those cells change as the body sends signals to deal with the new situation."

"So the trick is to discover which genes are sending out RNA in response to the condition under study," she said.

Kier continued chewing. "Exactly."

"And this DNA chip measures it."

"Sort of. To create a DNA chip, droplets of DNA from different genes are put on a chip. They can put thousands of droplets on each chip. When Tillman's researchers wanted to know what RNA was produced under a given bodily condition, they could extract RNA from the cells of whatever living tissue was affected and expose it to the chip. By seeing which DNA droplet matched the RNA, the researcher could tell which gene was activated as a result of the illness or condition under study."

"I follow that. You know in advance which DNA is in each droplet. The chip detects which droplet the RNA matches, and then you know which gene it came from."

"That's right. Then by studying a person who has recently been infected with a disease, for example, they can learn through the RNA from various organ samples which genes are involved in fighting the disease, and where relevant, which are involved in propagating the disease.''

''So this would help them understand disease processes.''

''Right,'' he said. ''Causes, cures, the works. But to do this efficiently, you would need human subjects. And you would need a sample of every disease you wanted to study. So it becomes clearer why all the diseases. But if they were, for example, using Tiloks, we would at the very least have a bunch of sick Tiloks. And for what I'm talking about, you'd be regularly punching holes in their bodies to get tissue samples from organs so it wouldn't be a secret.''

''So they're not doing that on the Tilok tribe. You're thinking if the reference in this RA-4TVM study was to human infants, then they were cloning people and using the clones for medical research.''

''That's right. First they used this chip technology on the same cloned infants. Later they just took organ samples and ran the RNA through the computer. And that's how they got light-years ahead of the rest of the world's scientists.''

''So they sacrificed babies to make progress,'' Jessie said.

''It seems too outlandish to be possible. But I believe it, even if I can't prove it.''

When they finished eating, they lay exhausted on the bed. Both fell instantly unconscious.

It happened in the middle of the night, after they had been sleeping for hours. Nothing that he could recall had awakened him, but he opened his eyes with a start. A creaking sound disturbed the still cabin. He couldn't tell its source. For no discernible reason he became very uneasy.

''We've got to leave right now.''

He was shaking her awake. He turned on a small light, grateful that he had covered the windows. Her mouth opened, probably to ask why.

"Get dressed. I'll throw the food in the pack and get some other things."

"What is it?" she asked, already pulling on her jeans.

"No time to figure it out." He had his pants on, then his outer shirt, leaving his T-shirt for her. They struggled into the camouflage outerwear. Kier began cramming more canteens, professional mountain-climbing gear, and snare material into the pack, all of which he had hauled from a trapdoor in the floor.

"Let's go." Five minutes had passed since it first hit him. Too long. "Out the back window."

He helped her through the window and led her straight away from the cabin into the forest so that someone watching the front would detect nothing. Once again, however, they left a trail in the snow. After two hundred yards, they circled, coming back to the creek that they had followed down to the cabin. Remaining in the creek so that they would leave no tracks they headed back uphill toward the caverns.

"Where in the hell are we going?"

"Hide in the caves."

"Why not follow the creek down? Your whole tribe could be—"

"If they figured out the creek, they'll be waiting below."

"But how do we know—"

"We don't know anything," he cut in. "It just didn't feel right."

As if in response, an explosion rocked the mountainside behind them, reverberating in the fog. M-16 automatic-weapon fire rang out.

"I'd say they just destroyed my friends' new cabin. With luck we have a minute or two before they start on our track."

Kier trotted up the creek now, hoping that Jessie could keep up.

It made no sense, he told himself. They had gone a couple

of miles underground. Tracking should have been impossible. Dogs couldn't follow their bodies coated in charcoal and pine scent, even assuming they brought bloodhounds this far into the mountains. Tillman probably was not fooled by the avalanche, lost no time, and had a man or two follow each creek down the mountain. If so, he had an uncanny ability to predict Kier's methods.

Kier heard her breathing and could see her sides heaving. Sprinting up this mountian with all the rubble and loose rock under the snow was physically punishing. Altitude with the resulting lack of oxygen made it worse.

For just a moment he would stop.

"How are you?"

"Maybe I should just end the pain—let you go alone and save the world. I'm holding you back."

"Give me your gun. Everything," he said.

Woodenly, she handed him the M-16, the pistol, and two grenades.

"I need you to give this everything you've got . . . like at the pond. I'm not leaving you and we're going to jog—even on the ledge."

"No." She shook her head.

"Yes."

He turned up the creek. The pep talk wasn't working. Awakened from a sound sleep, her belly full of food, and now sprinting, no doubt to the point of nausea, she looked wiped out. Probably making her angry was the best medicine.

"I don't know how they let women in the FBI," he mumbled.

She grabbed his arm.

"What did you say?"

"I don't know how they let Tillman get past the FBI."

"That's not what you said."

Then he started running up the mountain.

* * *

She was almost certain she understood him. It was such a stupid thing to say. Trying to suggest that she wasn't tough or lacked determination just to get her to run up a hill. It was infuriating. After all their talks, how could he resort to this sort of thing? She wanted to tell him to get lost, but she wanted to really skewer him, and he wouldn't slow down. Her chest burned, and killer pain squeezed at her temples. Making her yet more miserable, borderline nausea had begun creeping into her gut. She considered that she might be suffering a mild heart attack. God, she would get even with him.

Slick from the constant wet, the limestone made for ankle-jarring, knee-banging frustration. When they reached the bottom of the chute and her memory of it returned, she gave an involuntary groan.

"Wait here," Kier said.

"Is that a joke?"

Without a word he began scrambling furiously with hands and feet up the edge of the water-filled shoot. He disappeared in the dark shadows of first light. She heard a rock tumbling and then another. Instinctively, she stepped back. When at last she heard a yell she began groping for a line and was almost disappointed when she saw its outline in the gray light. Knowing Kier, she tied it firmly around her waist, managing only through great effort to stay on her feet as he pulled her up.

At last they were on the dreaded ledge. Before they began, Kier looked at her. Dawn was just breaking.

"The cavern is the one place they can't corner us or catch us. Not even infrared will work. Once we go in there, they have to either bring in an army or wait."

"Okay."

She was thinking about how exposed they would be. She forced herself to follow Kier's brisk walk along the ledge until he dropped flat on his face and she almost landed on top of him, lying between his legs, her chin on his butt. Kier looked 360 degrees, then pointed to something that froze her body stock-still.

An M-16 will kill at a mile, although aiming at such great distances was problematic because the bullet traveled in an arched trajectory. Shooting a couple of people at six hundred yards was a simple matter.

There were two groups of men, one on the slope far beneath their ledge and one on the mountainside at their elevation, but behind them. Each group stood perhaps six hundred yards distant. Both groups had emerged from the heavy forest at about the same time. She and Kier had five or six hundred feet remaining to reach the cave, at least half the length of the ledge. The worst part was ahead. It was inconceivable that they would not be seen.

Now they crawled. Sharp rocks grated over her thighs and belly. Nothing could be dislodged; not a single one of the hundreds of golf-ball-sized chunks could leave the ledge. One *ping* would bring field glasses searching around to their tiny outcropping. Watching Kier, she did as he did. An elbow and a knee moved together, but slowly, carefully, with exasperating precision. There was no option as to where to place her reddened elbows and skinned knees. Using the captured binoculars to study their hunters, Kier moved when the groups moved, stopped when they stopped.

Keeping Kier's pace while maintaining concentration was punishing. Soon Jessie found herself groaning every time an elbow caught the rock or came down too hard. Each little stone that branded a knee became hateful.

Then, in a split second, the glimmer of hope that had spurred her on evaporated. Just ahead of them two more men walked on their very same ledge, toward the entrance to the cavern. Kier and Jessie could not go up, they could not go down, and they could not stay put. If they shot the two in front of them, the bodies would fall and the men below would see them instantly. The near certainty that she would die hid in the darkened corners of her mind, waiting like a cancer to take it over. There would be no need to continue struggling once she accepted it.

For a few seconds, surrender seemed sensible. On further reflection, it seemed fully justified. It was only her innate grit that made her want to go out fighting.

Chapter 24

A strong arm needs a stronger heart.

—Tilok proverb

The two men on the ledge ahead wore camouflage whites. Any moment now, they would turn, check their back trail, and fire. When they did, bullets would start flying from three directions.

For once, Kier did not appear to have an immediate plan of action. Reaching up, she tugged at her M-16. Kier stopped to slip the carrying strap from his torso.

Something Dunfee had told Jessie came to mind. The most brilliant escapes relied on distraction. But how could these men be distracted?

Desperation hatched an idea. Crawling onto Kier's back, she whispered in his ear.

''We need them to drop on the ledge, right?''

''To shoot them without their bodies falling—yes.''

Quickly she explained her idea.

Time stretched out. The passing seconds seemed like pearls dropping through honey. At any moment, they might be spotted—and her plan required time. They backtracked twenty feet to a slight bend where they would be less visible. After removing his pack, Kier donned the mountain-climbing harness he'd retrieved from under the cabin, then scampered up the rock face at the point offering the best handholds. He would have to traverse the face of the cliff above the men, using nothing but natural handholds and footholds. If no such climbing aids existed, or if he made a sound, or if the troopers happened to look up, that would be the end.

As he scaled the cliff, Jessie started to strip. There was no sexual purpose in what she did. These men would not be seduced on a rocky ledge or dissuaded from their plan by anything so pedestrian as sex. Of that she was certain. Rather her idea was to appear harmless. A naked person didn't pose danger. In the second or two that it would take for them to take stock of her, she had to convince them that she knew something important, even vital.

Her toes were three or four inches from the precipice. She held herself against the rock. After finishing the shirt buttons, she tried to shed the coats. First the outer arm. Dizzying height froze her mind and her movements. She took one hand from its solid perch, then shrugged her shoulder, slipping off the coat while rocking precariously on the balls of her feet. Her calves began to burn from the squatting.

Finally down to her bare skin from the waist up, she dangled her feet off the ledge, using it as a bench. Quickly she slithered from her pants, ending up in nothing but her panties.

Again she let her gaze go down the cliff. The drop was bad, really bad. One little teeter or slip and she would plunge. God, she had to put her mind someplace else.

Both groups on the ground had been moving continuously for an unusually long time. Surely they would stop and study the cliffs at any moment. When that happened, she would die in a hearbeat. The men in front of her appeared as only partially visible shoulders and elbows. Maybe eighty feet ahead, they moved cautiously toward the cavern.

Glancing at her watch, Jessie saw that Kier had been on the cliff for five minutes. She leaned out to see, then clung to the wall. Leaning had given her a greater sense of the abyss. He looked to be up about thirty feet and twenty feet forward. Shaking his head in disgust, he had pointed at the men with his silenced pistol and motioned her forward. *Damn.* He would try it from where he was, with an obscured line of sight and too far for a one-handed pistol shot. She would need to lure them a long way.

Her hands trembled. She hated her fear. With every passing moment the two men were getting farther away. Over and over she pictured herself falling—alive and bullet riddled. She stood and shivered in the freezing air. She stepped over the pack, and almost stumbled. The ledge was barely a foot wide. Around the slight corner she continued. The men still moved. Faster now, over one hundred feet away, and still looking toward the cave. She scampered fifty more feet, then squatted in the wind.

"Help me," she said in a small, terrified voice.

The men whirled. One almost lost his balance.

"What the hell?" The first squinted and leveled his M-16.

"He's after me. . . . Please . . . please . . . he's coming. . . ."

"Shoot the bitch."

"He's coming." She began the tricky task of retreating from the thugs while continuing to face them. Initially, she moved more quickly than they did.

"Wait. Don't shoot. I've got Volume Six."

Now they were coming closer. At any second they could blow her off the ledge in a bloody mist. But it was working. Glancing everywhere but up, they kept coming, gawking. Dropping her arms, she exposed her breasts. It took many more breaths than she cared to count for them to pick their way along the ledge.

"Get down, get down . . . he's behind me." She lay flat as she spoke, praying that they would follow suit.

Thirty feet from her, the first man dropped prone, aiming past her. His partner fell to one knee, doing the same. Then, as if seized by a new thought, the second man spun around and looked toward the cavern. The first now trained his M-16 on Jessie's forehead.

The farther man finally dropped to the ledge as the first lifted a radio to his lips. Kier had to fire.

Pffft. The first man's head jerked, blood spraying from his neck. *Pffft. Pffft. Pffft.* Three more silenced shots jerked his comrade's body. *Pffft.* The last bullet went just below the second man's helmet. An arm went over the ledge. The body quivered in a spastic curl.

Already Jessie was up and running, hunkered down, trying to catch the falling dead man. He was slipping over the side. Kier dropped in front of her like a vulture landing on carrion. He grabbed the body as it fell. Twisting, turning, Kier and the man both went. She heard a snap, then the climbing line draw taut. Kier hung from the safety rope in his harness, clinging to the body of the slain soldier.

Now what?

Kier wrapped his legs around the dead man and, incredibly, began pulling himself up the line. Grabbing Kier's arm, she pulled as best she could within the limitations of her precarious position on an eighteen-inch ledge. She felt puny and weak, but her efforts seemed to help.

"Again," Kier grunted, this time getting his arms and torso on the ledge, still gripping the man between his legs. "Take the line off my harness and wrap it around him."

It would require her leaning far over the edge. Kneeling squarely on burning knees on the rough ledge, she undid the large snap on Kier's harness with relative ease. But the dead man hung three feet below her. As if reading her thoughts,

Kier threw his right arm over the back of her calves, pinning her to the ledge. His left hand clung to the ledge.

"I can't do this much longer."

"Jesus," was all she said as she leaned over the side.

For a moment, vertigo paralyzed her. If Kier lost his grip on her or the rock, they would both go. She lowered the line between the mountain and the lifeless body, letting the snap dangle. She could not retrieve it except by hanging lower.

"I don't think I can do this," she heard herself say.

"We'll die if you don't."

Crying, she let herself go headlong, slithering down Kier's body, then over the dead man. Kier's fingers bit to the bone behind her knee. Life seemed so simple. The only thing between her and her maker was a single human hand.

"Lower," she said.

For a split second Kier let her leg slide through his hand until he locked his grip on her ankle. His arm shook with the strain. Sick with fright, she reached under and around the body. Stretching for the line, her muscles screamed all the way to her fingertips. She grabbed it, wrapped it once, then again around the dead man, and fastened the clip at the rope's end back onto the line.

"God, get me up," she said, almost certain he couldn't do it.

His arm quivered even more as he groaned with the effort of the one-armed pull-up. Dangling crazily, she clawed up the back of the dead body, and up Kier's thigh. Straining to reach behind herself, she felt the ledge and pulled sideways and up in a painful lunge.

Kier released the grip of his legs, allowing the body to hang from the line. He climbed the line onto the ledge and quickly hauled the dead soldier after him.

By cutting the snowsuits off the bodies, they made the dead men less visible against the cliff. The soldiers walking the mountainside below had disappeared from sight into the pines.

Behind them the other group was moving through forest interspersed with meadows and at the moment were out of sight. Kier and Jessie raced along the ledge again as soon as Jessie had regained her own clothing. Now Kier carried two more radios, eight more grenades, and extra ammunition.

With any luck, their adversaries' expectations would work against them—any soldiers who saw them would assume the two white-clad figures walking the ledge were their own. Tillman would be powerless.

Chapter 25

Tell an enemy a lie he wants to believe, not the lie
you want him to believe.

—Tilok proverb

Either the dead men or their missing voices alerted Tillman's
men. As Kier and Jessie slipped into the cavern, M-16 rounds
poured through the entrance. Dozens of bullets smacked the
stone with explosive cracks as the fugitives collapsed to the
side, exhausted. Kier held one of the new radios, waiting for
the parley he knew would follow. It didn't take long.

"Listen up there, Mr. Kier." It was Tillman. "Maybe we
can make a deal."

He had an edge to his voice that was starting to sound like
nerves.

"Tell me about the lab books," said Kier.

Silence for a moment.

"Why don't you come down and tell me? You've been
reading them. You come down, we'll talk."

"Do we seem that stupid?"

"You're stuck in a goddamn hole. No way out that we can't watch."

Kier laughed. "You'll have to do better than that."

"Punch your birth date into the radio, then press star."

Kier did as he was told, wondering how Tillman knew when he was born.

"Now it's just you and me. If we can make a deal, you can live."

"Quit wasting time. Tell me why I should make a deal."

"We've got your whole family in the palm of our hand— your mother, sisters, everybody. This is the big leagues. Mess with me, they die."

"Go on." Kier's voice remained flat, but he felt his heart in his throat.

"You give us our stuff, we give you your tribe. We'll give you the medicine they need to survive. You sign some documents admitting this was a big mistake. We sign documents admitting everything you did was in self-defense. You sign a confidentiality agreement with the government. Big misunderstanding. Everybody goes home."

Jessie grabbed the radio. "How the hell can the government be in on this?"

"Early on they sponsored some of the research. Now they don't want anything to do with it."

"The government never condoned experimenting on people. Not in this day and age."

"What? Jesus, you are a virgin, aren't you?"

"Why don't you give us just one name?"

"Why don't you get a life?"

"May I?" Kier said to Jessie. She handed him back the radio. "We know you've cloned people. You experiment on the infants."

"Mr. Kier, you *have* been reading."

"You developed a means of reading the human genome.

Then you wanted to learn gene function so you started on a computer model that would correlate particular genes to particular proteins. You made clones so you could control variables like disease and then watch which genes were implicated. You developed a chip technology for use with the clones, but you don't need it anymore. You've got yourself the best computer model in the world. But to do it, you had to experiment on cloned people and commit various other crimes.''

"Sounds pretty fantastic to me. Nobody's going to believe you without evidence.''

"You found a person denominated 1220, who seemed to have some interesting immunity. I believe it affected susceptibility to a virus dubbed RA-4TVM. One of your little sidelines was building viruses. It was a natural because you could read and manipulate DNA and RNA. RA-4TVM was your accident. And with all your knowledge I haven't figured how you screwed up or if mother nature bit you in the ass or what. Anyway, you came up with a live-virus vaccine for RA-4TVM. You also developed an antivirus that kills cells infected by RA-4TVM. Together AVCD-4 and the nif-plus deleted RA-4TV mutation vaccine can prevent and cure RA-4TVM. So far so good?''

"You haven't told me what RA-4TVM is.''

Kier hesitated, his mind spinning. He didn't know. Not even a clue.

"I think it's something you made. Probably you were trying to build a vector and it ran amok. Maybe mutated. Maybe combined with inert DNA from long extinct retroviruses that have become part of our genetic makeup. At any rate, you were convinced it was a great little delivery wagon and rushed its development. Something went wrong. A surprise. Why don't you tell me?''

"You deal with us and maybe we will.''

"But if you can manipulate genes, you can cure viruses. I figure that before you could figure a way to explain how you developed cures, you had to understand how the cure virus would behave in a population. Somehow, some way you made guinea pigs of my tribe.''

"God, what an imagination. But you're just daydreaming, Dr. Kier. It's an interesting fantasy. The fact is your people have a naturally occurring but as yet undiscovered virus. I happen to have the cure. We may have helped some couples with fertility problems, but that's it.''

"We're not going to get anywhere if you feed me your trumped-up stories.''

"I know a hell of a lot about you, Kier. I've been studying your clones. Fine boys. Maybe you'd like to meet them.''

Kier was stunned, unable to think properly.

"The number 042863 588561289 that was on the various tables in Volume Six. I thought maybe you'd recognize it.''

Then Kier saw it. It was his birthdate and social security number. He hadn't looked at those numbers at all because he had never possessed Volume Six.

"Why me? Why would you clone me?''

"Well, you among others. I had to clone somebody and you've got excellent genes. Half-breeds often do. Everything from your propensity to muscle, straight teeth, and facile brain, Kier. It's a compliment.''

"How many are there?''

"You cooperate and I'll tell you.''

"What are you doing with them?''

"Yours or other people's?''

"Mine.''

"Your offspring. They're safe." Tillman lowered his voice to a soothing tone. "Kier, you can save them and your tribe if we make a deal. But you're fantasizing about a lot of things. Nothing wrong with making a baby. People do it every day. You've got some odd ideas about what we're doing. But I can straighten out the misunderstanding.''

Kier felt disoriented, but he knew he had to maintain absolute control. "You're scuffing your hind legs a bit much—like a dog trying to cover his scat."

"We seem to have a chicken and egg problem here. If you're on board, we can tell you things. If you're not, naturally we'd rather keep our own counsel. I'm afraid you'll just have to trust us a little. You give me back what is mine. Then you get the young Kiers. You get your tribe safe from an unfortunate and naturally occurring infection. Those mink farms are a real hazard. I can tell you one thing. A lot of your people are gonna die if we don't make a deal."

"Call your men off, go back down in the valley. Then we'll talk about getting you your fifth and sixth book." Kier was trying to decide exactly how to run his bluff.

"If I pull back and you don't show up for the powwow, you're going to piss me off."

"You're not going to make a deal with this maniac?" Jessie whispered fiercely.

Kier patted her arm in reply, and shook his head.

"You go back to the Donahues' farm." Kier stood with the radio. "Wait with your radio on. I'll be there day after tomorrow at nine A.M."

"It doesn't take that long to walk out of these mountains."

"You'll forgive me if I don't trust you and take my time."

"You don't show, a lot of people are going to die." Tillman signed off.

She put her hand on his arm. For once there was no anger in her eyes.

"I am at a loss for words," she said.

He had never felt so bewildered. Obviously Tillman wanted to throw him off balance, and it had worked. The table of contents stuffed into Crawford's boot had a section titled "Adult Cloning Methodologies." It was now absolutely clear that it meant adult people, not adult monkeys. There had been numbers of four digits and each four-digit number was followed by a letter of the alphabet. Undoubtedly the four numbers were an abbreviation. Probably the first four numbers of the birth date. By running the numbers together with no breaks or slashes, it had not been obvious.

Perhaps Kier's number had appeared several times followed by an "a," a "b," and so forth. Or maybe it was only listed in Volume Six. He couldn't remember how many letters were opposite each number. Undoubtedly each letter was the designation for a child clone. He wondered who "1220" was.

"I know what you're thinking . . . my not having anything to say," she said.

Kier half smiled.

"Is it that funny?"

"Well, you're talking," he said.

"I know. I can't help it. It's so weird. So bizarre. Here you are with a whole bunch of little people who are identical to you. It would be like finding out you had a bunch of twin siblings." She paused and moved closer to him. "I'm sorry. I wish there was something I could do. How much like you do you suppose they'll be?"

She put her arm around him. He thought about how good it felt.

"God, they'll be a lot like you."

He put his arm around her and held her close.

"He really rang your bell, didn't he?"

Kier looked down into her eyes, seeing the trouble in them.

"I guess he rang my bell as much as yours," she continued. "I can barely handle one of you in this world. Now I find out I'm sharing the planet with several of you."

They sat, holding each other for a time. "You know he never would have conceded what he did, if he wasn't completely desperate," she said.

Kier nodded. But, he could find neither energy nor consolation in that thought.

"Maybe they were expecting the plane to crash," she finally said.

"They had to be expecting something ugly. They were here in force. Tillman's guy told me the fiberglass pods were supposed to have been dropped."

"If you did want to deliver something secret to Wintoon County, why would you drop it from a jet? Why not just drive in on the county road?" she said. "Maybe the goal was some illusion. Maybe the point wasn't to deliver something to Wintoon County. Maybe the real point was to make something disappear."

It was precisely what he was thinking.

Chapter 26

A young man will fight a bear, but a wise man will
hang the camp meat in a tree.

—Tilok proverb

"Worm's Way? I don't like the sound of that," Jessie said.
"Why not go back the way we came in—at Tree Cave?"

"It'll be okay."

"Exactly how small is it? How long is the tunnel?"

"Tight for maybe forty feet. But I can fit. For you, it'll be
easy."

She stared at him.

"You aren't normal, Kier. You're not afraid of things that
scare the piss out of most people. So when you say it's tight
for forty feet, what about the rest?"

"You crawl for a hundred yards, then lie flat on your back
for probably thirty yards. Then comes the tight part. Hopefully
not much rock has fallen down. I haven't been through in a
few years."

"Do the kids go there?"

"No."

"Why?"

Kier started to walk and decided to change the subject. There was no point in having her frightened out of her mind before they even arrived at the tunnel.

It took almost a half-day's hiking through the darkroom-black caverns until they stood before the telescoping rock passage that Kier called Worm's Way. They had used up two lights and were on their third, but they had several more lights from incapacitated or dead enemies.

Stooping to look, Jessie would have sworn the passage petered out just beyond the first bend sixty or seventy feet away.

"Can't be."

"It's an illusion," he replied.

Bending, she looked again.

"Once you get there it's not as tight as it looks. Around the corner it opens up a little."

"It's 140 yards to daylight?"

"About that, give or take."

At first it was easy to crawl, and although it got low at the bend, it did open some, just as Kier had said. They enjoyed three feet of clearance for the next thirty or forty feet around the bend, then almost had to drop on their bellies. At this point Jessie still had a couple of feet on either side, which helped control her claustrophobia.

Because they could not risk a light near the exit point, they had to feel their way from here. Kier could do little to make it easy for her. When they stopped for a moment now and then to take stock, he encouraged her by telling her how he admired her strength and her determination.

The air tasted stale and slightly bitter in her throat. She found herself breathing more deeply without knowing if it was from exertion or fear. A choking sensation began to overtake her. Diseases like hantavirus came to mind. It became easier to imagine the ceiling caving in, or becoming trapped, or dropping into some unknown shaft because they had taken a wrong turn.

"Talk to me," Kier called out as her chest heaved with choking.

"How much farther?"

"We're about halfway."

That pierced her like a knife. The earth was crushing in on her. She yearned to stretch her arms out at her sides, but couldn't. She inched like a caterpillar, but still felt her back rubbing against the rock above her. And up farther it would be tighter still. She couldn't imagine it. She couldn't imagine surviving it. The chill of the limestone under her fingers sent the lonely cold to her mind. She couldn't raise her forearms or hands more than a few inches above her head—a constant reminder that she was locked under a mountain of rock.

At the academy they had put her in a sensory-deprivation tank that they flooded with water in the darkness. The marines used it to deter the faint of heart. It had been disturbing, but as the sound of her heart had filled her ears, she told herself over and over: They won't kill you.

What could she tell herself here?

"I don't know if I can do this."

"Listen to me," he said. "Turn over on your back and close your eyes. You can be wherever you let your mind put you. Remember the bed in the cabin. Remember the stars."

In desperation she did as Kier said, barely able to roll in the confined space. She filled her mind with the way she'd felt under the night sky. When she had calmed herself again, she listened to his voice.

"We'll be there in minutes. Just minutes. Reach and grab the rock, then pull." She did it. "Pull," he said again and again, making a rhythm for her of reaching, pulling, and sliding.

The regularity of it was calming, breaking up the terrible pictures in her mind. She found herself breathing with every reach and every pull, enhancing the rhythm. Reach, breathe, pull, breathe.

They did not stop or rest again until they came to the tightest section.

"Now don't let your hands come back past the top of your head. Stretch yourself out. Think string bean."

At that she laughed quietly. Kier chuckled back. They started again. Now she could almost kiss the rock. Her knees could scarcely rise to dig in her heels. It was so tight she couldn't imagine Kier moving. At that moment her hands touched his feet. Oh God, no.

He was stuck. She could feel him struggling. Her heart jumped. Inside her head a small, imaginary Jessie cringed at things too horrible to contemplate. The feet ahead of her still weren't moving. There was only struggle. Too much breath rushed in and out to even ask. She couldn't bear the wrong answer.

Something in her mind started pounding. *Perhaps I'm coming undone.* She noticed her head moving wildly side to side as if a giant hand were making her say no. She wanted to scream, but didn't. Then a voice spoke in her head. Her voice. She was back under the stars. There was something tiny inside her that wanted to reach out to something huge, something infinite.

You need to be at peace inside the mountain, she told herself, imagining herself rising up out of her body and passing into the stone. In a few moments, it no longer seemed so confining. The mountain was still above her, but it didn't contain her. She was part of it.

Then she saw the face of her late father. Before she had time to think what the tears meant Kier's voice cut through her consciousness. For a split second, she had thought it was the voice of her father.

"We're gonna make it."

The feet were gone. Calmer now, her mind urged her forward. In seconds the light of day replaced the utter blackness. A minute more of squirming and Kier pulled her hands into a wide-open world. The air tasted like her mother's fresh pillow-cases. The little Jessie inside her head danced for joy.

It did surprise her that the men in white suits had disappeared like a bad dream. Kier speculated that Tillman would try to pick up their track in the morning after they had passed farther down the mountain. Tillman would want to feel in control. He would want to ensure that they kept the appointment. But he would be too shrewd to risk scaring them off by leaving men in place. Kier planned to leave no trail by following creeks, and once they got below the snow line, by sticking to rocky slopes and washes.

With the wind whipping her unprotected ears with enough velocity to make her jaw ache, the reptilian mist washing over her, Jessie needed all her faculties to step precisely where Kier did. To do this, she wore no hood or helmet over her head. When Kier insisted on some protection, she agreed to wear only the helmet. More than once (she supposed as a form of encouragement), he remarked that she had saved them on the ledge. Even so, one more freezing hike over dangerous ground on a hungry stomach meant misery on a scale she never cared to repeat.

She developed confidence in Kier's theory about Tillman's willingness to pull back only after they had traveled miles without incident. When they doubled back, there was no one following. Below the snow line now, Kier took them down then up and over a high ridge and down into a different drainage.

They walked beside a beautiful stream in the afternoon sun. To her amazement it made her forget her weariness and her hunger.

" 'The whisperings of the mountain are like laughter—nourishment for the soul,' Grandfather says."

Jessie's senses began to catch the special feeling of this wild place. They traveled a river trail worn smooth in the verdigris granite. Around them echoed the many sounds of moving water: its murmurs, its bright tones like loose change, its pelting drumbeat, and in the distance, its cavalcade roar.

She felt the intrigue of the forest for the first time. Angled shafts of sun met the trees' hefty, gnarled old arms ending in hands of feathery, green-needled leaves. The chilly breath of the woodland on a winter afternoon left this world of light and shadow tinted with the sparkling wet of fresh rain.

On one side of them, there was a six-foot drop to rushing water; on the other, the firs grew thick, overhanging the ancient pathway.

"Watch your step." He offered a hand as if she were a porcelain princess.

She smiled, feeling foolish for enjoying the man's peculiar chivalry when they had such a sobering obligation.

"Moccasins, mules, and hard heels have worn these trails in the rock for hundreds of years," Kier half whispered, catching her eye, making it hard for her to concentrate on the history.

She wanted to stop and talk. Actually she wanted to be close to him, but the fear of being ambushed and the need to press on kept them going.

Running over bedrock ledges into shimmering pools in a series of cascades, the river became a foaming roar in this part of the canyon—known as Spirit Gate. At the end of the cascades was a pool, surrounded by lichen and moss-covered rock, and ringed with old-growth fir, hemlock, and cedar. Jessie tilted back her head, awestruck by the timeless immensity of it all.

They stood on a gray-white rock beyond the reach of the spray from the last cascade, where a small clear pool mirrored the mountain. They stopped for a moment to drink.

Kier pointed at tracks in the mud. "Those are otter," he

explained. He pointed farther away to the water's edge. "Those are coon."

All around the soft dirt told the story of the passing little feet.

"I'm chilled." She moved against him, feeling slightly bold. She let her gaze wander across the mountain. One lone fir grew crooked, high up, out of what seemed to be a smooth rock face. Wanting Kier's touch, Jessie felt a kinship to the solitary tree.

After a time, a gentle hand rested on her near shoulder.

"This hasn't changed for thousands of years, I suppose," she said, pulling his arm around her and leaning into his ribs.

"What hasn't changed, the scenery or the other?" he said.

"Well, both, but I guess at the moment I'm thinking more of the other."

The creek took them to the bottom of Mill Valley to the Wintoon River, but at a point far above the Donahues' or Kier's cabin. Quickly they darted across the Mill Valley Road, over a still-snowy ridge, and down into an area where they had not yet been—a place Tillman was unlikely to search for them.

At the far side of the ridge, Kier stopped and listened. They were in a dense forest.

"There's a cabin that's mostly hidden in the trees. We can approach it without being seen."

The owner was known as Indian Lady Margaret, Kier told Jessie, as they neared the dwelling. Her husband had been a successful fisherman, both on the river and in the ocean. Full of youthful energy at seventy, Indian Lady Margaret still kept the summer place that she and her husband had long ago built on the side of the mountain. It sat far away from any public road at the end of a jeep track in a tiny, natural meadow left to the sun by the conifer forest. As they approached the back of the cabin, Jessie could see that its walls were built entirely of stone; from the outside it appeared solidly enticing.

All one room, it was nevertheless a good deal larger than the now-destroyed honeymoon cabin. Kier knew right where to find the key and promised that its owner would heartily approve of their use of the place. In minutes, they had a fire going in the stove. Among the luxuries of this cabin was a feather bed and running water that flowed by gravity from a spring higher on the mountain. It took only a little doing to prepare their leftover food. Kier said Margaret wouldn't mind if they borrowed a canned ham that Jessie favored over reheated beaver tail.

For light they had kerosene lanterns. Not as bright as a normal array of electric bulbs, the lanterns bathed the cabin in a soft yellow glow. The rock walls would have been positively chic in a downtown New York restaurant—here they made good protection. The furniture consisted of a rocker with layers of blanket tacked on for padding, an old but serviceable sofa flanked by two handmade tables, and a five-board kitchen table with four rustic chairs.

Kier and Jessie still had enough energy left to speculate during dinner about the airplane and their adversary's machinations.

After dinner, Kier rigged sheets around a large bathtub in the corner. Using water that had been heating since before dinner, he made her a shallow bath. Almost falling asleep, he threatened to assist her in order to get his turn. Although they both talked of sleep with real eagerness, they were running on adrenaline and could not turn their drowsiness into the will to crawl in bed. Giving up on sleep for the moment, they sat down for a dessert of canned peaches.

"How the hell did he get a piece of you to clone?" she asked.

"I had my jaw wired together at the clinic. It was three years ago. They put me to sleep. They could have done anything."

"Oh." After taking another bite of peach, she continued. "Why are you so aloof? With women, I mean."

"How did we get from cloning to . . . ?"

"Biology to love? I think for most men that's the natural

sequence of events, except maybe they don't usually get to the second part. So don't change the subject. We're on aloof now."

"Maybe I'm not altogether sure."

"But you admit it?"

He nodded.

"Of course, you're sure. You've had years to think about it. You are introspective. You can't fool me with those terse Tilokisms of yours. Tell me. I want to know."

"I suppose my dad dying the way he did, coated me with emotional veneer. I suppose if I am numb I wouldn't know, after all these years, that there is anything but numb."

"I don't agree. I think you understand stir the oatmeal as a no-risk deal. To understand that, you've got to understand the possibility of something else."

Kier shrugged and touched her face. She didn't pull away.

"At this point I nod and you talk," he said.

She laughed hard.

"You're attractive when you're demanding telephones."

"You think you can sidetrack me with secret eyes?" she asked. "What do you take me for?"

"Who gets the bed?" Kier asked, abruptly sliding back his chair slightly as if to stand up.

"You. I can fit on the couch," she said.

As before, Kier wore only jockey shorts, she his T-shirt with her panties, while the rest of their clothes dried. She glanced at him as she sipped the cup of instant coffee they had borrowed along with the ham and peaches. She wasn't going to badger him any further. She was tired of badgering men. This time Kier did not try to make love to her with his gaze. He sat circling his coffee mug with a finger.

"Well, we should sleep for a few hours before I take off."

"Meeting's not until nine A.M. the day after tomorrow."

"I'm arriving before daybreak."

"Really. And why are we arriving before daylight?"

"I am arriving before daybreak to take Tillman hostage. It's the only way to find out what is going on."

This engendered a thirty-minute argument in which neither of them made a single new point.

"Well, at least you can't win the debate by locking me in a hole," she said finally.

"Wine cellar. But forget it. You wanna come, you come."

Now she could feel herself squinting, suspicious that she was being tricked.

"When you do that, it makes each little line in your face get deeper," he told her.

They smiled, and she inexplicably knew that he wouldn't trick her again. She held his gaze for as long as she dared. In his eyes she found a knowing strength that reached to her core. On the kitchen table his large brown hand contrasted with the whiteness of hers. She wished to feel his rough hand moving over hers. Such a simple thing, she imagined, would be so pleasurable. But she felt guilty for the wish. Each move they made toward one another, each little intertwining of emotion and personality, would in the end be undone, leaving neither the better for it.

"Frank Bilotti," she blurted out without really having made up her mind to do so.

"Who?" he asked.

"My boss."

"Yes," he said after a long pause in which she struggled to gather her thoughts.

"And Gail is my best friend from way back. I would have trusted either of them with my life. No question. You gotta understand. Frank was my mentor. We never crossed the line, but we felt deeply about each other—or I thought we did. After I introduced them, Gail had an affair with him. He's married to Eva. First big mistake."

Kier's eyes scrutinized her.

"Got your attention, didn't I?"

He nodded slowly.

"It had been going on for months. Frank is rich, by the way. Frank inherited lots of money, and unlike most of us, he doesn't need to work. The Bureau was an interesting hobby in more ways than one. He was bringing her travel brochures and talking honeymoon when there wasn't even a divorce in sight. He said they could take their honeymoon even before they were married. I begged Gail, pleaded with her to forget him."

Kier's eyes were somber, intent. She could feel herself about to cry, and tried to hold everything still from her stomach to her lips. "Gail, my dearest friend, was such a schmuck." Now tears were running hot down her cheeks. She paused to catch her breath. "She just ignored the facts. He was never going to leave his wife. She actually began thinking I was jealous. And maybe I was, but not the way she thought.

"See, I couldn't work with him like I used to. All his help, all his insight, the coaching about how to deal with the bureaucracy . . . it was gone, dried up. I suppose my disapproval about the whole situation was just oozing out of me. My respect for him disappeared, and he could feel it.

"I was supposed to meet Frank and two other agents at his summer home for a brainstorming session on a tough case. They were going to raid a place I had identified electronically. Anyway, I show up unexpectedly early by several hours, and even from the patio I can see that Frank and these two guys are watching this video.

"I'm a little quiet, wanting to surprise them, and they're so busy watching the TV they don't even see me. The window is cracked an inch and I can hear them. At first I think it's like an X-rated film or something. I'm embarrassed. Then I'm horrified. It's a video of Gail having sex with Frank, and these three guys are watching. And get this—Frank is *commenting* on it, and it's sick. All of a sudden I realize he's this cold detached bastard who's just using Gail in the crudest possible way. Frank's face is conveniently blurred on the tape, some special effect, but Gail's isn't. And believe me, from Frank's commentary for the boys you know it's Frank. And you knew Gail never had a clue about this.''

Jessie had finished her coffee long ago, but she held the empty cup in a death-grip.

''I blew sky-high, barged in and told them what I thought of them.'' She stopped for a moment. ''Frank turned on me. Just like that. My mentor, this man I would have trusted with my life, says that if three top agents say it didn't happen, it didn't happen. Then he threatens me. He actually threatens me if I say anything.''

''What did he threaten you with?''

''You know this case we were supposed to be meeting about?''

Kier nodded.

''I had done some sweeps on the computer that required permission from above. Frank had given me the authorization. It's like a wiretap sort of, only with respect to a hacker's computer. I didn't do much of it, but another gal in our section did, and he was going to say it was all my doing. That I was trying to get ahead and it was all unauthorized. He said I'd get a failing performance review because of it. He would tell everyone that I had concocted this crazy story about the tape when all they were doing was watching an adult movie to pass the time.''

''Usually the truth comes out.''

''Oh yeah, right. Sure it does. But you've got no idea how somebody as powerful as Frank, with as many friends as he has, can screw up your career. And in the end I didn't have the tape. When I grabbed it, they took me down. Beat the shit out of me.''

Jessie pushed the coffee cup aside and looked away.

''So what did you do?''

''It got bad, Kier. I had to use my gun to get out of Frank's summer home. Then I just walked out of the New York office, took a leave of absence, and came up here, but not without telling Frank's boss, Grady White. He's the head of the region. I told him the whole thing—off the record. He's sweating like hell. He believes me, but he says I gotta make up my mind: Do I want to leave this for Gail to deal with or file a formal report?''

''What does he think you should do?''

''I think he just feels sick, and trapped, and he probably thinks I should come forward and nail the bastards. Either destroy their careers or let them destroy mine. Without me, there probably won't be anything official. I'm not sure Gail would or could do it alone. If I talk, a holy war's gonna break out in the ranks of the Bureau. We can't all survive, but we could sure all go down.''

Kier leaned back in his seat. ''After all that, you think there's no way the government could have sold out to Tillman?''

''I promise you, Kier, this is different. This is three guys and their twisted sex lives. It's hormones. It's not bribery. It's just not the same. And Frank Bilotti is *not* the institution.''

Kier nodded as if he understood. ''So when I met you on the road, when we were in the barn, all this time you've had this inside you. And you've kept it there.''

''Yeah. Until now.'' She let herself begin to cry, completely weary of containing it. The fear, the anxiety, the heartache, the lost affection for Frank, it all wanted to squeeze its way out through her eyes.

She knew that Kier's hand would not move. At the other cabin he had rebuked himself; he would not allow himself to be drawn to her again. Sorrow and depression had replaced desire and settled over her. But now there was something worse than Frank Bilotti and his betrayal. Jessie could see the disappointment in all of her tomorrows: the mornings she would awake and wonder if she were in bed with the wrong person. Of course, she realized, that would be the lucky result. Just as likely, she would die—die missing this last opportunity to finally connect with this man, this guileless man. And outlive her cynicism, if not her singleness. She did not know how to begin.

In his fingers Tillman held the picture of Jessie, and his eyes periodically darted to it. A great pressure was building in his mind. Outside he saw a faint movement in the blackness. It was the llama wandering across the front porch. A man went quickly by the table, obviously trying to avoid him.

"When's somebody gonna butcher that damn llama?" Tillman asked. "Walking around like that gets the sentries used to movement. It's dangerous."

"I'll see that she's put in the barn, sir."

Tillman grunted as if he was half satisfied. Obviously the man had developed some ridiculous attachment to the animal.

Ready at last to talk, he called for Doyle, who came immediately with his mug of coffee. Doyle sat heavily as though the struggle were equally his.

"So what will he do?"

"I think he'll come." Doyle spoke without hesitation. "You've got his family and he's smart enough to know it. But I don't think he'll come when he says. And he won't come peacefully, that's sure. He'll come to take you."

"When do you think he'll get here?"

"Tonight sometime."

Tillman leaned back in the chair and poured himself another cup of coffee from the Donahues' pot. Only Doyle knew that Tillman had been on the mountain. The others thought he had just returned from Johnson City. He hadn't even told Brennan.

"I don't think we dare do anything until he arrives here. These men aren't smart enough to ambush him without being detected," Tillman said.

"With a chap like this who knows the terrain, it's nearly impossible to move on that mountain without tipping him off.

Especially when we don't know where he's going to leave that cavern."

"I'm going to go out by myself tonight."

"I have an idea," Doyle said.

"Go ahead." Tillman took another sip and let his stare test the man.

"I'd like to talk to Kier and the woman alone. I'd like them to think I'm an undercover FBI agent."

Tillman lowered his chair to the floor, intent on Doyle's every word. "I'm listening."

"When I worked for Her Majesty's government, one of the things they taught us was FBI procedure. Even went to Quantico for a fortnight. Their antiterrorist course was supposed to be the finest in the world. If I could get with the FBI woman, talk to her, I believe I could convince her that I'm on her team. Maybe I could convince Kier. If either of them believed me, it would be over quickly."

Tillman reappraised Doyle. "Why does a man with your background go to work as a mercenary?"

"Had a run-in with my supervisor. He had strong feelings about my taking some favors from some rich business types. Just vacations. They were recruiting for private security. It was the one really thick thing I did, but believe me, it was enough. Got demoted very quietly. At first I thought it was a disaster. Until I learnt the private money was a lot better, if you don't count the lost pension."

Tillman was silent while he thought about it. Something made him slightly uncomfortable, but he couldn't put his finger on it. Maybe it was the way Doyle told the story so easily, as if he'd never lived it.

"How do you propose to do this?"

"Tonight we leave the greenest men in the house. You and I get on the most likely trails. We put a few more men, the best ones, in the woods around the house. We try to capture him or her—either one. Preferably the bird. But we've got no control over that. If anybody gets either of them at gunpoint, I come along and promise to save them when I can. Then I pitch them.''

"You turn them loose?''

"Certainly not. But if I convince them I'm on their side—maybe I can get the sixth volume.''

"Sounds like a long shot. Might work.''

"To make it work I need something.''

"What's that?''

"I need to know whatever Kier would know if he read Volume Six. If I were the FBI and investigating, you see, I'd know why the hell I'm investigating. Only way to be convincing is tell them some seemingly secret stuff.''

It was a seductive pitch. Doyle was the brightest of his men. The subterfuge would be elegant if it worked. Tillman wanted to trust him.

"In short, I need to know what's going on or I won't be effective.''

Tillman wanted a drink and rose to pour one.

"You like a Scotch?''

"Please.''

Tillman had discovered that the Donahues had no liquor cabinet. An oversize kitchen drawer held the libations. He removed a bottle of Glenlivet, amazed that the Donahues would have a single malt.

As he returned to the table and poured them two Scotches, neat, he decided to begin by giving Doyle a rundown of the Marty Rawlins diary, then observe his reaction before deciding how much more he would disclose.

He might even tell Doyle just how far ahead of the rest of the world he really was.

Chapter 27

One sunset with a maiden surpasses ten Tilok feasts.
                                        —Tilok Proverb

It didn't matter in what light he saw her, the clothing she wore, composed or unkempt, perspiring or chilled—he found her beautiful.

Kier wanted her.

Jessie seemed resigned to losing him, judging from her sigh, from the sadness in her eyes, from her frown. The gulf between them measured mere inches, but added to that separation were the expectations of his family, friends, and, even though he had not proposed marriage, the innocent expectations of Willow. Once Kier reached across to Jessie, would it be the beginning of a betrayal or the end of one?

He could not think of what to say or how to speak what he felt.

"I never asked you about the mare. What were you doing with the pointing and the chanting?" she asked.

"Body language that a horse would understand. The chanting really just underscores the body language . . . helps get their attention with the changes in volume and tone."

Finally he managed to move his hand so that it was touching hers. Every millimeter that separated them was closed by him. She gave him no help. But the feeling was heady.

"Body language is important with horses too, huh?"

"The most important by far. They're herd animals. In the wild, horses have a pecking order in their band. The lead mare enforces behavioral norms. When she runs a horse out of the herd to enforce discipline, certain things have to happen for the horse to be accepted back. At first the dominant horse squares off, looking the outcast in the eye—challenging. When the subservient horse turns broadside and cocks an ear, it's a half-apology, so to speak. If the lead horse is satisfied, it also turns broadside, takes its eye off the bad horse, and ignores it. If the half-apology doesn't work, the outcast may have to drop its head to get back in—that's a sure sign it wants to come back.

"I was using the two horses as a herd; I was the lead mare. I got her thinking about joining the herd. It's a natural thing for a horse in trouble. I just followed the pattern."

"How did you learn all this?"

"Here and there. A little from Grandfather. Mostly though from horse trainers—even books." He chuckled. "And vet experience. It's not genetic. We Tiloks walked around the mountains. My ancestors didn't have horses nearly as early as the plains Indians. Only the chant was Tilok, and it's a medicine chant to ward off evil spirits and promote healing. I don't know if it works, I just prefer it to humming or yelling."

"I read that people sometimes use body language more than they use words," she said.

"Yeah. First, they square off, like this." He looked into her eyes. "But with people it's more of an invitation."

"And how does a person accept this invitation?"

"Prolonged eye contact," he replied while she continued returning his gaze.

"Will that do?"

"That will do. Then you come closer to me."

In response she came around the table. He rose and she pulled him tight. "Like so?"

"You pick up on this very well. Now you get heavy-lidded and half close your eyes. Then you turn your face up just slightly."

Before she finished he covered her lips with his, silencing her next line.

She finished it in her mind: *Should I put my head down now?* The kiss was better than good. But when she looked into his eyes, she saw the trouble there.

"I'm not sure what we're doing," he said.

"I think," she said, her voice husky, "I think you're asking the wrong person."

She let her eyes meet his. Slowly, as if each millimeter were a separate and painful deliberation, he reached for her again. In him she saw a quiet desperation that he could never voice. They stood wrapped in each other's arms as the flicker of the dying lantern lengthened the shadows and the darkness enfolded them.

She felt no constraint but her fear. His hands moved over her back as if they were at worship, relaxing her, comforting her, making her want more of him. Having once touched, neither wanted to pull away lest good sense intervene. After the failing lantern died and they were bathed only in the soft glow of the remaining one, his searching eyes met hers. In them the pieces of her dreams fit seamlessly together. The touch of his finger across her lips was real, like the rough boards under their feet.

Taking his first finger between her teeth, she tasted his skin and nibbled at his knuckle. Then they pulled each other closer so that her breasts were pressed against his chest, and her lips wandered over his face, placing kisses on his light beard and weather-toughened skin. She learned the nuances of his body. Her hands moved first at the back of his neck, then to his shoulders and the mass of his frame. She ran her hands over his smooth chest, following the contour of a giant pectoral muscle, then teased his nipples between her fingers. On his belly she felt the coarse hairs. Then she cupped the bow of his erection through his cotton shorts. Trailing her fingers along its length, she felt the shudder run through his body. Looking him in the eye, as if daring him to flinch, she reached beneath his shorts and took hold of him.

She felt the tightening in his thighs. Kier's hand trailed across her shoulders. She pulled the cotton briefs over his thighs, strewing soft kisses down his belly as she went. He groaned with longing, and the strength of his hands on her upper arms made her feel delicate. She sensed his body stir with need.

When she saw the question form on his face, she breathed his name and put her lips to his to tell him nothing more need be said or committed to. Jessie pulled him to the bed. Slipping off her T-shirt, she stood before him in her pale blue panties. His large hands caressed her shoulders as he bent to kiss her neck. She shivered at his touch, and she knew with certainty that he was worth the pain of the good-bye.

Putting her hands on his bare chest, she urged him onto the bed, where he leaned back against the pile of pillows along the old mahogany headboard. His fingers interlaced with hers, and in that touching she felt his reverence of her and what they were doing. Moving over him, she wrapped her arms tight around his neck; putting her lips to his ear, she let him feel the heat of her breath.

After a time, she released him and sat back on his thighs. Her breasts were the size of apples but more conical than rounded, high and firm, never having nursed a child. Her nipples, a pastel of brown and pink, stiffened with desire.

Around her neck, the golden hue to her skin contrasted with the starker whiteness around her breasts. Kier drank in the sight of her, his breath catching at the excitement shining in her eyes. The swell of each breast in his lips, the eagerness in her body, her smell, her nakedness.

When Kier used his tongue to feel the texture of her aureola, she shivered and pulled his lips hard on her. He began to lick her, tasting the sweat from the hollow between her breasts. With rhythmic strokes of his soft tongue, he drew from her an urgent moan. She arched herself backward, rising up on her knees. Her long fingers, buried in his hair, pulled at him while his hand gently traced up her leg to the edge of her panties, where he let a finger slip beneath. Jessie's deep breaths told him that the slightest caress would bring her to the edge.

Her body became a telegraph, and Kier the recipient of each nuanced message. Touching Jessie's smooth-skinned back like butterflies kissing the wind, he felt her body coiling around him, the flex of her thighs. Soon he could feel her determined desire, the increased strength of her grip, the arch of her spine pressing his face to her chest. Together they stripped off her panties.

Her triangle was silken and dark, matted down so that it seemed close cropped. Like the rest of her, it struck him as petite. He cupped her face and kissed her fiercely, marrying his tongue to hers, exploring its edges, then its underside. Her legs wrapped like vines around his and he felt the urgency of her pelvis pressing against his thigh.

"I want you," he said simply, looking into her eyes.

Sensing what he wanted, she abandoned herself to his touches and the sweet words murmured over her.

"You are more than I ever conceived, more than I dreamed about," he whispered in her ear.

He put one hand on her bottom, bringing her up on her knees

and with the other, he sent feathery-light touches between her legs, setting her to groaning shudders. Then the little touches changed. Around and around his fingers moved, never quite letting her reach the peak of her frenzy, making her crazy with anticipation. A buzzing began in her lower back, then spread up and over her shoulders.

Her fingers dug into the heavy muscle of his arms as she guided him into her. She put her hand down to his and pressed his fingers to her, moving them in a secret rhythm, teaching him. Her breathing now came deep and regular, like an athlete hitting her stride. She rode him on a sheen of sweat that made their thighs buttery slick. After a time a trembling began in her, an ache with the rhythmic squeezing of her legs around his middle. The sweet sensation caused her entire body to cling to him, as if by squeezing tight she might find release.

As she reached for the culmination of her pleasure, her breaths grew ragged again, sounding to her own ear like great gulps of life. Her lovemaking was pure, unfettered by any weight of guilt or worry—she gave herself to it and to him completely. Without a promise or a vow, he had somehow filled her with trust.

In the clenching of her legs he could feel a building rhythm and her pleasant desperation.

She pushed her pelvis even harder into his caressing fingers, clinging to his head as if it were her savior in a storm.

"Please," she said.

Feeling her rush, the wild thrusting of her hips, he pressed on until she screamed her solace, then groaned in satisfaction.

When her breathing had quieted, she lay like a rag against him. She played a little game, squeezing down on him, then giggled when, with his own flexions, he signaled back.

"What are we going to do with this now that I'm spent?"

"Spend you again," he whispered in reply.

Leaning back, she gave a wicked little smile, and Kier covered her lips and neck with gentle kisses until the deeper kisses began again to seem intriguing. After that, she thought of nothing but the pleasure of his tongue on hers, and marveled at the escalating stirring in her loins. While she giggled, he kissed her body endlessly. Patiently, his tongue made long, slow strokes everywhere, as if it had lost its way. Her desire was a tiny cloud over a parched desert, and that cloud grew with the heat of the day until it rained great droplets of relief.

After, when she was floating high above mere physical wanting on the rising currents of her contentment, after her thighs were loosened and as much in love with him as the rest of her, she held him very close as he climaxed in shudders that lasted like August heat into Indian summer.

It was just before she drifted off to sleep that something her mother had once said shot into her mind. She stirred and repositioned herself atop his body.

"What?" he whispered, making her smile.

"What?"

"You're thinking something."

"Hmmm. That old Tilok instinct that saved our lives. Well, I'll tell you what. My mother used to say that sanity lies on the far side of an erection. So now that we're sane, where are we?"

He couldn't answer.

Chapter 28

The rules of the hunt do honor to whoever honors
them, to the good and the bad alike.
                                        —Tilok proverb

Adrenaline fueled her racing heart as Jessie glanced around
the thicket where she and Kier had hidden themselves. Looking
and listening for the men who hunted them, she strained all
her senses. Kier remained still and peered through his stolen
field glasses around the pasture at the Donahues' farm. His
calm, she knew, was like the eye of a hurricane—never far
from the turbulence of the engine that powers it. She was certain
that not a minute passed when he didn't think of his mother,
wondering if she was tied up in Claudie's house.

Starting at eleven P.M., Kier and Jessie had recrossed the
ridge and walked briskly for five hours, most of it sideways
and downhill along the mountain, covering a great distance in
relatively little time. As Kier had predicted, the heavy rains of
the warm storm had melted the snow at the lower altitudes,

leaving the ground and vegetation sodden and thus quiet underfoot. Water dripped steadily through leaves and branches, a percussion that disguised the sounds of their passage.

The Donahue house was perched against the mountain on a slight rise that overlooked a tree-ringed pasture that ran like a widening funnel down the hill. Jessie guessed that they sat behind the several huckleberry plants some two hundred yards from the house.

Kier dropped one hand so that she could mesh her fingers with his. After twenty minutes of quiet observation, they had seen nothing except shadows moving against the curtains inside the house. They were not expected for another twenty-nine hours. Most of the men were probably still combing the mountain for their track.

According to Kier, at 5,800 feet, Elk Horn Pass was high enough that it would still be plugged with snow unless the largest plows had cleared the way. He suspected that Tillman had by now a stranglehold on access to the valley. The snow would be a perfect excuse to keep people out. Assistance, they decided, was unlikely.

Kier dropped the binoculars and turned to her. His hand went to her cheek; his eyes, she knew, were pleading.

"Just say it," she said, taking hold of his hand again in frustration. "You want me to stay here, only you haven't got a cellar to lock me in or a prisoner to leave me with."

Kier nodded in response.

"If you don't come back, I'm coming in."

Kier nodded. "I'll leave you a radio. But if I use it, things will be tough. I imagine they'll pick up anything we say."

They held each other for a few moments without speaking, each one trying to take in as much of the other as possible. Then they kissed—one of those kisses in which people try to transplant a part of their soul.

Kier removed his pack, took the M-16, two hand grenades, and a silenced .45. When he was ready to leave, he placed his

NECESSARY EVIL   309

forehead against hers. She bridged the darkness to his eyes by cupping a small penlight in her hand. Even though the light shone for only a few seconds, it was a risk, and she knew it. As he turned to leave, the image of his dark eyes burned in her mind.

In the deep forest, the night was like dark chocolate, and for Jack Tillman, just as palatable.

Moonlight sifted through broken, spiraling clouds made ghosts of the cattle. He sat yoga-style under a bush, absolutely still, save for the slight movement of his head, mind focused on his prey. Only the slight working of his jaw muscles and the gentle touch of his thumb to a razor-sharp knife would have told an observer that Tillman's meditation was of the devouring, hateful kind.

Down the pasture stood the house, looking like a small ship with gaudy lights floating on a black sea. But for all the light, the place stood absolutely silent as a church at prayer time. Inside many of his men waited, nervously fingering their rifles, thoroughly spooked by the Indian who had crippled or killed so many of their comrades. These were the sacrificial goats, placed in the house to cast shadows.

Tillman did not expect his invited guests until just before daybreak, which would be awhile in coming. He was almost certain the danger would make them want each other. He sensed their attachment from the track—from the way they walked together.

After they "made love"—he was sure they would call it that—the Indian would stash her and come alone. But she would be nearby. He was counting on that for his preferred plan. Actually, taking Kier's mother hostage had been too risky—although Tillman had her and the Tilok tribe just as surely as if they were hog-tied in the Donahues' living room.

For some reason, the jet had crash-landed over the drop zone largely intact instead of exploding in a billion pieces over the ocean, as had been the plan. The one merc lying on the snow had been shot in the head—as to the rest of the mercs and science types, there was no telling. By the time Tillman and his men arrived, the plane had been burning for minutes.

Now only the fifth and sixth volumes were missing—the sixth a renegade binder that never should have been made. Tillman needed to know what the Indian and the woman had seen at the plane. He had to know if anyone else had been there. With that information, he might put the pieces together and find the missing volume. If the wrong people recovered it, he was as good as dead.

As he watched the night, his mind turned to his man Jensen and their last conversation. He could recall nothing in Jensen's manner or words to indicate that he wasn't following directions. Of course, they hadn't talked much before Jensen breathed his last on the floor. Even so, he replayed it all again.

Stuffed animal heads hung on all four walls, all predators except the rhino and water buffalo, making it the most politically incorrect office of any *Forbes*-listed billionaire in the United States. Absent were the trophies of his corporate plundering.

Tillman had been waiting for Jensen, who was late and probably hesitant. It was in the nature of men, especially scientists, to go soft. People like Marty Rawlins began as vigorous pragmatists but, as they aged, became concerned that they were doing the "right thing."

A case in point was the three-ring binder, the so-called Volume Six, sitting on the green leather inset of his rosewood desk. In his desperation, Marty had written every damned thing down, or most of it—enough to hang them all. This was the only copy outside the lab. The faithful had smuggled it to Tillman to prove Marty's treachery. Once the lab records were separated from Marty, he would be dealt with—but not until.

The scheming had seemed endless, but at last things were in place. He pushed the com button on his telephone.

"Where's Jensen?"

"He's not in his office," the nervous voice of his secretary came back at him.

Tillman smacked the com button, and it occurred to him that his icy cool temperament might be heating up a bit. Taking a deep breath, he brought back the absolute calm and allowed reason to reassert itself.

Marty Rawlins, the master egghead, had to go, and so did most of his immediate support staff. Although Paul had just received his Ph.D., he was aggressive and brilliant like Marty. Tillman had groomed him carefully and absolutely convinced himself of the young man's determination. Nothing would stop them now. Paul had no trouble with the human tissue concept. And more important, he understood Marty's new DNA work— at least well enough to coordinate the work of the other senior scientists.

"Jensen's coming in," his secretary's voice told him without warning. He made a note to fire her in the morning.

"Everything set?" The tall, graying man approached his desk. Tillman noted Jensen's eyes running over the heavy canvas drop cloth on the floor.

"Just painters," Tillman said casually.

"Oh," Jensen said, looking as if the canvas might somehow gobble him up. "Everything is ready. Everything is exactly on schedule," he said. "They'll make the drop from four thousand feet . . . exactly five hundred feet above ground level. Then they'll pull up, and when they pass through twenty thousand feet—boom. They'll be off the Mendocino coast. Ocean's over a mile deep. I don't think there'll be a piece left bigger than a few square inches. It'll look like a fuel tank blew and then set off some oxygen bottles for the big boom. If they figure it was sabotage, we can blame one of those antitechnology terrorists."

"Mind locking the door?" Tillman asked from behind his

desk. He doubted the authorities would be so easily placated, especially given the magnitude of the explosion. But he would worry about that later.

Jensen went to the door and turned the heavy brass knob.

"I'd like to show you something," Tillman said, beckoning Jensen back to the desk.

When Jensen returned, Tillman removed a Beretta 9-mm., loaded with subsonic hollow point shells and a Nexus grease-filled suppressor. This kind of silencer was super quiet for two or three shots—then the grease would require repacking. If Tillman fired only one shot, aiming square in the center of Jensen's chest, it was a virtual certainty that the bullet would not emerge from what was left of Jensen. There would be no messy lead traces in the woodwork. But it was not his plan to fire that shot unless required.

"What are you doing?" Jensen gasped.

Tillman studied the man's eyes as they widened in terror. There were creatures of flight—these were usually the vegetable eaters. Then there were those who wanted to fight before they died. For the most part these were the predators. Surprisingly, Jensen was turning out to be an herbivore. This would be easier than he'd thought.

"Relax, Jensen. I just want you to take a little nap until this is all over." Tillman removed a plastic bag from his desk, then rose to come around to Jensen.

"But why . . . ? I . . . I've done everything you asked . . . everything—"

"Stay calm and I won't kill you. Otherwise you're going to end up on the canvas, bleeding from a punctured heart."

In the bag there were several large, soaked cotton balls.

"What are you doing?" Jensen's eyes flashed to the canvas as panic began to control him.

Tillman stepped behind him, congratulating himself on his judgment. He knew he had been right. The man was weak. He could be broken. With practiced ease Tillman slipped a pair of handcuffs on Jensen. He took the bag from the floor where he had dropped it and slipped it over Jensen's head.

"Please . . . you can trust me—" Jensen choked as much from panic as the lack of oxygen. It took only seconds for the chloroform to do its work.

Jensen's eyes seemed to bulge, remaining open as if he were staring at some far-off place. They were brown eyes, but now appeared clearer and lighter, which Tillman found interesting. Foam collected at Jensen's lips and his hands opened and closed as if trying to grasp something. Out of interest in what might happen, Tillman undid the cuffs, but Jensen was too far gone to even try to save himself. Perhaps it was involuntary, or perhaps he could see eternity rushing at him, but Jensen now grasped at the air in front of his face, reaching for something only he could see. Around his fingernails the flesh was turning blue.

Tillman caught Jensen as his knees began to buckle, and then he smelled the man's defecation. Tillman knew from years of experience that mammals sometimes evacuate their bladders and bowels in their death throes. He had prepared for just such an eventuality with the plastic-lined canvas.

With some care, Tillman wrapped the body in the plastic-lined canvas and placed it in a giant nylon bag that would otherwise have housed his hang glider. Hang gliding was a sport whose benefits, he now decided, extended beyond the obvious.

Tillman would personally put the body in the trunk of his car, take it to the jet, and put it in the cargo hold.

Later, a witness would swear he saw Jensen walk onto the doomed plane with the other passengers.

Tillman reattuned all of his senses to the night landscape. His eyes worked the edges of the ravine and the pasture below. He listened for the slightest variation in the forest's sounds, for any sign of a creature's alarm that might signal an intruder. There were rustlings, small noises, but nothing he could identify as human.

So far Kier had preferred to fight alone, leaving the woman nearby, where he perceived she would be safe. Odds were he would follow the same pattern now—bring her partway, then leave her.

The question was where Kier would leave the woman. If she was an ordinary woman, he would leave her far back; but in her case, where she herself had killed and killed well, it could be much closer. She would be aggressive, insisting that she should come along. Perhaps she would come the whole way. Tillman would wait near the base of the ravine until daylight, when he would hunt the woman. If Kier and the woman hadn't arrived by dawn, he would change his strategy.

It was from the corner of his eye that he caught the flicker of light. What he saw lasted no more than a few seconds, but it was all he needed. It was not worthy of the Indian to make such a mistake. He knew it was either the woman's carelessness or a trap. It had come from below at the edge of the pasture. If he was correct about the light, they had slipped past him undetected or taken another route.

If Tillman could capture the woman, he would not follow Doyle's recipe in its entirety. Instead she would be suitably tormented, then brought to the Donahues', where Doyle would slip into her room and reveal his FBI status. Tillman would have her in a controlled environment where she couldn't escape. The thought of softening her up sent a wave of anticipation through Tillman. His heart quickened with the mental image of her bound and helpless. It struck him as an odd reaction. Rape was normally the province of lunatics, the exception being in war, where for centuries rape served as an effective means of subjugation. If the best means of rattling Special Agent Mayfield was to take her sexually, then that certainly made it an appropriate tool. Sexual submission would make a woman like her feel especially helpless. For that reason alone he would consider it. Once she felt weak and vulnerable, Doyle's story would come as sweet relief.

Tillman rose, using his peripheral vision to navigate in the darkness along the ravine and to the edge of the forest. The pasture grass had spread beneath the trees. Its moisture and the sodden leaves made for quiet walking. With care he could approach within inches of the woman and she wouldn't even know he was there. A cluster of three tall fir trees stood near the spot where he had seen the flicker. He guessed the distance along the fence to the fir. By his estimate, it was one-third of the way across the back of the pasture, which he knew to be approximately seven hundred feet. Merely to arrive at the juncture of the back fence and the side fence would require twenty minutes. He took one step at a time, listening before taking the next. In the forest the dark was so heavy that it seemed to have texture. Only out of the very corner of his eye could he discern rough shapes.

With every step, he made an instinctive calculation of his vulnerability to detection. In the pasture there was enough light that someone hiding in the forest might see him as a silhouette unless he kept trees between himself and the open field. As he turned down the fence line that would take him to his goal, the brush became less dense, the forest more open. Even so, if she was hiding perfectly still and low to the ground, it could take hours to find her. And then, if he did, she might see him first.

It was an interesting problem. She had obviously begun as an utter neophyte in the woods, but since fleeing with Kier, a real tracker, she had no doubt learned much. The two men who had stalked her on the mountain were dead—and one of them had been shrewder than most. The thought that she was dangerous made her powerful, and power made her appealing.

Silence pervaded the night forest in winter more than at other times of the year. On this late fall night, there was little to disturb the quiet except the *tap, tap* of water on the forest floor.

A scampering on a tree might have been a squirrel or tree vole. Farther on came the barely audible splashing sound that Tillman took to be a coon washing its dinner. Cattle occasionally rose and moved about the pasture, but none blew in alarm as he glided by.

After getting within thirty paces of where he thought she would be, he slowed so that he moved no faster than a few feet a minute. Tillman allowed his mind to think of nothing but the woman. Somewhere nearby she waited—perhaps with the Indian, but probably not. Remaining absolutely silent was essential, if he was to detect her first. Since she carried a silenced pistol, she could kill without alerting any of the sentries posted around the house.

The tension was exquisite.

He moved into an area overrun with oaks and a few smaller, scattered Douglas fir. In the shade of the trees grew large sword fern with an occasional huckleberry and more manzanita. He felt a needled bough in front of him, and could barely discern the outline of the tree, which was maybe twenty feet high. The top, which drooped in an arch toward the ground, identified it as a hemlock. Beneath its bushy boughs would be a likely hiding place. Squatting slowly so as to remain silent, he listened and sniffed for several minutes. There was no sound, nor could he smell any odor, but he felt a presence, like a pause in a speech, where the forest was the orator, and he the audience. Or was it his imagination?

Light as soft as satin sheets, as subtle as the warmth of winter sun, began to spread across the eastern sky as the full moon came from behind a cloud. Soon the pale light would encroach on the mystery of the darkened forest and find its way beneath the hemlock. But before its faint glow lightened the part lowest to the ground, it would expose him. Gradually, he moved to his belly, knowing that now he would have to work even more slowly.

Unless she had moved, she must be close.

Chapter 29

Value patience over the chase and you will have
meat for winter.

—Tilok proverb

It was what they called a deer trail, but it looked too big and
obvious for just deer. Here, at the base of a steep hillside well
back from the pasture, people and livestock had taken to using
it. For that reason the trail was easy to follow. Kier stepped
well off the worn pathway to the slope above, going slowly,
expecting to find a sentry lying in wait.

When he was no more than one hundred feet from the house,
a single snap, probably the sound of a boot heel on brittle dead
wood, alerted him. His hand caressed the grip of the silenced
.45. Just in front of him there was a large huckleberry with
interlocking stems. By turning sideways he managed to get
through without making a sound. Nearby there was a small
conifer, which he stepped behind, waiting. Whatever had made
the noise stood close. The air shivered with the silence.

In moments of stress, the mind moved oddly along several parallel tracks, but always shouting the question: When? When? When? Drawn like all men to induce the tragedy, to anesthetize the agony of anticipation, Kier felt the temptation to move, to explore.

But he was calm and he let his meditation make him part of the whole of the place where he stood. He relaxed his muscles, relaxed his breathing to become deep, and perfectly controlled, allowing his senses to expand, to reach out. He became, in his mind, content with this place, as though he might remain here forever. All urgency departed him. Only the smooth metal of the trigger under his finger connected him to the struggle. He waited longer still. A tiny rustle of a night breeze, just enough to nod the foot-high grass, passed by. Then a muted, throat-clearing sound jarred the stillness.

It was an incredible blunder. Perhaps too incredible. He remembered Tillman on the mountain, shadowing his own men, and pondered whether this might be a similar ploy. He once again scanned 360 degrees. In the shadowy grays of forest in the moonlight, it would be hard to discern a man. He saw nothing.

The man making the sounds would be on the far side of a dense manzanita just ahead. Curving around the brush clump and through a tiny clearing, the trail would lead Kier into an ambush at very close quarters. Behind the manzanita was a large stump, perhaps four feet wide, which no doubt provided a shield. Kier waited.

The first awareness of the second man was not an instant in time. It was more like an itch that had no true beginning. While he believed he smelled the body odor of a man, there was no certainty. A rabbit's track in a vestigial snowdrift veered as if the little animal had detected something on the side of the trail opposite the manzanita, where a car-size boulder protruded from a hillock. An old dogwood stood stark and almost leafless against the granite. Suspicion that someone might easily hide behind the boulder became a conviction without conscious thought.

Another throat clearing from the stump failed to distract Kier's attention from the boulder. He searched the hillside for areas where he could observe the trap. Because of the dense foliage, there appeared to be no spot that would afford him a good view. Darkness had now given way to the full moon, finally broken free of clouds. It was the brightest of nights, and Kier knew he would need to move quickly. Slipping back through the brush along the trail about thirty feet, he placed a small flashlight in the pathway and turned it on. Next he retreated up the hill and into the forest about twenty feet, where he pointed his silenced pistol at the ground and fired.

"Mother of God," he groaned in his best Irish brogue, a decent imitation of Jack Donahue's father.

Silence. No movement. Careful to avoid the snapping of twigs or the sound of branches on fabric, he made his way through the forest back toward the manzanita. As he approached it, he saw a soldier moving along the edge of the trail toward the flashlight. Slipping quietly to the ground, he lay still, straining to hear the man's hurried whispers over the radio. He tensed as he considered that they might call in an army of shooters, but held his fire, gambling that they would not. First they would reconnoiter.

In seconds, the man had the flashlight. Then there were more whispers on the radio, which Kier again couldn't understand. Finally the man began to cast about in the brush near where he had found the flashlight. Kier turned his attention to the terrain around the rock across from the manzanita, observing a movement so subtle that to be certain of it was difficult. Perhaps there was a watcher.

The second time he saw movement, he could just discern the outline of a helmet. Next he was able to define shoulders and a torso, and then it became apparent that the movement was the slight nod of a head, full in the moonlight, as the watcher listened to his radio and shifted his gaze from side to side for danger. Kier began to get a sense of him. This fellow was much more careful than the first. He appeared calm, but it was a purposeful, deadly calm, revealed in ways that Kier could not yet pinpoint except for the slow deliberation in his movements and a certain detachment that they betrayed.

Kier suspected he was a leader, but not Tillman. Perhaps the second in command. With this came the realization that his task was becoming infinitely more complex. The watcher was a man who needed to be captured or killed—not merely wounded. To take his time and undertake a stalk would not work. Daylight would come too soon.

In his pocket he carried a garrote—a piece of wire snare with a stout wooden handle at each end. Now he removed it, moving back toward the man who searched the brush near the flashlight. In three minutes, he stood beside an old alder, its base immersed in a big manzanita that afforded him cover in the filtered light.

Forty feet away, behind some black oak and a smattering of head-high fir, was the man who hunted him. He was using the barrel of an M-16 to probe the brush diligently, perhaps expecting at any moment to find a wounded Irishman.

Watching him make ever-widening circles, Kier realized it would take too long for the man to pass close enough for the garrote. The silenced pistol would be too loud. Several feet away lay a faint trail through the brush, a natural corridor. Perhaps Kier could somehow use it. He crawled to the narrow opening and sat down in the middle of it. A large oak spread itself over the trail. One hefty branch passed through the tops of some incense cedar. Quietly, Kier climbed the oak, hooked his legs over the branch, and hung by his knees over the trail. Against the thick foliage, he would be invisible unless somebody shone a light skyward. Kier groaned loudly like a dying man, and immediately the footfalls of his quarry went silent.

He groaned again, twisting his voice into a wounded man's despair.

With luck the man would come with his eyes cast down, his light creeping just ahead of his feet, and his mind on a half-dead man who must surely be lying on the ground. Footfalls moved rapidly through the forest, and a light beam scurried among the trees. The movement stopped, started again. At first Kier got only glimpses; then his heart sank. The man had wandered off the trail.

Not aware enough to find the natural passage through the brush, the hunter, obviously tired of looking, forced his way through the manzanita, the tick weed, and the red bud. Kier tensed and drew the .45 from his belt when the fellow stopped short. Twenty feet separated Kier from his hunter. Kier barely breathed. He knew the man was listening for any sound, searching for any clue.

The light began moving around the brush. He came forward—ten feet away. Kier's concentration sharpened; his body was a taut-muscled spring. Damn! Veering off, the merc passed just out of reach.

Blood pounded in Kier's head and his feet began to tingle from the loss of circulation. He asked himself how long he could hang this way and still remain effective. The weight of the .45 put a slight ache in his extended arms. The discomfort would grow until finally Kier would be unable to maintain a firing position. By pulling the gun to his chest, he reduced the muscle fatigue.

At last, the man found the break in the foliage and began following it, apparently giving up his random search. Slipping the pistol into his belt, Kier once again readied himself. At about five feet from Kier, the man stopped, knelt down, and began moving the outer branches of the cedar. He was crawling, searching beneath the foliage.

Kier knew he had to act. If the man went beneath him he could drop from the branch using the wire as he fell. Seconds stretched to minutes and still the man stayed away. By now Kier's feet were numb and his head felt swollen. He clenched the wooden handles of the garrote, his fingertips unconsciously caressing the coarse wood pegs. He concentrated again on his target until the man moved almost directly beneath him. Kier looked for the watcher, the smarter one, but saw nothing. He positioned the wire, took one deep breath, and released his knees.

The damp leaves of the forest floor under Tillman's bare palms, the cool of autumn rushing down his throat, the feel of his instincts guiding him to yet another quarry—these things enlivened him. Only the threat posed by an unsuccessful outcome nagged at him. Once again it occurred to Tillman that his personal intervention was required at every turn. When they desperately needed a breakthrough in testing methodology, it was Tillman who first insisted on cloning infants in a Brazilian laboratory. It was he who determined to use Tilok women as surrogate mothers, and it was he who had the foresight to make the baby clones brain dead. Although some of the others recognized the necessity, it was Jack Tillman who had to come in one Saturday to apply the needle to the thirty infants. No one else had the courage to move the project forward.

He had assembled the babies in New Mexico at a high desert viral research laboratory. Marty was due to arrive in two weeks. Of course, Marty could never be told explicitly what had been done. For the record, the two men Tillman had told of the plan said it was unethical and they were absolutely opposed. Yet on the day in question, the five senior lab personnel managed to be absent for the afternoon without any further discussion or explanation.

In the room normally reserved for autopsies and tissue samples, six of the babies were lined up like little loaves of bread on three stainless-steel tables. They were still wrapped in their blankets and strapped to miniature eggshell-foam mattresses. The other twenty-four babies lay in plastic cribs lined with the same material.

The lights had been dimmed, but that would not suit his needs. When he turned on the high-intensity fixtures, many of the babies began to wail. It perturbed Tillman that all the babies were positioned to stare into the manmade sun. Someone should have provided for a means to shade the babies' eyes. Nobody was paying attention to details.

Tillman had received hypothetical instructions. Plunge the hypodermic into the diamond-shaped fontanelle, the soft spot at the top of the baby's head. Someone mentioned anesthesia, but Tillman hadn't the time. He viewed his next act like a late-term abortion, except that the remaining tissue would mimic life and serve the cause of critical research.

He reminded himself of this several times as he filled the first hypodermic. The syringe's ten-gauge needle, a relatively large bore, was calculated to make the process go as quickly as possible. In a few minutes, the infants would become human tissue—no more and no less.

Since it was important that there be no infection, he used a small razor to shave the downy hairs from the scalp before applying alcohol with a swab, followed by Betadine. Grasping the head firmly in his left hand, he felt the fontanelle. Only skin, the epidura, and the meninges separated the brain from the external world at this stage of development. He would angle the needle toward the frontal lobe with his right hand. He wondered if he ought to feel something. But noting that he felt nothing, he told himself that he had achieved a clinical detachment.

Now, in the high mountains of northern California, on a lonely stalk, Jack Horatio Tillman struggled to find that same clinical detachment. His frustration with Kier and his own men made it difficult, but finally he thought he had succeeded.

He had entirely circled the small hemlock before he realized that something bulky appeared wrapped around its base. If it was the woman and she had seen him, he was in trouble. This was the last thought he recalled before his chest exploded in a kaleidoscope of pain and he felt the bone-crunching thud of a subsonic .45 slug strike the steel plate in his body armor. It was the angle that saved him from serious internal injury.

His instinctive cunning left Tillman looking like a ground-sluiced dove. Slumping as though dead while in extreme pain was not something most men could do well.

His ribs were just bruised, he told himself. Nevertheless, it would be hard to have his first FBI agent while in this much pain. Ever since the thought had sprouted in his mind, it had been growing. Something about possessing the woman behind those eyes had stirred the pit of his being in a way he wasn't often moved. Now that she had shot him, his urge had become a passion. The picture of Jessie he had taken from the Donahue lady still lay in his pocket. Odd that he could become so intrigued based on nothing more than dead bodies and a photo.

Above the screaming pain, Tillman felt the quiet. She was waiting. Smart. Then he heard a rustling as she slithered over to him. He lay absolutely still, rolling his eyes back in his head. When she lifted his lids and shone the little light, he would appear gone.

Chapter 30

The test of rabbit is winter. The test of bear is
spring. The test of man is his wanting.

—Tilok proverb

The great cliffs overlooking the Donahue farm and rimming
the river valley looked impressive, even at night. With the
passage of clouds, the moonlight shafted down through billowy
openings, revealing the texture of the mountain, its overlapping
rock slabs and tree trunks in several shades of black. The nearby
pasture had turned almost gray with light, its cattle moving
lazily as they grazed.

Sitting was much tougher than doing something. Still, Jessie
had elected to huddle under the tree. She was glad she had
when the man came crawling through the forest at the pasture's
edge. At first, all she saw was a shifting pattern in the darkness
so elusive she couldn't be sure it was anything. Then, looking
from the corner of her eye, as Kier had taught her, she distin-
guished a head. When the head disappeared, she found a torso,

or so she thought. Whoever it was, he was frighteningly close. He hadn't whispered the Tilok password given her by Kier.

She wanted to squeeze the trigger, but all she could think was: What if I puncture a lung? What if I explode a heart? She was not an executioner. And there was plenty of time before the squeeze to think these and the other thoughts jumbled in her head . . . until she let her finger pull and heard the muffled spit of the heavy-caliber handgun.

The dull thud of the bullet preceded a gush of air from the lungs that made her stomach roll. If he'd been wearing a jacket, he might have suffered only bruised ribs and some thumping of the internal organs. As much as her trembling hand would allow, her gun remained riveted on the almost-invisible form. At the least movement she would shoot again. But nothing, not even a groan, indicated the man had survived the shot. No conscious person could lie motionless in that kind of pain. She waited a minute more, then crawled forward.

It was only a few feet, but she went slowly, watching, listening, with the gun pointed. When she knelt a foot from the stalker, she put her fingers to his carotid and found a pulse. Feeling the torso, she found a bulletproof vest under the camouflage coat and in the sheath across the front a dented steel plate. She had struck only a glancing blow.

She pulled off his helmet, keeping the gun at his temple. "If you can hear me, asshole, don't even twitch or I'll blow your head off."

He did seem to have a large head. Pulling out her penlight, she shined it in his face, then rolled back the eyelid.

As she did it, she leaned over him, pressing the gun to his temple. More quickly than she could have imagined possible, his head jerked up. Automatically, she fired the gun. Missed!

One of his hands buried itself in her hair, yanking her head to the sky while the other grappled with the gun. Two more shots discharged into the night. Now pulling the trigger would do no good because he was stronger—he was aiming the gun.

When she brought her knee slamming up into his ribs, he moaned through gritted teeth. Her head went backward with his hand. Drawn by the fierce pain, her left hand went to the back of her head while the other stayed with the gun. Jessie was fighting a man with the strength of a maniac. He easily wrenched the gun away, and when she rolled, he was on her, clawing at her throat.

Jessie went crazy, kicking and tearing at him and the earth. Like a hungry animal he came after her and after her, bearing down on her until his grip closed on her throat and his grunts turned to satisfaction.

Her head felt heavy. She wanted only air. The hand gave way just a little and she breathed. Still, she was fading. The blood to her brain was being cut off. Like a drunk drowning in a puddle, she was watching herself die.

Her arm flopped. His grip relaxed a little more. She saw only a large round shadow where his face should be. He climbed on top of her, parting her legs around him and moving in tight. God, no. The realization spread like a dread disease. She sensed the sex. He brought the barrel of the gun under her throat.

"Where's the Indian?"

Try to think. The gun would blow her head half off. His hand was already clamping harder again, pinning her in place. She wanted to whimper.

"Where is he?"

"I don't know."

"Don't mess with me." The hand suffocated her. Her vision shrank to a tunnel. She could feel herself sinking. It was blacker than the night. Thoughts swirled, but wouldn't stay, everything turning and mixing.

"Talk." He was shaking her.

"I don't know where he is," she choked out when he released the pressure for a breath.

"You're lying." Then she felt the knife on her cheek, down her neck. It was pricking the skin.

"Oh no." God, she didn't want to be cut.

The knife was back at her cheek. "Tell me."

"He left me here." She could feel the sting of the knife cutting. The horror of it consumed her. The words came fast, staccato. "He left, looking for you. Didn't say how."

"He was going to the house, wasn't he?" The knife stopped cutting. "You're not answering me. I don't want to make a mess of you."

"I imagine he started for the house. Where he is now, I haven't the faintest."

"Tell me about the plane."

She spoke, desperate to keep the knife still. She told him about the brilliant light in the sky, the explosion, the trek through the snow, even the angry squirrel.

"What about the plane? Tell me about the plane. Was anybody alive?"

"One guy, covered in blood. He threw a grenade after shooting at us."

"What did he look like?"

"Older than the rest ... glasses. . . . But he was covered with blood ... you couldn't tell . . ."

"Was there anyone else? Anyone around the plane?"

"Not that we saw. Only a set of tracks leaving the plane."

"What did Kier tell you about the tracks?"

"Nothing. Just a man ... that's it."

"He knows more."

She felt the blade again. "Well, he didn't tell me," she almost shouted.

"What did you take from the plane?"

"Five bound volumes."

"Did you read them?"

"Not much. We had no time, and they were technical."

"You're lying. He knew a lot. Where is the sixth manual? Were there six of them?"

"There was a spot for a sixth, but there were only five books."

"Don't patronize me." The knife cut her cheek; she gasped at the sting.

"We left the four in the cabin and took one with us. The sixth we never found. Maybe the guy who left the tracks." She felt the knife again. "I'm telling you, I don't know where!"

His hand crushed her throat. "Shut up. You scream like that again and you're dead. Where is the fifth?"

"Kier hid it near a cabin—he didn't show me where."

Now he controlled events. She imagined having a scarred face, death. Her mind fought the obvious conclusions. Think. She had to think, not just cower. He was fumbling with something.

"Roll over."

He turned her easily, like a cougar with a rabbit. She felt the cuffs snap in place. Escape seemed impossible, but she could not let herself surrender. How could she disable him? How could she run?

Now he was unzipping her coat. Then he was pulling it open. As she felt his hands on the buttons of her shirt, her head began to spin. It couldn't be. Not here, on a freezing night in the dirt. Dizziness swept her. He yanked Kier's T-shirt to her neck. She could feel his fingers moving on her belly. He unfastened her jeans. Blackness began to fill her mind—her spirit wanted to crawl to some far-off place.

What lunatic would . . . her mind snapped back. Her pants were around her thighs, then her ankles. He rose over her, his hands and mouth on her. He rutted like a pig.

"No—"

His large hand knocked her almost unconscious. Her mind swooped to the brink of hysteria. From somewhere, she didn't know where, she remembered a man from training—a rapist—talking about his anger on tape.

"Did your mother or father fill you with this much rage?

Did the neighbor lady play with you? What?'' Her tones to her own ear sounded amazingly matter-of-fact.

His breathing grew more rapid. He crawled on her, his powerful knees forcing hers farther apart. Her mind staggered around like a drunk in a busy street—the wet earth, twigs and brush grinding into her bare buttocks—the odor of his breath.

''You never told me about Mom—this sickness you seem to have . . .''

A slap stung her face, smearing blood, sharpening her mind. With a start, it occurred to her that he wasn't entering her. That something wasn't . . . he was flaccid.

''God, after all this you can't get it up?''

The words just came. Then a giant sneer took over her mind. This pig couldn't do it. With all his rutting he couldn't pull it off. Raucous, crazy laughter escaped her lips.

''You poor bastard. You want to rape me. No, you want to hurt me, subjugate me to your sick fantasy. And you can't get it up.''

The slap distorted her face, probably broke something, but didn't stop her. ''Or was it the mommy talk?'' Her jaw cracked with the thud of his heavy fist, but still she couldn't stop. Now his bloodied hand was thrust between them; he was working himself.

''When it's this bad you try playing with yourself, do you? Maybe if you undid the cuffs . . . damn it, with my bloody lips I can't even say it . . . if you undid me, maybe I could—''

She began to laugh her crazy laugh and couldn't stop until she coughed on the blood. ''Maybe I could give you a hand.'' Her laughter pierced the night.

A minute passed while she felt the rhythm of his hand and then his frustration. Faster and faster he moved, as if he were jerking on a soft, seasoned rope. Her lips felt like balloons— she couldn't absorb another punch. Still, like a moth drawn to the flame she couldn't resist speaking again. ''My ass is freez-

ing, why don't you call it a night? This is no way to get even
with whoever screwed you over."

He stopped. "Later," was all he said as he rolled off and
put his clothes back together.

"Would forcing sex on me really buy you something?" she
asked as he pulled her pants back up around her waist.

"I promise, you'll beg me to do it."

This time she said nothing. He fastened her pants, zipped
her coat, and told her to walk.

Leave clues. She must leave an easy track. She began to
scuff the ground every third step. If she could break a branch,
she did it. They walked at the edge of the forest, him behind
her with a gun at the back of her head. For a split second, she
pondered whether Kier would be better off if Tillman pulled
the trigger.

Chapter 31

Some men would invent evil spirits if they learned
they did not exist.

—Tilok proverb

Kier landed squarely on the man's back, flattening him to
the ground. One twist around the neck with the garrote and
Kier had a lethal hold. Soon the mad flailing gave way to
unconsciousness, allowing Kier to release the pressure. The
guy had no cuffs in his pack like the rest. Instead, Kier used
the laces from the man's boots to tie his hands, then cut one
Achilles tendon. What ammo he didn't keep, he tossed in the
brush. To make them useless, he removed the firing mechanism
from the two pistols and the M-16, discarding the vital parts.

Kier worked quickly, knowing that the watcher—by far the
deadlier of the two—might arrive at any moment. As soon as
they knew a soldier was down they would send out a squad.

Passing through the densest part of the forest, mostly on his
belly, Kier returned to the rock and the dogwood. No one

remained there. Kier had no thought as to where the man might have gone, except down the trail to find the flunky.

Kier decided to wait before proceeding to the house. A feeling that it was the wrong target began to take hold. If Tillman was around, he would likely be near the Donahues' house, watching and waiting. It was much more like this man to be part of the trap than the bait.

Something made him look back in the direction he had come. A chipmunk sat in a moon ray, frozen on a log, watching, flicking his tail as if it had been disturbed. There was no sound, but a shadow stood against the leaves of a nearby myrica. If it was a man, he was good. No more than twenty feet separated them. Despite his will to remain watchful and still, Kier's heart quickened. Every fiber of his being said he was in danger. For just a second, he wondered why the man didn't strike.

Without a plan, without thought, he bolted to his right just before he heard the sound of a clip sliding into a pistol. Then he sprang for a log, rolling next to it. At any second, a grenade could drop beside him. If the man was throwing a grenade, he wouldn't be able to shoot for a couple of seconds. It was a horrible gamble, but Kier curled to a crouch, then jumped the log. Straight at his target he ran, knowing that at any moment he could be shot to pieces by an M-16.

He saw the hand cocked, poised to throw, the bulk of a pistol in the other hand. Kier fired into the metal breastplate that would cover the man's chest. The bullet knocked him backward. Then Kier fell upon him.

A tangle of gouging fingers and raining fists fought the encumbrance of the so-called bulletproof jackets. Of their vitals, only the men's faces were unprotected. The soldier fought with a ferocity that Kier had never encountered. Kier could feel thick fingers closing on his neck. They had come to rest almost head to head. At the same moment, each struggled to get atop the other. As they both came to one knee, Kier grabbed a thumb to break the man's chokehold. When the fingers started to slip, the man pulled back and swung with his fist. It caught Kier straight on the jaw, stunning him. Kier shook it off and plunged at his opponent, pinning him back to the ground.

He realized the man was looking in his face, talking, no longer struggling.

"Stop fighting. I'm the FBI. Special Agent Doyle."

Kier barely comprehended the words. With the opening, he swung again, landing the punch squarely on the smooth-shaven chin. The man's face went slack and Kier struck again. He didn't move.

"FBI, my ass," Kier muttered to himself, cuffing the man with his own handcuffs. Still, something in the back of his mind made him uneasy. What if he was the FBI? No. Couldn't be. This was a hired killer. He had been about to throw a—Kier's eye went to the green metal shape. Unbelievable. It was a stun grenade—wouldn't kill anybody.

A groan made Kier turn. Returning to Doyle, Kier knelt and shook him until he became fully conscious.

"I'm Doyle," the man said. "I was trying to talk."

"How does the FBI get with a madman like this guy?"

Doyle shook his head as if trying to think. "We were tipped off that Tillman—Jack Tillman's his name—was doing criminal things. I got hired through a merc agency overseas just like everyone else, only I'm undercover FBI."

"Why should I believe you?"

"You've got to. And when you hear what I have to say, you will believe me."

Kier crossed his arms, silent. "You were holding a pistol."

"Check the clip. You probably heard me pop in the rubber bullets," he said. "It might help if I speak with Agent Mayfield."

"She's not here. What's Tillman up to?"

"It's a very long, involved story."

"Try me."

"What I know is mostly from FBI files. But yesterday I got him to confide in me, and I was able to fill in some gaps."

"So?"

"First off, we think he created a number of cloned infants for medical research. He mapped the human genome."

"I know that. What else?"

"You read it in Volume Six?"

"Volume Five."

"Have you got Volume Six?"

"Not so fast. Tell me more."

"Right. Well, you know he's using the Tilok clinic to get surrogate mothers for the clones?"

"My cousin gave birth as a surrogate—they said it was for adoptive parents," Kier said. "Beautiful baby."

"I'm sorry to hear that." Doyle fingered his bloody lip with cuffed hands. "They make the babies brain dead with a chemical cocktail they call Whiteout. Call the babies tissue samples. The child barely functions. Just eats, defecates, and sleeps."

Kier felt as though he had been dealt a blow to the stomach. He stared at the dark outline of Doyle, hatred boiling in him.

"Were these kids all mutilated after they were taken?"

"None of the babies was adopted by wealthy families like they said."

Kier was dizzy with disgust, with loathing. "Tillman cloned me." His voice shook when he said it.

"I'm sorry. I had no way of knowing. How did you find out?"

"Tillman. I believe him when he says one of those birth dates and social security numbers was mine. I've seen the I.D. numbers for other people in the summaries."

"I'm telling you all this so you'll believe I'm not just some mercenary," Doyle said. "Okay?"

"Go ahead."

"Tillman made one move that didn't work out the way he planned."

"The vector-virus work."

"You figured that out too?"

Kier didn't answer.

"It was only a tiny part of their work," Doyle continued. "But it went really wrong. They rushed too fast to make a vector of an African virus thought to be harmless. Which wasn't and was worse after the bug mutated in a Tilok. It's very slow acting. Goes to the bone marrow and could take years to kill you. Or it can go faster depending on your immune system. They ended up studying the DNA makeup of the Tiloks."

"Was 1220 a Tilok?"

"She was. She was exposed to the naturally mutated vector-virus RA-4TVM when they discovered quite by accident that she was immune. They studied her, they studied others. She was the reason they became so intensely interested in the Tiloks in the first place. It was the immunity thing."

"According to the summary the antivirus and vaccine AVCD-4 appeared to work," Kier said.

"Our guys think so too."

"So it was the immunity theory that kept them studying the Tiloks."

"Yup. But the Tiloks apparently have another genetic difference. Evidently a retroviral event in the Tiloks' history left a DNA segment in their genes that combined with Tillman's vector virus, RA-4TV, through natural reassortment. Out came a mutated version of the RA-4TV, called RA-4TVM, and it's a killer. Actually the original RA-4T virus was not as harmless as they thought. They got in a hurry because they were so excited about the vector application.

"Tillman's people couldn't cure either RA-4T or RA-4TVM until just recently. But it escaped into the U.S. population and Tillman's known it for two years. Often people have no symptoms for four or five years. Then they start dying. Some could live a long time. We think Tillman's been working over the past months to make it look like the virus originated on a mink farm on the Tilok reservation.''

"So how did the Tilok get RA-4TV in the first place?"

"The short answer, we don't know, but we sure as hell want to find out. We do know he was using the Tilok people to test the progress and cure rate of the AVCD-4 antivirus when used to control the run-amok RA-4TVM virus. And any of its mutations. When the RA-4TV reassorted itself and mutated to become RA-4TVM—that part we're sure was an accident. Probably isn't likely to happen in anything but a Tilok body. The bad news is that we don't have the cure for the RA-4TVM. Tillman does. It's in Volume Six. And the antivirus and vaccine were on that plane.''

"So my tribe and the rest of the country are at risk if we don't get the cure?"

"Yes. From the now long escaped RA-4TVM. Do you have Volume Six?" Doyle stared into Kier's eyes when he asked.

"How widespread is it?"

"We don't know exactly. Tillman purposely gave it to quite a few Tiloks at the clinic because he and Rawlins were desperate to know how it would spread and how it would act with the vaccine and the antivirus. Through some absolute fluke Rawlins's wife got it early on. By the time they got the cure fully developed, she was too far gone. If left untreated long enough it invades the brain. Although it's curable if you treat it early, the later stages cause neurological damage with symptomatology similar to Alzheimer's. The brain damage is irreversible, even if you kill the virus. The virus spreads from person to person in a manner similar to AIDS, but frankly more easily. It can be passed by saliva, I'm told.''

"That would really make them desperate."

"It sure would. Imagine the liability. Even if they could cure it. Now, do you have Volume Six or don't you? I must know.''

Kier's face was a stony mask. "I don't know how the FBI could let this happen. You know so much."

"Listen, we've got to find the cure for this mutated virus *before* we take in Tillman. Otherwise he bargains with it for his freedom. We've also got to find Volume Six and get the evidence. A lot of our information came from a witness who was on that plane and is now dead."

Kier shook his head.

"Their technology is the discovery of the century, if not the millennium." Doyle struggled to get up, but Kier kept him down. "Rawlins made this sixth volume to take the power out of the hands of an absolute nutter. If the FBI can get Volume Six, we might find the house of horrors where they keep all the brain-damaged clones. Maybe what he's done with the Tiloks and how to fix it. Heard enough to help me?"

"What about the plane and the soldiers?"

"Tillman must have learned Rawlins was turning on him. He had to bury Rawlins and all records of illegal activity. So he thinks up a plane crash. Step one is to get Rawlins to agree to move the lab. Step two is to make sure that all the evidence of illegal or controversial stuff is destroyed except what's being moved on this plane to the secret new lab. Step three is to load Rawlins and his closest cronies on the plane with all their records. Four, drop the important research materials to Tillman before a preset bomb explodes the plane over the ocean. Five, convince the government that all the records are gone, destroyed in the 'accidental' crash.

"We watched while the bastard got the plane off right under our noses. Somebody on our team screwed up. I'm guessing that when Tillman's men pulled their guns and prepared for the drop, the scientists were ready. They had prepared for something like this, brought their own guns maybe. The thugs were supposed to parachute down with the lab equipment and records. Instead, there's a shootout and the plane crash-lands near the drop site instead of exploding over the ocean."

"That would explain the second explosion."

"They picked your mountain for the drop because it was near their clinic and in line with a runway on the coast. Those footprints from the plane must have been somebody who survived the crash."

Kier shrugged in reply.

"Where's Agent Mayfield?"

Kier hesitated.

"You gotta tell me."

"How do I know you're the FBI?" asked Kier. "How do I know you or the FBI haven't made a deal with the devil? It wouldn't be the first time."

Doyle sighed. "Look, I don't know where you get your ideas, but this isn't the movies. Sure, Tillman has friends in high places like you'd expect, but if we can get hard evidence, he's cooked."

"Where's Tillman, then? Let's find him."

"What's not getting through here is that Tillman's going after Mayfield. It's the best way to get you alive."

Kier felt the words like an electric shock. Of course. Tillman knew about him and Jessie. The way she walked so close. From the track.

"I should have realized," he said, standing. "He's already tried that once. I've got to backtrack. Alone."

"You'll have a lot better luck with me. Think about it. The two of us can walk right out in the open as long as we're together."

Kier considered. Doyle was right.

Chapter 32

The lessons we're taught as children must be
learned again in hard times.

—Tilok proverb

Kier and Doyle backtracked Kier's trail toward Jessie. When
they reached the edge of the forest next to the pasture, Kier
stopped. Using a small light, he examined the tracks in the
earth near a puddle. All of the imprints were made by large
boots. After proceeding another fifty yards, he once again examined the ground. He found a track—Jessie's boot—and a print
immediately behind hers. Kier recognized it as that of the lone
stalker on the mountain. A few yards farther Kier could see
that Jessie had been scuffing.

The look on Kier's face told Doyle what he needed to know.

"He found her."

Kier nodded, his hatred of Tillman and fear for Jessie displac-
ing everything else.

"What's your name again?" Kier asked, now able to see

the man's face clearly for the first time. He was square jawed, with handsome Anglo features dominated by bushy red eyebrows and long, neat sideburns.

"I'm Quartz on the radio. The men know me by Doyle."

"Okay, Doyle, it looks like he's taking her to the house. I'd guess if we wait, we'll hear from him over the radio. If we follow them, we'll walk into a trap."

At that moment, Doyle's radio crackled. "Base to Iron. Do you copy?"

"That's the guy you killed back there. I'd better answer." Kier uncuffed him. "Base, this is Quartz. Iron went to check on some suspicious movement."

"This is base. Why can't he tell us that?"

"Don't know. Last I knew he was on his hands and knees in the bushes."

"It sounds like you better check it out. Find out for sure. Everybody else stay put and keep your eyes glued."

The man from base then completed a roll call. Kier counted twenty responses, which meant that at least that many ringed the house.

As the roll call ended, Kier's radio, set to a different channel, came on. "Dr. Kier, do you copy?"

"Tillman?" Kier asked Doyle.

"The very same."

"I hear you."

"I've got your friend Jessie. I think it's time we talked."

"Tell him yes," Doyle whispered. "We'll go in and see what he has in mind. Before we go, you've got to tell me where the sixth volume is."

Kier's mind whirled.

"Well?" Tillman persisted.

No option seemed good. Gambling everything on Doyle and his scheme didn't seem wise. On the other hand, it was direct, simple. He had no better plan. And stalling while his family, his whole tribe, could be infected with Tillman's virus made no sense. Jessie was in the most immediate danger. This would get him in the house, near her.

"Listen, Dr. Kier, I wasn't kidding. I've got your mother, your sisters, the whole damn tribe. I've got them. Every one of them has viruses inside them. They'll be in a world of hurt within a week or so. I've put a little goody in the Tilok reservoir that raises their susceptibility to this disease like a tinder-dry forest feeds a fire. I've got the only stuff that'll kill the virus. Come and talk to me, or your tribe and your girlfriend here die."

"Okay," Kier finally replied and ended the transmission.

"Where's the volume?" Doyle asked again.

"Not yet."

Claudie's kitchen had been turned into a command center. Maps were spread around, their corners held in place by cups of stale coffee and butcher knives. Judging from the glass filled with cigarette butts and ash, somebody was a heavy smoker. Probably they were nervous. The only sound in the place was the creaking of the hot metal of the stove.

Tillman's arms were folded across his chest, his face a mask of arrogant confidence. Coldness glistened in his dark eyes. The man had a hard angularity that came from a lean, muscled body without an ounce of rounding flab. Four men in addition to Tillman stood by. They all wore taut faces and leveled guns at Kier, mindful of their fallen comrades. At first Kier did not see Jessie, but as he moved into the kitchen, his eye found the corner of the living room where she sat handcuffed and tied to a kitchen chair. He winced at the lines of dried blood on her swollen face.

He took two steps toward Tillman, a low moan escaping his lips.

"Hold it!" Tillman shouted, holding up his hand. The guns

in four hands quivered with tension. "One more step and you're dead."

Kier stopped, his gaze returning to Jessie. Around her torso were bands of heavy plastic tape confining her belly and upper arms. Her hands were cuffed in front of her. Each calf was fastened to a chair leg. She was totally immobilized, unable to do no more than blink her eyes in frustration.

Only Tillman appeared relaxed, leaning against a countertop with his gun holstered. Kier had surrendered his pistols to Doyle before entering. For appearances, Doyle held a gun fixed on Kier's back. Of course, it was a real gun, it was loaded, and it could just as well be used for killing as for appearances. Kier wondered if he had made the right choice.

"So, Dr. Kier Wintripp, tracker and survivalist extraordinaire, special deputy sheriff on occasion, youth leader, martial arts expert, and country vet—not to mention wine connoisseur—how nice of you to come and see us." Tillman's face broke in a self-satisfied smile. "Tell me, Doyle, could you have gotten him in here with the FBI story if I didn't have little Miss Muffet here?"

Kier reeled at Tillman's words, forcing himself not to turn and stare at Doyle. So it had all been part of the game.

"Frankly, I doubt it. He's a mistrustful bloke. Doesn't have much confidence in the government," Doyle replied. Kier could hear him smile.

"Well, we have that in common, Kier and I." Tillman pushed off the counter and moved to Jessie. "So tell me about the missing volume and the footprints." Tillman pulled a thin, black knife from his pocket. "I'm listening."

"Not much to tell. There was one set of tracks leaving the plane, and I found a hole big enough for one missing volume in the metal box."

Tillman unfolded the blade and began scraping the underside of his nails. "Did someone come from the plane?"

"I saw no tracks leading into the area, only a set of tracks leaving."

"You're a tracker. You know a lot more."

It was true. It hit him like a bolt from the blue. Kier *did* know more. Yet until this moment even he had been unable to solve the puzzle.

"It was a man who swaggers, makes a lot of noise. Puts his heel down heavy, a lot of snap, crackle, and pop. Except for once," Kier said. "One time he took a stalker's stride, with straight feet, one almost in front of the other. The two or three steps that followed were an Indian's walk. The rest was all city man. He was small and traveled fast. He couldn't find natural breaks in the forest. He just bulled his way through. Seemed headed in a lost man's circle that would have intersected with the county road. No blood in the track, but he did walk with a slight drag like he was hurt."

"Old man or young?"

"I can't always tell the age of a man by his track, but in this case it was an old man who wanted to make fools of us all. You will never find the book by yourself." Kier said it with the utmost conviction.

"What do you mean?"

"This man who has your book is the only living Spirit Walker of the Tilok tribe. He lives in the mountains. You will not find him unless he wants you to find him."

"And why would this old man be at the crash site minutes after the plane hit the ground?"

"I don't know if I can give you an explanation that would make sense to a white man."

"Try me."

"The old man believes in omens. Think of it as the past and the future meeting at a point in time and space with a silent witness."

Tillman snorted.

Kier looked at the ceiling before he continued. "Yeah, well, if you're small-minded like the rest of us, consider that you left an elephant-size trail in his mountains. I saw your tire tracks going up by the old Murdock place. Don't think he would miss them, or the details of your camp, or your number, or the maps you studied, or the guns you carried, or your whispering in the night, or the food you ate, or the spoor you left. If you camped near Murdock's, then you were within three miles of the crash site. It would only take a tiny bit of intuition, or a single crow's head for clever luck, for him to be at the crash site if he was already on the mountain, watching you. And he surely was. You were like a circus in his living room."

"He must have a place where he goes."

"He goes where the wind blows him. His living room is Iron Mountain on this side; his bedroom in the summer its north shoulder; his kitchen in the summer the north face; his playroom the backside; his backyard the Wintoon wilderness; and his exercise area the Marble Mountains. His church is the sky, where they say he walks if he becomes tired of the earth. So you tell me—where would he go with your horror?"

"Could you track him?"

"You haven't been listening." Kier allowed a look of amusement to cross his face. "And why would I want to?"

"Because of the little extras I will do to your woman if you don't. Because I'll kill your tribe."

Kier imagined Tillman's words floating over a road map of unspeakable things, all of them etched in the sickness of his mind. "If he doesn't want to be found, I can't track him. But I'm the best hope you've got."

"Maybe he won't resist being found by you."

"How will he know I'm the one who'll come? I expect he'll assume there's a whole army of rednecks after him."

Tillman unholstered his gun and pointed it at Kier. He had one of his men put handcuffs on him. "Leave us alone," he said to his men, who then began filing out. "You too, Doyle," he added when Doyle hung back.

After they left, Tillman spoke in a whisper. "I'll kill your damned tribe with the RA-4TVM virus. I've already infected dozens."

"How could you have done that?"

Tillman looked like he was thinking, perhaps reconsidering his disclosure.

"Remember the free cholesterol test at the fair?"

Willow had taken the test, Kier recalled distantly.

"Kissing, spitting on the food enough, living in real close proximity, it'll spread. Not well, but it spreads. Then we dosed the water here with a catalyst."

"Were you going to cure it?"

"Oh, sure. I mean, we aim to please. In the beginning you can stop it with the antivirus and a vaccine. Later it takes the addition of a special little protein molecule that clogs up the host cells so the virus can't dock. We also planned to neutralize the catalyst we put in the water. If we wait until the little bastards have taken root, so to speak, we've got to kill most of them with the usual, then the rest of them with a very powerful drug that kills the bone marrow. If we wait long, to save your friends we'd have to do a bone marrow transplant or else increase the natural immunity in each individual. So you don't want to dally. We can fix it, but if we don't, your tribe will die slowly. If we continue the test, and you do as we say, we'll call it the flu at the clinic and treat everybody before it gets serious. But if I don't get the sixth volume, I won't bother stopping the disease. I swear to you, Kier, if you don't find it, a third of your people will die in the near term. And among that third will be your mother and your sisters. It will go down as a fluke of nature."

"The CDC is gonna ask a lot of questions about where the virus came from."

"We've got that covered. It's in the mink at the mink farm owned by the Grove family. It mutated slightly and crossed over to people."

"Look, I can't find the old man if he doesn't want to be found. Especially in a day or two."

"I don't care about your theories or Spirit Walkers or any of that stuff. Your girlfriend stays. You go. If you aren't back in twenty-four hours with Volumes Five and Six— No. Better yet, you radio every hour and give me a report. If I like the report, well, nothing happens. If I don't like it, we start cutting little pieces off little Miss Muffet. First toes, then fingers, then"—he reached and cupped his own ear—"imagine what she'd look like without ears. Then maybe we'll de-lip her." Tillman smiled again. "We'll leave kind of a mewling hole for a mouth—like a newborn. Then we'll take some more interesting things. Maybe we won't do you a favor and kill her. Maybe we'll let you keep what's left."

"I get the books, you'll kill us anyway."

"I'm sure you'll come up with something. Smart Indian like you . . . some way to trade." Tillman paused, placed his hands behind his back, and stared out the kitchen window. "I'm tired of this. Either leave and get me the book or kiss the Tiloks good-bye and I'll start the surgery on your girlfriend."

Kier turned toward the door after one last glance at Jessie. The pain of walking away without her was a great, aching wave inside him. He held up the cuffs to Doyle, who had the key.

"I'd hurry, mate," Doyle said with a smile.

Kier knew at that moment that he would kill him. As he opened the door, he looked Doyle square in the eye. Doyle winked almost imperceptibly.

Only the chill of the air and the gray of dawn tickling the eastern sky were good. Never had he felt so lost. Jessie was in an armed camp with a man who wanted to dismember her. His family and tribe were in the process of dying. Kier growled his desperation. No time to wonder about the cold-steel edges of Tillman's heart or the brutish thing that passed for his mind. He needed his grandfather. Where to begin? Where on the mountain would Grandfather hide? What other mountain might he choose?

Then a little light in his mind became a dancing torch on the face of the water. Grandfather would be at the caverns. He could survive undetected there endlessly. Kier walked quickly now, mulling things over. Grandfather had once told him that he'd squeezed into a coffin-size cave and stayed for three days to experience the rock. No one could find Grandfather in the caverns unless he wanted to be found. So Kier would leave signs leading to the pond in the cavern and wait for Grandfather. It was all he could think of to do. And it was logical.

But Kier was desperate. *If Grandfather had my problem, what would he do?* Kier asked himself as he jogged on the trail back toward the cave high on the mountain. Stalking Bear was a Spirit Walker, a mystic. He would use his instincts, not his logic. For Grandfather that was fine, but Kier needed the comfort of reason.

He ran past the alders on the flat, across the creek, hopping stones up the hill, and, with dawn breaking over him, climbed for the true fir forest as fast as he could.

Something was wrong.

Of course, something was wrong, he told himself. *Tillman will likely filet alive the woman I love.*

He stopped. It wasn't that. It was different.

He threw back his head and looked at the stars and the fading moon. What? A dawn wind rushed through the trees.

In his mind, he could see Grandfather by the lake in the early morning. It had been not three months ago. The way he slowly turned his face to the rising sun, as if it were magic, as if it were full of the wonders of life. The joy in the old man's face had been unmistakable. Kier focused on that joy, seizing it to make it his own, even in the midst of his despair. But where did this get him? He was not going toward the cave. He was not going anywhere. For the first time in years, he wanted to weep at the hopelessness of it all. But he did not know how to cry.

Indian men did not weep. For all the white man's culture that had taken over in him, this one thing had never changed. Now he wanted to cry. For reasons he couldn't fathom, he didn't move. Minutes ticked by. He noticed a tear on his face, and could feel its track as it ran—a terribly odd sensation.

He was oblivious to the approach of the old man—until he felt his grandfather's hand grasp his arm.

"I thought you would never stop," Grandfather said. "I have been following you, waiting to see where your thoughts would carry you. . . . You were going so quickly."

Grandfather's eyes sparkled with interest, the gaze penetrating. Somehow Grandfather had always managed to stand ramrod straight, even in old age. Only the creases in his face and the long, flowing gray hair betrayed his years. The Spirit Walker never spoke in terms of "worry." Worry was not a habit he considered appropriate to this or any other life.

"You watched me walk away?"

"It was important."

"Never mind. Where is the sixth volume? Were you at the jet?"

"Did you not see my track?"

"Yes, yes. You laid a white man's track."

"Didn't it cry loudly?" The old man barely cracked a smile.

"Yes. Too loudly. Now where is the volume?"

"Why do you ask?"

"I need it so I can at least pretend I'll trade it for Jessie."

"I do not have it."

"I need it for Jessie to live. I need to save our people."

"From what?"

"A disease, a virus, from the man who owns the plane."

"I have the cure for the disease. I gave it to the newspaper man."

"What do you mean?"

"A man on the jet, he gave me a thick book . . . told me to give it to a man at the *New York Times,* along with the big case. He said it was the cure for the Tilok. He stayed with the plane. He said others would come."

"What book?"

"He said it explained everything about the cure and about the plane."

Kier was stunned. The man who threw the grenade had been friend, not foe—only there had been no way to know. He had died believing Kier and Jessie were part of Tillman's private army.

"Where is the case that has the medicine for the cure?"

"James Cole has half of the medicine—the other half I hid. James is on his way to the *New York Times* with the diary and half the medicine—he went where the man on the plane told me—to a reporter in San Francisco."

"Do you know anything of Claudie?"

"She is safe in a cave. I am now a godfather to the two boys. Claudie and her boys are very strong."

"We've got to save Jessie. Somehow I need to fake a trade for Volume Six. And I have to have something in my hands to prove I've something to trade, to stop him from hurting Jessie."

"Let's go get her."

"How?"

"Come on. I'll show you."

Chapter 33

Powerful men are moved by their wills; great men
by their spirits.

—Tilok proverb

Although the horizon was now exploding with the red dawn,
the light remained low, darkness holding itself fast in the shadows where Grandfather and Kier moved soundlessly. As he
went, the old man called out occasionally like a chickadee.

Once, when he must have seen or felt Kier's frown, he said,
"It is so that if there are any watchful ones, they might mistake
the spirit of the one who passes."

Since they were making no sound, Kier took him to refer to
some spiritual sense. He only shook his head and wished he
had a gun. Then he recalled his pack, and reached a hand to
Grandfather's shoulder.

"I have a gun off that way, at the head of the pasture."

"I don't think there is time if we are going to do this before
full daylight," the old man said.

They made their way to the edge of the forest. At their closest, the trees were a good fifty feet from the house. Kier wondered how they would get across the opening in the gray light of the dawn. When they reached the last patch of brush, they lay flat and looked over the foot-high bunch grass. Two men were visible, one at the edge of the front porch, the other by the back door. Each had an M-16. Without guns, it was hopeless. Kier glanced at Grandfather, who simply nodded before turning and grabbing the nearest Scotch broom. It had been uprooted and fashioned into a hedgework that a man could hide behind. Back on his belly, Grandfather moved it out into the grass, then motioned to Kier, his first two fingers making a walking motion; then he pointed to himself. Obviously, he intended to show himself in the clearing as a distraction.

"When I get inside, you turn out the lights at the fuse box," Grandfather said. "White men see nothing anyway. But you must move in your spirit."

Inwardly, Kier winced. Nobody is invisible, not even Stalking Bear, he told himself. Still, he would keep himself so flat to the ground he might as well be a spirit.

"I will also make you invisible," the old man whispered, trotting off into the forest.

Kier waited. The odds of this working were miniscule. Grandfather was the stealthiest man he had ever known, but he still had to lug around a body susceptible to a bullet. Once inside the house, lights or no lights, everyone but Grandfather and him would have a gun.

However insane it was, there was no time to ponder it, for Grandfather was now out in the open. About one hundred feet away, he had emerged from the forest. But he didn't just walk. Instead, he danced and chanted. It was an elaborate pantomime that told the story of a great hunt.

"What the hell?" The man on the back porch by the fuse box advanced toward Grandfather, while Kier began to crawl.

The man went for his radio. "We've got some old Indian out here, crazy as a coot."

"Repeat, did you say old?"

"Wrinkled as a prune. Just dancing and chanting."

"Bring him in," Kier heard Tillman say.

Both men now walked quickly to Grandfather, while Kier crawled as fast as he dared toward the rear door. More men came out of the front door, walking around the kids' toys, and another man came around back just an instant after Kier had slipped under the back porch.

Kier hunkered down while the new man took up position above him. His eyes peered through the space between the planking. From the shadow of the man's feet, he knew he was standing well back toward the house. No solution came to mind. Damn. He was stuck. Crawling out from under the porch was out of the question. He would be dead before he got over the porch railing. And now Grandfather was captive, waiting, helpless—like Jessie.

The chair was from Europe of all places. Before this Jessie had thought it was comfortable. It was unbelievably stout, but even if it hadn't been, she would have had no opportunity to free herself. A man stood next to the chair, guarding her. Periodically Tillman would appraise her from a distance, like a dog checking its dinner bowl. It was only a matter of time before he tried to complete what he had started in the forest, she knew. His humiliation burned in his eyes. Now it was a contest.

Incredibly, she was starting to believe that the man Doyle was not really one of Tillman's mercs. He had signaled her twice with an almost imperceptible nod. She wondered if he could be FBI. It could easily be some elaborate trick, just as Tillman had said.

Pain shot up her back through her shoulder blades, and her

knees felt as though they had needles in them. Being immobilized was far more painful than she would ever have imagined. She couldn't move anything that counted, and the only time she could get up was to use the bathroom—and each time she did, they retaped her more tightly than ever. Although caked in blood, the cuts on her face appeared superficial in the mirror.

Her first indication that something unusual was happening came when she heard about the old Indian over the radio. She was almost certain it would be Grandfather. Then they were bringing him in. Two men picked up her chair and put it close to the wall dividing the kitchen from the living area so that she could not see or be seen.

When they got the old man inside, Tillman wasted no time. "What can we do for you?"

"I did not know there was anything you could do for me," the old man answered.

"Why'd you come?" Tillman sighed.

"No reason." There was a pause. "You're here with a lot of men. A lot of fancy guns. You have reasons?"

"What's your name, old man?"

"Chunk Tawa."

"In English."

"Chunk Tawa."

"What's it mean?"

"You would say 'Stalking Bear.' "

"Do you know the one they call Kier?"

"The animal doctor."

"And do you know somebody whom they call a Spirit Walker?"

"You believe in that stuff?" The old man chuckled.

"Do you know him?"

"Broken-down old man like me."

"Where is he?"

"Who knows? Tavern in town, maybe."

"I don't think you're telling me the truth. Now why did you come here?"

Tillman's voice had become a snarl, and Jessie wondered if he had hold of Grandfather.

"I like Claudie and Jessie. Do you like them too?"

"How do you know Jessie?"

"She's been here a few days. I heard about her. I met her in my dreams. How do you know her?"

"Shut the hell up and answer my questions, or you'll die. Now where in the f—"

The lights went out. Jessie heard a shriek, followed by a choking sound that she imagined was coming from Tillman's lips. Frantically she began rocking in the chair, but in an instant she felt a gun at her temple. Then, inexplicably, the gun dropped. There had been a silenced shot.

"FBI, remember Dunfee?" someone whispered in her ear.

Then they were gone. Shots from next to her sprayed the room around her.

Doyle.

Desperation clawed at him, tightening his throat. He knew he had to move quickly or they would kill Grandfather. Feeling around on the damp earth for any kind of weapon, he came up empty. Then he remembered. Under the front porch, there was a pike pole from a logging pond that the Donahues used for pulling down fruit-laden branches when harvesting apples. He scurried under the house to the front porch. As he went, he could hear Tillman firing questions at Grandfather. In less than two minutes he found the pike pole and brought it back beneath the back porch. A gap between each of the porch's board stairs allowed ferns to grow up through the steps. Moving under, Kier aligned the pole with the openings in the steps. He made a rustling sound with his hand, then waited. The guard didn't move. Again he did it. Still the sentry didn't come. Next he tried a snake's angry hiss. But it was as if the man were deaf.

Finally he called out madly—the chickadee and the snake— a fight. A shadow appeared on the steps. The man was on his knees, trying to peer through the fern. He fumbled with his light. Kier used his hand to make another scurrying sound. He raised the pole, looking for a face. Nothing. Nothing. His arm shook with the tension. A light. A face. There. With all his power, he drove the pole straight for an eye. Only a grunt and the sharp exhale of breath marked the piercing of the man's skull. The long point and the large barb had disappeared into the man's head.

When Kier tried to pull the pike pole from the man's eye socket, the barb caught and the head came forward.

Kier needed the pole. Quickly he crept from under the porch, then dragged the body out to free the long handle that protruded from beneath the steps. The man's body gave an ugly quiver. One firm jerk did not free the pole. Kier placed a boot on the dead man's face and yanked. There was a wet snap as the skull fractured and the tip came free. He grabbed the man's sidearm and rifle on the run. On the porch, he threw the main breaker in the fuse box, then broke it for good measure.

He tried the knob only once. Then, slamming into the door with his shoulder, he broke it off its hinges, knocking it inward and flat to the floor. Inside all was black. The feeble rays of winter dawn displaced the darkness only near the entrance. Men were calling in muffled voices. He stayed very low, hearing the *pffft* of silenced pistols as he went. There was some kind of firefight going on—people shooting at each other. Since he knew the layout like his own home's, he went to the corner of the living room where he had last seen Jessie—but found only an empty space.

Somewhere, he knew, a man had a gun to Jessie's head. He had to take the man down, and quickly, before someone found a light. *Pffft. Pffft.* More shots fired wildly in the dark. For a fleeting second, he wondered who was shooting at whom. He crawled in ever-larger circles. His fingers found a boot. A body. A dead man. She could be anywhere. They might have moved her to the back of the house.

Panic rose inside him. He resisted the urge to call out. Sensing was more important than thinking, his Tilok mind told him. He moved across the carpet toward the other corner of the living room. If she was in here, she was probably next to the wall, hidden from the kitchen.

Kier reached an empty chair on the opposite side of the room. He had seconds at best. He heard his grandfather.

"Kier."

Pffft. Pffft. More shots from men shooting blindly. Grandfather must be shooting as well. Kier fired a volley from the M-16, punching holes in the tops of the walls. It would keep people down.

A hand grabbed his arm, pulling him. It was only a moment before his hand found another chair—Jessie. But she was lying on the floor, struggling, trying to escape her bonds. Kier heard a sound like a knife through cardboard. A light flashed, bouncing off the ceiling. With a single shot the light went out. Now his fingers found Grandfather, kneeling low by Jessie's chair. She was moving, crawling along the floor.

"Jessie."

"Kier."

"Grandfather."

"Let's go," Jessie snapped.

Grandfather led the way toward the light. As they reached the back door, he finally saw her. Then they were outside, running. They should have been shot going through the door, silhouetted by the dull morning light. They hit the trees still alive and for a moment an exuberant joy sang through Kier.

"I can't believe we're alive," Kier said.

"White men can't see spirits," said Grandfather.

"Somebody in there was on our side, shooting like hell.

That's why we're still alive," Jessie said. Then she stopped running abruptly. "We can't run now while Special Agent Doyle's still in there."

"He double-crossed me," Kier said.

"He didn't double-cross anybody but Tillman. He's a real agent."

"Then he's sold out."

"You're wrong," she said. "Get it in your head. The FBI are the good guys. We've got to help Doyle. If they figure out he was shooting, he's dead."

Kier grabbed her arm to draw her forward, but she shrugged it off.

"We have more important things to worry about than one man," Kier argued, "even if he is legitimate."

"You would never say that if it was Grandfather or me."

Kier sighed and looked at Grandfather. "I suppose you could go," Kier said haltingly. "We have the diary and the cure. You could tell the newspapers." He struggled. He didn't want to risk Jessie's life again. At best, Doyle was a government agent with a facility for lying. Jessie's blind faith in the damn government was ludicrous. He kicked the dirt, then turned away from her, staring at nothing.

"I can't live in a world where everything depends on the Lone Ranger, Kier. You've got to believe in more than yourself and the Tiloks. Nobody in this country can tolerate the Tillmans of the world. This government can't. Give me the pistol and let's go back. Let Grandfather take care of the Tilok." She studied him. "On everything else in life you are so wise. I just . . ." She shook her head and remained silent.

He guessed she had said her piece. He took a deep breath knowing he had only seconds to decide.

"Whisper to me where the cure is," he asked Grandfather.

The old man responded so quietly that Kier could barely hear. Then Kier turned to Jessie, seeing the question in her eyes.

"There is nothing they can do to make me tell," Kier said, as if to explain. "The stuff with James Cole should be safe. But we may need the other half that Grandfather hid."

Her gaze went to the ground. He knew she was wondering whether she could protect the information from Tillman if she were caught and tortured.

Grandfather nodded. "We are surrounded," he said.

Kier neither saw nor heard anything, but somehow began to sense something. If only Jessie hadn't insisted they stop. Maybe if it were Grandfather and him alone. But with Jessie . . . It seemed hopeless.

Grandfather touched his arm, looked Kier full in the eyes. Kier had never before witnessed such calm in the face of such danger.

"I should go now," Grandfather said.

The old man squatted and duck-walked into a patch of young fir, seeming to get very small. The forest fell deathly quiet. Even the birds sounded muted. After a moment, Kier heard the faintest snap followed by a rustling sound a little farther off. Men were coming.

"You go. I'll do the best I can to hide." Jessie stood close to him.

"This time, he'll torture you. He's worse than we imagined."

"I know." Tears filled her eyes. "Go now. You've got to get away."

Another snap came, much closer.

Kier hesitated. "I can't leave you," he said simply. "Let's go. If we get away, we'll find you some firepower, more ammo, and come back for Doyle."

Moving low to the ground, they passed through some manzanita, oaks, and patchy fir, then came to an opening. Several men, he thought at least seven, were spread out in a line behind a stand of fir trees, all within 150 feet. It looked tough. He pushed Jessie back into the brush. The throbbing sound of a helicopter emerged from the distance. Seconds later, it hovered directly over them, just above the trees. They retreated, moving to the left, staying low and out of sight. As if it had eyes, the chopper hung squarely over them. Kier knew it must have infrared sights. Even Grandfather could not hide from this.

He caught a glimpse of the helicopter's belly, and his mind began to spin. In giant letters, FBI read obscenely across its underside. He pointed.

"They'll save us," she said.

Now there was no good answer. Kier reasoned that the Feds were either on Tillman's side, or they had been misled. Whichever, they were being used to track them more surely than any man could ever accomplish.

"They aren't saving us. They're following us. They're killing us."

"You can't know that," she said. "We're saved, I tell you."

He considered shooting the rotors with his newly acquired M-16. It was the only way to escape the chopper. But doing so would put him squarely at odds with Jessie and the government. It could turn them into criminals. Again he moved left and motioned to Jessie. With a dubious look, she followed. But the giant bird would not back off. If he didn't do something, they would be captured. He brought the gun to his shoulder. Through the trees he aimed at the whirling rotors. His finger went to the trigger.

Jessie grabbed his arm, swinging the rifle away. "Don't. They're trying to save us." She was screaming in his ear now.

He knew her mind as if she had an hour to speak it.

"For once in your life trust the government."

It was her expression that filled him with indecision. She was so certain, and she wanted so much for him to believe in her and her FBI. For whatever reason, the men back in the clearing did not seem to be following. He looked up. The copter was lowering two harnesses, offering to lift them out. Once in the harness, they would have no escape. He looked at Jessie, could see the hope written in her eyes.

"Please," she said simply. "You aren't the only justice for the Tiloks."

He nodded, wanting to believe she was right, but almost certain she wasn't. He walked woodenly beside her into the tiny clearing, where they fastened themselves into the harnesses. In an instant, the helicopter began to rise, hoisting them above the treetops before whisking them straight for the Donahue ranch and Tillman's men. It broke his heart to watch Jessie's face as the horror became real to her. They were being delivered to their tormentors.

The men in the woods below marched back to the house, where more men stood waiting in the yard. One was lighting a fire. Kier's gut tightened as he watched a man with a coiled rope. The copter delicately lowered them into a circle of at least a dozen men, all aiming their automatic rifles at Kier and Jessie from point-blank range. Kier looked for Tillman. Not surprisingly he remained safely out of sight.

Kier could shoot, but only at the drones. And they would kill him and Jessie long before he got them all. Leading the pack was Doyle, waiting for them with a sly smile. When they hit the ground, one man took Kier's rifle and the pistol. In seconds, he and Jessie had their hands and feet shackled. They could only move in a slow, shuffling walk. Kier wondered how long it would take for them to die. Tillman, he knew, would make it as slow as he could, especially after deciding they couldn't or wouldn't deliver to him the sixth volume.

Chapter 34

A man knows the goodness of life when he would
sacrifice his own for the village.

—Tilok Proverb

"I wish we had more time, Kier. I'd enjoy giving your
girlfriend a little thrill. But the old man seems to have vanished.
For some reason, the heat-seeking stuff hasn't picked him up.
Leaves us with a big problem." Tillman spoke above the noise
of the landing helicopter. "Putting FEDERAL BUREAU OF INVES-
TIGATION on the chopper was another great Doyle suggestion."

Doyle still grinned, but there was something about his eyes.
Like he wanted in the worst way to send a signal. Kier ordered
himself not to believe it. Then he asked himself what exactly
he had to lose.

"Hang her in the tree," Tillman said.

There was an oak not twenty feet away. Three strong men
shoved Kier to the ground and dragged him to it.

"I want you to watch this very closely," Tillman said.

Kier lay on his back, immobile, as they hung Jessie by her hands, then tied her feet to the base of the tree so that she was stretched taut against it. Her breathing was labored. It was like a crucifixion. If she hung that way long enough, she would suffocate under her own weight.

"Begin with a toe," Tillman said casually.

Kier just stared, hating himself for trusting Jessie's judgment. They brought out a giant pair of bolt cutters. It would take off the toe like a twig. A man thrust an iron into the newly lit fire.

"That's to cauterize it after it's cut. We want her to last a long time. Without that, she'd lose one hell of a lot of blood. Unless, of course, you want to tell me where the old man is and get me the book."

"The book's on its way to the *New York Times*."

Now they had her shoe off. Kier glanced at Doyle and something came to his mind.

"Doyle told me you were cloning babies for research and then destroying their minds."

"Enough," Tillman said, turning to Doyle with a shocked expression.

"You mean your men don't know that you're destroying babies' brains to get rich? They don't know that in a few days the whole damn country is gonna know, and they're going to be accessories? They don't know you're going to turn a virus loose that'll make AIDS look tame, just so you can get rich on the cure?"

"He said shut up," Doyle cut in. He reached down and grabbed Kier's coat. "Shut up or die now."

Kier could see Tillman's men looking at each other, edgy but not yet agitated.

"Did anybody tell these men about the virus they were exposed to as a result of the plane crash? Any of you guys—"

Doyle clubbed Kier with the butt of his gun, but not hard enough to do any damage.

Sensing what Doyle was doing, Kier curled up fetally and feigned unconsciousness.

"Wake him up," Tillman shouted. "We aren't gonna get anything out of him this way. Damn it, Doyle, I thought you were smarter than that."

"He's talking too much," Doyle shot back. "You want the whole world to know?"

Through half-closed lids, Kier saw Tillman coming closer. Then he felt Doyle leaning over him. Doyle put something in his hand. A key! Could it be . . . ? Was this another—

"Have you fucking lost it?" Tillman was in Doyle's face. "Nobody knows anything. But if you don't shut up—"

"It's all in the sixth volume, isn't it? Well, isn't it?"

"Listen, I don't know—" Tillman said.

"And it's on its way to the *New York Times*!" Doyle raised his voice.

Kier had his cuffs loose. Doyle and Tillman were standing right over him.

"Nobody but me is going to see that volume—"

"Because if it's going to the press, we'll all go up for murder, won't we? It's all in there. You let those idiots write it all down."

Kier opened his eyes to see Tillman grab Doyle. All eyes were on the two men. Kier huddled around his knees to unlock the leg irons.

"You work for me, you mother—" Tillman paused "I didn't know the bastards were writing it all down until—"

"Until just before you killed Jensen."

"How did you—"

"Know about that?" Doyle finished the sentence for him. The mercenaries had gathered closer, converging on Doyle.

Tillman went for his gun, but Doyle was faster, stopping Tillman's hand at the holster.

To Tillman's left a man pivoted, turning his rifle on Doyle. Kier rolled, catching that man and flipping him with his legs.

Kier had knocked the man unconscious before a single shot was fired. Kier knew that any of the men might have shot him but for the gun that Doyle held to Tillman's head. Tillman's hand remained frozen on his holstered sidearm. A dozen guns turned on Doyle.

Shots from unsilenced weapons rang out from inside the copter. Two men from the copter jumped out and dropped prone, their automatic weapons trained on the group. Two others slumped in the cockpit. Kier's eyes went to the automatic on the ground.

"Don't even think it, Indian," Tillman said. He ordered two guns on Kier.

"You're under arrest," Doyle said calmly. "The two guys alive at the copter are mine."

"Screw yourself. Shoot if he moves," Tillman called out.

"Nobody here has to go down for murder except Tillman here," Doyle shouted.

"Nobody here has to go down for anything." Tillman made his best pitch to his men.

"I've got more guys coming," Doyle said. "Now you men stand down."

But not a man flinched. Kier sensed they were used to taking orders from the man with the money, Tillman. Then, for no reason that Kier could have articulated, he knew Grandfather was near. He could feel him.

"Make sure the woman dies," Tillman called out. Two men trained their guns on Jessie. "Put a bullet through the middle of Doyle's head if he so much as moves." A dozen guns locked on Doyle's head. "So, Doyle, I suggest a deal. We all stand down. We all go our own way for the time being. I take Tonto here."

Doyle said nothing. Kier threw back his head and began a death chant. From the trees Grandfather's voice rang out in an eerie reply.

"There's a hundred Tiloks in the woods. Nobody will get out of here alive."

"This is bullshit. There's one old man—"

An arrow sliced through the air and sank into Tillman's throat, cutting off his words. His mouth went wide, his eyes wider.

Doyle stepped back, keeping his gun trained on Tillman.

Tillman stumbled in a slow circle as if he wanted one last look around. Oddly, the wound seeped little blood. Staggering, he knocked over the can of gasoline near the fire. The liquid ran downhill away from the flame. A loud wheeze escaped Tillman's lips, but nobody moved. The flat beat of another chopper could be heard just over the ridge before it burst over the shoulder of Iron Mountain, swooping toward the group.

"Anybody shoots again and it's a war," Brennan, Tillman's senior man, said nervously.

As if in slow motion, Tillman raised his gun from his holster. Doyle tensed.

"I said nobody shoots," Brennan said again.

Seeing Tillman aim at Jessie, Kier tried to move after him. "No," he said. Three automatic rifles poked Kier's chest.

"Put it down, Tillman, and we'll get you to a hospital," Doyle said.

What happened next only a few witnesses saw. A body flew like a projectile out of the trees, leaping between Jessie and Tillman. It was Grandfather. As if he had known the moment when the bullet would arrive, the old man took Tillman's shot full in the chest. Before another round could be loosed, Kier took two giant strides and dived, knocking Tillman's gun skyward.

Nervous trigger fingers twitched all around, but no one fired as Jack Horatio Tillman fell to the dirt.

* * *

A cry escaped from Jessie's throat as Grandfather fell. Through tears she watched Kier kneel and put his ear to Grandfather's lips. Grandfather spoke for maybe a minute. Then Kier threw back his head with a wail that seemed to pierce the heavens with his sorrow. The Spirit Walker, she knew, had gone to the sky.

As they cut her down, her eyes never left the small, elderly man whose calm dignity would remain frozen in her mind forever. Why he had chosen to die for her was more than she could bear to ponder. When Doyle removed the shackles, she stood by Kier, who remained bent over his grandfather.

She put her hand on Kier's back. His hand reached back to join hers. Again Kier began the death chant that she had heard moments before. After a time, she didn't know how long, he stopped. FBI men came for the body, but she and Doyle shooed them away. They didn't need an autopsy. What had happened was plain. Why it had happened was not. When at last Kier spoke to her, she was hardly prepared for what he said.

"Grandfather said to tell everyone that he caught the bullet for his great-grandsons, whose spirits he saw dancing in the sky. They cried out for the life of their mother. Because of the soldiers in the woods he had only the one arrow. He told me: 'I put my life force into my feet and leapt for the sky to save her. It was good.' "

Doyle went to Tillman, who lay on his side, the tip of the arrow having passed out the back of his neck. Somehow it must have missed his carotids. His mouth made the motions of the gag reflex, but only a tiny sound came. He had to be swallowing a lot of blood.

"Kill me." The words formed and died on his lips.

"You must have had some things from your laboratory hidden somewhere," Doyle replied evenly.

Tillman formed the words again. "Kill me."

"It could be a rough ride back in the helicopter. They might even save your worthless hide. Although I'd guess even if they put your throat back together, you'll never talk again. . . . What the hell, they'll execute you anyway."

"Please." Tillman gargled the word.

"As an officer of the law I can't kill you. But I could give you this lighter. You're lying in the gasoline."

Tillman clenched his hands. Jessie thought it doubtful that Tillman could actually flick the lighter. But her body moved forward—she couldn't let Doyle give him the chance. Kier's hand took her arm, and she stopped, trusting Kier's instincts.

She wondered if there were more pain for Tillman in the loss of his power than in the hell of having an arrow through his throat. For him, the lighter might be the only power left.

"Before I give you the lighter, tell me where you hid the hardware and the software for electrolytic reassortment. Tell me where the cure is for the RA-4TV mutation. Keep in mind I've got to believe you, Tillman. The helicopter is here. You get one chance."

"Summer home." He mouthed the words.

"Not good enough."

"Underneath."

"Where underneath?"

"Old bomb shelter."

"Bravo. I believe you."

"Now kill me," Tillman choked out again, desperate.

"Sorry, old chap. They'd have my badge if I let you burn."

"It's odd that with our chopper and all the gadgets, it was a simple wooden arrow that got him."

Doyle watched as they carried a ghastly pale Tillman off on a stretcher.

Jessie responded first. "It wasn't the arrow that got him."

Doyle's bushy brows raised in a question.

"It was a Spirit Walker."

"Yeah, well, according to my men, your Spirit Walker never

did show on the infrared detector. When he left you two, he just disappeared.''

Jessie and Kier looked at each other, and the look grew until it became the beginning of a bridge big enough to span the chasm between them. They both pondered whether they would finish that bridge, and if they did, whether either of them would cross it.

Epilogue

As Jessie drove, she found herself very quiet inside. Before she left Johnson City for Washington, D.C., she had asked Kier for a photograph of Grandfather. Every morning she would stare at the eyes, and memorize the lines in the face, trying to find the man. She toyed with his last words, hearing them like a hammer on an anvil, each one falling with a jarring ring. She wondered at their audacity.

But for the memory of Grandfather, she would have been rehearsing her greeting, speaking out loud her intended conversation. Perhaps she would have looked in the mirror, stopped a second time to brush her teeth, or checked her clothes for lint. Nothing in her life to date had been as important to her as her upcoming visit with Kier.

He didn't know she was coming. Although it had been a month since she left Johnson City, she had spoken with Kier several times. Some of their talks had centered around Stalking Bear and her need to know the man who took her bullet. They talked about the upcoming prosecution of Tillman and their respective interviews with the prosecutors. Neither of them ever brought up Stalking Bear's last words, Kier's girlfriend, Willow, his marriage plans, or lack of them. The words "Do you miss me?" were perched on the edge of Jessie's tongue during every call, but never seemed to take flight.

According to Claudie, who had insisted she come, Kier talked about her constantly. The intrigue of the unspoken romance was driving Claudie nuts, so after numerous entreaties, Jessie decided to surprise Kier. Now that she was here she felt like an idiot.

Arriving in the parking lot of Kier's veterinary clinic, her tires crunching over remnant ice and snow, she recognized his adjoining cedar-shingle house from photos and from Claudie's description. It was late Thursday afternoon, just before closing time, and according to Claudie he was always in his clinic on Thursdays. She found herself gripping the wheel. Maybe this was all a big mistake. She should have warned Kier she was coming. What if he had plans? What if he had a date with Willow? She could end up looking as if she was out here to catch Kier. After a moment's pondering, she realized that the fear of looking foolish was not the essence of her problem. It was simply that he might not be interested.

"Are you lost?" a young woman said through the cracked-open window of Jessie's rental car. She was obviously Native American; Jessie wondered if she might be Tilok. She was slender and her carefully groomed, jet-black hair was trimmed to just below her ears.

"No. I was, I was just going into the clinic."

"Do you have a pet?" The girl asked, obviously curious.

"I don't. I came to see Dr. Wintripp."

"Oh, he's my uncle."

"Your name wouldn't by any chance be Winona, would it?"

"Why yes. Are you the FBI lady my uncle keeps talking about?"

"That would be me."

"Well, come in. I know he'll be delighted to see you. Thrilled actually." The girl flashed her a smile and led her inside, before quickly disappearing through a back door.

Jessie found Kier in the lobby of his clinic, talking to an elderly white-haired lady with a Labrador.

"Hi," she said abruptly. "I thought you would be tending to the animals or something."

"I am, I mean I was," he said. "I was giving Mrs. Abernathy a tour of the facility. Mary Abernathy, meet Jessie Mayfield, the lady who was in the mountains with me."

"Oh my, I can tell all my friends I met a celebrity."

Kier gave a rare smile, watching Jessie.

"Well, you two probably have a lot to discuss. But I just want to say that in these parts we are very grateful for what you and Kier did," Mary said.

"Thank you very much. The FBI had a lot to do with it."

"Well, I don't know, I read that you and Kier were pretty heroic. So don't be afraid to take a bow." The woman smiled at her. "Come on, Shep," she said to her dog. Waving to Kier, she said, "I'll be back next month so you can see how he's doing."

"Okay," Kier said. Then turning to Jessie: "What a great surprise."

"Yeah, well, now that I don't have Bilotti to kick around anymore, I thought maybe I'd come and look you up."

"He's resigned, huh?"

"Completely. He was a good man," she said. "He just forgot who he was for a while. Finally told the truth. Shocked the hell out of me. Anyway, I'm done with Frank's midlife crises. I came to see you."

Winona came back through the door from what appeared to be Kier's residence carrying a baby swathed in a tiny blue comforter.

"You remember I told you about Winona's baby?" Kier said, beckoning Winona. "He is great. Tillman hadn't gotten around to harming him. He was too busy chasing us. The original genetic work to build the computer model was over. I guess they wanted this beautiful boy for some bizarre new experiment.''

''I don't even have to adopt him because I am his birth mother. At least that's what the lawyer says,'' Winona spoke up.

''Is he you?'' Jessie blurted out as if the thought had exploded from her mind.

''No,'' Kier said gently. ''He's not me. He is cloned from a man who died in an auto accident. They took the cells when he died at the hospital.''

The child had a full head of black hair and wide brown eyes. The infant's lips seemed to form a slight smile that was reflected in his gaze.

''A happy baby,'' Jessie said, surprised to feel tears welling in her eyes. There was something very special to her about this child's survival. All the time they were with Tillman out in the woods, they were keeping this baby safe.

''Tillman's trying to kill himself,'' Kier said.

''I heard he managed to pull out his respirator,'' Winona said.

''But he didn't make it,'' Jessie said.

''Been okay with me if he succeeded,'' Kier said.

''They only now have everybody on the way to being cured of that RA-4TVM virus. It's a wonder we didn't get it.''

''Or something else.''

''We were lucky it was as cold as it was.'' Kier led Winona over to a big leather couch as they talked. Jessie followed and settled close on the other side of Kier. She heard the phone ringing on the reception desk, but neither Kier nor Winona moved to answer it.

''You know the irony of it is that scientists say his companies did more to advance medicine than any other research group in history. Even most cancers are treatable using their methods," Kier said.

A woman appeared from around the corner.

"Mrs. Olson is on the phone and insists she has to speak with you. Alfred's stomach is acting up again."

Kier sighed and stepped over to the phone at the receptionist's desk.

Jessie could tell that Winona wanted to say something to her, so she encouraged her with her eyes.

"I wanted to meet you," Winona said while Kier talked to the woman on the phone. "Everyone does. The only woman I know that ever managed to give my uncle a hard time."

"Who told you?" Jessie asked.

"Uncle Kier's mother."

Kier stopped talking for a moment and turned his attention to the two women, looking first at Jessie.

"I didn't hear about this." Jessie returned Kier's glance and noticed that he looked as cool and steady as ever.

"Your husband really needs to go to the clinic. It's safe now . . ." Kier was saying to the lady on the phone.

"Yeah, she told us about all your talks with Kier," Winona said. "I think you've made stirring the oatmeal a forbidden task for women of the Tilok tribe. Did Kier tell you that Willow doesn't stir his oatmeal anymore?"

Kier was hanging up, but obviously still paying attention to Jessie and his niece.

"Kier told you all this?" Jessie said.

"Oh, Kier didn't tell me. Willow told Kier's mother when Willow went off to be with her new boyfriend. A white man."

"Willow went off with a white man?"

"Well, that's her new boyfriend. He's nice."

"I notice your uncle hasn't told you to stop talking," Jessie said, acutely aware of Kier's 6'4" frame now hovering over them.

"Yeah, but he'd sure like to. But that wouldn't be cool. It wouldn't be Kier."

"So what do you suppose Kier will do now that he doesn't have a girlfriend?"

"We're all waiting to find out. You know some of us think a white woman wouldn't be so bad."

"Winona, let me see your young son," Kier said, reaching down to take the baby in his arms.

"Uncle Kier is dying, can't you tell?" Winona said.

"Kier, would you like your niece to stop telling stories?"

"Maybe if somebody stopped encouraging her, she might devote herself to some more interesting topic."

"To a Tilok nothing is more interesting than Kier Wintripp's love life. Jessie seems Tilok enough in that regard," Winona said.

"We better be careful, Winona. Kier's afraid of things he can't control. Right now I'd say you fall squarely into that category."

"Why don't I take the baby back to the house and feed him?" Winona said.

"Good idea," Kier said, handing the child back to Winona.

Glancing over her shoulder, Winona said, "I think Uncle Kier wants to go with that knocking-the-bed-down stuff."

"She has no respect," Kier said.

"Evidently, you must have told Willow a whole lot."

"I was trying to explain what you were saying. I was telling her how wrong you were."

"Obviously, she agreed with you."

Kier looked at her with a half-mad, half-puzzled expression, while she returned a clear-eyed stare.

"Trust me. Everybody loves you," Jessie said. "Is Willow serious about this new man?"

"I don't know. She's not serious about me."

She twirled the strap on her handbag around her finger.

"There's a job managing the Mountain Shadows Clinic,"

he said. "The government has taken it over. It's a big deal. It will serve all three tribes in the area, plus Johnson City and all the gentleman farmers. They need an administrator. Computer background is really important."

"That's an interesting bit of news." There was a long silence while she continued to twirl the strap. "You know, I'm scared to death. How about you?"

"I'm nervous," he said with a half-smile.

"So we're two very nervous people sitting in your lobby. You know we've been talking quite a bit these last weeks. And then we have these awkward silences. I was just wondering if you've said the things you really wanted to say. I mean if you boil it all down to its essence, have you said it?"

"No. Except just now about the job."

"I haven't said what I came all the way to California to say either. So why don't we talk about what we really would like to say, but never quite get around to. You first."

Kier shifted on the couch as if he couldn't get comfortable.

She felt uneasy and part of her wanted to erase the pregnant pause and make the conversation easy. But she didn't.

"You could be really good at this job here in Johnson City," he said.

"So you think I have job skills," she said haltingly. "And that is what you wanted to say?" She leaned back. Then in a soft voice: "I could go first, but then you'd have to remember that you didn't." She sought his eyes and resolved not to look away. He returned her gaze.

"I love you, and I don't know what to do about it," Kier said at last.

She could imagine Grandfather's face softened by a near smile.

"I think it will come to you."

The Wingman Series
By Mack Maloney

Call toll free **1-888-345-BOOK** to order by phone or use this coupon to order by mail.

Name _____

Address _____

City _____ State _____ Zip _____

Please send me the books I have checked above.

I am enclosing	$_____
Plus postage and handling*	$_____
Sales tax (in New York and Tennessee only)	$_____
Total amount enclosed	$_____

*Add $2.50 for the first book and $.50 for each additional book.

Send check or Money order (no cash or CODs) to:

Kensington Publishing Corp., 850 Third Avenue, New York, NY 10022

Prices and Numbers subject to change without notice.

All orders subject to availability.

Check out our website at **www.kensingtonbooks.com**

A World of Eerie Suspense
Awaits in Novels by Noel Hynd

"Book 'em!"
Legal Thrillers from Kensington

HORROR FROM PINNACLE . . .